ANNE PAOLUCCI

SLOW DANCE TO SAMARRA

A Mystery Novel

Copyright @ 2007 by Anne Paolucci

Publishers Cataloging-in-Publication

Paolucci, Anne

    Slow dance to Samarra : a mystery novel / Anne Paolucci – Smyrna, Del. : Griffon House Publications, c2007

    p. ; cm.

    ISBN-13: 978-1-932107-22-7
    ISBN-10: 1-932107-22-3

    1. Missing persons—Investigation—Fiction. 2. Absence and presumption of death—Fiction. 3. Police—Ontario—Ottawa—Fiction. 4. Police—New York (State)—New York—Fiction. 5. Mystery fiction. I. Title.

PS3566.A595 S56 2007
813.54—dc22   0612

Published for
THE BAGEHOT COUNCIL
by
GRIFFON HOUSE PUBLICATIONS
P. O. BOX 98
SMYRNA, DE 19977
griffonhse@aol.com

CONTENTS

Author's Preface 7

PART ONE: *KATIE (2002)*

Chapter One 11
Chapter Two 25
Chapter Three 43
Chapter Four 64

PART TWO: *FRANK (2001)*

Chapter Five 81
Chapter Six 91
Chapter Seven 105
Chapter Eight 118

PART THREE: *McCALLEY (AFTERWARDS)*

Chapter Nine 135
Chapter Ten 147
Chapter Eleven 164
Chapter Twelve 188
Chapter Thirteen 209
Chapter Fourteen 229
Chapter Fifteen 251
Chapter Sixteen 271
Chapter Seventeen 292
Chapter Eighteen 307
Chapter Nineteen 326
Chapter Twenty 343
Chapter Twenty-One 364

Death Speaks: There was a merchant in Bagdad who sent his servant to market to buy provisions and in a little while the servant was back, white and trembling, and said, Master, just now when I was in the marketplace I was joined by a woman in the crowd and when I turned, I saw it was Death that jostled me. She looked at me and made a threatening gesture; now, lend me your horse and I will ride away from this city and avoid my fate, I will go to Samarra and there Death will not find me. The merchant lent him his horse, and the servant mounted it, and he dug his spurs into his flanks and as fast as the horse could gallop he went. Then the merchant went down to the marketplace and he came to me and said, Why did you make a threatening gesture to my servant when you saw him this morning? That was not a threatening gesture, I said, it was only a start of surprise. I was astonished to see him in Bagdad, for I had an appointment with him tonight in Samarra.

From *Sheppey,* a play in three acts
by W. Somerset Maugham (1933)

AUTHOR'S PREFACE

This mystery, like my first (*In Wolf's Clothing*) is a brain teaser more than a *whodunit*. Inspector Luke McCalley of the Ottawa Police Department again is featured, together with his friend and colleague, NYPD Detective Ed Markarian. They had proved stimulating, when I first introduced them; I found them just as much a challenge in this work. It was like meeting old but not altogether predictable friends. Again, I let them call the moves and followed in their wake.

The two make their appearance in Part Three. The earlier sections feature, separately, Katie and her husband Frank. Each serves as the "I" of the narrative, the major player in a series of events which, in reverse chronology, lead up to the present and the appearance of McCalley and Markarian. The chronological reversal came naturally and was essential for the unraveling and meshing of past and present events I had in mind. The dramatic beginning in St. Tropez set the mood I wanted, introducing something of the bizarre and grotesque.

Human nature being what it is, the tragedy that struck the nation with the terrorist attack on the twin towers on September 11, 2001, could certainly have prompted the kind of escape I describe. My account, however, is pure fiction — just as the characters who inhabit this fiction have been created for the occasion. Any resemblance they bear to people living or dead is purely coincidental.

Many thanks are in order, but I can't possible list the many readers of my earlier mystery, who urged me to bring McCalley and Markarian together again, or the many friends who encouraged me in the task. I hope I have not disappointed them.

I would like to express my personal gratitude to my researcher, Azar Attura, for her efficient cooperation through the long haul. She was always there when I needed her.

To Bob Searby who, unlike those who wrote they "couldn't put it down," is still reading *In Wolf's Clothing*, unwilling (so he tells me) to part with McCalley — go on and finish it, Bob. I've got another one for you.

PART ONE

KATIE (2002)

Evil is not a thing in itself but a privation;
it is not *something* but the absence of the
light and love of God,
(ST AUGUSTINE)

CHAPTER ONE

I watched the sun on his face and hair, as he smiled at something I'd said. I rested my hand on his arm for a few seconds. "I have to catch a plane," I said. Neither of us moved.

"I'll call a cab." He stood there examining his nails.

"It was good seeing you after, what? Seven years?"

"Your sweet-sixteen birthday party. Mom and I stopped by, remember? You lived in Larchmont, then. We had a hard time finding your house, and your mom scolded us for being late."

I laughed. I had forgotten. He looked up frowning.

"Will you do something for me?"

"Shoot."

"My wife Emma."

I stared. "Come again?"

"Shoot my wife Emma."

He didn't blink once. He just stood there and waited for an answer.

"You can't mean what I think I just heard," I said.

"You heard right." He became animated then. "I've got it all worked out. Trust me. It's like any other piece of business I take on. And I'm very good at what I do."

"Then why don't you take this on too?"

He smiled. "Because the husband is always the prime suspect."

"What about relatives and house guests? Aren't they going to be suspects, too? Won't they be questioned?" I heard my words coming at me from a distance, as though someone else was speaking them.

"No one will think of questioning you. If they do,

11

you'll be hundreds of miles away within a few hours."
"Oh? Where am I going?"
"Back to the States."
My head was spinning. I must have stared. Finally I said in a strained voice I scarcely recognized: "I have ten more days to go —"
"You can come back any time you like."
"Really?" I threw down my coat and tote on the nearest chair. I crossed my arms and studied his face for a few seconds. Then I took a deep breath and said:
"I work at a very demanding job. I saved up enough vacation time and money to spend a month in Italy and France. Italy was great. It was nice running into you here. You have a beautiful place. The party you gave for me last night was a real surprise. I enjoyed it. We had a chance to catch up on things. I knew Aunt Millie had died in January, but your talking about her brought back some good memories when our families used to get together in the summer." I raised my hand to ward off any interruption. "Later today, I'll see my old college buddies. It's been two years since we went our separate ways. I saved these last ten days for them. I expect they have lots of things lined up for us. But when I get back to the States, and that won't be until ten days from now, because I'm not cutting this trip short for anyone, least of all for a distant relative who — "
"Cousin. Our grandmothers were sisters — "
" — a distant relative whom I happened to run into while I was having coffee outside my hotel and who wants me to shoot his wife, . . . when I get back home, these three days will be erased from memory. Got that? What it means is that I never want to hear from you or see you again."
He seemed strangely calm. My words had not made much of an impact. "Later on, you can come and go back and forth as often as you like."

"Oh?" I meant it sarcastically, but it came out a real question. I went on quickly: "I'm not quite on your level, I can't take time off whenever I feel like it, even if I could afford it!"

"You won't ever have to work again."

Again, I stared. He had a way about him. I couldn't quite figure out why I was still standing there, listening to him. I was beginning to feel something else, too. I was afraid. Not of him, but of my curiosity.

"Will you call me a cab, please?" He looked at me as though waiting for some signal. "Look," I said, impatiently, "I'm your guest. I'm stuck here in the middle of Nowhere, France. Oh, your villa is incredibly beautiful, St. Tropez is heaven on earth; but I have to catch a plane to Paris. My friends are waiting for me at the airport."

I didn't really expect him to do it, but he surprised me by walking to the phone and speaking softly into it in French. He put down the receiver and turned to me.

"I meant it," he went on, as though there had been no interruption. "You'll never have to work again."

"Just like that."

"I've opened a Swiss account in your name. It has a token sum of a hundred thousand in it, as a starter. A gift. No strings attached."

I had to admire his style. I had no doubt what he said was true.

"You know what I'm saying is true," he went on, as though he had read my mind. "Later, you'll find an additional deposit of ten million." I tried to take it in. Was he insane? Mom had often said her cousin Millie was a bit strange. He went on in that soft clipped voice of his. "Your mother must have told you that I made lots of money over the last four years. When my father died, I inherited a mess of things. I wasn't really good at anything, but I decided to play around with what I had. It was a game at first. It became a curse. I didn't need it or want it, but money came in with every breath I took. It was something to do, something to keep me from thinking too long about other things. Rich or poor, my life is the same."

"You wouldn't have all this if you were poor," I waved my hand in a grand, philosophic gesture.

"I can live without it. It was Emma's idea. I need very little. I don't have the usual vices. I use my money to make my friends happy."

"But not your wife." He didn't answer. Instead, he took my hand and led me across the beautiful drawing room, like a parent gently pulling a child, to the large windows overlooking the south side of the estate. He opened the lower part of the huge windows, first one then the other. He did this without letting go of my hand. The fragrance of roses wafted in. Outside, the bright summer lawn sloped down gently, and beyond it was the breathtaking view of the Mediterranean. I had stood in that very spot, taking it all in, the day I arrived. I was impressed all over again, standing there now.

"Beautiful, isn't it. Oh, I enjoy this place. But I can live without it." He paused briefly. "When I wake up in the morning and see her sprawled on the bed next to me, I want to die. She poisons the air I breathe. Just thinking of her makes my flesh crawl."

"Hey, nobody forced you to marry her."

"She did. She told me she was pregnant."

"Nobody gets married these days just because they goofed."

"Well, I admit I was infatuated. Besides, I thought it was time to think about a family. It wasn't as though we couldn't afford children. . . . There were other reasons, too."

"So it *was* your choice," I said with a grim smile.

"Do you plan to make it a habit? You'll need all your money for that."

"Don't be flippant, Kootie." It was the first time in the three days I'd been in his house that he had addressed me with my childish mispronunciation of what my dad used to call me when I was young. I had almost forgotten it myself. Now, a picture flashed before me. I was about four. Someone had come to see dad, and, as the visitor was leaving, Mom came downstairs with me. The man leaned down and touched my cheek. "So you're Katie," he said. "No," I had corrected him, "my name is Kootie Pie."

"When I married her she was like Botticelli's Venus. Everyone would turn to stare. It seems an eternity ago. Then. . . . Well, you met her. She never gets up before one or two in the afternoon. Then she disappears until dinner, if there are guests. Otherwise she just disappears."

"So she's gained some weight, drinks more than she should. She likes to insult you in public. It's still no reason to kill her. Just get a divorce, for godssake!" I couldn't believe I was actually reasoning with him!

"Our family goes back quite a way, you know that. And there's never been a divorce."

"There's never been a murder, either."

"Ah, you're wrong there, but no, not recently."

"I can't believe you're serious." Outside, a car had pulled up in the driveway. I turned away from the window and watched him walk back into the room and sit on one of the soft-cushioned sofas. I went on, my heart racing: "I can't believe this! You want to kill your wife and here I am, a widow at twenty-three, a widow a whole year already, who'd do anything to get my husband back!" I heard myself laughing uncontrollably.

My cousin gave me a curious look and said: "You can have him back any time."

My mouth must have dropped open. I turned from the window and leaned against the wall. My lips felt dry. Outside, the driver honked several short bursts.

"So, you're Christ now. You raise the dead."

"No, the living."

Oh, he was full of surprises! I closed my eyes, my heart pounding. I rested my head against the wall and took deep breaths. When I opened my eyes, he was beside me with a tall glass of water. I turned away from those searching, untroubled eyes.

"Here, drink this." He stood by as I gulped down the water. "Why don't you sit down?" When I didn't move, he went on. "He's alive. There's a new woman."

I couldn't get any words out. I simply shook my head in disbelief. Outside, we could hear the taxi drive off after one last impatient blast of the horn. I closed my eyes again.

"I wasn't going to say anything. What's the point? It's almost a year now. But since you brought it up — "

Without opening my eyes I said: "He was killed with all those others!"

"No. He survived."

My eyes suddenly flew open. "I don't believe you. You're crazy, you know that? What's come over you?"

For a moment he seemed ill at ease, but it was only a fleeting impression. "I make it my business to find out things. Since we're at it . . . . I didn't run into you the other day. I knew you were coming, found out where you were staying. The other morning I waited for you to come down for breakfast. I came up to you as you were drinking your coffee."

I heard the words but they registered dimly. My mind was elsewhere.

"What did you find out about Frank?"

"I came across him by accident." The look on my face must have reflected disbelief because he went on quickly, "I was scanning quarterly reports of companies I do business with, glancing at new names added to their Board of Directors, things like that. Last November, one company had replaced two directors. I didn't have a clue at the time, but I did what I always do. I asked one of my assistants to compile a brief background resume of the new people. I like to know who I'm dealing with. It was purely routine." He gave me a long searching look before going on.

"One of them was from Berlin, the other living in Ottawa, originally from New York. There were photos too. The second man looked familiar. I finally realized who it was. I pulled out the wedding picture you'd sent Aunt Millie — you and Frank on the steps of City Hall — and sure enough, the man in the picture was your husband. I did some more checking and discovered — oh, never mind the details. What you want to know is, he's changed his name and started a consulting business that's doing pretty well. He's made new contacts."

After a while, I said: "They're living together, isn't that what you said?"

"No, I said — "

I didn't let him finish. "They're married?"

"Yes. There's a baby, too."

I went to sit on the couch and he followed. We sat in silence across from one another for what seemed an eternity. Thoughts banged against the cavity that was my head. Feelings I didn't recognize and didn't like exploded deep inside me, bursts of flames. White heat enveloped my insides, my stomach churned as in a storm at sea, my nerve ends prickled right down to my toes, as when Dr. Forman drew blood from me for the very first time, when I was fourteen.

Suddenly I was angry. "But he died! He never made it out of the North Tower!" At first, I didn't think he would say anything more, but then he began again, softly, looking down at the floor, his hands clasped between his legs:

"No, he made it seem that he died. In a way, he must have planned his disappearance very carefully, and for some time back. Then, that incredible opportunity presented itself and he took advantage of it. I don't know how he managed it, but he did!" He snapped his fingers and shook his head, almost in awe. I must have winced. When he spoke again, his voice was soft. "Yes, he must have been thinking about it for quite a while. How to leave you and —" Whatever else he was about to say, he decided against it. Instead, he went on, with a touch of awe: "You've got to give him credit for fast thinking!"

I held back the scream that rose in my throat. Touching my arm lightly, he went on:

"It was quite extraordinary, you know." I shook him off and turned away, but he continued, as though talking to himself. "Anyway, his colleagues confirmed he had gone there for a meeting. Naturally, when he didn't return, everyone assumed he had been killed with all the others. There was no need to go further with it. No one questioned his death. Oh, he was clever! Just walked away from it all!"

I couldn't absorb it. I heard myself ask: "Why?"

He shrugged. "He wanted out." I must have groaned, because he reached out again and put his hand on my shoulder. When I rested my head against the back of the sofa, he straightened up and crossed his legs. "You *can* get him back if you really want him. He's still legally married to you."

I must have tried to laugh. It came out like someone choking. "What I'd like to get back is this last year of my life," I managed to get out. Then, after a few deep breaths, I frowned. "How do I know what you're telling me is true?" I knew what he would say before he said it.

"Why would I make up a story like that?" He was right, of course.

"A whole year! A whole year thinking he was dead, mourning him!"

"Did you really? Mourn him?"

I shot up from the sofa and paced to the window and back. "You're a cruel and evil man," I told him when I had regained control. "Nothing touches you!" I stood over him, struggling to keep my composure.

"That's not true," he said. "I know you're hurt. But not for the reason you think."

"Whatever our differences," I went on, trying to stay calm, "they were unimportant. What was important to me was the promise we made, the pledge we had taken. We cared for one another. We swore to build a life together. We'd been married just over a year."

"But your heart wasn't really in it." He held up a warning hand. I held back what I was about to say. "You made that very clear," he went on, almost gently. "Just now you said 'differences,' 'promise,' 'pledge,' 'cared for one another,' 'swore to build a life together.' Not once have you mentioned love, happiness. Did you love him? Did he love you? Were you happy together?"

I shook my head, like a dog shaking off water. "Love! Love obviously comes and goes. He made that clear enough!"

"No no. *You* made it clear. *You* wanted something else. I'm not criticizing you. But it's true, isn't it? You wanted security, a family, a routine. Love was a foolish thing to build on. And you may be right." I said nothing. He went on. "You can understand why I felt it was best to leave things alone under the circumstances. He seems serene where he is, with the new family he has created for himself. And you still have a very good chance to get what you want, whatever it is you feel you need." I sat down again. He came to sit beside me and lifted my head. "Look at me and tell me I'm wrong." I couldn't speak.

After a while, he sat back and just looked at me. When he talked again, it was almost a whisper. "Strange how lives cross, people come together, separate, come together again. The patterns are predictable, you know. There are only a few and they cover just about all possible human behavior." He gave a bitter laugh. "Oh, yes, I've researched that too. I'm afraid I don't hold much hope for the human race. I have a theory you see, contrary to all that has been said." He gestured with his hand, a large sweep that took in the entire room, the world, the universe. "I don't believe man is top of the heap, that God singled him out for special privileges on this planet or any other planet. We think of ourselves as unique, in a special category as humans, but what sort of God would give us all the goodies we enjoy — art, lust, music, new technology, exotic foods, all those things that we like to think make life worth living — what God would give all that and then destroy us? We're human, after all, we are told. What we mean is, we die like the other animals. We can't get around that!

"But if that's so," he went on, searching my face, his eyes glittering with an unexpected emotion I couldn't quite take in, "if all that is true, why don't we act like other animals? Instead, our pleasures fade and we have to pump them up with perverse priming. Animals mate when nature tells them. They eat only when they're hungry; they don't stuff themselves or go looking for excitement out of season, for anything that appeals to them, any time, day or night. By contrast with animals, our so-called sensibilities are nothing more than highly developed nerve-ends that respond to our acquired perversities. There's nothing natural about the human race, unless you call our gorging on pleasures, a natural pastime. We take what we want and justify the havoc we wreak on the grounds that, as the highest form of intelligence, we enjoy special privileges. We've even created an invisible overseer to authorize all this. I call it self-indulgence writ large." He frowned at some idea that had intruded, then went on:

"We're just a fluke. We've even learned how to justify our self-serving behavior by creating morality. It all started with the great Socrates." He burst out laughing, a harsh sound, then went on breathlessly: "Just so we can lord it over all other things around, grab what we want in the name of some divine purpose." He leaned toward me as far as he could, bringing his face close to mine. "We're a big joke!"

I was riveted to the look on his face. It glowed with a kind of religious fanaticism, and, yes, a suggestion of madness too. At the same time, I must have taken in every word because I remembered that conversation long after. I wanted to get away from him but couldn't move.

Something in my face made him pause. He was calm again when he spoke.

"We're all egotists, you know — in spite of our good intentions." He frowned. "What I'm trying to say is, put it all behind you and pick up your life again."

Utterly exhausted, I took a deep breath. I felt as though I had been sobbing. "The taxi came and went," I said weakly.

For a moment, he looked at me with the same wild intensity with which he had delivered his brief lecture and then burst out laughing, a rather pleasant laugh this time. "So, I didn't impress you?" He picked up my coat and tote. "I'll drive you to the airport myself. You won't miss your plane."

I followed him out into the bright sunlight, on to the gravel driveway. I looked out over the wide expanse of garden, with its graceful gazebo on one side, the beautiful fountain with its *carrara* cupids on the other.

The burst of colors was like a Renaissance painting. I glanced behind me at the chateau for one last look as he brought the Mercedes around.

We drove in silence, but there was heavy tension between us. At the same time I was acutely aware of some inner struggle he was experiencing. My own nerves were raw. I felt drained. At the airport, he called a porter and watched as my luggage was checked in. He took both my hands in his. A rueful smile played around his lips.

"I won't try to apologize or excuse myself. I meant every word I said." He dropped my hands and kissed me quickly on the cheek. "Don't judge me, please. I haven't judged *you*."

"I have nothing to be ashamed of," I countered lamely.

"Nonsense. We all have secrets, we're all weak."

Just as I turned to leave, he said: "What are you going to do about Frank?" I had no answer, but he must have read something in my face because the look he gave me was sharp, a kind of warning. "Don't rush into anything," he said crisply. "He's not worth it. And in any case, you're not exactly free of blame." I wanted to slap him. Instead I stood there struggling for words.

"You said you didn't judge me."

"I don't. I never will. What I'm telling you, you already know, deep down inside. Look at the plus. You've gotten rid of him. I should be as lucky!"

I knew I was doing something I would regret. He was telling the truth and I didn't want to hear it, but I slapped him anyway. He grinned. It was the only time I'd seen him do that. He suddenly seemed much younger than his twenty-nine years. I didn't trust myself to say anything more, so I turned and walked away. I felt his eyes on me but I didn't want to give him the satisfaction of looking back. I walked straight into the terminal. After I'd checked in, I found a bar and had a martini.

When the flight was called, my mind was almost blank. I didn't want to recall any part of my visit to the chateau. My cousin receded into the dim past. My husband had been killed in a terrorist attack.

I had to believe that he had been in the North Tower, killed with all those others. . . ..

I had to believe I had not made a horrible mistake.

I had to believe —

The little voice I was trying to stifle finally broke through my flimsy excuses. It had a curious resemblance to my cousin's voice.

Why are you closing up like this? It's no good. You'll have to live with it, you know.

Or, I could report him to the proper authorities. I could denounce him as a bigamist. He would lose his job, maybe the woman too, if she didn't know about his past, about me. About our marriage. He'd go to jail. . . .

Then what? What satisfaction would I find in doing that? What about his child?

What about the child? the voice inside me asked. *Have you thought about the baby? what you'll be doing to it? Are you really going to feel better, reporting Frank to the authorities?*

Yes! No. . . . I wasn't sure. . . .

Then, the dam burst and I was sobbing. The flight attendant was coming through the cabin. He leaned over the other passenger in the aisle seat, an elderly man reading *The Wall Street Journal*.

"Anything I can do?" he asked me.

"Nothing, nothing," I said quickly with a forced smile. I waved him away and took out some tissues to blow my nose, wipe the tears from my cheeks and neck. I tried to keep my thoughts at bay, but it didn't work. What had happened and what lay ahead flashed before me, crowding out the present: my friends waiting for me in

Paris, my job back home, the high-rise in mid-town Manhattan, where my husband and I had lived for just over a year; my cousin asking me to kill his wife, the bank account with a hundred thousand dollars in it. . . .

I pulled out the small paper I'd seen him slip into my tote, just before we parted. It had the name of the bank in Geneva, where he had set up the account in my name, the number of the account and the date — three days earlier — when he had deposited the money, just after he had "run into me" at the hotel. I folded the paper carefully and put it inside my wallet. Did he really think I would go along, keep that money? I would call them, no, better yet, I would fly to Geneva before returning to the States and personally make sure the money was sent back to him.

Having made that decision, I began to feel better. In the toilet, I brushed my hair and put on fresh lipstick. I tried a smile, but the lips in the mirror quivered and the eyes that looked back at me were dark with an unutterable premonition.

CHAPTER TWO

Back in my seat, I must have dozed. I surfaced unwillingly from the depths of a sleep induced by fatigue. I felt as though I had been running a marathon. At first I was completely disoriented; I was still somewhere in that other world of night and oblivion. My nap had not brought relief; awake again, reality crashed into my consciousness, a physical pain that left me breathless.

The stewardess was tapping me on the shoulder.

"We're beginning our approach. Please put your seat in the upright position." I followed her instructions, then took out my compact and stared back at the tired face in the small mirror. Was that me? I powdered my nose again. Would Josie and Marge see anything in my face, any sign of what I had learned, the agony I was going through? I knew I couldn't share with them what had happened, what I knew. Not until I had thought everything through carefully.

We hadn't seen each other since graduation two years earlier. They had taken jobs in Paris; I stayed in New York; but we managed frequent e-mails. I had looked forward to spending these last ten days of my vacation with them. But now I wondered if I could get through even the next few hours. One thing was certain. I would have to cut my visit short to get to Geneva before returning to New York. The account must be closed as soon as possible, the money returned to my cousin. Somehow I had to get that in and dredge up a good excuse for my change of plans.

I groaned silently. What could I tell Marge and Josie? Not the truth, that was out of the question. Besides, what could they possibly recommend that had not already occurred to me? I couldn't bring myself to burden them with my dilemma. I realized that I might

even be putting them at risk, confiding what I knew. Just how, I didn't know. It was a gut feeling I couldn't ignore. If something were to happen, a crime committed —
Crime?
What was I thinking?
I shook my head in frustration. No. Under no circumstances would I drag them into it, no matter how much I wanted to share my misery, how much I needed comforting. I felt myself give in to anger and, yes, fear, too. An ineffable insight warned me to be careful. I recognized and accepted it, without trying to understand.

He had put money in an account for me. Why? A gift, he said, no strings attached. Or was it a bribe to keep me quiet? Well, once he got his money back, he would know how I felt. Case closed.

Would it end there?

I had made fists in my lap, my breathing was forced, as though I lacked oxygen. The plane touched ground and raced forward as the brakes came into play to slow us down. My whole being seemed to be racing with the plane, rushing forward toward some undefined end, unable to stop.

Pull yourself together, I told myself. *Your best friends are waiting for you at the gate. Since you can't tell them what happened, you've got to hide it, look normal. Act as they expect you to act after two years apart. You can't cancel this visit; and even if you did try to explain, there's nothing they can do to help you. Why burden them with the floating anxiety that has taken hold of you since this morning, since your cousin destroyed your peace of mind in just a few seconds, with just a few words? It would be cruel and insensitive on your part to force them to share your uneasiness — to confide in anyone at all, for that matter. You've got to see it through by yourself.*

I hated him then, hated my cousin for having put me in this position, thrusting me in a predicament from which I could not free myself. I suddenly realized, too, that somewhere along the line, I might have to make a terrible decision.

No it wasn't over, by any means. Wishful thinking on my part. I had to face the unpleasant fact that I could not expose anyone else to the consequences of what might happen down the line.

I had to see it through on my own.

I rested my head on the back of the seat and closed my eyes as the plane came to a stop and the stewardess gave the usual last-minute directions.

People gathered their belongings and started to move into the aisle, falling into line even before the stewardess opened the steel door. I waited until most of the passengers had gone past me before moving forward toward the exit. I grimaced, trying to adjust my face to look normal, to manage a smile at least, or something that could pass for one.

Instead, I cried. The joyous shouts that greeted me just inside the gate brought tears to my eyes.

"When we didn't see you right away, we thought you'd missed the plane!" cried Marge, giving me a big hug that made me stumble.

Josie pushed her aside to hug me in turn. "You look great! A bit tired, though." She took my tote. "Give me your stubs," she went on, in her familiar businesslike way. I gave them to her. It had been the same at NYU. It was Josie who took charge of things.

"Still giving orders, I see," I managed with a little laugh.

Marge put an arm around me and we all headed for the luggage carousel. "I can't wait to hear all about your trip so far. How was Italy? Did you get to Assisi? Did you meet anyone interesting? What was your cousin like? I bet you couldn't tear yourself away!"

I'd called them from the chateau to tell them I'd

run across a cousin of mine and would be spending a few days with him and his wife, instead of going on to Nice. I would be arriving in Paris, as planned, two days later. Now I took a deep breath and made a face. "Hey, I just got here! Give me a chance to catch my breath!" I could hear my voice from a great distance, answering their questions. "Nothing interesting to report on all counts," I said. "My cousin is the same as I remember, although much richer than the last time I saw him, before his father died. He's made a fortune in just a few years."

"God, it must have been difficult tearing yourself away from all that!" said Marge, her eyes wide with excitement. "We've been reading all about him. He's a legend in his time, apparently. More clever than Donald Trump. Almost as rich as Bill Gates."

"It's just money!" I tried to sound light.

"Listen to her! 'Just money!' Is that all you have to tell us?"

Josie said: "Every other day, there's something about him, about both of them, in the newspapers and magazines. We saved some to show you. Wait till you see! He's a celebrity!"

"Is his wife as gorgeous as she looks in the photos?" asked Marge.

I found myself nodding. "Yes. She's beautiful."

"What did you talk about?" asked Marge.

"Nothing much. I was there only three days, remember? People coming and going all the while. I didn't even have a chance to spend a couple of hours on the beach. By the time I got on the plane this morning, I was exhausted. Believe me, I couldn't wait to get away, relax, do normal things, be with you guys!"

It was true enough, she thought grimly.

We had reached the luggage carousel, which was already moving. Josie picked up on my last comment. "Get away from all that? Me? I'd want to settle in for the duration! Well, for as long as I decently could!"

Somehow I managed to laugh with them. Just then, my bags appeared on the carousel and we busied ourselves retrieving them. Marge and I waited for Josie to bring the car around.

On the drive to the apartment my friends had shared since they arrived in Paris, they brought me up to date: Josie, with stories about her job at the Embassy; Marge, about her colleagues and students in the private school where she taught English.

"Do you think you might want to settle here?" I asked Marge, trying to keep up my end of the conversation.

"Depends," said Marge, somewhat embarrassed.

"What she means is," Josie chimed in, "depends on whether or not Jean Brovert is serious about her."

"Ah, so you've met someone," I prodded.

"You meet a lot of people when you're an American in Paris. Josie drags me to all the Embassy events."

"Jean was not an Embassy event, darling," her friend said with a knowing smile. She turned to me: "He teaches geography and history at the school."

"How long have you known him?" I asked Marge.

"He was hired this past year. We've had lunch a few times —"

"And a few dinners, and a few trips to museums, and a few concerts. . . ."

"Do you like him?" I asked, sensing in Marge a certain reluctance to discuss the subject.

"He's a colleague, that's all." Marge seemed annoyed. Josie tossed her head impatiently.

"She doesn't want to admit she likes him because he hasn't even kissed her once, believe it or not."

"Oh, stop it Josie! We're just good friends."

Josie laughed and winked at me.

"If he's serious, you'll know in due course. Right?" I put my arm around Marge's shoulder. It was comforting to feel her close. We sat like that until we reached our destination, on the outskirts of the city. The building was old but imposing.

"We couldn't get anything this size in the center, not for the price," Josie volunteered as she stepped aside to let me into the apartment. "We even have a garage around the corner. It came furnished, but we added a few things."

"The basic pieces we found aren't too bad," added Marge. "Better than most of the cheap stuff you usually get in furnished apartments. We didn't have to throw out anything. Just added what we wanted. The couch we bought," she went on pointing as she spoke, "those two chairs were here."

"The table is ours, we needed a bigger one," Josie added. "The one that was here we put out in the entrance hall, just inside the door."

"Looks nice there," I said, trying to focus on what they were telling me.

"It was worth spending a bit of money here and there," said Josie. "We'll be around at least two or three more years — at least *I* will. Don't know about *her*!" She gestured toward Marge. "*She's* apt to pick up and leave me stranded, give up all of this to run off with Monsieur Brovert, if he asks her to share his humble abode!"

"Oh, stop it," cried Marge slapping her friend on the arm."

"Then Katie would have to leave her job and move in with me," Josie said laughing, as she led the way down the corridor. She opened the door at the very end of the long hall and brought my bags into the room. "You have a bathroom all to yourself, how about it?" They watched as I put down my purse and looked around. The space was almost too large for the few pieces in it: a bed,

30

a large wardrobe, an upholstered chair, two straight-backed chairs, and a table that served also as desk. The bath was enormous with old-fashioned fixtures, including a footed bathtub and, totally unexpected and somehow out of place, a dressing room vanity with a pretty satin skirt and lights all around the framed mirror.

"We bought that. Adds a touch of home," said Josie. I wondered what she meant. I had never seen theater dressing room lights in her bathroom back home. "Plenty of room for your things," she went on, opening the doors of the high oak wardrobe.

"And plenty to spare," I agreed. "I doubt I'll fill even a quarter of it!"

The rest of the apartment, like the room they had given me, was large and furnished with the barest essentials: an odd mix of inexpensive pieces put there by the owner and other items that clearly reflected the more personal taste of the tenants. The impression was of a large space not clearly defined but pleasant enough.

"It looks comfortable," I said at last.

"We like it," said Marge.

After a full tour of the place, Josie took it upon herself to lead us back to my room.

"We'll let you rest a while. Do you need help unpacking?"

"No no. Thanks anyway."

"Let's see. It's six-thirty. We're taking you to dinner at one of the local places. They know us and the food is good. Is eight-thirty all right? People eat later, here. But we can go earlier if you like."

"No, eight-thirty is fine."

"We'll be downstairs. There's plenty of hot water for a bath, if you want one."

"Thanks. . . . Thanks for everything."

They had started to leave. Something in my voice made Josie look back.

31

"Is everything all right?"

"Of course! Why shouldn't it be?" A rush of emotion came over me then. I wanted to cry out to her, to both of them, hug them, tell them everything — but I knew I couldn't. I walked over to where they were standing by the door and drew them to me in a tight embrace. "You have no idea how happy I am to see you both. To be here with you! It's been too long!"

I meant it. They smiled. Josie patted my shoulder.

"We'll see you in a little while, then."

Inside, I shut the door and leaned against it. The day had exhausted me. I was tired physically, drained emotionally as well. I had come to realize that one's life could indeed change overnight. In a matter of minutes, in my case! My life, I knew, would never be the same again. My cousin's words had left my familiar world in ruins. Whatever sorrow I'd felt at Frank's death less than a year ago, whatever grief I had continued to nurture through all those terrible months, seemed insignificant now, compared to the new sorrow at discovering that he was in fact still alive. Betrayal by someone you thought loved you was far worse than death, infinitely more devastating.

What I had learned had plunged me into despair. I seemed to be caught in a maelstrom that carried me far from the comfort of familiar things. I felt frustration, anger, fear; what I had taken for granted, had grown accustomed to, had been swept from my universe into a great black hole. I knew then the power of evil. It took hold inside me, bringing darkness into my soul. Outside, the sun was shining, but it did not lighten my mood.

I lay down, too tired for a bath. My thoughts were a jumble. I couldn't rest and I couldn't focus. I kept trying to close off the memory of what had happened that morning, but the images came rushing back — my cousin looking down at his nails, searching my face to read what

I was thinking, studying my reaction to his words. I saw again the intensity in his eyes as he expounded on life as he saw it; his calm voice, his even tone as he traced his relentless pursuit of an unspeakable goal, as he betrayed his indifference to moral imperatives, as he gave way to a sense of quiet urgency. Every detail was etched in my memory.

My head was spinning. One thing was certain. In a few days I would go to Geneva and send back the money he had deposited in my name . . . but deep down I knew that nothing would ever be the same. I had been compromised. His presence could never be erased. I could not hide from it, even with an ocean between us.

I must have dozed. When I woke, my room was still full of bright summer light. The heat of the day still lingered. My watch said seven thirty.

I sat on the side of the bed, trying to clear my head. I told myself, worrying wasn't going to make it any easier. Neither would brooding.

It didn't take me long to unpack. After everything was put away, I took some aspirin and washed my face. I dressed slowly: a simple blue linen dress, straw sandals, a shoulder bag to match. I powdered my nose lightly and put on fresh lipstick. My face stared back at me blankly from the other side of the mirror.

I found Marge and Josie out on the tiny terrace overlooking the square below the high windows of the living room. They were sipping white wine. Josie pulled up a chair for me and handed me a glass.

"Try this. It's local. Marge found it. Or rather, her friend did. He knows where to go for the good stuff at discount prices."

I sipped, tentatively at first. The wine was tart, chilled to perfection. It went down easily. Marge asked about mutual friends back home. Josie talked about French investments in Iraq. She had majored in economics and finance at NYU. The embassy had hired her as an assistant to their trade analyst. She seemed to be well-informed about things.

"I don't understand all the criticism back home, about France supporting the Iraqi," she was explaining. "We do our thing, the French do theirs. They have trade agreements with Iraq. Why should they give them up to suit us?"

"It's not that simple," I ventured. "We're trying to control terrorism. The French are trading with a country that harbors terrorists."

"Terrorists are everywhere," Marge chimed in. "You might as well close up shop in every foreign country with that kind of attitude."

"It's not an attitude. It's a reality. Besides," I went on quickly, "it's not trade in general, it's selling arms and even nuclear materials to our enemies. I don't think that's ethical, do you?"

"It may not be ethical," Josie countered, "but neither is war, or killing. All I'm saying is that we have no right to dictate to another country that way. They're only looking after their own interests."

"It's hard to forget nine-eleven," I said, even as the horror of what that event had done to my life threatened to drown my efforts to remain calm. "You're right in a way: it's not a question of ethics or logic. It's a question of survival. This is a different kind of war."

I saw Margie glance at Josie. They couldn't begin to imagine what was going through my mind, but they suddenly seemed to remember that Frank had been one of the victims of that unforgettable terrorist attack in New York the previous year and suddenly grew contrite. Josie brought an end to the discussion by getting up and stretching. "It's eight-twenty. Time to eat," she said.

We followed her back inside. Marge closed the doors to the terrace.

It was a short walk to the restaurant. Josie ordered a bottle of wine right away and we started to drink at once. By the time the food came, we were pretty high, laughing, teasing one another. I don't remember what I ate, roast duck I think. After the dishes were taken away, the owner came over. When Josie told him I had just arrived, that they hadn't seen me in two years, he pulled up a chair and treated us to *espresso* and cognac.

Someone made a toast. "You won't believe this, Monsieur Talman," said Marge, putting down her glass and reaching across me to tap the man's arm. We were all pretty drunk by then. "Guess what! This nice lady, our friend here, is related to —"

I tried to hush her but she ignored me and came out with my cousin's name. Monsieur seemed impressed. He turned in his chair to look at me directly. "She just came from a big party he gave for her at the chateau!" she went on, as though I had won a gold medal at the Olympics. By that time, the wine and cognac had worked their magic on me as well. I actually laughed.

"Money, money, money!" I said, with a wide gesture that struck something that turned out to be Josie's shoulder. "Wives and money!" I'm not sure what I meant, but it seemed relevant.

Monsieur Talman rose and took my hand. He was a polite little man, a Kabyle from Algiers, I learned later. All his mature life, his father had been taking care of the extended family of eighteen. He plowed infertile land, struggled for every ounce of barley or couscous needed to feed themselves and keep the oxen they had to borrow in return for a portion of the harvest. But the harvests were minimal; life was a daily struggle. Mr. Talman had finally gone to work in Algiers and from there had moved on to Paris, as so many Kabyles before him had done, in their desperate need. In Paris he'd found a job washing dishes in the restaurant where they were now sitting.

Used to long hours and hard work, he was given more and more responsibility; and after several years, when the owner retired, Mr. Talman bought the place at a very good price.

"It was a pleasure meeting you, Mamselle," he said, bending over Katie's hand, Then, turning to Josie: "Are you ladies all right? Do you want me to walk you home?" It was late. The place had gradually emptied. Josie shook her head and said something reassuring to him. "Well then, good night for now," said Monsieur. He bowed and walked away, toward the back, where two waiters were upending chairs on bare tables. He stopped to help them.

I heard myself still talking. Josie had gotten up, ready to leave, and was urging Marge to do the same; but Marge shook her off and continued to stare at me, listening raptly to what I was saying.

"The Midas touch. Everything he touches turns to hard currency. Except Emma. Emma turns to fat. Ha, ha! Oh, he thinks he can buy me. You know, he's crazy. Did I tell you? He's off his rocker! I should know, right?" I felt someone tug at me, get me up out of my chair. "No, let me finish," I said somewhat annoyed. I picked up my glass and drank the rest of the cognac. "Ah! That's better." Later, when I tried to remember what I'd said, all I drew was a big blank.

We staggered home, Marge on one side of me, Josie on the other. Marge stumbled a few times, but Josie held her own, still the caretaker. The last thing I remembered was Josie pulling my dress over my head and settling me under a cool fresh sheet.

Sometime during the night, I threw up. Afterwards, I sat on the edge of the bed, my memory still clouded, my mouth dry, my head spinning. I fell back down and after a while must have fallen asleep again. In the morning, my head throbbed, my body was too heavy for my legs to carry. I fumbled in my tote for some aspirin, but getting water from the bathroom tap to wash it down was more than I could manage. I lay down again. Finally, I forced myself to walk the distance from the bed to the bathroom and in one desperate gesture scooped water into my hand and washed down the two tablets I had been holding.

A new worry surfaced. What had I said last night about my cousin? About Emma? About money? I shook my head as though by doing that I could get rid of the dreadful truth waiting to be stirred up. Tears of frustration ran down my cheeks. I cradled my wet face in my hands and swore out loud.

If this was the best I could do, I might as well give up, I told myself. How was I going to explain what I had said the night before. . . . What exactly *had* I said? If I could only remember! I groaned out loud. Then, as suddenly as the tears had come, I felt myself grow calm, shedding the lethargy that had taken hold of me earlier. My head cleared. I found myself doing what I always did in a difficult situation: I went through my options. In the end, I decided the best course of action was to say nothing about how I'd behaved the previous night, unless Marge or Josie asked questions. The bottom line, after all, was that we had all drunk too much. I could honestly say that after a certain point I couldn't recall anything, and therefore whatever it was I said was a lot of hogwash: my thoughts, as well as my words, were steeped in alcohol.

My concern, I realized when I walked into the kitchen, had been unwarranted. Josie was preparing breakfast. Marge was sitting at the table, her head thrown back. She held an ice pack against her right temple.

Josie turned, as I came in. "Well, well, alive and kicking, I see."

"Barely alive. Certainly not kicking," I said. I poured myself a cup of coffee and sat down next to

Marge. "Bad, huh?"

Josie answered for her. "She can't move and can't talk."

"What about you, Josie? Are you immune or something?"

"I could always outdrink you two, have you forgotten?" She sighed. "Actually, I didn't have that much last night." She came to the table and sat down opposite Marge. "I guess I'll put the eggs on hold." It wasn't really a question. She turned to me. "Would you like some toast?"

"No, thanks. Coffee is all I can take right now."

"How did you like the place?"

"C'mon, Josie, I was too far gone to really notice."

"Stressed out, I'd say. What I can't figure out is *this* one," pointing to Marge, who let out a small groan. "She should have known better. She would have ordered another bottle of wine, if I hadn't stopped her."

"We were celebrating, remember?" I protested.

"Okay, Okay," she said, dismissing the subject with a wave. "But what about the rest of it?"

"What do you mean?"

"All that jazz about money and wives?"

"What did I say?"

"Oh, I don't know. It was all a big mush."

"It couldn't have been important."

"You sounded . . . I hate to say it, you sounded jealous."

I couldn't help laughing. That certainly had not crossed my mind as a possible explanation. I heard myself say: "Who wouldn't be jealous? The lucky dog!" Relief flooded over me. I watched as Josie went to pick up some magazines that were lying on the counter top across the room.

"Like I told you, he's all over the place. Here, see for yourself." She put down the magazines and sat down again. "We saved them for you."

    I opened the one on top and leafed through until I came to the story. It was about an opening at one of the major galleries. Lots of photographs. My cousin was in almost all of them. My cousin alone, my cousin with close friends, my cousin with Emma, my cousin with his Excellency the Mayor, my cousin with Henry Kissinger, my cousin with a Rockefeller who happened to be visiting, my cousin with the head of the UN. One caption described him as "the American billionaire who has made the Riviera his home"; the text gave some of the highlights of his successful rise.

    In another magazine, a picture story of some other event carried the headline: "All that, and Emma too!" And there she was, still incredibly beautiful, wearing a thin silvery tulle which made her look ethereal, even though her figure seemed more full than svelte. Emma's gown was described in detail, as well as the jewelry she wore — emerald chandelier earrings and a sculpted necklace of gold and diamonds, with a large emerald pendant —the only touch of color. It served to highlight dramatically her almost platinum hair and the silver gown.

    Every detail of her appearance was faithfully recorded. Together, she and my cousin gave off an aura of wealth and luxury, royalty one might be tempted to say, but there was also — or was it my imagination? — a suggestion of self-indulgence, boredom even, in their expressions. Still, to the ordinary reader who could only dream of such a life, the two seemed the perfect couple blessed by success and all good things.

    Emma, it seemed, had replaced Princess Di in the French press. I wondered vaguely who dressed her, got her ready for these social occasions, prepared her for her public appearances. I marveled, too, how nothing of their difficulties, of Emma's drinking, my cousin's indifference to her, no hint of their private lives had managed to leak out. There were, after all, plenty of people around, day and night: maids, a valet, a cook, a butler, a housekeeper, and guests, often enough. Surely someone would have noticed, as I had, soon after my arrival, the strain between husband and wife? But then again, knowing my cousin and his many talents, having witnessed his charm, I could easily grasp how he might subtly bribe, insinuate, even threaten if necessary, servants and friends to keep their mouths shut.

I picked up another magazine. This one carried a feature story about the chateau, beautiful photographs of the rooms. Emma alone, this time. Emma in deceptively simple clothes, explaining, pointing, chatting, smiling. I wondered what threats my cousin had used to get her into position for the reporter who had come to write the story, for the photographer who'd taken the pictures. Had he temporarily taken away the booze, the drugs?

"Did you know he was such a celebrity?" Josie interrupted my thoughts.

"I knew he had made a fortune."

"Were you surprised when he invited you to visit them?"

"The surprise was running into him. Or rather, his spotting *me*. I told you on the phone, remember? I was having coffee at my hotel, one morning, St. Tropez was on my itinerary, and suddenly there he was. He'd recognized me. That's when he invited me to the chateau. I checked out of the hotel and went to stay with them for the next three days. Skipped Nice."

"When are you going to tell us all about it?"

"What's to tell? He's a clever man. I really don't know him that well. Hadn't seen him in years. It isn't as though we played together as kids. He's much older than I am; I almost didn't recognize him at first."

"But he remembered you all right!"

I almost broke down then, almost told her how he had staged the accidental meeting at the hotel. Instead, I made a face and said: "He did, although I've changed quite a bit since he'd seen me last. I was only sixteen."

"Has he changed much?"

"Not physically, but, . . . I can't really explain it, there's something about him . . . a different look — "

"The sweet smell of success — "

I laughed. "Can't say I smelled anything, but there was a certain confidence, a certain ease in his success. But it was always there, potentially at least. I remember, nothing seemed to faze him, even back then. Even as a teenager, he was different from the rest of us. Never awkward or uncertain. Even as a boy, he found his own way of doing things, was never part of a group. Deliberately so. He always seemed in perfect control. Still is. Only more so, if that's possible."

Margie took the ice pack off her head and picked up the coffee Josie had set in front of her earlier.

"It must be cold by now," I said. Josie reached for the cup.

"I'll pour you a fresh one. Nice and hot."

Margie waved her off. She hadn't spoken since I had come into the room. "This is fine." It came out as a hoarse whisper.

We both watched her as she took a tentative sip. Her movements were slow, her face still pale and drawn. Josie and I must have betrayed our concern in the way we were watching her, because she suddenly broke out in a wide smile.

"Loosen up! I'm getting better with every minute. It was worth it, even though, right now, I feel like hell!"

We puttered around, skipped lunch. By late afternoon, we were ready to move out and around, but it was getting late and we decided to save the Louvre and other places of interest for the next day. Instead, we spent a couple of hours browsing in the shops. I treated myself to a lovely sweater and a large straw hat. We came home early and sat down to a modest dinner Josie put together for us. The next day, true to their promise, my two old friends took me sightseeing. The morning went by quickly. We had a relaxing lunch at a bistro and again ate dinner at home, catching up on all the latest gossip. The next few days were more of the same. Somewhere along the line, Josie took us to a reception at the Embassy. I met some interesting people and had occasion to practice my French. Twice we went dancing, six of us. Josie recruited colleagues to escort the two of us; Marge had her friend Jean, on whom she lavished attention. The days flowed into one another. I began to relax.

CHAPTER THREE

By the end of the week, I had almost forgotten my resolve to cut short my stay in order to stop in Geneva and close the account my cousin had opened in my name. Very soon, I would have to tell my friends I was leaving earlier than expected. I still hadn't decided how to explain to Marge and Josie the urgent need to cut short my visit with them.

I finally managed to come up with something.

"A colleague asked me to deliver a letter to his banker," I told them. "Something personal. I don't know what made me say 'yes,' but I did. He's been a great help to me, ever since I started this job, a good friend. It would have been impossible to put him off. I'm really sorry. I'd almost forgotten about it."

That last, at least, was true. I felt terrible for having to deceive them. I felt even worse for having to leave: Marge and Josie had provided me with a short reprieve from the inevitable gloom that was waiting for me when, alone again, I would brood about what had happened. With them, I'd almost felt like my old self. Most of all, I would miss their innocent questions, their friendly teasing, I envied them their inner peace. As I hugged them goodbye, I promised I'd try to get back soon. I meant it.

In Geneva, I grew increasingly tense. I knew nothing about transactions of this kind. I had read about them in books, in newspaper stories about organized crime — how illegal profits are "laundered"; that money that can't be reported to the IRS is sent to the Caymans or to Switzerland.

In the end, it proved very simple. The account was there, in my name, to do with as I pleased. I was pleased to close it. I was pleased to have them send the entire amount to this person at this address, or could it be transferred directly into one of my cousin's accounts?

The bank director gave me a very special smile. In his eyes, I had suddenly been thrust into a higher realm: I was related, *related*, mind you, not just *acquainted* with but actually *related* to the eminent Charles Benson! The man's voice grew softer, more confidential, his manner more ingratiating. Did I know the account number? If not, Monsieur would recommend the first option and have the check sent directly to the gentleman. He, personally, would make sure of everything. Her cousin should have the check in his hands within the next three days. Was there anything else he could do for her?

When all was arranged and I was ready to go, he asked how long I would be there, and I told him I hoped to leave the next day but still had to change my ticket and find a flight to New York from Geneva, instead of Paris. Monsieur insisted on taking over the arrangements. In a matter of minutes, he had managed to get my ticket changed: I would be leaving the next evening on a Swiss Air flight. He also booked a room for me for that night.

The next day I took a tour of the city, had a leisurely lunch, visited the shops near the hotel and bought myself a gold wristwatch. Late that evening, I was on the plane, headed for home.

Back in New York, I tried to focus on the here and now. I returned to work two days later and took up my usual routines, the visit to my cousin an unpleasantness that grew more distant with every passing day. I e-mailed Marge and Josie, thanking them for their hospitality. I had truly enjoyed being with them; they had made me forget, for a while at least, the nightmare of my first few days in France.

The weeks, months, flew by. In November, I was promoted to the executive level job I had been waiting for. My first assignment as Assistant Head of Public

Relations took me to Paris, early in January, where I met with a group of Japanese clients. The firm had chosen me because I spoke Japanese as well as French. I knew the protocol too. I'd taken a short seminar not long before, on cultural networking. In fact, I had been seeing quite a lot of the man who headed the communications group our firm had hired to train its executives in protocol procedures. His name was Francis Delancourt, a sandy-haired cheerful, pleasant man, altogether different in looks and personality from Frank Hastings. We had grown close. . . .

I was understandably excited by the assignment but there was also a certain tension about returning to France — especially since, just before leaving New York, I had received a card from my cousin. There was no return address; just the St. Tropez postmark. All it said was: "I said it was a gift. No strings attached. Enjoy it. You deserve something special." Rage welled up inside me: he had opened a new account! I would have to find a way to close that one too, of course, send back his money. I was furious. How could I make him understand? I wanted absolutely nothing to do with him. I was determined to get rid of his "gift," once and for all, realizing at the same time that I might possibly have to confront him again to make my point. . . something I dreaded.

I was beside myself, angry that he was causing me so much trouble; but even as I raged at his audacity, I knew I had to postpone dealing with the matter. I could not be distracted from my assignment in Paris. Moreover, I needed time to work out some sort of strategy to put down, once and for all, his arrogance and presumption.

In Paris, my research and preparations paid off. Our Japanese clients were ready to make a deal. I had answered their questions honestly but discreetly. At the end, they had wined and dined me. I was invited to visit Japan.

I was sure the report that would be sent back about the meeting would be a favorable one. My own written account was terse but left out nothing important. I had been working on it every day, summarizing the exchanges that took place, noting what I thought needed attention, suggesting certain measures for dealing with these particular clients in the future. My writing had always been good. I was pleased as I read my summaries at the end of each day.

This time, I decided not to call Josie and Marge; I would have no time for them. Later, I found they had left several messages on my e-mail, about what I was about to discover for myself, on my last day in Paris.

I was returning to my hotel, late that afternoon, mission accomplished, quite satisfied with the results of my meetings, when something in the evening paper caught my eye as I walked past a corner kiosk. I picked up a copy and read about the inquest that had taken place the day before to determine the cause of a mishap in which the wife of noted billionaire Charles Benson was killed while negotiating a curve on the Amalfi road on the second of January. She was returning to Naples from a holiday visit with friends. It was a difficult road, even in good weather; the snow and ice had made it extremely hazardous.

Most of the story was a rehash of what apparently had been printed some days earlier. Emma had spent New Year's eve and day with friends and was driving back, alone, to her hotel in Naples. It was growing dark. The car swerved on the slick pavement, as it came out of a steep curve, then fell into the side of the cliff, turning a number of times before hitting the bottom. The story had lots of fillers about my cousin's business, his wealth, how he came into his money, how everything he touched seemed to prosper. I read the account over and over again, not at all surprised to learn that the inquest had ruled Emma's death "an accident." The story ended: "Not everything can be bought."

I remember laughing hysterically for a minute or two. Then, in spite of my effort to distance myself from the event, the past came surging back like a rogue wave, drowning my resolve.

He'd done it! Or was it really an accident? Even if I wanted to do so, what exactly could I report? I had the weird feeling I was caught in the same trap as before. Was there a convergence of incidents here? I'd received my cousin's card just before leaving New York on January third. Emma was killed on the second of January. Was it a coincidence? Or was the card a warning of some kind?

Don't go paranoid, I told myself. He's crazy.

But I had to do something! What?

He had, once again, put one hundred thousand dollars into an account in my name. I had returned his money and he had put it back.

A reminder?

A bribe?

He hadn't killed Emma. *But he wanted her dead.*

I realized with a jolt that I could do nothing. I was helpless. He had contrived to bring me into the middle of the mess that was his life.

I had no proof of anything, but nothing could convince me that Emma's death was an accident. Everything in me cried out for justice. But, what could I tell the police, if I went to them? Knowing my cousin, I knew there would be no loose ends. If it *was* foul play, he had covered it well. He had thought about it too long. There was nothing I could do. If I were questioned, how could I explain away the money he'd placed in my name in a Swiss bank account, knowing what I knew, having heard him say what he said!

Anger slowly gave way to despair. It eroded by well-being, my confidence. When I returned to New York, my work began to suffer. I began to loose weight. My attention often strayed. People began to notice a difference in me. I was no longer lively. I rarely smiled. Eventually my helplessness grew into a kind of lethargy, then acceptance. I resigned myself to the ugly reality that my cousin had found a way of shattering my world.

He had effectively silenced me. I had been compromised in a way beyond my control or my understanding. How different he had seemed in the old days! He was funny, then and never talked down to me. Once, briefly, I even had a crush on him — the older cousin, the young man who wore expensive clothes easily, who knew how to listen, how to make you feel special; the cousin who could look you straight in the eye and tell you the truth. "The truth shall make you free," he'd said to me once.

What a joke, I thought, recalling how profound those words had sounded when I first heard them. It was summer. I was twelve. My mom had taken me to visit her cousin Millie out in the Hamptons. Charlie had taken me for a walk into town. We stopped for an ice-cream soda. He'd asked me about school. "It's okay," I'd said, with a shrug. He crossed his legs and sat watching me as I swirled the straw around. "What you mean is, you can't stand it." I had giggled. "Who needs all that stuff?" "You'd be surprised," he said. "Wait a few years and you'll find out how handy even math can be." "I doubt it," I'd snapped back, then asked in turn: "How about *you*? Do *you* like school?" "No, but I force myself to work hard. Especially on those subjects I hate the most." "Weird!" I'd said with a dramatic gesture. "Why would anyone want to do *that*? It's crazy!" "To discipline the mind," he replied, studying my face all the while. "To learn to face challenges. You'd be surprised how important that is. The earlier you learn to face reality, the better off you'll be." "That's not reality," I said, feeling smug, "that's torture." He'd laughed, leaned over and mussed up my hair. I liked that. "Maybe so. But there's another side to everything, you know." I stretched my legs out into the aisle and crossed my arms. I felt very grown up just then. Suddenly I remembered something my dad had said once, when he was kidding around with me. "Like, the opposite is also true?" My cousin looked surprised. "That's good. Very good! Where did you get it?" "Why? Am I too dumb for it to be mine?" "Well, Kootie," he'd replied, as he took out money and laid it down on the table. "The truth is, the truth shall make you free." "So, where did you get *that*?" We both laughed as we left the shop.

    The truth had not made me free; it had bound me inextricably to terrible secrets I couldn't get rid of. I could never shake him off. The words I had dredged up from that long-ago past, rose to taunt me. My world had been simple enough then. Had it all been a lie? Whatever the truth, surely I could discipline myself the way he said he had learned to do.

    Slowly, I forced myself back to reality, picked up the pieces of my life. I began to concentrate on my work again, made an effort to be pleasant, to listen, to dress carefully. In time, I regained something of my former self. Those around me began to relax in my presence. Now and then someone teased me about the dark mood I'd harbored for a while. I laughed with them. Then, early in May, I received a short note from my cousin. He'd remarried, sold the chateau, lived now in Paris, where he had his main headquarters, was coming to New York on business in a few weeks. He'd like to see me.

    For days I debated whether or not to answer him. I knew if I saw him I wouldn't be able to refrain from asking how he managed to have Emma killed. How he got away with it. And just as surely he would reassure me it was really an accident. I needed time to bring myself under control.

I tore up the note.

I hated myself for not being able to act rationally in the matter. The truth was, I was afraid of seeing him, of reading whatever was there, in his face.

By then, I had moved in with Francis, but the mail addressed to my old place was still being forwarded to me. That's how I learned, in June, that Frank had been killed. The envelope had a Paris postmark but no return address. No note even; just a clipping from a Canadian newspaper. It reported a hit-and-run accident in Ottawa. There was a photo with the story. It showed Frank in front of a cottage, probably where he lived with his wife. He was smiling, facing the camera and holding a toddler. He seemed happy.

I looked at the picture for a long time, with a feeling of emptiness for things past, precious years lost. I thought of the man in the picture, the man who had been my husband, who had found a way to get rid of me, who had found happiness. His death had freed me. Is that what my cousin was trying to tell me? I could make plans, now, I could marry again, be happy. Was my cousin happy with his new wife? Had he found a new Emma, just as beautiful, and just as disappointing? How many Botticelli Venuses would he go through before settling into his own shortcomings?

I pulled myself back to what was nagging at me.

Was Frank's death really another coincidence? I didn't think so, but I couldn't bring myself to entertain the other possibility. At that moment, I was almost ready to meet with my cousin, after all. I felt there were lots more questions I wanted — no, *needed* — to ask him.

I dispelled the thought even as it surfaced, telling myself that the only reason I was toying with the idea of seeing him was that I had thrown away his address and knew I couldn't reach him easily any more. I just wasn't ready to see him, find out the truth.

Oh, but you do want to see him, said the little voice inside me, not so innocent any more. *And you can easily track him down on the internet, if you really try. You're afraid. You're afraid of what he might say. Not just about Emma or Frank. . . . About* you, *about* him!

Had he found love? Had he found happiness?

Had he stumbled on to something worth all that old trouble?

You're afraid he won't share it with you this time, my little voice whispered.

What is happiness?

What is love?

I knew with certainty, then, that I would never want to hear the answers; but my intention was shattered when my cousin arrived in New York.

I was standing by my desk one morning in July, shuffling though the mail I found neatly piled on my desk, when Lucille, my secretary, came in with a message.

"The best for last," she said smiling, as she handed me a slip of paper. "This gentleman called just before you got in. Said he was your cousin. Said he's in town briefly and wants to have lunch."

"Today?" I heard myself ask.

"Said he could meet you after his morning appointments. Any time after twelve. His name is —"

"I know who it is," I snapped. Lucille moved away from where she had been standing, holding the door ajar, and stepped inside the room. The woman could always read my moods.

"He apologized for calling so early but he had a meeting in a few minutes and wanted to get to you before then." I said nothing. "He got in very late last night."

I stood by the window, looking out over the tall buildings around me. Did I really have a choice? I still had not closed the new account he had opened.

51

I walked back to my desk and sat down. "He's not my favorite person — " was all I could manage.

"I gathered as much," said Lucille. "You don't have to see him, if you don't want to," she reminded me.

"You're wrong there," I said cryptically.

"He'll be calling back, first break he gets. You want me to tell him you're busy?"

"No. He'll only badger me until I give in. Might as well get it over with."

I looked down at my hands, clasped on top of the stack of papers on my desk. Clever bastard, I thought. Leaves nothing to chance. Lucille said: "He suggested meeting at the Regis. I guess he's staying there."

I made a show of impatience and drew myself up, ready for business.

"Tell him, when he calls, I'll meet him at twelve-thirty in the hotel lobby." Lucille nodded and turned to leave. "And Lucille," I said, leafing idly through the papers on my desk. "I won't be back after lunch. There are a couple of things I have to take care of."

Alone, I burrowed in my chair and took some long deep breaths.

What was he up to now? I vowed I wouldn't let him see how much his presence bothered me. At that moment, I truly wished him dead.

The rest of the morning, I buried myself in work: cleared the papers on my desk, dictated memos and letters, set up appointments for the next day. By noon I was ready to leave.

"Try to enjoy your lunch," Lucille whispered, as I dropped last minute memos and instructions on her desk. "After all, it *is* the Regis!"

It turned out not to be the Regis. He had made reservations at a tiny French restaurant on one of the side streets between Fifth and Madison.

For some reason, I expected him to have changed,

that evil would have left its mark; if anything, he looked sharper, livelier.

"How's you wife?" I found myself asking, as we waited for a cab to take us to the place he had chosen for lunch.

He gave me a strange look. "Fine, fine."

"Does this one suit you?" The nastiness in me was taking over. I didn't even try to stop it. I felt I had a right to be sarcastic. After that first look, he seemed to take it in stride.

"Janine is wonderful," he said, with a smile.

"The Queen is dead. Long live the Queen!" I said, a little too loudly.

"You must meet her."

"Not if I can help it." He didn't reply right away. We had reached the restaurant. In the tiny vestibule, I stopped and faced him, my adrenaline pumping courage into me. "I don't ever want to meet her. And I don't ever want to see you again. I don't know what you have in mind, why you've come, but you'll never win me to your side. Just so you know. This is the last time I will ever meet with you."

He nodded as though I had asked him to look after my plants while I was out of town.

The restaurant was cool and bright. I chose a salad. I refused the wine he had ordered.

We ate in silence. I finished first and sat staring at him as he finished his food. When our plates were taken away and we were left with coffee, he said, in his calm steady voice:

"I wanted to see you. We are cousins, after all."

"An unfortunate accident."

"That's not fair. I've done you no harm."

I laughed but almost choked on it. He pushed the glass of water toward me. I took a large gulp. "Really?" I finally managed. "You destroyed my peace of mind. That means nothing to you?"

"I'm sorry, if I've done that. I never meant to. I sent you news I thought you would want to have. Was I wrong?"

"You know damn well you were wrong. About that and a lot else."

"It was a bad time for me."

"And now everything is okay?"

He turned his wine glass back and forth, between his hands, before drinking again. He looked away for a while and said nothing; then he turned back to me, his steady gaze fixed on my face.

"Nothing is ever okay, not in this life," he replied softly, still toying with his glass. "But if you mean things are better for me at home, yes, that's true. I'm entitled to that, everyone is. Do you begrudge me some happiness?"

"Hell, who am I to begrudge you anything? I have no say in the matter."

"But you seem to resent me. Why? I don't deny Emma had become a burden. You saw for yourself."

I waved his words away. "Yes, yes, I saw, I heard, I watched her put you down. But you wanted her dead, and it wasn't just wishful thinking. Do you think I can ever forget that? What you asked me to do the morning I left for Paris?"

He looked down at his hands. I felt like shaking him. "And why the hell do you insist on putting money in the bank for me?" I went on heedlessly, not really expecting any answer. "Haven't I made it clear that I want no part of it?"

I had brooded for weeks on how to convince him that I didn't want his money. This was my only chance.

"To prove to you that it was simply a gift. No strings attached."

"Oh, there are strings attached. We both know that."

"No. I don't know that. It *was* a gift."

Everything was spilling out now. I didn't care how I sounded or who heard me. All my pent-up frustration was gushing out. "For your information, I read all about Emma in a French newspaper. Last January, when I returned to Paris on business. I read about the inquest and how she died. Who did you get to do the dirty work for you?"

There was a flicker of something in his eyes, but it was quickly gone.

"I can't imagine what you're thinking, but Emma's death was an accident."

"No, I don't think so." I stared back defiantly.

He shook his head and looked away for a few seconds. "You've obviously made up your mind about it; but she was in Italy and I was in Paris."

I broke out in a Dracula laugh, managing not to choke on it this time. It was almost funny, as though we were playing a game to see who could keep going longer, without caving in. Instinctively, he darted his eyes right and left, as if to see if I had drawn attention to myself. No one seemed to have noticed.

I began to feel heady, although I hadn't touched the wine he had poured for me.

He leaned back, pushed his coffee cup aside and clasped his hands on the table.

"Don't play games with me, Kootie — " he said in a hoarse voice.

"Don't call me Kootie," I interrupted in a vicious whisper.

" — it's too late for that," he continued over me.

"It's too late for a lot of things. Words have wings. Once said, you can never pull them back in." He cocked his head to one side, shifted in his seat, and drew his hands into his lap. He smiled at me, an amused look lighting up his face.

"I know what you're thinking," I went on, feeling a rush of confidence. "You asked me the same question when I was twelve." I mimicked his voice, assumed a kind of calm indifference. "'Where did you get *that?*' As though I'm some kind of retard!?"

"I remember." he said evenly. "You're still full of surprises," he said, with a thin smile. "I've always liked clever, witty people. I envy them, in fact."

"Right. Now you envy me."

"In many ways I do." He leaned across the table as though to reach out for my hand. I quickly withdrew it. Once again, he had assumed that calm unruffled look. "You mustn't jump to conclusions," he went on, as though reading what was uppermost in my mind. "About the money: I give gifts to so many people — employees, friends, colleagues. It pleases them and I enjoy sharing their pleasure. Why can't I give you a gift?"

"Because I don't want it."

"A gift is not something you want. It's something you accept. It's as simple as that."

"Not this gift."

"All right, then. If it makes you feel better, if that's all it takes to make us friends again, you can close the account. I won't reopen it. I promise."

I must have shown my relief, for he smiled, pleased with himself.

"You bet it makes me feel better, but don't think for a moment that we can ever be friends again." I needed to say much more. There was so much I wanted to know. . . . It was a mistake, but I heard myself ask:: "What about Frank?".

"What about him?"

"The clipping you sent said he was hit by a car." I stared at him, my heart pounding. For a while he said nothing.

"Whatever are you thinking?" he asked finally.

"You know what I'm thinking!"

He frowned, the first time I'd seen him do so. "You've been brooding too much. Snap out of it."

"Another coincidence?" He never took his eyes off me. He seemed truly dismayed. I felt my certainty beginning to slip.

"Dear Katie, what else could it possibly have been?"

"The same as Emma's death?"

"That's nonsense, and you know it. I sent you the clipping because I thought you would want to learn what had happened."

"I would have found out sooner or later. I had every intention of checking things out for myself. Out of curiosity, if nothing else."

"But now there's no need to do that, is there."

"There never was a need to do that. Frank was declared legally dead, after nine-eleven."

When I didn't go on, he said: "Do you really think I wanted him dead?"

"You don't want to hear what I think!"

"Obviously I made a mistake in sending you that notice."

"You know damn well it wasn't a mistake. It was your way of drawing me in again."

His eyes opened wide. He seemed genuinely surprised. "What do you mean?"

"To silence me?"

He shifted in his seat and shook his head in denial, as he gestured for the check. "You've been fantasizing. I can see now how troubled you've been all this while. I'm truly sorry if I had anything to do with it."

The waiter came with the bill and was paid in cash. Neither one of us rose to leave. My cousin looked thoughtful. Now, he crossed his arms on the table, leaned toward me and said:

"Listen to me. Whatever it is you have imagined or brooded about, forget it. I won't deny that Emma's death was a relief to me. I'm not a hypocrite. She had been drinking. Her friends urged her to stay the night; there was plenty of room in their villa. But, she insisted on driving back. And your thinking even for a moment that Frank's death was anything other than what was reported is simply absurd. I have no interest in Frank. Never had. I really have no vital interest in you, either — except, you *are* my cousin and I *do* like you. I thought we could be friends."

"You've made that impossible. . . ."

"I don't see how, but I'll have to accept your decision."

"Not mine. Yours. *Your* decision."

"I hope some day you'll realize how wrong you were." We both stood up, ready to leave. "You're set then, on carrying on this grudge?"

"Is that what you call it?"

"These doubts?"

"Did you think you could convince me your intentions were, . . . are . . . pure?"

He looked sad. "Honest, not pure. I don't know what pure means." I walked past him, out the door. "I wish you wouldn't leave like this," he said as I moved toward the curb. The doorman whistled for a cab. "I only wanted to see how you were. Didn't expect to find you so wrought up. I wish I knew how to ease your mind."

A cab pulled up. I looked back, my hand on the car door. "Nothing you can ever say can ease my mind. Some stains never come out. Like blood —"

He touched my arm, gently. "You've misjudged me, Kootie," he said, forgetting my earlier reproach for using that childhood nickname. "There's no blood on my hands."

"There's blood money, though. You've shelled out

plenty of that, I bet."

He shook his head in disbelief. "You don't know what you're saying," he said sharply, holding the cab door open. I gave the driver my home address and wrenched the door shut. He looked, suddenly, dejected, almost helpless standing there.

"Ah, but *you* do," was my parting shot, out the window. "You know *exactly* what I'm saying."

The afternoon stretched out before me, a bleak prospect. I regretted having told Lucille I wouldn't be back after lunch. Work would have distracted me; but I realized I was too upset to return to my normal routines.

Inside the apartment, I grew restless. Francis wouldn't be home until six-thirty, at the earliest — four and a half hours from now. What would I do with myself until then? I was too wound up to read or watch TV. The conversation with my cousin kept playing inside my head. Snatches of it kept coming back. I knew I had to say the things I said, get it all out; but his reaction had only confused me. He had betrayed nothing. In fact, he had almost convinced me that —

What, dear God, if I was really wrong about him? Would I ever be able to forgive myself? All those horrible things I'd said!

No, no, that's crazy, I argued against my caution; if I *was* wrong, why had he flown to New York just to see me? What was so urgent? We both knew he didn't have to go anywhere for meetings; he called the moves, people came to *him*. No. There was a purpose behind this trip, but not the one he had offered. Oh, he wanted to check up on me all right, but for reasons of his own. To make sure I wouldn't spill the beans, what else?

Or, was my imagination really working overtime?

How I hated him for making me doubt myself! He had won this round too. I was stuck with his secrets. If I decided to go to the authorities, even at this late date, what would I tell them? "Charles Benson, the billionaire whose wife was killed in a tragic auto accident near Naples, is a murderer!"

Hell! *I* would be the one they'd lock up. And who could blame them? What solid evidence did I have?

The only solid thing that wouldn't wash away, that I kept coming back to, was the offer he'd made, before I left the chateau. He did utter those words. He could never take them back. Still, what it boiled down to was my word against his. Who in his right mind would believe *me*? Even if they listened, what proof did I have? Sure, his wife had been killed, but it was an accident. The inquest ruled it that; and who would question their findings? There wasn't the slightest hint that it had been anything but an accident. Whoever he had gotten to do it had done a perfect job. Nothing would ever connect him in any way to his wife's death. If I accused him of anything, he might even sue me for libel . . . or do much worse. Oh, he was capable of anything, to protect himself, to get what he wanted. He wouldn't hesitate for a minute to have me killed too, if he thought I was a threat to him. Even if I *was* his cousin!

I was certain too that he had paid enough to get the job done well, that whoever did it would never have to resort to blackmail. After all, he had offered *me* ten million! Enough, surely to keep someone quiet for all time. Enough for someone to lead a life of luxury for several lifetimes. Knowing him, I knew he would have planned every detail, down to the smallest.

So, who would believe me?

With painful clarity, I also reminded myself that in the worst possible scenario the one hundred thousand dollars he had deposited in Geneva, in my name, could easily be construed as payment for keeping my mouth shut. The money had been received and had been spent

— or so it would seem. We both knew I had sent it back to him, that I refused to accept it, but he probably had covered those tracks well enough. And, to top it all, he had placed (or so the record would show) another hundred thousand in my account. Who would believe that it was just a gift, "no strings attached"?

At best he had compromised my reputation. At the worst, the money could be construed as payment of some kind, to silence me about his intention to get rid of Emma.

Something else now began to bother me. It had been lurking inside me all along. Why, in heaven's name, had he asked me to shoot his wife in the first place! He didn't need me to kill Emma! And he certainly wouldn't have wanted her shot! It just didn't make sense. So why broach that horrible request at all?

The more I thought about it, the more I became convinced that there was something seriously wrong with him. Surely he knew what it would do to me! I thought again of my mother telling me more than once that there was something wrong with her cousin Millie. Had her son inherited it, whatever it was?

Imagine if I told anyone that he had promised me ten million to kill his wife! I'd end up in the loony bin. Sure, Emma had been killed. But not shot. He was too clever for keeping to that plan after he'd made the offer at the chateau — if it really had ever been a serious option. By now I was sure he had worked out the real scenario long before I arrived in St. Tropez, a much more efficient plan, as it turned out.

My thoughts were racing wildly, way out of control. One thing I knew for certain: he would not hesitate to destroy me, if he felt I was a threat.

He'd come to New York to see how I was taking it. And I'd made sure there was no doubt in his mind. Lashing out at him, telling him what I suspected, was a relief but, also, I now realized, a big mistake. Too late, I chided myself. All I'd done was give him good cause to worry. I'd let him know how much I hated him and that, given the chance, I would do everything in my power to make him pay for what he'd done. I'd been reckless, stupid....

In an effort to distract myself from such painful speculation, I went marketing. I decided I would surprise Francis with his favorite dinner that evening: my version of chicken cordon bleu. I bought boned chicken breasts, *prosciutto* and *mozzarella*, and for dessert I picked up some *cannoli*, Francis's favorite dessert.

Later, with my preparations done, I changed into a new silk lounging pajama I'd bought on sale the week before. By the time Francis came home, I had settled into what by now was a familiar role. Tonight there was champagne. I placed it in the cooler, my two Waterford glasses next to it on a tray. Then I lit candles in the long silver holders that had belonged to my mother and grandmother. They cast soft shadows on the walls. The Cole Porter tunes drifting into the dining room from the CD player in the living room added to the romantic atmosphere.

After dinner, we sat close together on the sofa, and Francis told me how much he loved me. With his arms around me, I felt safe. In that small oasis of contentment, I was, for those few precious moments, my old self. Francis made me whole again.

I glossed over the call that morning and lunch with my cousin.

"Am I going to meet him?" he asked, after I had given him a brief account of the visit, mostly about the food, how my cousin looked, that he had remarried, things like that.

"I don't think so. Not this time around, anyway," I managed to improvise. "He's flying back to Paris tomorrow."

"Next time, then."

With my head resting on his shoulder, I felt the past receding, a new life taking hold. At that moment, I was at peace; the earlier uncertainties and worries fast disappearing. I gave silent thanks for having decided to share my life with this man who gave me strength and purpose and would take care of me. I rejoiced in my decision.

The evening before, Francis had asked me to marry him and I had accepted.

CHAPTER FOUR

The ceremony at City Hall, early in August, was a quiet one, much like the one when I married Frank, three years earlier, right after my graduation from New York University. Back then, my brother Matt had to rush off to a new job in California and couldn't be there for me. This time, he insisted on flying to New York "to give me away." We had been very close, Matt and I, still were. We'd exchanged e-mails often enough, but I didn't realize how much I'd missed him, until I embraced him again after three long years. At the same time, I couldn't help thinking back, much as it hurt, to Frank Hastings.

I'd met him during my senior year. Frank was five years older than I and had a Master's degree in accounting. When I first met him, he'd already been working for several years as a medical claims investigator for a large insurance company. We were comfortable with each other from the very first date.

When my parents were killed in a car crash two months before I graduated, Matt took over. A trust fund made the paperwork easier. In no time, with the help of a lawyer friend, he cleared probate and sold the house.

Also at my insistence, we had split evenly the money recovered from the sale of the house and the rest of my parents' belongings. My brother had wanted me to have most of it, to help Frank and me get started; but I convinced him I didn't need it. Frank, I had to admit, had not been able to save much, but things would be different — I insisted — since I now had a job, too, a very good job. My study of French, Italian, and Japanese had turned out to be a major asset and had given me an edge. I could tell, when interviewed, that they were impressed with my credentials, in spite of my lack of experience. Given time, I could rise easily to an executive position. I decided when I was offered a job with a major electronic firm to make every effort to improve the skills I already had and to take on new responsibilities whenever an opportunity presented itself. I was determined to make a mark.

Frank and I eased into married life effortlessly. My brother seemed happy with his new job as district manager for a large computer company and wrote back enthusiastically about it. There were moments, in those early days, when I wished my parents were still around to see how well their kids had managed. The feeling of wanting to share your happiness with those dearest to you is natural enough; but in my case, there was a special reason for wanting Mom and Dad — Dad especially — to know how well I'd done for myself.

He'd been discreet about it, but I knew he was disappointed with my choice. There was a coolness between them, when Frank visited. It made me sad, but I kept telling myself that, like most parents, they simply thought I could do better. Given time, they would surely feel as I did about Frank. After all, he was a mature, reliable man, with a good job and salary. He was not a drinker and didn't smoke. What more could a girl ask for? I concluded that their reaction was normal and that they'd come around in due course.

Only once did Dad refer to Frank openly and betray his feelings. It was after dinner, one evening in April, just before he and Mom were killed on their way back from visiting friends in Stamford. I had rushed home with the news that I had received an offer from an international firm that had interviewed me on campus some weeks earlier. They smiled, nodding their pleasure as I shared some of the details with them.

"That means Frank and I can be married next year, maybe sooner!" I went on heedlessly.

Mom said nothing, a smile still lurking around

her lips but her eyes suddenly alert. It was my father who asked, quietly:

"Are you sure you want to marry him, Katie? You've had no other serious dates all this time. Shouldn't you have? How can you be sure you want to spend the rest of your life with Frank?"

I was stunned. "Of course I want to!" I answered, frowning. "Would I be wasting my time on someone I wasn't serious about?"

I realized he was genuinely concerned, but I couldn't understand why. My mom said nothing, as though they had agreed in private that my father would speak for both of them. You could see they were embarrassed, but worried too.

After some more of the same, I asked bluntly: "What is it exactly, you have against Frank?"

"He's distracted, Katie. Not all there for you." The surprise on my face must have given him pause. When he resumed, he held up a hand to ward me off: "All right, all right: I confess it's more a feeling than anything concrete."

"You just don't know him as I do," was all I could say. "He's withdrawn at times. So? Not everyone's a Jolly Joe. You certainly aren't! That doesn't make you a risk as a husband does it?" I turned to my mother. "Does it Mom?" She chuckled but said nothing. That broke the tension somewhat. But Dad had not finished yet.

"He's restless. Somewhere down the line, he'll disappoint you. The decision is yours, but I wish you wouldn't do anything right away."

I couldn't take in what he had said. It was so unfair! Only later, did that conversation come back, the truth of those words rise to haunt me. At that moment, I was understandably annoyed. The expression on my face gave him pause. He got up and held up his hands, as if to say, 'That's it. I'm done.' What he actually said was:

"I've said my piece, Katie. We love you dearly, you know that. And though we don't quite agree on this, we'll be there for you, whatever you decide."

I hugged him then, the tension between us gone.

The incident had come vividly to mind a number of times since I'd first learned from my cousin that Frank was indeed alive and well in Canada. What had my father seen that I had missed?

What I still couldn't figure out is why he had gone to so much trouble to be rid of me. Why hadn't he simply asked me for a divorce? Sure, it would have been hard for me to accept at first: I would have been shocked, devastated at the idea of divorce after a year of marriage; I would have cried and objected; I would have been embarrassed at my naiveté, but eventually I would have given in. There was another woman and, damn it, I had my pride!

Thinking him dead all those months, before my cousin informed me about what really had happened, I had genuinely mourned him. I mourned the happiness I thought we had shared. Many nights I cried myself to sleep, thinking of the years together that had been denied us, a marriage that lasted only a year. Later, I kicked myself, thinking how I'd missed any signs of trouble along the way. Brooding about it, I'd figured out that he must have met the woman at a conference he attended in Toronto in April. He had returned to Canada twice that summer to be interviewed — so he'd said — for a really good job.

What a fool I'd been to trust him! All those lies! I remembered his enthusiasm when he returned from the conference in Toronto, all excited about new possibilities. I'd suspected nothing, had encouraged him in fact — although I began to worry somewhat about what would happen if he received an offer and asked me to move to Canada.

Did he really expect me to pick up and follow him, wherever he decided to go? I thought it best to say nothing more at the time. After all, no firm offer had been made, and the whole thing could prove a false alarm. Still, I thought his enthusiasm strange, since he had obviously not given much thought to the impact a move of that kind would have on me. I was doing very well in my own job. I grew apprehensive about the choice I might have to make. I certainly wasn't ready to leave New York. I tried to reassure myself that if it came down to it, Frank wouldn't budge either.

Little did I know that he had already made up his mind and was desperately looking for a way out! I had no inkling that he meant to abandon me for another woman, that he didn't give a hoot about my job and my future. He wanted out and fate had conveniently lent a big hand!

Well, I had a new life now, a new husband, someone who really loved me. And I loved him. Oh, he was successful too: president of a consulting firm that specialized in training American executives in Japanese social and business protocol. We got along very well, enjoyed our time together. I knew we could help one another realize our ambitions, reach our goals. Eventually, enjoy a family together. . . .

My brother was just as happy to see me again, even if briefly. Over our modest and very private wedding lunch at the Plaza, right after the brief ceremony at City Hall — Matt had to fly back to the West coast, later that afternoon — my brother told us how he was planning to set up his own company. He made a very nice toast and presented us with a substantial check, asking us to pick out our own gift for the apartment we now shared as husband and wife, since we knew best what we wanted. I hugged him with genuine affection — he had looked after me as far back as I could remember and I loved him dearly. I was pleased that he and Francis seemed to take to one another. They talked easily about many things. Before leaving, my brother urged us to visit him soon.

It was a week later that I received a long-distance call at home, one evening. Francis was in his study, working at the computer. I was in the living room, reading.

I picked up the receiver almost at once, since it was on the side table beside me. I was annoyed at the interruption.

"Hello," I said, somewhat sharply. The line was open but no one spoke. I repeated the greeting and added: "Who is this, please?"

A voice at the other end asked: "Is this Katherine Hastings?"

I put down the book, frowning. Whoever was calling apparently wasn't aware that I had remarried.

"Who is this?" I asked again, this time with a certain curiosity mixed with sudden apprehension.

"Is this Mrs. Hastings?"

"Yes, yes, this is Katherine Hastings," I replied, realizing only after I had uttered the words that I had misled the woman.

"I'm so glad to have reached you, Mrs. Hastings. My name is Flora Chadwick. I don't know if you've talked with Inspector McCalley yet; he flew to New York today, to see you and others who knew Frank. I was married to Frank — James Chadwick, that is, that's the name he took on when he came to Ottawa —"

My head began to whirl. I jumped up and moved about, as far as the phone cord would let me, back and forth, as though my uneasiness could be dissipated by pacing. Why was this woman, Frank's other wife, the one he'd married after staging his own death, calling me? What could she possibly have to tell me? How did she find me?

I felt I was about to plunge into a dark abyss. I forced myself to focus on what was being said at the other end.

"— didn't want to bother you; so much has happened. I won't even try to put myself into your shoes" — but you have, haven't you! you did exactly that! I thought to myself — "but I need to talk to you. It's important. Could we meet? I can fly down any time. Just tell me when."

I sat down again, before answering.

"What is there to talk about?"

"James. I mean Frank. How he died."

I was about to retort: The first time or the second? Flora went on: "Did you know that he had staged his own death, that he escaped nine-eleven?"

Of course I knew! I knew that and much more! But I had no intention of telling her that. How could I?

Instead I said, after a pause: "What are you trying to say?"

"I'm truly sorry," she said quickly. "I couldn't stop him. He had made up his mind." She went on to give me the details of Frank's escape, their marriage in Ottawa, his death in June. I can't remember what I said to fill in the pauses. When she spoke again, her voice sounded raw, as though she was fighting a bad cold. "I didn't want to be the one to tell you all this, but I had to, given what's happened. Not a day goes by that I don't think about what James — I'm sorry, I keep forgetting — what Frank did just to be free again."

That "free again" hurt. "There are other ways of being free besides causing the kind of grief he caused!" I burst out, beside myself with anger and self-pity.

"But I didn't know, I still don't know all the details; and I never asked. It was too painful. But he told me enough for me to piece it together. It was awful what he did!"

I laughed into the phone. "Well, fate caught up with him, didn't it! Don't be shocked if I don't feel sorry for you."

Suddenly the voice took on a different tone, came out stronger and clearer. "All of this is irrelevant. The past is done with. I need your help here and now."

"We have nothing to talk about," I said woodenly, all my anger suddenly spent.

"I assure you there is. My James, your Frank was killed here in Ottawa recently. It wasn't the hit-and run that was reported."

The full impact of what she had just said did not register right away. My suspicions were one thing, but Flora's conviction was something else. I confess my curiosity was aroused. I heard myself saying, rather bitterly:

"You're telling me that maybe he staged another death to free himself again? Start another new life in South America or Australia?" It was cruel of me, I knew; but I wanted her to feel something of the pain I had felt, on learning what he had done to free himself of me.

My sarcasm had no effect on her. "He was killed, but there's more to it."

All I could muster was, "Oh?"

"When can I see you?"

I heard Francis flush the toilet . He'd be in the living room in a matter of seconds, ready for me to join him and relax over a glass of wine.

I was petrified. He knew I had lost my husband in nine-eleven, but that's all he knew. I still couldn't bring myself to confide in him what my cousin had asked, what had happened during my vacation abroad, Frank's marrying again. I had kept all that from him; it was simply too hard to explain. Besides, always, in the back of my mind, was the thought that sharing what I knew would place the other person in a precarious legal position. Francis might even urge me to go to the police. I just couldn't do it. What could I possibly tell them? More important, what would happen to Francis and me? I simply couldn't risk it.

I shut off all argument. The water was running. Francis would be strolling in any minute. Quickly, I suggested meeting the next day, at noon, in the lobby of the New York Public Library.

Francis came in just as I put down the receiver.

"Who was that on the phone?" he asked, as he turned on the TV.

"Someone at work about a special meeting tomorrow." He handed me the glass of wine he had poured for me. He picked up his own glass and lifted it in a silent toast, as he placed an arm around my shoulder. Then he kissed me, raised his glass and said: "To us. To my only love. To my Katie."

I closed my eyes and prayed that I would never have to tell him anything that might make him sorry he had ever said things like that to me.

The next day I cleared my desk, gave Lucille the preliminary draft of a presentation that was coming up and that would keep her busy typing and checking figures for the rest of the day, and took a cab to the Library. I knew the small trim woman watching the entrance was Flora Chadwick the minute I saw her. There was an air of expectancy about her, a look she must have seen reflected in my own face as I approached.

"Mrs. Hastings?"

"I don't have much time to spare," I said somewhat curtly, avoiding any formal introduction. I led the way to a nearby bench.

Her plain green suit made her face look very pale. She wore no make-up, didn't have to. Her complexion was flawless, not a wrinkle anywhere, her light brown eyes large and luminous. Still, she was not pretty or striking even; but her face, when animated, took on a special quality.

"Thank you for coming."

I went right to the point. "You said Frank didn't die the way it was reported."

"That's right."

"Does it matter?"

"Yes. It does. You see, he was killed deliberately. It wasn't a hit-and-run accident. He was murdered." She didn't take her eyes off me when she said that. I shifted in my seat, a new dread settling over me.

"That's absurd. Who would want to murder Frank!" Even as I uttered the words, the devil reared his evil head to smirk at me. I suddenly recognized the possibility, no, the certainty of it. Everything fit; all that had been plaguing me since my cousin had sent me that clipping about Frank's death came together.

"That's what I'm trying to find out!"

"There was an inquest, right?"

"They had nothing to go on."

"And you're telling me that it was deliberate, even though there's nothing to go on."

"I can't explain. Not yet. But I'm certain he was meant to be killed. Someone wanted to do away with him."

"Well, I have to tell you, I'm not surprised if it really happened that way. You're telling me he disappeared, took on a new identity.... Who knows what he had to do to maintain that fiction, make sure no one would ever find him!" I didn't try to hide the bitterness in my voice.

Flora was watching me intently.

I was tempted to tell her I knew all that she had told me, but how could I? He was despicable, my cousin, but I had nothing on which to base my own private conviction that he was capable of anything and in no way was I prepared to confide in this woman, who was obviously bent — for reasons of her own — on finding some excuse to shift the blame for Frank's death, make it out as murder instead of an unfortunate accident. She was probably right, but I couldn't let her know that.

"I really don't want to get involved in any of this, even if there were something I could do for you," I said, by way of conclusion. "I recently remarried. I have a new life. I don't need any of this. Frank hurt me enough. That part of my life is over."

We sat there for a while, without speaking. I could see Flora struggling with her own demons, trying to adjust to what I had said. I wondered if she had any idea of the nagging suspicions she'd revived in me! I said, trying to get over the awkwardness of the moment:

"You have a little boy?"

She nodded. "He's almost a year old. I left him with my mother."

"Does your mother know about Frank? That he was married before? . . . . And did you know he was still married to me when he married you?"

"Yes . . . and yes."

"It didn't bother you?"

"Of course it bothered me!" she whispered hoarsely. "I was horrified. But he was determined. He had burned his bridges. There was no going back. We both knew it. . . . I went along, yes."

"You think he told you everything?"

She looked at me boldly, a challenge in her eyes.

"I never asked to be told anything. I trusted him. We trusted one another. He told me what he wanted me to know. It was enough."

I couldn't resist it, so I asked bluntly: "Did he tell you why he left me the way he did?"

There was no hesitation on her part. "Yes." I said

nothing, and she went on: "He didn't want to hurt you, but he wasn't happy. It had been a mistake, he said. He was sorry to do it, but it was the only way."

My cousin's words echoed somewhere inside me. "He was happy with you, then?" I heard myself asking.

"Yes. We were happy together."

"No qualms? No guilt? Having me believe he had died so horribly?"

"It was his decision. I had to accept it."

"You realize you could be charged for helping him in all this?"

"I didn't help. I had no knowledge of anything at the time."

"But he told you about it, later. And you didn't report any crime."

"What crime?"

"Bigamy. Fraud, in assuming another identity." It sounded silly, even as I said it. She looked genuinely distraught. I went on recklessly. "Were you so far gone that you could allow yourself to become part of a conspiracy?" I didn't know anything about the legal aspects of the matter, but I didn't care.

"We loved each other."

I swallowed, remembering my cousin's words. "How did you meet?"

"Frank came to a convention in Toronto. I met him there. I was working for a dentist at the time, and he'd asked me to go along, help him over the hurdles, as he put it. It was all on the up and up. He's a very shy man. A good dentist but still needs a caretaker. Hasn't married. Lives at home with his mother."

"And that's where it started."

She looked down at her clasped hands on the table. "Yes."

"Love at first sight?"

She raised her eyes and gave me a defiant look.

"Yes."

"And you went through that ingenious charade to get rid of me!"

"I had nothing to do with it. He told me he would take care of things, to be patient. I did that."

"It didn't bother you to learn what he had done?"

"Look, I don't have to defend myself, or James, for that matter. He did what he thought was best for everyone concerned."

"Letting me mourn him for a whole year was just an unpleasant side effect, is that it?"

"I couldn't linger on that."

"Of course not. No one, nothing else mattered, except satisfying your own lust."

She stood up then, her face a deep red. "You don't deserve an answer, but I will tell you that it wasn't like that at all."

"Oh, sit down," I exclaimed irritably. "And stop acting so innocent. You both did an unforgivable thing. Deliberately. Fully aware of the terrible pain you were inflicting. How can you live with yourself, knowing you were causing another human being so much pain ?"

She was upset, I could see, but she sat down again. "Can we skip over all that? I didn't come here to hear your resentments or your self-righteous indignation. What happened is past. That part of it, at any rate. What I'm concerned with is why my husband was murdered."

I didn't try to hide my frustration. "You yourself said there's nothing to suggest foul play. So, why should I accept your unfounded suspicion as fact? Besides, where do I come into all this, even if it's true? And what makes you think I would want to help you, even if I could?"

"Why wouldn't you want to help? You may have information I could use. Why wouldn't you want to help me get at the truth?"

"I don't see what help I can offer." Frank was out

of my life, I kept telling myself. Sure, I had my own suspicions about his death, about my cousin's possible involvement in it; but nothing I could share with her, or with anyone else, for that matter. In any case, it was too late for me to care. In my book, Frank was history. Dead and buried, physically as well as in my soul. I had much else to occupy me now. Whatever he had done to get himself murdered — if indeed that was the truth — had absolutely nothing to do with me.

Flora was watching me all the while. Out loud I said:

"I can almost sympathize with you, but you're wasting your time."

She had assumed an air of calm, a determined set to her face. "Just hear me out. Forget all the other things for now and just listen to what I have to say."

I had not moved, debating whether to leave or stay, when Flora began, in a low voice:

"You know that Frank was a compulsive gambler, that he owed thousands of dollars to a mobster in New York at the time he disappeared?"

I could not hide my shock. She waited patiently until I could speak. "That's impossible," I said.

"It's true. I gave Inspector McCalley all the details, everything Frank told me. He owed roughly seventy-five thousand dollars." I must have gasped. "Are you all right?" I muttered something, and Flora went on. "It was the reason he had to play dead."

I was speechless. After a while, I heard myself stumbling over the words that had came up from deep inside me. "How . . . No, never! I would have known! No, his only hobby, his only passion was flying. Every Saturday. He took out a Cessna every Saturday. . . ."

"I'm sorry if I shocked you," I heard Flora say softly, "but you do see, don't you? They must have tracked him down and had him killed."

Even if I had wanted to leave, I couldn't. I stared at her, frozen where I sat. For a moment, I felt her hand on mine. I had no strength to brush it off. Then she withdrew it and began to speak again, in her soft voice.

I sat there and listened to the rest.

PART TWO

FRANK (2001)

Nel mezzo del cammin di nostra vita
mi ritrovai per una selva oscura
che la diritta via era smarrita.
(DANTE, *Inferno*, I, 1-3)

Mid-way along life's journey,
I found myself deep in a dark wood,
for the straight path had been lost.

CHAPTER FIVE

The big guy opened the door and stood to one side as I walked into the room. The man sitting behind the massive mahogany desk was on the phone. He glanced up at me as he continued to talk. When he was finished, he sat back in the large high-back leather chair and scrutinized me, nodding as he did so. His smile did not reach his eyes. They were very dark brown, almost black, and the bushy eyebrows above them reinforced the effect the man had on even the most casual observer: *don't mess around with me.*

But I wasn't exactly a casual observer. I had good reason to be worried.

"C'min, c'min Frank. . . . Sit down . . . . Say hello to Bonz," Everyone knew Bonz. He'd been a wrestler then a bouncer in Las Vegas, before Joe Sarace took him in and made him his bodyguard and strong-arm man.

His presence worried me even more.

I gave a small nod in his direction. All I got was a stony stare from where he stood to one side of the door, feet slightly apart, his hands folded in front of him. Dressed in a dark maroon tweed jacket, maroon shirt and black tie, he looked exactly what he still was in a way: a bouncer gone to seed. His hands were large and puffy, his face, heavily-pock-marked, had a grayish pasty tone, as though he rarely went out into the sun. His jacket was buttoned and bulged over his broad chest.

"Been with me since his mother passed away. How long ago was that, Bonz?" asked the man behind the desk, without taking his eyes from me. Bonz answered, his lips barely moving.

"Twelve years ago come Christmas eve."

At a wave from my host, I reluctantly sat down on the plastic chair, directly across from him.

"Yeah, God rest her soul," Joe was saying. "Yeah, well, Bonz has been my right hand and my left hand all these years, right Bonz?" Bonz said nothing. The man at the desk lit a cigarette and took a deep breath. As an afterthought, he held it up and raised his eyebrows in a question. "Sorry. Would you like one?" I shook my head. "Yeah, I know," the other went on, as though they were two old chums waiting for take-out orders. "All my friends out there are quitting, and here I am, still puffing away. I guess until it happens you don't believe it ever will." He laughed at some private joke. "Anyway, I still got a few good years to think about it." After taking another deep breath and exhaling the smoke slowly, with obvious relish, he rested the cigarette in a large crystal ashtray and leaned forward, crossing his arms on the desk in front of him.

"Well, Frank, I'm glad you're here. I was beginning to wonder. You were supposed to come yesterday —" I cleared my throat and moved slightly forward on the familiar molded chair. I was beginning to perspire. I wasn't sure how to begin, but I had to say something. I couldn't avoid what was coming.

"Like I said, on the phone, Joe, I need a few more days, three at most . . . ." I scarcely recognized my voice.

Joe watched me through narrowed eyes. When he spoke, his voice had a different timbre, the words came out sharp-edged. He sat back in his chair.

"Well, I tell you Frank, I've got a bit of a problem myself. Maybe we can help one another." He picked up the cigarette and puffed on it for a few seconds, all the while scrutinizing me across from him. When I didn't answer, he got up and walked across the room, then back to where I sat. He looked down at me before returning to his desk, where he stood behind the leather chair, leaning into it slightly. He studied me for a few more seconds, then waved his hand with a smile.

"Yeah, I could give you a bit more time to pay me back." I couldn't help betraying my relief, as he walked away from the desk again and went to stand near Bonz. I turned my head to follow his movements, not altogether sure what was coming. "But, to be honest with you, Frank, I don't think it'll do any good. As of today, you owe me the original five, plus two thousand interest, as we agreed, plus a penalty, as of today, of another thousand for being twenty-four hours late with your payment. You owe me, this minute, eight thousand dollars. By next week, that will have more than doubled. Will you have that kind of money for me in seven days?"

When I didn't reply, he went on: "I explained all this when you came to me the first time, Frank. I can't make exceptions. My word is at stake here. I give what I promise, no questions asked. I expect others to do the same." He watched as I took in the familiar argument. After a minute or two, he went on:

"So you're telling me you can't come up with the money, right?" I nodded feebly. Joe strolled back to stand behind his desk.

"Truth is, Frank, you can do us both a favor," he said as he sat down. "Friends help one another, right? I helped you out of a tight spot, when no one else was around for you; but, now you tell me you can't pay up as we had agreed. A deal is a deal. You know the rules. Everybody knows. We're here for you, but you gotta respect the rules. Right?" I didn't say anything. "So even if I could, which I can't, but even if I wait until next week, tell me Frank, if you don't have the money today, where will you get it to pay me next week? Like I said, if there's no money coming to me, well, rules are rules. Even if I wanted to help you, I don't have the last word. My boss doesn't take excuses."

"I'll have the money next week. I've got calls in."

Joe frowned. "Calls get you the answering

machine. No, Frank, you've got to do better than that. Anyway, the bottom line is, I can't wait. I have others to think about. My cash flow depends on people respecting their obligations. I've got my own bills to pay. I don't get extensions any more than you do. Nothing personal, but in this business, Frank, we can't run to Judge Judy. You made a deal with us. We are the court, the judge and jury. You can't run to the police."

I must have looked genuinely shocked. "I'd never do that!" I blurted with honest indignation.

"Nooooo, . . . of course not. . . . What I'm saying here, Frank, is that you've got to make good on your loan today. Pay up now. Not tomorrow or next week. This afternoon, Frank. Before you go home."

I spread out my hands in a hopeless gesture. My whole body seemed to cave in where I sat. "Can't do it. I don't have it."

Joe looked across the room and addressed Bonz. "Hear that? He doesn't have the money." He walked to where I sat and circled slowly around me, returning to his desk again after a few seconds, where he sat down and cupped his face in his hands. "He came today to tell me he can't pay me back."

I said, contritely, feeling sorry for myself, for having placed myself in this horrible predicament: "I just don't have it. I'm sorry Joe. I haven't slept for three nights thinking about it."

Joe sighed. Bonz shifted slightly where he stood.

"Well, now, Frank, you put me in a tough spot. I'll have to tell the boss about it, and that's trouble. And you certainly don't want to get your wife involved —"

"Keep her out of it!" I lashed out. "She has nothing to do with this!" I jumped out of my chair and rubbed my sweaty palms on my trousers. Joe watched me for a few seconds then waved me back down.

"Sit down, sit down." He waited for me to resume

my seat. "Hey, I wouldn't want *my* wife to know either. And we want to keep it that way, right?" I nodded. I felt the pressure building up behind my eyes, suddenly tired. "Sure we do. Let's see, you've been married just a few months, right?" I shifted nervously in my seat. "Believe me, I know how you feel. But it doesn't solve the problem, Frank. You know it. I know it."

"Take it out on me, if you have to," I ventured, with a touch of bravado. "Just leave Katie out of it." The words echoed emptily in the cavity of my head.

"Frank, Frank," said Joe softly, assuming a stricken look. "I don't want to hurt anybody. We can settle this, believe me." He waited a few seconds, then went on. "I figure, given the circumstances, your not having the money to pay me today, and not likely to have it next week or the week after that, and with every passing day getting in deeper and deeper, making it tougher and tougher for me . . . ." He sighed as though it was too painful to finish the sentence. After a small pause, he went on. "Well, like I said, we can work something out." I said nothing, anticipating the worst. Joe pushed back his chair and crossed his legs.

"Here's the story, Frank. I need someone to do a little job for me. No big deal. You just do what Bonz tells you. Easy as sucking on mother's milk. You not only get your loan paid off, you get a bonus too. Fifteen big ones." He let that sink in. I took a large breath, afraid to think even one small step ahead. *Why me?* Was my first reaction. He must have read my mind, but the expression on his face precluded my asking the question. He had lit another cigarette but seemed to have forgotten it in the ashtray. Now he picked it up and puffed on it. "You'll be driven uptown and driven back. No sweat. When you go home, you tell your wife . . . or, you don't tell her — it's up to you — how you got lucky, how you won big on a bet the guys at work all placed on a reliable tip one of them got from somewhere. If you like, we can give you stubs to prove it — "

"Damn it!" I interrupted, "She doesn't even suspect that I gamble, and you know it!"

"Right. So there's nothing to explain. That's the best way. Just hide the cash in some safe place."

He watched me through narrowed eyes then came around the desk to where I sat like a zombie, staring out at some point above his head. He bent low over me, bringing his face close. "You can do a lot with fifteen grand. All free and clear. Behind me, Bonz laughed. It sounded like a growl. Joe straightened up slowly and went on: "Not bad for less than an hour's work. Like Wheel of Fortune, right Bonz?" The big man laughed again.

"Here's the story, Frank. Believe me, the last thing I want is to hurt anybody. But we have to protect our own. Our investments. Our integrity. I'm caught in a bind, too. So, this little job settles everything between us. The loan. The interest. The penalty. Nobody outside this room will ever know about our conversation. In a few minutes, you walk out of here through that door and about an hour from now you come back directly into this room again, through that same door."

I looked where he was pointing, but saw no door. I turned back to him as he went on: "Bonz will drive you uptown. You do what he tells you. He drives you back here. After a while, you leave up front, just the way you came in. You get into your car that's been parked outside all the time, and you drive off." He paused but only for a moment. "Gina has been at her desk all morning, and at least a dozen other people are waiting their turn out there. They'll witness your leaving, like they saw you come in."

I looked at him helplessly, as he put out his cigarette. I realized it was my turn to say something.

"What are you asking me to do?"

"You've piled up a nasty debt, Frank."

"I've got it under control." I tried to sound convincing, but the words came out flat.

"Not by a long shot." He shook his head. If I didn't know better, I would have said he felt sorry for me. "Don't kid yourself," he went on. "We both know you can spend the fifteen grand in a couple of days. You'll come knocking on my door again before the week is up. Just wanna make sure you know what's coming. And Frank, I won't always be able to help you out, like I'm doing today. *Capisce?* Just to remind you. . . . "

We were silent for a while. I wondered what I had to do to make up for what I owed him. It couldn't be anything good.

By this time, I had a major headache. From the corner of my eye, I saw Bonz move away from the wall, cross the room to a painting on the left of the desk and press the side of the frame.

The painting swung out to reveal the door of a safe. I watched as Bonz turned the knob several times. When the safe opened, he took out a shoe box. He put it down on the desk, then closed the safe. Joe opened the box and with great care took out a small revolver.

"You can't miss. Even without all those trophies you piled up when you were an active member of the rifle club your father had you join when you were a teenager. I guess he thought it would keep you out of trouble."

I jumped up as though a bolt of lightning had shot through me. "What are you asking me to do?" Bonz took a step forward, but Joe waved him off. It flashed through my head that he knew all about me, how my father had died before I finished school and that I hadn't touched a gun since then.

"Bonz will explain everything on the way."

"You're asking me to kill somebody?"

"You owe me, but you don't have the money. I'm giving you a way out."

"Murder? You're asking me to murder someone I don't even know?"

Behind me, Bonz laughed. Joe smiled. "If you knew him, there would be a real problem," he said.

"There's no real problem?" I yelled. What came out was a hoarse whisper. Joe seemed unmoved. I shifted my gaze to Bonz, then back to Joe, the enormity of the situation stifling me. "Why me?" I finally asked.

"Because nobody knows you, nobody would ever suspect you. Oh, they always question us, when anything happens, we're the "usual suspects," as they say in that movie . . . ." he turned to Bonz, smiling, "what's the name of it, Bonz? I can never remember —"

"Casablanca," muttered Bonz, through tight lips.

"Yeah, that's it." He started to sing. "*'You must remember this, A kiss is still a kiss . . .'* yeah, a great movie — " He seemed lost in a reverie of his own, his eyes closed, for a few seconds. When he looked at me again, his eyes were hard points of darkness. "As far as we're concerned, everybody out there, you signed in to see me early this morning and came in around eleven. You'll leave around twelve-thirty, one, at the latest, depending on traffic. I'll have the cash for you when you get back."

"I don't think I can do this, even if I wanted to. I *know* I can't do it!" I heard myself say. My heart was pounding. I couldn't breathe.

"Sure you can." He picked up the gun and turned it over again slowly, with exaggerated care. Bonz watched him.

"Took it apart coupla hours ago, cleaned it, loaded it. It's okay," he offered, in his thick hoarse voice.

Joe nodded and handed the gun to Bonz, who replaced it in the box, after wiping it with a soft cloth.

"It's business, Frank, just business. Just remember

that and you'll be fine."

Then, as though a silent signal had been given, Bonz picked up the box and went to where Joe had pointed earlier. There, he took out a small device from his pocket and pressed down on it. A panel opened in the wall. He jerked his head, motioning me to follow him.

I took in the secret entrance, the box tucked under Bonz's left arm, Joe walking over to the opening and standing there, with his hands in his pockets, waiting for me to move out with Bonz. I tried to stand, fell back into my chair instead, all energy drained from my body. With a tremendous effort, I stood up again, holding on to the arms of the chair for balance.

Even before I started to follow him, Bonz had disappeared down the dark passageway. As I began to walk unsteadily behind him, I heard the panel close softly. A glimmer of light some few hundred feet ahead told me the passage was not a long one. Long or short, I knew there was no turning back. What choice did I have! And yet, I knew in my heart that a choice had been made and that I was indeed responsible for it. The truth of the knowledge gave me a strange release. My adrenaline kicked in, and a new burst of energy quickened my step. Somehow my mind had closed down on all arguments and doubts. Even my headache was gone.

As I followed Bonz to the end of the passage and into a small private yard, where a car was parked, I wondered at the change that had come over me in those few seconds since leaving Joe's office. I had accepted the inevitable, the realization that the only way to survive was to swim with the current, go through the motions that could buy time. Meanwhile, I would do what was asked and pull down the shutters of my soul.

As though on cue, I saw again Bonz's broad back as he led the way into the hidden passageway. A rush of fear flooded my stomach. The unbidden image slowly receded, but the earlier illusion of strength had dissipated with it. I was trembling now; and much as I tried to push it aside, I saw vividly, as in a silent nightmare, what the future held. They had me trapped. My life was no longer my own. There was a poison inside me that would eventually take its toll.

I knew for certain that my debts would pile up, grow bigger and bigger. Joe was counting on it! He had me by the short hairs.

I thought of Katie. Sooner or later she would find out. What had I done to her? To us? To our marriage?

I didn't have to wait for Hell. I saw with clarity the completed deed, felt the weight of it in the pit of my soul, a festering growth.

CHAPTER SIX

It's easy to say that gambling, smoking, or what have you, is an addiction. Calling it an inherent weakness in the genes, something inherited, maybe, or congenital is a convenient way out. It gives lawyers a great incentive for suing the tobacco companies for you and make a neat profit for themselves at the same time. Pretty soon they'll hit the casinos too, and the OTB, for pulling you in!

I could never swallow such arguments: putting the responsibility on someone else for your smoking or your gambling. Saying you're born with it or calling it a disease. Even if it were a disease, the cure for this kind of disease is not outside you: it's not a pill or a patch. It has to come from inside. To think someone else is responsible for your actions is convenient but irrational.

I've made a lot of mistakes in my life, but I've never confused expediency with morality. To me, logic and rationality are what religion is to most people. Reason tells me, whatever else one might like to hear, that gambling is just a dirty habit. No point trying to justify oneself by calling it something else, putting the blame on genes, on some pull from the outside.

I like to gamble. I know it's wrong, I know it's destructive. I also know, I'm not ready to stop.

Of course, very few people are ready to listen to logic when they want something badly. They turn reason into rationalization. One has to feel good about whatever he does. It's human nature. Fine. Who am I to judge? But, for me, it doesn't work that way. I remember a friend of mind saying once: "Go ahead and sin if you want to, just don't ask the Pope's blessing."

Thinking about all this and my own problem, after my visit to Joe Sarace, an incident from my college days comes to mind. It was in a world culture class. Professor Baxter started us off with some pages from Aristotle's *Ethics*. I've never forgotten that brief exchange. Aristotle had written somewhere: "Vice is a bad habit; virtue, a good habit." George Jennings, the smart ass in the class, boomed out from the back of the room: "That's supposed to be profound?" A few guffawed with him. We all looked expectantly at Baxter, standing by his desk up front. I felt embarrassed for him but curious too, as to how he would answer. He didn't seem at all flapped by George. I realized he was probably used to it. On this occasion, he simply said: "I don't know about 'profound.' Transparent, maybe, but true."

Those words stuck with me, for some reason. They surface at the oddest moments. Yes, I'm convinced that gambling, like smoking, is a bad habit, something one allows to take over. I should know, right? The arguments put forward by well-meaning people who make a living plying you with promises, are false. I know. My gambling — like any other bad habit — gets worse the more I give in to it. I know as surely as I know my physical body that until my will is purged, until I'm ready for it in my soul, I don't have a chance.

Katie told me once — not realizing how close to the mark she was — about her father quitting smoking cold turkey. He had made up his mind, he'd told her; he'd accepted the inevitable consequences if he continued and then and there decided to avoid them. "I didn't want to be dragged to the hospital at my great inconvenience," he had told her. He knew that the longer he went on smoking, the more his lungs would suffer. He already had a hacking cough, his cheeks were swollen, his nose was often bloody. So he'd made up his mind and redirected his will. It was not a casual decision. There was great deliberation and determination behind it. His mind was made up. So, one day, instead of lighting up another cigarette from the stub he was discarding, he'd put it out and never lighted another. Her father had told her all this after finding her experimenting with cigarettes with her friend Daisy, when he came home from work early one afternoon. "No," he'd told her when she asked: "I never craved a cigarette once my mind was made up." He said he never wanted to have that terrible taste in his mouth again, never wanted to breathe the foul air smokers left behind. He had made up his mind and had never backtracked.

I wished, then, I had that kind of determination. Maybe it's a gift, like grace from heaven. Oh, I've cut down from time to time. Then, some days, I make up for it with a vengeance. And when recently I blew everything on what was supposed to be a sure bet — not only what I'd put aside to serve me on such occasions, in a private account I'd opened on my own and which Katie hadn't the faintest idea existed, but also a sizable sum from our joint account. I was desperate. I could forget about my secret account for a while (there was only a token fifty dollars left in it); but the money I'd taken from our joint account had to be replaced quickly, even though I was the one who dealt with bills and taxes. Sooner or later, Katie was bound to find out, if the money wasn't there.

I'd reached bottom, or so I thought. I knew Joe could easily break my arms or crush my knee caps, kill me, even. And there were other problems, other dangers I couldn't bring myself to think about. . . .

I almost wish he *had* killed me. Instead, he not only cancelled my debts; he actually lured me with a fat bonus of fifteen grand to feed my habit, to be sure I would eventually go back to him for another loan.

Well, I'm stuck with it. I'm stuck with Joe. I'm stuck with obligations I detest. I hate myself even more for being so weak. I used some of the fifteen thousand to replace what I'd taken from our joint account, but the rest went the usual way.

The devil lurking inside reminds me there will always be a "bonus" from now on. I shudder even as I entertain the thought.

After that unforgettable afternoon in and out of Joe's office, I lived in silent terror, wondering if someone had recognized me, or if the police were on my trail, or — worst of all — when he'd call on me to do another job. I cringed at the thought. But I knew he was good for the money, and he knew he had me.

I was getting more and more depressed with each passing day. I grew restless. My work suffered. I knew my job was a dead-end. It paid well, but it was humdrum, boring. My mind kept straying to other possibilities, but in my heart I knew it was more than just the job that was bothering me.

There was something missing in my life. As I became more and more anxious, I grew lethargic as well. Gambling was pulling me deeper and deeper into a state of numbness. I felt trapped. I'd lied to Katie about my salary, so I could keep part of my paycheck for OTB. (Dividends from an investment I'd made some years earlier went into that OTB account as well, but these were spaced too far apart and not always available when the money was needed.) Now I found myself lying to her about a lot of other things, including our relationship. I felt awful about it. Katie was a wonderful girl, but I started to question our marriage, my feelings for her. What had been pleasant routines, our time together on Sundays, even our love-making, had become oppressive duties.

Several weeks had gone by since my last visit to Joe. I owed him again, but I thought I might get out of the hole this time with a check I was expecting. He laughed when I told him about it and asked for some time. Instead, he offered me another deal, a familiar script. This time he sent me out to deliver some packages. He didn't tell me what was in them, and I knew better than to ask. The "bonus" was a paltry sum compared with the earlier amount — but I was grateful for it.

Then, early in April, I read about a three-day meeting on medical malpractice claims that was being held in Toronto, later that month. Katie encouraged me to attend. I decided to register for it, but not before telling Joe I would be out of town for a few days. He was pleased I had stopped by to tell him.

None of us could possibly have imagined what lay ahead.

I sent in my registration fee and made flight arrangements. The idea of getting away, if only for a few days, perked me up.

Katie was pleased at my initiative. I mentioned vaguely new job possibilities up there — just aimless chatter — but Katie grew silent at the idea (I realized later) of having to move to Canada if I did find better work there. I didn't blame her. She was making a good salary, and her job held much more promise than mine. It would be a difficult decision for her, if it came to that.

The flight relaxed me. After checking into the hotel, I strolled into the large area where information booths had been set up, and public relations people were standing by to answer questions and hand out brochures. I spent some time talking to several of them and found that I was glad I'd come. Later, after a quick shower and change, I wandered back down again, and found myself in a large hall where one of those get-to-know-your-colleague cocktail parties was going on. I picked up a gin and tonic and chatted for a while with someone from a Canadian-based insurance company.

If nothing else, I told myself, getting away has lifted my gloom. For a while, my troubles seemed far off.

I was about to leave — it had been a long day, and

there was an eight o'clock meeting the next morning that I had flagged in the program listings and wanted to attend — when I saw her: a diminutive woman, about five-two, with light brown hair pulled back in a ponytail. I don't know what made me take a second look — she was plain almost, her navy skirt and white cotton blouse dull compared to the eye-catching cocktail dresses other women were wearing.

She was standing alone, near the entrance, her arms crossed, a glass of what seemed to be ginger ale in her hand. She was completely at ease, taking in the scene; nothing to suggest she was looking for company or wanted to strike up a conversation. A small smile played around her lips. I was drawn to her. Her mood seemed to reflect my own.

Her name tag said Flora Mosely. She read mine out loud.

"I've never been to this kind of convention before," I said, somewhat lamely.

"They're not bad. You learn a lot about what the others are doing."

"I'm afraid I just needed a break," I said, feeling somewhat foolish.

"Nothing wrong with that," she said. "It's a break for me too, in a way," she smiled as though letting him in on a secret. "I'm with my boss, Dr. Herman, David Herman. He's a dentist. He wants to learn more about malpractice suits — although there aren't as many in his field as in the medical profession. I manage his office," she added, as an afterthought.

I thought, mistakenly as it turned out, that I understood her presence there and decided to move away as soon as I decently could. Conventions provide an easy opportunity for trysts, for people to meet and relax, without having to count the minutes before each has to go back to familiar routines, spouses at home. I wasn't about to intrude.

She gave me a curious look and said bluntly: "It's nothing like that. I'm his caretaker. He's very absent-minded, misses appointments if I'm not there to remind him. Mrs. Herman, his mom, calls the office every day to check up on him," she went on, holding back a smile. Then, suddenly, she burst out laughing, a pleasant laugh, not mean or sarcastic. I joined in, surprised to discover how relieved I was to find out that nothing was going on between them. "He's a very nice man," Flora went on; "I've been with him since a year after I graduated high school. He was our dentist. Still is. Not a mean bone in his body. His mom and I are good friends, by now. She knows I can be trusted to get him home in time for a dinner party, or getting him out in time so he won't be late for the theater, that sort of thing. A couple of years ago, I started going with him on trips like this. Although she'll never admit it, I think Mrs. Herman has learned to depend on me almost as much as her son does." She laughed lightly again. "It's not a problem. It's rather nice to get out once in a while. Last year, we went to New Orleans."

"Do you have time for dinner?" I found myself asking.

She cocked her head to one side, but there was no hesitation. "Why not? But I have to find Dr. Herman first and make sure he's settled for the evening." She glanced at her watch. "About an hour from now, in the lobby?" I agreed, and we parted.

I felt something strange and alien as I walked back to my room. I tried to convince myself it was nothing more than a companionable dinner date, a way to fill in time. Everyone did it. Nothing unusual about that, I told myself. But even then, something was stirring inside me, a feeling I didn't want to examine too closely.

In my room — my conscience prodding me — I

placed a call to Katie, and we chatted for a few minutes. I told her just about everything, except my dinner date.

"Well, enjoy your stay," I heard my wife say. "Sleep well."

I felt guilty as hell, but shoved the feeling into some dark corner of my soul. I'd done nothing to be ashamed of! I was simply having dinner with someone. Big deal!

I was early downstairs. Flora was late. I was surprised at the disappointment I was already feeling that she might not show up. But then, suddenly, she was beside me. She hadn't changed or put on lipstick but had brought a sweater along. I must have shown my relief at seeing her, because she gave me a quizzical look and a big smile.

Neither one of us knew our way around Toronto, so we asked the concierge for a restaurant within walking distance. He was very helpful. In less than ten minutes we were seated at a modest but clean little pub and had ordered the specialty of the house: shepherd's pie.

When I tried to remember that evening, all I see is Flora, her hands cupped around her face, listening to my uninspired chatter. I talked about my job, about my college experiences, about everything under the sun — except my wife Katie. I held back on that; I didn't want to face the possibility of not seeing her again. And I stifled any suggestion of deceit and guilt by telling myself there was nothing wrong in what I was doing.

But when I left on Sunday afternoon, I found myself asking if I could visit her. Her eyes sparkled. I could tell she was pleased. For my part, I was exhilarated; a kind of madness had taken hold of me. I had decided that Flora wasn't the kind for casual affairs and that I was getting way over my head, but I couldn't help myself. She attracted me in a way I couldn't and didn't want to analyze. All I knew was, I wanted to see her again. Nothing else mattered.

Of course, I was a fool. I had a wife waiting for me at home. We had been married only a few months!

On my return, all I could think of was Flora. More than once, I wanted to call her but resisted. The next week, I told Katie that I had heard from one of the Canadian companies and was taking a quick overnight trip the next Monday to have an interview. It was true that during the convention in Toronto I had spoken about possible openings with someone from a Montreal-based company, but there had been no call.

Katie had no reason to suspect I was lying. She went along with the idea, but the small frown on her pretty face told me she was apprehensive. We both knew that if I went to Canada, she couldn't come with me; not at first, anyway. If it came to a decision, she probably wouldn't leave New York for a long time, if ever. But of course, I didn't want her there. If I went, it would be because of Flora. There was no place for Katie in my plans.

I told myself things would fall into place . . . if and when. Meanwhile, I sustained the fiction I had created and showed some concern about the effect my hypothetical move would have on her, if I did accept a job in Canada. I could see that the possibility was bothering her. I told her not to worry. Nothing would probably come of it. All through that charade, I felt strangely detached — not because I knew it was a piece of fiction, but because the only thing that mattered to me was Flora. I couldn't wait to see her again.

On Sunday night I flew to Ottawa. where Flora lived. I was due back on Tuesday morning and had told Katie I would go straight to the office from La Guardia. I did plan to return on Tuesday, but I wasn't going back to the office. My time with Flora was precious; I wanted to be with her as long as possible, so I'd booked a flight for late in the day and planned to take a cab home directly from the airport, as though I were coming from work. I had made arrangements to be back in the office on Wednesday morning; no one would expect me back before that. The likelihood that Katie would learn about all this was pretty slim; even if she did, it could easily be explained by last-minute delays in departures, which forced me to change my flight.

On this second occasion, Flora and I were more restrained, more conscious of what was happening between us. I still couldn't bring myself to tell her I was married. After checking in at a motel near the airport, I drove to her house for dinner. I met her mother then, a very pleasant, well-informed woman in her early fifties. She was a librarian at a private high school.

We had a very comfortable and pleasant dinner and spent the next morning walking around the city. After a leisurely lunch, I found myself fretting, wanting to declare myself, tell Flora how I felt, before leaving the next day. But the hours slipped by. I was scheduled to fly back to New York the next afternoon.

It had come as a shock, this new feeling that brushed everything else aside. I thought I loved Katie, but I had come to realize what a huge mistake I'd made. Oh, Katie was the best! And I certainly didn't want to hurt her. But what I felt for her, I now realized, was something quite different from what I felt for Flora. Flora was my life, my very breath. I simply couldn't live without her. I never dreamed a person could be so taken, so compellingly drawn to another human being. I loved Flora with a passion I had never felt for anyone before, including Katie. It made me ecstatic and depressed at the same time. All I knew was, I wanted to be with Flora, I was unhappy away from her. When she wasn't with me, I felt cut off from life itself.

We lingered over coffee. An awkwardness had

come between us, threatening to spoil the wonderful time we had spent together. Without realizing what was happening, I placed my hand over hers. I saw my own sadness reflected in her eyes.

"Flora, I have to say this before leaving. I want you to know how I feel."

"Don't, Frank, not yet, not now," she said, patting with her free hand the one that held hers.

"No, it can't wait. I have to say it before I leave. I love you, Flora. I can't bear being away from you."

"I know," she said so softly I almost missed it. She looked away, then, as though weighing what should be said next. "I feel the same way, Frank," she said turning back to me after a while, with a sad smile. "But you have a good job in New York. You can't just pick up and leave. And, well, I have Mom. I can't pick up and leave, either."

"I know." I still didn't dare mention Katie. Or the other problems I had, which I kept pushing aside. I hated myself for the deception, but I couldn't risk telling Flora about my wife, my gambling, all the other things eating away at me. . . . not yet, anyway.

"We can get around all that, can't we? If we love one another?" She nodded and smiled. I squeezed her hand. "I know we can swing it, trust me on this — "

"Oh, Frank, let's not make any rash decisions. There are things we both have to take care of, before we think or do anything else."

"That's my girl!" I said, leaning back. At least, now I knew how she felt. I could be certain of her love and loyalty. I told her that in the weeks and months ahead, I would make every effort to see her, to find the time. I was being brash, and I knew it; but at that moment I felt I could do anything.

Before heading for the airport, I put her in a cab. But before letting her go, I kissed her for the first time, a long passionate kiss. We clung to one another, then she moved slowly out of my embrace and stroked my cheek before getting into the cab. I watched her go, a pall of misery settling over me as the car sped away.

I had prepared a plausible story for Katie. She had no reason to suspect anything other than what I told her. I was so restless by this time that I felt I had to bring up, as soon as possible, for my own peace of mind, the difficulties that might lie ahead, if a job were offered me in Canada. The excuse I gave was that there was no point avoiding the hard realities we would have to face if that happened. I still had no idea how I would handle things, when the time came — for sooner or later I knew I would have to leave New York. There was no doubt in my mind about that.

"This might turn out to be a big decision for both of us, Katie," I began, in the wake of my announcement that the interview had gone well but it was all very tentative. "There are no openings right now, but . . . well, they sounded optimistic. . . ."

"You would have to move up there, of course." I noticed she didn't include herself in that scenario, but then she went on quickly: "It would certainly be a hard decision for *me*," she said tentatively, perhaps waiting for some kind of reassurance. I didn't say anything, and after an awkward pause she went on: "To be honest, Frank. I don't know if I could pull up roots here and move to Canada. But let's not rush things. Like you said, it's all very iffy." I nodded. "Besides, there are other options. This is as good a time as any to consider them." I nodded again, and she went right on, as though she had rehearsed it all beforehand.

"Let's say you do get a good offer. You can use it to advantage to get what you really want, right here in New York. You wouldn't have to move at all."

"I thought about that." I lied, "but there's a long

waiting list for the kind of promotion I'm looking for. The competition is fierce."

"But Frank, if the people in Canada are willing to take a chance on you, if they think your credentials and experience are good enough for you to work for them, you can argue persuasively to get what you want right here, in New York. Maybe in another company. It means taking time to write letters and make inquiries. Together we can do it. You know I'm ready to help every step of the way."

"I know you are; but honestly Katie, I don't feel we should count on offers in New York," I ventured. "It was hard enough to get the job I have."

"No harm trying," said Katie, with a smile and a hug. Her concern made the deception I was weaving all the more despicable. Katie meant it, good soul that she was; I knew she would indeed do everything possible to help me, even though in the end she would be the one to suffer. Whatever solution I came up with, she would be left behind. Of course, what I really wanted was very different from the story I had concocted. I wanted Flora, I didn't give a hoot about a better job. I would work at whatever I could find, so long as I could be near Flora.

But the script had to be played out carefully. Too much was at risk. I needed time to work out carefully the details of how I would disappear, how I would be declared dead. Because anything less than that would not work. Divorce was not an option, even if and when Katie agreed. It was Joe and the rest I was running from. The plan had to be foolproof, so that nobody could ever find me.

The irony was that since Flora had come into my life, I'd scarcely visited the OTB. I was beginning to put away some new cash, not much, nothing close to what I owed Joe. But it gave me confidence, so that without even thinking about it I had not placed any bets for almost a month. With Flora, loving her as I did, wanting her more than anything else, I knew I could overcome my addiction. The prospect of losing her because of that terrible habit brought me close to madness. I couldn't eat, work, or sleep thinking about it. This time I was determined not to fall back into it again. I knew Flora would give me the strength I needed to keep my resolve. The alternative was unthinkable.

Early in May I flew to Canada for a "second interview." Seeing Flora gave me new energy, a sense of power. I felt cleansed. I was happy.

On the plane back, a plan was beginning to form, one that had to be perfect down to the minutest detail, if I was to escape. There was no room for even the smallest error. Katie's grief, though misplaced, would be nothing compared to Joe's anger, to the retaliation I would be subjected to, if things didn't work out. . . . If my plan failed, if I were to be discovered, my life was over.

Even the deadly dangers I knew I was courting could not dissuade me. I nurtured my plan as it took shape, tended it carefully. All my energies were now directed toward one goal. To be with Flora. Nothing else mattered.

CHAPTER SEVEN

I had a second addiction. It was not a secret, like my gambling, but a legitimate hobby.

My grandfather, who had been a pilot in the second world war, wanted to continue flying when he came home in 1945. My grandmother had put her foot down, when he told her he was thinking of retraining so he could fly the new commercial jets. They were about to be married, and he had to go along; but he did the next best thing: took a job supervising the assembly of airplane parts out on Long Island, where he soon had enough saved to put a down payment on a house in the new community of Levittown. In 1949 they moved into their new home with their infant son — my father. By the time I was born, in 1974, they had moved to a larger place in Huntington, where my grandparents had offered my parents the upstairs apartment. The arrangement suited everyone: the women got along; my grandfather was generous and, with a few under his belt, quite jolly.

By that time, my grandfather had found a way to continue flying with my grandmother's grudging approval. Saturdays — he made clear — were his, to do with as he pleased. No one was to count on him for anything on that day, even if it rained. After breakfast, he would drive out to the small airport in Islip and wouldn't be back until late in the evening. If his friends had a small plane available for him, he would put in some flying time. (I'm not sure just what the arrangement was, but I learned later that some money did exchange hands.) If there was no plane available, he was perfectly happy, just hanging around with the mechanics, the dispatchers, the pilots. Soon, everyone got to know him.

When he came home on those days, Granpa was exhilarated. As I grew up, I was allowed to wait up for him. Squirming or kneeling on a kitchen chair beside him, as he ate his cold supper, I'd ask a mountain of questions: where he'd gone, what he had seen, the kind of plane he'd flown, everything I could think of. He would make a show of fending me off, but even though I was just a child I could see he was pleased with my interest. My father, I learned later, had proved a disappointment to him in that Dad never outgrew his fear and dislike of flying and avoided it whenever possible. His interest had been guns; and for a while I shared in it. He taught me how to fire and would periodically take me to the range, to practice with him, once a week when I was about eight. It didn't last long. My real passion, I soon discovered, was planes.

In me, Granpa found a ready and avid listener. I was an ideal audience. On my tenth birthday, which conveniently happened to fall on a Saturday, he took me with him. I'll never forget that day, when I flew with him for the first time. By the time we got back home, I was hooked.

I took to it like the proverbial duck to water. I soon became as enthusiastic about flying as my grandfather was.

After that, he brought me along whenever he could. When the weather was bad, we'd sit around and talk with his friends, or go into the hanger and watch the mechanics work on the planes. We'd break for a quick lunch nearby and come back to the airport until it was time to go home.

During the next few years, Granpa and his friends saw to it that I got to know everything there was to know about planes — engines, propellers, controls, landing gear, emergency equipment — as well as air traffic and other regulations, which I studied more assiduously than any school subject, including math, which I enjoyed and was good at. I had learned the names of dozens of planes, having spent hours assembling models from the kits Granpa would bring home for me. The shelves in my room were filled with those miniature replicas. I could recognize most planes on sight, including the old German and Japanese war planes.

By the time I was fifteen, I knew everything there was to know about airplanes of all kinds, including the large new jets. I had become an expert mechanic, as well.

On some days, when a plane was available and we flew, Granpa would let me take the controls for a few minutes. By the time I finished high school, I had put in lots of flying time and was ready for my license. I got it that Fall, when I started my Freshman year at City College; but my pleasure turned bitter when just before Thanksgiving my grandfather suffered a stroke and died.

I continued the Saturday excursions on my own, Granpa a constant presence. His buddies were now my buddies, and soon I had worked out arrangements that enabled me to rent one of the planes when it wasn't being used. Well, it wasn't exactly a rental; the arrangement was an informal one (as I'm sure Granpa's had been), no questions asked. And I always did what I'd seen Granpa do many times (and what I'm sure Lou, the traffic control supervisor, expected me to do). Although nothing was ever said in so many words, at the end of the day I would thank him and hand him some bills "for his trouble." He always managed to look surprised and pleased, as though he never expected money. Well, it was only right that I should pay for the use of a plane. As far as I was concerned, it was the equivalent of renting it. Lou simply made it possible.

I was at peace up there in the clouds. Flying made me forget the humdrum routines waiting to claim me down below. Looking down from above, I always experienced a tremendous release, a sense of power that lifted me briefly above my ordinary and predictable life.

Up there I felt like a god.

On several occasions, when we were first married, I'd asked Katie to come along with me; but she wasn't interested. Her work kept her busy more and more; she often stayed on late at the office; some weekends she even took work home. Saturday soon became her personal day, too, as it had been mine for so long. She used it to advantage: attended all-day seminars, went to matinees or to a museum with her friends. Saturdays refueled both of us. We came together in the evening, refreshed, with stories to share.

Katie loved her work and never considered the extra time spent at the office or taking projects home over the weekend an imposition. She was eager to learn whatever she could to improve her skills and make her supervisors aware of her many talents. Her immediate goal was an executive level job.

Sunday became our special day together. We idled most of the morning, reading the *Times* over a leisurely brunch. In the afternoon, we'd take long walks through the Park and end up having dinner near Columbus Circle or Lincoln Canter. We rarely varied from this routine; occasionally we dined with friends or went away for the week-end — in the summer especially. Then we would drive to Saratoga Springs for theater or a concert at the Performing Arts Center (carefully avoiding the race track); or, when we could get a couple of extra days off, to one of the New Jersey beaches or down further, to Delaware, to relax in the sun.

It was a comfortable life. Katie was never demanding; she was easy to get along with. When she suggested this or that, I fell into step. I basked in her enthusiasm for whatever she took on. I was content. I'm sure Katie was happy.

All that changed suddenly. My priorities shifted and new and unexpected plans surfaced. Flora Mosely had come into my life. I didn't want to hurt Katie; I vowed to do everything in my power to minimize her suffering. But when the idea came to me, how I could literally fly off to a new life, all concern for Katie was pushed into the background. My attention was now riveted elsewhere. I had found a solution. Nothing else mattered. At home, habit carried me through the evenings and into the next day. Even as I chatted with my wife, over dinner, my mind often was busy working out the logistics of my plan.

It had to be perfect. I had to disappear so that no one could ever find me. There were other things to worry about, but Joe was my nemesis. He had to be convinced that I was dead. There could be no loose ends, as far as he was concerned.

Although my purpose never wavered, I actually grew lethargic and dispirited during the next few weeks. I became irritable and restless, trying to work out an infallible strategy. Watching Katie grow more and more confident, always trusting and happy, ready to move up to a better job so we could rent or perhaps buy a larger and better place, made me sick. I couldn't help feeling self-pity as well. My own job paid well but had turned out to be not only a dead-end but hopelessly boring. I couldn't figure out what had made me go into the insurance business in the first place; but after more than five years, I'd come to hate it. At twenty-seven, I was still young enough to move into a totally different field of work. The first thing that had come to mind was flying, of course. If I qualified (and why wouldn't I?), any one of the major airlines would pick me up and train me to fly the newer planes. When I brought it up, Katie — like my grandmother — had put her foot down.

No doubt to compensate for cutting off that possibility, and also because she had begun to notice my restlessness, Katie had prodded me, one sunny Sunday afternoon, as we walked across the Park to 72nd Street, to take some days from work and just relax. It was at that time that I received an announcement about a three-day conference on malpractice insurance claims, to be held in Toronto, in April. Little did either of us know how our lives were about to change! I remember Katie saying it would be a pleasant distraction.

I marvel to this day at the irony of fate: how that pleasant distraction brought me to Flora Mosely.

Back from the trip, I brooded more than ever about how to get away from Joe Sarace — from what I owed him, from other worries plaguing me, from a routine and boring job, and, yes, from Katie. I couldn't see my way clear yet, but my mind was made up. I rationalized that I couldn't continue living with a woman who, I had discovered (too late, unfortunately) I didn't love as I should, or remain at a numbing job; and I certainly wasn't cut out to be a hit man for Joe, or more precisely for the Ambrosini family, for whom he worked!! My future was bleak. My gambling debts had reduced me to a sorry state. Things were getting worse with each passing day. But, of course, the real reason, the only reason, for my wanting a new start was Flora.

Perversely, from time to time, part of me still entertained the dream of a huge payoff on a long shot, matched only by the even more improbable dream of owning my own Cessna. I knew of course that, without going into even deeper debt, Joe's fifteen thousand (already squandered on the horses), would not have been enough for a plane and everything that went with it — periodic maintenance and a place in the hanger, for starters. And even if by some miracle, I had stifled my gambling impulse, even if I never placed another bet, I still owed Joe in a big way. Which meant I was trapped into doing whatever he asked, for years to come. The mere thought terrified me. I didn't have the stomach for what he wanted done. I dreaded what I knew was inevitable; but I had no choice, if I wanted to stay alive.

I had to find a way out, I reminded myself each morning when I woke and each night as I lapsed into sleep. I had to have Flora.

Even before the plane arrived at La Guardia, I'd begun to map out the plan that would free me from my bondage. Whatever guilt I might have felt about abandoning my wife, had all but disappeared by the time the plane landed. It was strange to realize that my feelings for Katie had not really changed; totally different emotions had simply pushed them aside. If I hadn't met Flora, I probably would have stumbled along, would never have left Katie, would never have questioned our relationship. We were comfortable together. She was a loyal and loving woman; any man would be proud and happy to be with her. She knew how to dress, was easy with people, very smart, good company, attractive — Flora, by comparison, was quite plain. Yet, I loved Flora, and Katie was no longer important to me.

I don't remember coming to a decision about all this: it just happened. And once it happened, I knew I could never settle for less.

My big worry all this time was Joe. If it hadn't been for Joe, I would have told Katie the truth and, somewhere along the line, we would have gotten a divorce. Much more civilized that way. Poor Katie. She probably would have gone into mild shock at first, then tried to reason with me, maybe yelled some (although she rarely raised her voice). She would have retreated, suffered and wept in silence; but eventually she would have come through. She had her pride, after all.

The real problem was Joe.

Joe would move heaven and earth to get back at me. I had to disappear. No. Not just disappear. I had to die and stay dead.

The plan, when it flashed before me, was like a revelation, like the conversion of St. Paul. It hit me like lightning. In that moment of absolute clarity, I saw what had to be done. It wouldn't be easy, but I knew I could swing it.

When I was ready and everything was in place, I would take a plane out on a Saturday and not come back. I would stage an accident. The plane would go down and burst into flames and its occupant burned beyond recognition. Every moment had to be carefully planned, each detail foolproof.

Some Saturdays, when the weather was bad, I went to the New York Public Library instead of flying, researching what I needed to know. Afterwards, I would meet Katie and we'd go home together. I told her I was looking into some legal issues that might serve me in my job. She was encouraging.

For a long time, I couldn't bring myself to face the central element in this equation, the one thing without which success was impossible. I steered away from it and started with the lesser preparations.

The airport at Islip had grown over the years; there were a lot of new faces around; but the dispatchers and some of the others knew me well. Some of them had known me since I was a teenager; some even remembered my grandfather. They were used to seeing me but usually too busy for more than a wave and a greeting when I checked in. I'd started parking my car on a deserted road at the far end of the field, away from the tower. Once in the plane, I would taxi to where my car was parked, get in and out of the plane several times — as though checking things out before asking for clearance — setting the pattern that allowed me the time and distance needed to bring extra fuel and other things on board on the projected day. No one asked questions. No one took any notice.

I also made a point of telling the dispatchers and some of the mechanics I knew that I was planning a few overnight trips before the weather turned, maybe fly my wife to Vermont for a long weekend. I even asked about inns and B and Bs. It was all very casual, with a few jokes thrown in.

All through May and early June, I flew for longer and longer periods of time, scouting wide areas on our side of the border, looking for deserted stretches where the plane could crash and burn without doing serious damage to houses, farms, or people. I finally found the ideal spot: a large meadow of high grass, near the border, where I could also hide the car I planned to rent to get me into Canada. I carefully mapped out the routes.

I bought two parachutes from an army discount catalog and had them sent to a post office box I'd opened in Islip, then transferred them to a storage unit I'd rented, near the airport. The fuel containers were already stacked in there, waiting. After the parachutes arrived, I made a point of stopping to check them out on Saturdays, before going on to the airport. I would practice folding and unfolding them, to make sure they worked properly. When the time came, only one would be used, of course, although I hadn't as yet worked just how that would be accomplished. These, like the containers of extra fuel, would go into the plane at the last moment.

I wanted desperately to try out the parachutes, but I knew that doing so would raise questions and suspicion. Instead I found videotapes of parachute jumps and studied them carefully. Not that I hadn't jumped from a plane before. My grandfather had made sure I could handle that and other kinds of emergencies. Even before I got my license, he had me go through a series of tests with an expert and had me jump several times. He was very proud of me, I could tell; but we were wise enough not to mention it to my mother or grandmother.

On those occasions, usually after the jump, he would warn me not to parachute unless the situation was really crucial. He would then tell the story of how, flying as substitute co-pilot with another team during the war, the pilot had ordered them to jump on the way back from a bombing mission in Germany because of a malfunction that turned out to be minor. The pilot brought the plane in without difficulty; but his order to jump hospitalized the navigator and bombardier. My grandfather suffered a broken leg.

Well, in a crazy way, even my grandfather would have to admit my situation was a crucial one!

The car rental I chose was about an hour's drive from the site I'd picked for the crash. There were closer ones; but I wanted to avoid any possible connection with a plane going down in the area. The week before, I would rent a Jeep and leave it hidden in the high grass, near a boulder I used as a landmark. These preparations, like the others, presented no real problem.

I went over them again and again, to be sure I had not overlooked anything. Finally, I had to face the most critical part of my plan: finding someone whose body would be strapped in the pilot's seat, burned beyond recognition: someone to substitute for me.

I used the internet to locate pilots' organizations, veterans' groups, air force personnel, local clubs, whatever was out there that I could tap into for what I needed. Hours were wasted weeding out long lists of names, researching backgrounds, exchanging e-mails with anyone who seemed to qualify. It wasn't easy. The person I was looking for had to love flying, had to be someone who would be all too happy to find a buddy with the same passion for planes. Most important, absolutely essential: he had to be a loner with no immediate family or relatives. He could not be missed.

This last requirement, which I felt was essential for the success of my plan, greatly narrowed the pool of candidates. By the beginning of June, my search still hadn't turned up anyone who answered the profile I'd worked out. My hopes began to ebb. Once again, depression set in.

In spite of the difficulties, or maybe because of them, I made a huge effort to appear cheerful and loving with Katie during this time. When she got a rather large raise, I surprised her by taking her out to dinner and ordering a bottle of champagne.

As the days went by, however, my anxiety grew. I became increasingly despondent, impatient with those around me. I used my lunch hours at work to search the internet and e-mail frantically, leave messages for likely candidates, trying always to sound casual, as though I had all the time in the world to exchange friendly banter. It was late in June that I found him, the perfect candidate, just what I was looking for. His name was Kevin Masters. He was a few months older than I and had been divorced three years earlier. He told me he had no intention of marrying again: it was too much of a drain on one's emotional life, trying to please a woman. I felt sad for him, in a way, but — I quickly reminded myself — the divorce had made him a free agent. He lived on the West side, had some bar buddies but no close friends, avoided relationships with women but enjoyed them and was never at a loss for sex partners. What clinched it for me was his dream of one day having enough money to take flying lessons, eventually being able to buy his own small plane. Absolutely perfect for what I had in mind!

I did some checking; everything was as he had told me. We started to exchange e-mails on a regular basis. When I invited him to fly with me early in July, he was ecstatic. That first day I made sure I got there ahead of him. I had him park on the same road where I'd left my own car. I'd explained that we had to be careful: I wasn't allowed to take anyone up with me. He bought it. We worked it out so he wouldn't be seen getting into the plane. Once inside, he crouched low until we were in the air. We did the same thing coming in for landing.

I quickly discovered that he had done his homework and knew a great deal about planes. It made my task that much easier. He was an apt pupil.

The third Saturday in July, I had him take the controls after we'd cleared the airfield. I did that for the next few weeks.

On our anniversary, early in August, I took Katie for a leisurely dinner at a small French restaurant near the Plaza. She looked especially smart that evening, in a simple black dress, her long hair framing her pretty face in stylish swirls. Over dessert (thanks to a hefty loan from Joe), I gave her an antique pendant of white filigree gold with a large pink sapphire, a beautifully faceted stone, nestled in the center. The braided chain I'd bought to go with it was perfect. Katie was stunned. Her eyes shone with pleasure when she opened the velvet box. I reached across and took her hand in mine. There were tears in her eyes.

All I could think of was Flora.

I don't know how I got through that evening and night. When we got home, we made love with more passion that ever before. On my part, there was a sense of urgency mixed with sadness that it would all soon end for Katie and leave her grieving. I truly wished then that I could spare her all that was coming, but there was no way I could. No way I *would*. I had no intention of changing my mind. Still, I felt bad — not guilt, not remorse; it was too late for that. She was a good wife, a wonderful companion; it just wasn't enough. I truly wished I could explain to her what had happened to me, make her understand. Instead, I would have to live with the knowledge that I had betrayed her in a most shameful and unforgivable way.

In the end, it was more a heavy thought than a real feeling. I knew with utmost certainty that my new life would soon lift that burden too. Even as I kissed Katie that night, whispered to her, caressed her, did all the things I'd learned she enjoyed, and finally brought her to climax, it was as if I were playing a role while watching myself from the wings. I must say that Katie rose to the occasion. She was more receptive than usual, aggressive even, in her love-making. I knew she would remember that night for a long time. Fleetingly, I wished I could return her unwavering trust.

By the end of August, Kevin was ready. He'd had enough flying time to feel confident in the pilot's seat. That's all I wanted, but I made a show of introducing him to the basics of take-off and landing. Keeping up the fiction, I told him at the end of the day that in a couple of weeks I'd let him take the plane up and bring it down on his own. I'd never seen him so excited.

That week passed quickly. During flight, the next Saturday, we reviewed everything connected with take off and landing. I promised him a crack at it next time.

All the while, I was thinking of the real event I had scheduled for that coming Saturday, the day I'd chosen to carry out my plan. While I parachuted to safety, the Cessna, with Kevin strapped in the pilot's seat, unable to free himself, would crash and burn. I was truly sorry having to use him in that way; he was a likeable guy. But I had made a choice and had to see it through.

As it turned out, a bizarre set of coincidences fashioned another plan — one that was unexpected, foolproof, and infinitely more effective.

CHAPTER EIGHT

The following Tuesday I left for work earlier than usual, for a nine o'clock appointment a few blocks from my office. I checked in with my secretary, who had folders ready for me to take to the meeting with a Mr. Katzman, a lawyer with whom we were negotiating a settlement for one of our clients.

It was a glorious morning: I checked my briefcase for the documents I'd asked my secretary to get ready for me and walked the eight blocks to my destination. It was a little after eight-thirty when I arrived. Mr. Katzman was already in his office. We shook hands, and he led me into the conference room next door, where he had laid out his papers. His client was suing a cosmetic surgeon, who carried insurance with us, for having botched up what should have been a simple "face lift." Something had indeed gone wrong. My task was to avoid a trial and bring down the three million dollars Katzman was asking for his client.

Coffee was perking. I welcomed it, since I had rushed out that morning without breakfast. We were standing, sipping from our plastic cups and chatting before getting down to business, when a tremendous impact startled us. The building rocked. Coffee spilled onto my shirt as I reached for the back of a chair, to steady myself.

"What was that?" I asked. Katzman put down his cup and hurried out into the corridor. Others had come out of their offices, wondering what had happened. Some went back inside to call Security in the lobby. One man called for an elevator, but the cars were not moving. From somewhere above us, we heard muffled shouting. Soon, two men appeared at the door of the stairwell. They stood there while one man held the door open and

118

called out: "There's a big fire up above, at the top! You should get out. Use the stairs!" Having relayed the message, he and the other man disappeared, as the door closed after them.

"Are they evacuating the building?" I asked.

Katzman shook his head. I followed him back inside. Several of his colleagues were huddled around a large man, who was on the phone. The name on the door read, "Timothy Ryan." He was a partner in Katzman's firm.

"I can't hear you!" Mr. Ryan was saying in a loud clipped voice, spacing out the words, two fingers covering the ear that wasn't glued to the receiver. "What?" he kept asking. "What was that? Speak more slowly!" Shaking his head, he finally put down the phone. "There's a fire up in the restaurant. The fire trucks are on their way. I'm sure everything is under control. No need to panic." We inched back with the others, as Mr. Ryan pressed to clear his room. "I'll let you know if there's any change," he said, as he shut his door, dismissing everyone.

Someone stopped by and addressed Katzman. "There's a lot of confusion about what's happening, Ernie. Are we safe here?"

"Ryan thinks so. You heard him."

A new commotion brought us back into the wide corridor outside. A small group had assembled near the stairway exit, as though waiting for a signal. A man hurried out from one of the rooms down the hall and waved them forward. "Go! Go!" he called to them. "Take the stairs!" With that, the cluster disappeared into the stairwell, the man who had called out bringing up the rear. There was murmuring among those of us left in the corridor. Katzman led the way back inside.

"Maybe we should postpone our meeting, " I said tentatively, as a new sound reached us from the stairwell. Someone opened the exit door and we all heard it: the muffled sound of shoes on the hard cement stairs, as some people worked their way down at a steady pace. I turned to Katzman again: "Maybe we should leave?"

"There's a fire up there," someone volunteered, as he went by.

"Did security tell you to leave?" Katzman asked.

"No. Our supervisor did," answered the man, over his shoulder.

I could see Katzman was worried, I was too. A medicinal smell was beginning to taint the air and wisps of smoke were filtering down.

"Let me see if I can reach Security." He dialed from his cell phone and talked with someone briefly. When he looked at me, his phone still open, he had a dazed expression on his face:

"A plane crashed into the building."

"A *plane*??" I was stunned.

"That's what they said."

"But . . . that's impossible! How could a plane not see the building? The weather is perfect. Why would it be flying so low?"

Katzman shook his head. "I have no idea!" he said with a hopeless gesture.

"Maybe we should postpone our meeting," I ventured again.

"I guess so."

"I'll call you later to reschedule." I returned the folders to my briefcase, put on my jacket, and started to leave.

"Aren't you coming?"

"I'd better wait for Mr. Ryan — " he said, with a frown.

"I think it best to move out as quickly as you can." You could see, he was itching to do just that.

"You heard him. I can't leave, not with everyone else still at their desks."

I shrugged and left him standing there.

The smoke in the corridor was much thicker now, the sound from the stairwell, a constant flow. The strange odor — a mixture of scorched plastic and burning metal — was much stronger. A group of people were standing by the elevators, as though waiting for the cars to stop and take them down. I said, as I went past:

"You shouldn't use elevators, when there's a fire." Most of them ignored me and kept pressing the buttons; others glanced my way uncertainly but didn't move. I wondered how many were already stuck in one or more of the cars.

Katzman walked out, spotted me and came over. "I just talked with Ryan. He's set on staying put. Doesn't think the fire will ever reach this far down." He scratched his head, then looked toward the elevators. "Are they working?"

"No, I don't think so. The cars are not moving." I could see he was ready to leave. "Even if they were, it wouldn't be safe. People may be stuck in them already." He nodded and walked a few steps with me. His anxiety was palpable. I said, "You should get out right now."

He stopped to face me, nodded, and suddenly made up his mind. "Yes. you're right. I will." He went back into his office. I was about to take to the stairs, but curiosity and some other as yet undefined impulse shaping inside me forced me down along the fast-emptying corridor. I watched groups of people take to the stairs. Looking back, I saw Katzman and three or four others from his office join those waiting to enter the stairwell. The cluster by the elevators soon followed them.

Suddenly, I was the only one left in the corridor

And then it hit me. The vague undefined feeling I had ignored earlier suddenly became a roar in my ears. I was afraid to acknowledge it, even as it flowed through me, making my heart race. I stood there taking long deep breaths, not daring to look too closely at the possibility that was shaping itself in my head. I was so distracted by my own thoughts that I barely noticed the second impact. This one didn't rock the building as much as the earlier one had. The new sounds seemed somewhat removed, coming from outside. I tried to concentrate on what was happening around me, but the excitement building up inside my brain was crowding out everything else. Even though caution warned me I shouldn't allow myself to harbor, not for a moment, the incredible, improbable solution that a little voice inside me was suggesting — it was too far-fetched, too many variables were involved! — my confused thoughts were already falling into place. All precautions were brushed aside. I knew exactly what I had to do.

I pulled out my cell phone and called Katie at work.

By now the sharp smell of burning was pervasive. The smoke had thickened. The phone was working and I got Katie without any difficulty. I thought, recklessly, Fate is on my side!

I told her where I was and the reason for my being there.

"What?" she gasped into the phone. "Frank, get out of there, get out as fast as you can!" She went on to tell me about the planes that had hit. I listened carefully to what she was telling me. I had to know exactly what had happened, what was happening.

"A terrorist attack?" It was the one thing that had never occurred to me. "Are you sure?"

"That's what everyone is saying! Someone caught it happening on tape, the planes going into the buildings! The television cameras are there now, we're watching the towers burn! God knows what else is going to happen, Frank. Get out of there, please, now, this minute!"

The poor girl was on the verge of hysteria. I

reassured her I would be leaving soon.

"What do you mean, 'soon'?"

"There are disabled people up above who need my help to get them to the stairs." It wasn't exactly a lie.

She paused, but only for a moment. "Frank, no one is safe there! I'm looking this very minute at the smoke billowing from Tower One, where you are. I'm looking right at it. We have the TV on. There's black smoke and flames everywhere. What floor are you on?" I told her. It was below the middle. "It's spreading, Frank! She said again. "You're not safe where you are!" I could hear her voice break.

"Don't worry, Katie. The fire trucks are here. They'll have everything under control in no time."

"You're not listening, Frank!" she went on, her voice sharp and desperate. "It'll take time for the firemen to get up there. And the fire is intense, you can see it spreading. You've got to get out of there. Now, Frank!"

"Katie, there are people still working in the offices, up here — " It was probably true. He hadn't seen Mr. Ryan or the rest of his staff leave. Or had they left without his noticing?

"Please, Frank. Tell me you're going to take the stairs down right now, right this minute!"

"Don't worry sweetheart," I heard myself say. "I'll be out soon." She was still talking when I cut her off.

Would it work? Could I pull it off?

I went back down the corridor, glancing into the empty offices. In one, I found a seersucker jacket draped over a chair, where someone had left it. I picked it up. Inside was a large wallet, the kind that folds only once and is about the size of a small notepad. In one compartment there were seven twenties, three fifties, three one-hundred dollar bills. The driver's license was made out to a Peter Swentner. There were major credit cards also and a pocket-size photograph of a young man with his arm around an older woman, his mom probably.

I stuffed the jacket and wallet into my briefcase and finally entered the stairwell.

"What's happening?" I asked a man who was rushing by.

"Fire on the top floors!"

I realized I probably knew more at that moment, about what had happened, than anyone else around me. I joined the crowd. It was moving in surprisingly orderly fashion. There was no panic. No one spoke. As we negotiated the stairs in a kind of eerie silence, the only sound was that of our shoes hitting the narrow stairs. People were joining us at every landing. At one point, we ware forced to stop and press against the side wall to let through firemen, carrying all their heavy gear. They came up in single file, as we watched. Silently, we let them pass. I wondered if they were just starting up or if others were already putting out the flames at the top. I wondered too if they could really control the inferno Katie had described. . . .

Then the momentum picked up, and we were moving down again.

It wasn't until much later that I sorted out everything that had happened, how I'd accepted a decision I was scarcely aware of, letting the pieces of the puzzle fall in place without any conscious deliberation. Hours after the event, I began for the first time to review the images that had registered in my mind while I was still in the North Tower. Still later, days and months afterwards, images of that silent moving flow of people, of firemen trudging up the narrow stairs, of confused faces looking for answers, would startle me, without warning. At such moments, the panic and fear I had managed to hold back at the time would threaten to engulf me, the remembered scenes made even more vivid by distance, playing themselves before my eyes like an old film. The shock I felt at those moments was more intense than anything I felt while still in the tower.

But right now, going down the stairs of Tower One, all I felt was elation, exaltation, an incredible sense of accomplishment, even though success was yet not a certainty. Much else was needed to wrap things up. But deep inside me, I knew Fate had dealt me a winning hand!

In the lobby, there was utter confusion. Dozen of fire fighters their gear all ready, stood about impatiently, waiting for orders. I wondered, fleetingly, why they weren't up there, with the others.

Once outside, I didn't stop to ask questions. When I saw a TV reporter shouldering her way toward me, I quickly moved behind some ambulances and sprinted in and out of clear spaces until I had put several blocks between us. I was panting by the time I finally looked back to see the devastation I had left behind.

The sight of the burning towers took my breath away. I was appalled at the massive cloud of smoke that engulfed the top half of Tower One. I wondered if it had reached the floor I'd been on. If so, anyone still there would be unconscious or dead by now, from smoke inhalation. The pervasive odor of intense burning filled the street. I could see bright flames spewing out through the smoke. Tower Two had been hit near the middle, but the devastation was no less dramatic.

I started walking uptown again, my thoughts in a whirl. Could the burned bodies be identified? Were the flames intense enough to destroy everything, including teeth? Could DNA tests reveal anything under these circumstances? I knew I couldn't move ahead until I had an answer to these questions.

The answer was not long in coming.

Mid-Manhattan was utter chaos. The sidewalks were jammed. People were streaming across the Fifty-

Ninth Street Bridge, heading into Queens. There was grid-lock everywhere. I had reached the lower seventies when I heard shouting from a distance and saw people around me turning to look back. I did too. A dense cloud of smoke obscured the view of the towers. People around me gasped., some began to yell and shout. With a shock, I realized that the smoke I thought was obscuring the towers was in fact the debris of the towers themselves, which had collapsed!

I forced myself to keep walking, trying to keep my excitement at bay. It would work! The new plan would work!

It was almost eleven thirty when I stopped at a luncheonette on Broadway, where I ordered a sandwich and coffee. While waiting for my order, I watched the replay on TV of the towers collapsing.

I ate slowly, taking in what was coming through on TV. The more I heard, the more confident I grew. It soon became obvious that many had been lost in the initial impact, in both towers, but hundreds, perhaps thousands had died when the towers collapsed.

Only then did I admit success. I had scored. My earlier plan could be abandoned. The terrorist attack had provided me with an infinitely better one!

My phone call to Katie had been a stroke of genius. She knew where I was when I called her, knew I intended to stay there for a while, to help others find their way out. My disappearance would be mourned but never questioned.

I was confident the new plan would not only work but that it was foolproof. It was better than anything I could have dreamed up, much better, certainly, than staging a crash, with all the complicated preparations such an accident entailed. It now seemed a preposterous idea, that first plan, foolish even. I saw the opportunity granted me just a few hours earlier an eerie coincidence, as well as a sign of good fortune. It pleased me no end that Kevin would be spared. I'd grown to like him. I was glad he didn't have to die. I also realized that he would, in fact, serve as an excellent witness to my kindness, my generosity, my friendship. I pictured him coming to meet me on Saturday, only to find out that I was among those who didn't get out of the North Tower in time.

Before leaving the luncheonette, I checked the phone books for hotels in the area. I took down a few names; but the first one, several blocks away, seemed adequate for my purpose. It was in the middle of the block, the interior small and dark. I walked into an empty lobby. The clerk was just inside the lounge, where a small group was gathered around the TV, watching replays of what had happened earlier. I went to stand with them and saw again the plane turning into the first tower and some fifteen minutes later a second plane hitting the second tower. I shuddered to think how close I'd come to really being killed.

I went back to where the clerk was still standing and told him I wanted a room for the night. He was all apologies and hurried back behind the desk. I explained, somewhat breathlessly, that I'd just come from the scene of the disaster and had had to leave my personal belonging behind, including my raincoat and a tote with my wallet inside. I pulled out my money clip, wondering if he would insist on an ID. I had put Swentner's driver's license in my pocket, just in case such an emergency arose. As it turned out, I didn't have to use it. I paid cash for the one night and signed the register with a fictitious name.

The clerk, I could tell, was dying to hear all about my escape. I answered some of his questions, trying to look spent and nervous, and soon he gave up. I took my key, and went up to my room, where I put out the "Do Not Disturb" sign and locked the door.

I took out Swentner's wallet and examined its contents carefully. Besides the driver's license, already in my pocket, there were three credit cards, a club membership, the photograph I'd already glanced at, and a slip of paper with the name, address, and phone numbers of an attorney. A note on the back read: "Please contact in case of an emergency."

I slipped the paper inside the seersucker jacket, which I put on in place of mine, and returned everything else to the wallet, which went back into my briefcase. With my case in hand, I hurried downstairs. The TV had drawn even more people. A grim voice was giving the latest news about casualties. The clerk who had checked me in was busy talking to someone. I left unnoticed.

At a nearby clothing outlet on Seventh Avenue, I bought a tote, roomy but small enough to carry on a plane; an inexpensive raincoat, a plastic zipper bag for toiletries, two pairs of socks, two undershirts and shorts, a white shirt, and a red and blue patterned tie. The man at the cash register was on the phone. He rested the receiver on his shoulder, rang up the amount and gave me my change, without interrupting his conversation. He barely glanced at me.

I hooked the tote over my shoulder and went looking for a drugstore. I found one at the corner of the block and purchased a razor, toothbrush, toothpaste, shaving cream, aspirin, and a few other odds and ends that I thought I might need in the days to come. In a nearby Genovese, I bought a one-quart teflon pot.

By now it was close to three. I found a deli and ordered coffee and a pastry. After paying the bill, I went to the phone booth in the back, closed the door and dialed the number on the slip of paper I'd found in Peter Swentner's wallet.

Mr. Preston, the receptionist told me, was on his way out. I told her it was an emergency. When he came on the phone, I said bluntly:

"Mr. Preston, do you know a Mr. Swentner, Peter Swentner?"

"Yes. Peter is a good friend of mine."

My mind was racing, but I had prepared for this while waiting for my change.

"Has he called you any time today?"

"No, no. What is this about? Is Peter all right?" I could hear his voice falter, as though he was anticipating the worst. "What did you say your name was?"

"Turnbull. Archie Turnbull. Look, the reason I'm calling —"

"Mr. Turnbull, Peter and I are old friends. Good friends. We both graduated from Cornell the same year. I haven't heard from him all day and I'm beginning to worry. He works in one of the Twin Towers, an investment firm. Do you know where he is? I have to know. Is he all right?" His voice was sharp, strident almost. More than good friends, I thought. Out loud I said:

"I really don't know. The reason I'm calling is that, just after the plane hit, there was a lot of confusion. Things were hectic. People were yelling and pushing, scrambling to get out. . . ."

I was improvising, but what difference did it make? Preston asked:

"Is Peter with you? Did he get out all right?" His voice had risen a notch.

"I don't know. . . . What I wanted to tell you is that, while I was running toward the stairwell, I saw a wallet on the ground and picked it up to give to the police when I got outside the building. Then I saw a slip with your name on it and thought I'd call you first. I thought I might send the wallet directly to Mr. Swentner at his home. His wife will want to know that —"

Preston interrupted. "Peter isn't married. He has

129

only his mother, but she's in a home."

Now that I had the information I wanted, I moved to end the conversation.

"Well, I thought I'd call this number, to let you know I'd found —"

Preston interrupted again. "Where are you now?"

"What? What did you say? I'm losing you," I lied. "Can you still hear me?" Then I hung up.

Back in my room, I rested the pot inside the bathtub and took everything out from Swentner's wallet except the driver's license and one of the major credit cards. I cut up the rest of the plastic and, as best I could, the empty wallet and put everything inside the pot.

I put the money found in Swentner's wallet inside the kraft envelope I had tucked away in my briefcase, where no one had access, except me. In it was what was left of the money in the hidden account I had closed, as well as six thousand in small bills — what remained of Joe's last loan to me. I counted out six hundred in twenties and added them to my wallet. The Kraft envelope went back into my briefcase.

I put Swentner's driving license and one of the major credit cards inside my own wallet. I had no intention of using anything with his name on it, except in a real emergency. The fact that Preston or Swentner himself would never receive the wallet I'd promised to send could scarcely matter, under the circumstances.

I put a match to what I'd placed at the bottom of the pot and watched the fire take. The paper burned quickly; plastic took longer, giving off a strong odor which soon dissipated, when the flames died down and I ran cold water over what remained. I opened the window for good measure.

I could have burned the stuff without the pot, there wasn't that much; but I wasn't taking any chances. The bathtub had no trace of anything having been burned in it, but I rinsed it carefully anyway. I left the pot near the window, to cool, and went down the hall for some ice. Back in the room I poured myself two of the small scotches from the mini-bar and lay down on the bed, sipping my drink.

I thought of Flora then. All that she meant to me. I basked in the memory of our last meeting. How I missed her! Because of her, I had managed to steer clear of OTB for weeks now. I was proud of that. I had some ready cash to start with, when I reached Ottawa.

I must have dozed off. Loud music from an ad on TV woke me. It was after six. I went into the bathroom and put what I had burned into one of the plastic bags I'd saved from my purchases; the charred pot went into the bag it had come in. I freshened up, put on the seersucker jacket again, picked up my briefcase and went downstairs.

The night clerk had come on duty. He was busy and didn't look up. Not that it really mattered, but I felt the less anyone remembered about me, the better. I slipped out, unnoticed.

At the first trash bin I discarded the charred pot. Further on, I threw away the bag with the contents of what I had burned.

As I continued to walk, and all through my dinner in a small Irish tavern I came across, just off Broadway, I began to plan for the next day.

PART THREE

*INSPECTOR McCALLEY
(AFTERWARDS)*

CHAPTER NINE

At four-thirty, the small deli Katie had chosen for the meeting, on a side street two blocks down from her office building on Third Avenue, had — as she had rightly anticipated — only a few customers. She had never eaten there; it wasn't the kind of place she would choose for lunch or even for a snack, although it was clean enough. She knew she was safe from curious eyes here, not likely to run into anyone from the office, especially this time of day, when most of her colleagues were clearing their desks and getting ready to leave for home.

She had skipped lunch and left early, telling her secretary Lucille that she had to rush home to get ready for dinner with friends. She gave herself at the most an hour. If it took more than that, she'd have to call Francis and work up some story about having to finish a presentation for the next day — a normal routine when Frank was around, but one that she had willingly given up since she'd married Francis. She didn't want to chance even a suggestion that she was returning to her old work habits, especially since it wasn't true. She had promised Francis, from the very start, that she would cut down on overtime, keep regular hours, come home for dinner so they would have time to relax together in the evening. She had done just that, surprising herself at how quickly and easily she'd adapted to the new routine. No more overtime, no more taking folders home to study for meetings the next day. It was a life new and unexpectedly welcome: it had in fact become a delightful habit.

It had grown on her more and more. She looked forward eagerly now to leaving the office quickly at the end of the day, taking nothing to work on at home, arriving predictably around the same time, often finding Francis had set the table, lit candles, poured wine, sometimes started dinner. The long pleasant evenings were spent talking, planning, exchanging stories and reminiscences. They grew close in a way she never dreamed was possible, certainly had never experienced before. She wondered at times how she had managed to live any other way. Francis had brought a new dimension into her life; he meant more to her than she could begin to explain or even understand. It had surprised her, that strange sensation, a feeling of belonging that was both painful and full of joy. It made her fearful and happy at the same time. It had lit up her life. She thought she recognized, no, she finally *knew*, what it meant to be in love. Often, her cousin's words echoed in her memory. She felt guilty somehow, knowing that he had been right about all that. Emma had been his mistake, as Frank had been hers. She had to admit that he had touched a raw nerve. Would she ever get over that meeting?

No, she couldn't spoil it for Francis, or for herself. Besides, too much was at stake. Francis was very good at sensing her moods. If she came in later than expected, she would have to lie, something she wasn't prepared to do and wasn't good at. If she tried, he would know right away that something was wrong. What could she tell him?

Certainly no more than she had told him, soon after they met. At that time, she had convinced herself that all Francis needed to know was that her husband had died in the twin towers tragedy. It was official. The rest was a horror story best left untold. And even if she wanted to tell, how would it be received at this late date? How could she tell anyone, least of all the man she loved, that Frank Hastings had managed an incredible feat: had staged his own death and fled to Canada, where he married a second time under an assumed name, while he still had a first wife? The very thought repelled her. How could she share it with anyone else, especially her new husband? She couldn't risk sharing all that with Francis, not now; nor was she ready — probably never would be — to answer the questions he was bound to ask. Even more frightening; where, if it came to that, would she find the right words to explain why she kept it all from him, and for so long? She had no answers.

Besides, it still hurt. She had been betrayed in a terrible way. How would Francis react to that? Would he think it was something she had done, something lacking in her that had driven Frank to do what he did? The thought had buried itself inside her, rising to haunt her when she least expected it. It was a burden she must carry alone. Francis would be spared. He was her whole life now. She would protect him at whatever cost. Without him, nothing mattered. Her old life and the incredible circumstances that had threatened to destroy her were now behind her. It would remain her secret.

Or was — until Flora Mosely, or rather, Mrs. James Chadwick, sought her out, to tell her what Katie already knew, of course, but had to hide from the rest of the world. She wondered if she had managed to show surprise, sound shocked, whatever would normally be expected under the circumstances. Had she shown the proper amazement and disbelief at what Flora Chadwick told her about Frank, as though she hadn't known about his unbelievable escape and his real death in Canada?

How could she tell anyone that she knew, before Flora told her, that her husband had not died on nine eleven, that he had managed to get to Ottawa, where he married a second time, as though she, Katie, had never existed; and that almost two years later he had really died, the victim of a hit-and-run, in Ottawa! She herself could hardly grasp it, even now. How did she expect others to understand?

Her peace had been shattered. Not only had Frank risen from the dead, taken on a new identity, married again, as her cousin had informed her on that unforgettable day when he had offered her ten million dollars to shoot his wife; not only had she been grieving for him all those months — in addition to all that, she had had to cope with his real death, which Flora Hastings/Chadwick had flown to New York to tell her was not a hit-and-run accident but murder!

That had really shocked her — Flora's insistence that Frank had been murdered. Who would want to murder Frank? As the secret life of her former husband was laid before her, Katie's initial shock turned into a deep despondency. How could he have kept his gambling a secret from her? His huge debts? The loans? He had told Flora all about that, and much else besides. And what Flora had learned from Frank had made her seek out Inspector Luke McCalley of the Ottawa Police, who had come to New York to investigate Flora's story.

There had to be something behind that story.

McCalley had, in fact, already arrived. Soon after her meeting with Flora, Katie got a call at work, where Flora had told him he could reach her. She'd grudgingly agreed to see him after work. So here they were, sitting opposite one another in the back booth of a drab luncheonette off Third Avenue: — he, quietly sipping coffee, waiting for Katie to absorb what he had just told her; Katie staring down at her cup of tea.

The waitress came by to ask if they wanted refills. McCalley shook his head. After a while, he began to speak again. His voice was soft and oddly soothing.

"I know how difficult this must be for you, thinking your husband dead for almost two years, then finding out that he was very much alive all that time and was only recently killed."

She looked up with a twisted smile. "Don't leave out the part about his new wife and his son!"

"That too," he offered calmly. "I'm truly sorry to have to bring all this up at this time, but Mrs. Hastings, that is, Mrs. Chadwick has made some very serious allegations that we feel should be looked into."

"Why can't you leave me out of it?" she burst out, unhappily. "I can't help you. Frank has been dead to me since nine-eleven. He was declared legally dead!"

"I realize that —"

"Then, leave me alone!" she cried out, unable to hide her frustration. She could feel the tears just behind her eyes and turned away quickly.

"I can't, you see," McCalley said quietly. "There's enough in Flora Chadwick's story to make us want to investigate it. I'm saddled with the case; I can't walk away from it." He stopped, waiting for some sign, eager himself to get the interview over with. Katie's silence forced him on. "I need to find out everything I can, so we can get to the bottom of this. There seems to be more to Frank Hastings than anyone imagined."

"Do you listen to all the rubbish that comes your way?"

"No. But there's enough in Mrs. Chadwick's story for us to have taken an interest."

Katie turned slightly where she sat and crossed her legs. She wasn't prepared to shed tears or show just how deeply Frank had wounded her. She would not humiliate herself in front of this man.

"You're kidding, right? You believe all that, about Frank having been killed by mobsters?"

"It's possible. . . . What can you tell me about your former husband, Mrs. Delancourt?"

"Oh, for goodness' sake! What's there to tell? Ask Flora. She knows everything. Frank apparently trusted her more than he trusted me!" She couldn't hide the bitterness in her voice. McCalley gave her a curious look as she plunged on. "Why should I give a hoot, will you answer me that?"

"You're not the only one who is suffering. And

there's the little boy. He misses his father. We owe them something. How his father died. Why he died."

Katie took it in, feeling even more defenseless against the truth of those words, but angry, too. "I'm not a monster, Inspector. I know she's suffering. It may not be her fault, what happened, but, forgive me, I can't reach out to her, to anyone right now. I feel I've been punched senseless and am just coming around. I ache in every way possible. Can you understand that?"

"Of course, I understand!" McCalley said through tight lips, betraying a vulnerability Katie had not given him credit for.

"Frank Hastings was a scoundrel," she went on, in a rush, "both in life and in death. Those he left behind will never be the same." The words tumbled out of her.

McCalley pushed his coffee cup to one side and, leaning forward, crossed his arms on the table. "You're absolutely right. No one will be same because of what Frank Hastings has done. Still. it's my job to bring some kind of closure to it all, for the sake of the living, for you and Flora, and for the child. I can only do that by finding out what really happened." Katie sat motionless, staring off at some distant point beyond the counter. McCalley went on, in a low whisper. "Do you think she hurts any less than you do?"

Katie looked at him with angry eyes. "Spare me, Inspector. I don't know how much Flora Chadwick hurts. I know how much I hurt, how much I've been hurting. And now you come along and force me back into that whole mess because you want to find out who killed Frank Hastings, if he was really killed. Well, whoever did, it's none of my business. And, if you really want to know, I'm glad he's dead. Really dead! I hope there is a hell and that he's rotting in it this very minute!"

McCalley glanced away, frowning. Katie felt as if she had been in a physical fight. Her head was pounding.

She heard the sharpness in her voice with morbid fascination, the rush of words as they tumbled out. Before she could regain some measure of composure, McCalley had turned back to her and went on, as though he had not heard the last outburst:

"Did it ever occur to you that Frank may have placed you in danger by his actions?"

"What do you mean?"

He realized her surprise was genuine and that she probably didn't know everything that Flora Chadwick had learned from her husband and relayed to McCalley.

"I know Mrs. Chadwick told you about his gambling, about the debts he'd piled up." Katie did not respond, and he went on in his slow, even voice. "What she didn't tell you was how he managed to pay off debts that went into five figures. These weren't exactly bank loans, Mrs. Delancourt —" he paused with a wry smile. "The bottom line is, he didn't have the money to pay them back, never would have. Just before he disappeared, he'd asked for another large sum. Do you realize the kind of interest that accrues every day in this kind of . . . shall we say. . . informal borrowing? For those who can't pay back, it becomes a dangerous game. Anyway, Frank found himself forced to do favors."

Katie stared at him. "What are you telling me?"

"That mob involvement in Frank's death is not exactly far-fetched. We know who Frank went to for loans. Flora gave us a name. The man is part of a notorious organized crime family." He waited. Katie's eyes were riveted on him but she said nothing. "We're pretty sure that in order to pay his mounting debts, Frank had to . . . carry out orders, do illegal things. . . . ."

He heard the quick intake of breath, watched her body grow tense, her hand clutch her throat. Her eyes, unblinking, never left his face.

"You're telling me you think Frank committed

crimes to pay off his debts?"

"We know he did. That's what he told Flora; and we have no reason to doubt it, since everything else he told her seems to check out. We know how he got out of Tower One that day, what he did to cover his tracks, everything fits. We'll be double-checking, but we even have the name of the hotel he stayed in that first night He even told Flora, after they were married, that he had cut back on his gambling after he'd met her, told her about his flying and about the first plan he'd concocted. He was going to crash the plane he used to borrow on Saturdays from a friend in Islip. All the preparations had been made" — he waved aside the details— "including luring a likely candidate to fly with him and die in his stead. Found him on the internet, a young man called Kevin Masters. I plan to see him tomorrow, but I'm sure he'll tell me what I already know. Masters would be at the controls and Frank would parachute to safety, having made sure Masters couldn't bail out. He'd even picked out the spot for the crash, had everything worked out — a rented car would be waiting nearby so he could clear out of the area quickly and head for the border, with a stolen ID in case of an emergency — everything was in place, down to the minutest detail, including extra containers of fuel on board so the body found in the wreckage would be burned beyond recognition. He also made sure that no one would suspect anyone else was in the plane with him. Masters had never been seen at the airport. Frank had managed that too, incredible as it may seem."

The look on Katie's face stopped him. Flora obviously had not told her everything. She had turned deathly pale, her eyes fixed on a point over his shoulder.

"Are you all right?" he asked. She seemed not to have heard. He reached out and placed his hand over hers. "I'm sorry. I thought you should know."

She turned to him: Her gaze slowly came to focus

on his face again.

"Crash a plane? With someone in it?"

"It would have worked, too, I'm sure. But on September eleventh, a much simpler plan came his way. What was a terrible tragedy for thousands of people turned out to be, for him, a stroke of unimaginable luck, at least he must have seen it as such. He made good use of it. We'll never know what went through his mind at the time, but he worked it all out in a flash. Pity he didn't apply that subtle mind of his to improving his life — yours too — in legitimate ways." He watched as she took it all in, her face drawn, her lips a grim tight line, her brow furrowed, her eyes registering shock and horror.

"Flora told you all this? Frank told her all this?"

"Yes." He could see the emotions flit across her pretty face — incomprehension, a sense of helplessness, anger, jealousy even, at learning that Frank had confided so much to Flora. McCalley thought he saw also in her body language — she was squirming in her seat, as though anxious to be released from the unpleasantness that kept her there — the doubts that had surfaced about her marriage, about her responsibility for what had happened, her integrity and worth even. Frank had trusted Flora as he had never trusted her.

In a kind of desperate gesture, she looked at her watch. "I must be going," she said quickly, extricating herself from the booth. McCalley reached out and placed a restraining hand on her arm.

"There are some more questions I need to ask —"

She stopped, her body poised at the edge of the booth. "My husband is waiting for me. I have to run. . . ."

McCalley went on, without releasing his hold. "I need to talk to you some more."

"Why? You already have all the answers!"

"Not all, Katie." Too much had been said, too many personal matters had been shared for him to continue addressing her formally as 'Mrs. Delancourt.' "There's a great deal that I need to find out before we can lay the matter to rest."

She stood up and rummaged in her bag until she found a small pad. He watched her scribble on it and took the paper she tore out and offered him. "That's my cell phone," she said dully. "Call me there if you really have to. And only during the day."

He put the paper in his wallet. "Your husband doesn't know?"

She gave him an anguished look. "He knows Frank died in nine-eleven." He sensed her deep unease but could say nothing to reassure her.

"You don't want to tell him the rest? Do you think it's a good idea to keep it from him?"

"For God's sake, Inspector! How would you feel if I dumped this horror story in your lap?" McCalley looked away, somewhat embarrassed. He understood only too well what she felt but knew with equal certainty that eventually it would all come out and Francis Delancourt would have to cope with what had happened to his wife. McCalley wasn't prepared to make the point so bluntly; the woman had been through enough. But he'd seen too often the grim results of keeping such secrets. They never remained buried.

She picked up her tote, ready to leave. McCalley stood up. "I'll be as discreet as possible. . . ."

He saw the relief in her face.

"I really have got to run. I'm late as it is." She was moving toward the door even as she spoke.

McCalley sat down again and counted out money to pay the check the waitress had brought him. He accepted more coffee and sat quietly sipping it for a few minutes. He wished he could have spared Katie from learning what he had told her, but actually there was much more that still remained to be said. He had held back a good deal.

He could still see her face, flushed with anger, her lips a thin hard line, even as she spoke. Something she said kept ringing in his ears. What was it exactly? He racked his memory trying to pinpoint the words, the phrase.

It had been around the time nine-eleven first came up. No, after that. She had been angry and lashed out at him about hurting. Yes, that was it. He had said, referring to Flora: "Do you think she hurts any less than you do?" And she had answered about how much she was hurting and — he searched for the words, the phrase —

She'd said in her anger: "And now you come along and force me back into that whole mess because you want to find out who killed him." What was it that bothered him about those words, uttered in the heat of anger and frustration? Was it his imagination playing tricks on him or was he right in thinking that she already knew about Frank's death in Ottawa, knew long before he or Flora told her?

Back in his hotel room, he washed up and went down to dinner. But even as he ate the excellent steak he had ordered and sipped a glass of Merlot, his favorite wine, Katie Delancourt's words, the sound of them, with all the emotions they betrayed, kept playing in his head like a record. McCalley "had forced her back into that whole mess. . . ." Yes, that was the phrase! *"Forced her back into that whole mess."* Was he reading too much into it, letting his imagination run away?

He wasn't one to trust his instincts, although they had proved correct often enough. But he was a sensible man; everyone knew his aversion to speculation. Sergeant Bill Kenney, whom McCalley had chosen as his assistant several years earlier and with whom he worked closely, had been warned many times not to jump to conclusions, not before all the available data had been collected, when all the pieces of the puzzle had been carefully studied and in place. The entire Department knew that McCalley did not tolerate hunches and unfounded theories. And now, here he was, speculating about a phrase Katie Delancourt had tossed out in frustration and anger.

He shook his head, as though to clear it of such baggage. Impossible for the woman to have known before now that Frank did not die on nine-eleven, that he had gone to Canada, remarried, and had been killed only recently in Ottawa! But then, what had she meant by saying McCalley had forced her *back* into that whole mess? Impossible as it seemed, improbable as it sounded, McCalley could not help thinking, could not rid himself of the notion that Katie Delancourt had known about Frank's escape from nine-eleven and his death in Ottawa before he and Flora told her, and that somehow the knowledge had driven her to make hard decisions, not the least of which could well be her determination to keep it all buried.

It was just a hunch; but in spite of his better judgment, he could not let it go.

How could she know, before Flora arrived in New York and spoke with her, that Frank Hastings had not perished in the twin towers tragedy? For he was certain that in the heat of her anger and pain Katie had betrayed herself. Was he right? And did she realize that she had given herself away?

Was he reading more than he should in that one phrase?

CHAPTER TEN

When Kevin Masters walked into the hotel lounge just after six the next day, McCalley had already settled into a nook that boasted the only two large armchairs in the room. He was glad he'd come down early. It was the cocktail hour, and the place had begun to fill up.

McCalley rose as the waiter pointed the young man in his direction. When they were both seated, McCalley ordered a beer for Masters; mineral water for himself. They chatted pleasantly until the waiter returned with the drinks. The Inspector had decided on a casual strategy, a "need to know" approach. Just how much to tell the young man would depend on what Masters had to say — except for one piece of information: McCalley had decided not to tell him what Frank Hastings had in mind when he befriended him. Not today, anyway. It would come out soon enough.

On the phone, he had explained that he was looking into Frank Hastings' death to clear up some misunderstandings that had arisen about his estate. The man had been officially dead for some time, of course; his wife had remarried; but claims initiated by relatives who had unexpectedly surfaced in Ottawa called for some sort of investigation. Masters had accepted the story, didn't even ask for an ID. McCalley brought out his badge anyway, before going on. He hated the deception he had concocted; but he felt it was the best approach. For a while at least, Masters would be spared the ugly truth about the man whom he believed to have been so selfless and kind.

"Tell me about Mr. Hastings," McCalley began easily. "What was he like?"

"A great guy, Inspector."

"How long did you know him?"

"Since June, but we hit it off right away."

"How did you meet?"

"On the internet — where else, these days?" McCalley laughed and sipped his mineral water. "It was strange really, how it happened. I love small planes. Hope to own one, some day. I've read a lot about them but never been in one. One day, I find this message on the website."

McCalley made himself more comfortable in the big chair. "Your website?"

"No. I don't have one, but we both subscribe to the same aviation magazines, clubs, informational online services, that sort of thing. Members have access to those websites; they post information, ask questions, things like that. Frank had put a notice on several of them about wanting to share expenses with someone who was interested in owning a Cessna."

"And you answered him?"

"Just out of curiosity. I can't afford even a small piece of a Cessna. I just wanted to chat about planes. You know how it is on the internet. Even strangers can communicate without any trouble. I thought: if he's out to buy a Cessna, he must know how to fly one. Something I'd never done."

"Did he?"

"Oh, yes! He told me right away, he'd been flying for years. Got his license when he started college."

That much was true, at least, thought McCalley. Out loud, he asked: "And after all that time, he wanted to buy part ownership of a Cessna?"

"I guess he couldn't afford it before."

"What else did he tell you?"

"He explained that he had a friend who had bought a plane for tax purposes but had no intention of flying. He didn't mind if his buddy used it once in a while. Can you believe someone owning a Cessna and not flying it?" He shook his head and finished the beer.

"What happened after that?" McCalley asked, stretching his legs and trying to show nothing more than a casual interest in these details.

"We started exchanging e-mails. Frank would tell me how far he'd gone the last time he'd flown, or about some new gadget he'd found, what he'd seen during the flight, things like that. And lots of stories about his grandfather, who first took him up in a plane when he was still a kid."

McCalley caught the waiter's eye and gestured for refills. Masters had found his stride and went right on.

"I don't make friends easily, but with Frank I was at home, right off. Even before I actually met him, he was already an old friend." There was a faraway look in his eyes. McCalley said nothing.

"The beauty about e-mail," the young man went on, "even a shy person has no trouble communicating. You can remain invisible forever if you want to, and still say anything you like without feeling self-conscious. You can write an essay and fifty strangers will read it, some might even comment on it. There's no limit to what you can do. The whole world is accessible. You might find yourself talking to Donald Trump one day."

McCalley said nothing, having no personal experience with e-mails or websites, and no particular interest in talking to Donald Trump one day. His assistant, Sergeant Bill Kenney, had tried on several occasions to get him to learn how to use the internet. It was easy enough, but he stubbornly refused to be drawn into it. Even tape recorders were a nuisance. "Too risky," he never tired of saying. Knowing this, Kenney had learned shorthand before he applied for the job as McCalley's assistant, and it had proved a wise decision. He had also mastered the new technology, a fact that was not lost on McCalley, who was wise enough to make good use of Kenney's skills with the computer and the internet. Kenney himself took a lot of ribbing from his colleagues about the Inspector's refusal to move into the twenty-first century. Hearing the quips and jokes about the "dinosaur" he worked for, Kenney would grow fiercely protective. It was rumored that he had turned down a promotion, so that he could continue working with McCalley. He rose to the Inspector's defense every time and was especially sensitive to comments about McCalley's notorious dismissal of "hunches" and idle speculation before all the facts were in. In the local pub with his colleagues, or over coffee during a break, Kenney took the ribbing and in the end would join in the laughter. It was all good fun: McCalley's track record precluded real criticism.

McCalley was, in fact, taking in as many details as he could, comparing them with what Frank had confided to Flora, and the woman, in turn, had told McCalley. Listening to Masters' enthusiastic account of e-mails and websites, he shuddered to think how close the man had come to programming his own death through the internet.

The waiter came with fresh drinks. Masters picked up his glass and raised it in a silent toast. McCalley did the same with his Perrier.

"I worked up enough courage to answer Frank's notice," Masters went on. "I told him I was interested in Cessnas, and would he mind telling me more about them? I told him right off I couldn't help him — didn't want to give him the wrong impression — told him I'd never flown in a small plane, but it was something I was dying to do."

You almost did, McCalley thought. A wave of sympathy made him clear his throat. Frank Hastings couldn't have found a better victim.

"When did you actually meet?"

"Late in June. He asked if I wanted to come out to Islip, one Saturday. I couldn't believe my luck! I'll never forget that first time!"

"He invited you again?"

"Oh, yes. Every Saturday after that. Before then, I'd spend the weekend loafing around, sometimes I'd go to a ball game or a movie. I've been at loose ends, since my divorce." Masters suddenly seemed to crumple where he sat. "I still can't believe he's gone, that I'll never see him again." His voice was hoarse with emotion.

"When was the last time you flew with him?"

"The Saturday just before nine-eleven. The eighth, I think it was. I parked my car in the usual place, just off the service road that goes past the airport." McCalley cocked his head and raised his brows in an unspoken question. "It's a busy place, Inspector, it's grown a lot since the old days and handles many more planes, large ones even. I got the feeling they don't like casual flying or amateur pilots, especially on one of their busiest days. Frank explained it had been hard enough getting them to let *him* fly on Saturdays — luckily he had friends who'd known him for years, some even knew his grandfather — but, well, he had to find a way to sneak me in."

"How did he manage that?" McCalley asked, when Masters paused to sip his beer.

"It was easy enough. He told me to park at the far end of the field, near the service road. He was always there before me and would be waiting close by. I'd climb in the plane and keep my head low until we cleared the tower."

"Quite a risk he was taking," ventured McCalley, allowing his curiosity some room.

"I know." Masters' eyes clouded over with the memories he had evoked. He went on, almost to himself: "I'll never forget the sensation, the exhilaration of flying in that plane. I'd dreamed of it forever, and suddenly it was happening. . . . I must have made a nuisance of myself, with all my questions, but he didn't seem to mind. In fact, he was pleased at my enthusiasm. In a couple of weeks, he had taught me everything about the controls, about climbing and settling into the flight pattern, what all the gadgets were for — I couldn't have done better if I'd hired an instructor!

"The third Saturday in July, we changed seats, and he told me to take over. I couldn't believe it! I remember Frank smiled and said: 'Hey! There's always a first time!' It wasn't perfect, but he was there for me, every second! Then, on the last Saturday of August and the following week, he went through everything about taking off and landing. That last time, Saturday the eighth of September, he told me I would take the plane up and bring it down in a week or two and that I was ready for the pilot's test, anytime. He was going to get the application forms, help me through the paperwork, brief me about everything!"

"All that time, no one ever suspected Frank had someone with him in the plane?"

Masters shook his head. "No. After the plane had been checked out, he'd taxi to the far end of the field, where he'd told me to wait. I was usually early. I'd run crouching low and climb in. Then he would work his way around again for clearance and take off. No one ever dreamed anyone else but Frank was in the plane."

"How did you learn he had died?"

"When I turned up on the fifteenth and he wasn't there, I was concerned; but I really began to worry when there were no messages in the days that followed. I never dreamed he's been in the towers on the eleventh! When my e-mails weren't being answered, I realized I had no address or phone number for him. Didn't even know where he worked. Then I did what I should have done earlier. I checked the phone book. Sure enough, he was listed. I called the number and talked with his wife. She told me what had happened. That's how I found out that Frank had been at a meeting in Tower One and never made it to ground level." Masters blinked, his eyes moist. "A nice woman. I told her about my flying with Frank on Saturdays. She didn't know anything about it. We were on the phone a long time. She thanked me for calling."

Masters sipped his beer in silence, nurturing his memories. McCalley made no effort to break into his meditation. He let his own thoughts fall into place.

From what he already had uncovered and what Kevin Masters had just told him, McCalley was now able to piece together new details of Frank Hastings' original plan that Flora Hastings had not been able to provide. He had to give the man credit: he'd thought of just about everything. The picture that was emerging was all too clear. The only thing missing was the date he'd planned to carry out his gruesome plan. It would have had to be sometime in September, McCalley guessed. The fire had to be intense. Rain and bad weather could foul things up. But, of course, fate had intervened.

Luckily, McCalley mused, Frank had not had a chance to erase every trace of his preparations. Had he not taken the opportunity that unexpectedly presented itself on the fateful day that changed his life, if that hadn't happened and he'd carried out his first plan, he would certainly have had time to erase every trace of what might have aroused suspicion. By now, McCalley knew enough about the man to give him credit for careful planning, as well as fast thinking: he'd grabbed the escape offered by nine-eleven and quickly used it to advantage; but he'd also meticulously planned a difficult crash scenario, which no doubt would have worked. But what turned out to be his lucky break also forced him to abandon whatever was still on his home computer, which Katie Delancourt had stored in a closet and had agreed to turn over to(McCalley that morning, after Francis had left for work.

There were no messages to or from Masters. What he did find, among other things, what Frank no doubt meant to erase later but had no opportunity to do so, was Masters' e-mail address.

Actually, it was McCalley's colleague and good friend, NYPD Detective Ed Markarian, who pulled up that and some other interesting information from the computer and diskettes McCalley had brought back to his hotel room that morning. He'd called Ed on his arrival in New York and, as he had predicted, his friend was more than happy to help in any way he could. And so today, Markarian had spent his lunch hour in McCalley's hotel room — two hours in fact — searching the computer for anything that might be relevant or useful to McCalley's investigation, while nibbling on sandwiches from room service.

He was just as efficient this time as he had been when McCalley had come to New York to continue a murder investigation that had started in Ottawa. The Ellis Bantry case might never have been solved, except for Markarian's unstinting cooperation. He'd gone out on a limb for McCalley, even taking records from official files to allow his friend a chance to study them at leisure. McCalley was forever grateful for the time and effort his friend had spent on the case, even before his role in it could be officially acknowledged by the New York City police. It had been a difficult time for both of them. Now, here he was again, ready to do whatever McCalley asked and needed.

Unlike McCalley, Ed liked computers and was good with them. McCalley had watched him pull up, in addition to Masters' e-mail messages, the phone numbers of army discount houses and of some storage rentals out on Long Island. It suggested to McCalley that whatever

Frank Hastings had had in mind required buying and storing things near the airport.

They drove out to Islip early in the afternoon, a search warrant in hand. It was easy enough to find the storage facility Hastings had rented. They had started with the two closest to the airport; the very first one they tried yielded results. The man who had rented the space identified Frank from the picture shown him. Their search yielded two brand-new parachutes and five large containers of fuel.

The storage unit was sealed off, and with Ed's help, an officer posted there. Before returning to the precinct — he had paperwork to catch up on — Ed agreed to return to the hotel for a late dinner that evening. McCalley would fill him on the interview with Masters.

The sound of the other man's voice roused the Inspector from his musings. It was now well into the dinner hour, and the lounge had almost emptied; but he wasn't ready to let Kevin Masters go yet. He cleared his throat and moved forward, clasping his hands between his knees.

"Frank never talked with you about his work, about relatives in Ottawa, other hobbies?"

"No."

"But he knew all about you. . . ?"

"There wasn't much to tell."

"He never spoke about his relatives, his wife?"

"He told me he was married, but that's about it."

"Never mentioned wanting to visit Canada?"

"Never."

"Did he say anything about a new job?"

"No. Was he was thinking of moving to Canada?"

McCalley shrugged and smiled. "I'm not sure. . . . Did he ever mention owing money, having to pay off loans, things like that?"

Masters shook his head. "No, but he must have

had some ready cash, Inspector, if he was out to buy a piece of a Cessna."

"Yes. You're right." He stood up. "I may call you again, Mr. Masters. Thank you. You've been a great help. I hope I haven't kept you from your dinner."

Masters registered some surprise at the abrupt dismissal. The two men shook hands and parted — the Inspector marveling again at Masters' never having questioned his new friend's extraordinary generosity in giving up his precious air time to teach an utter stranger how to fly a small plane. Frank Hastings must have rejoiced at having found such a trusting soul.

After making some calls, McCalley returned to the lounge to wait for Markarian. It was close to nine before he arrived, looking drawn and somewhat dishevelled. McCalley met him halfway into the room.

"The dining room stays open for after-theater snacks, but the manager assured me we can still get a good steak if we want it."

"Sounds fine to me," said Markarian. They both added a salad to their order, as well as a beer for Markarian and a glass of Merlot for McCalley. As they sipped their drinks, Markarian told him about the case he was on — an aggravated assault with weapons — which he was ready to close. He would be free to help McCalley full time, for as long as needed, since the Hastings case was of great interest to the New York police, especially the possible connection with organized crime in the city.

While they ate, McCalley told him briefly about his interview with Masters. Markarian for the most part nodded, pausing once to ask a question. Finally, relaxing over coffee, Markarian summed it up for both of them.

"So, Masters didn't have a clue —"

"No. How could he? I don't know if I did the right thing not telling him the truth —"

156

Markarian shook his head. "You've saved him some sleepless nights, Luke...."

"For now, anyway. He was so trusting...."

"Even you and I might have been taken in, Luke. The worst betrayals, and the easiest, are by people we love and trust. Anyone pulling that kind of stunt belongs in Hell."

McCalley couldn't help smiling. "I think they're already there. Dante put them at the very bottom of his *Inferno*."

Markarian laughed. "Okay, so I haven't had time to read the *Divine Comedy*. It's on my list, though!" They both laughed, pleased to be sharing a meal, good friends as well as experienced investigators, ready to share what they knew.

McCalley moved on to what was uppermost in his mind. "I want to pass something by you, Ed." Markarian perked up. He relaxed in his chair: "Katie Hastings, I mean Katie Delancourt, said something yesterday that has been nagging me."

Markarian couldn't help laughing. "Inspector McCalley following up a hunch? I don't believe it!"

McCalley smiled, taking in stride the friendly nudge about his no-nonsense approach to investigations, his refusal to entertain speculation and theories before all the evidence was in. During the Bantry case, he had repeatedly warned everyone, including Markarian, against jumping to conclusions.

"It's not really a hunch, in this case. Something she said alerted me to the possibility that she might be hiding information."

"What did she say?"

"She was understandably upset by what she'd heard, first from Flora Hastings, Flora Chadwick that is, and later from me. She was really shocked when I told her we thought Frank might have committed crimes as payment to the mob for his big gambling debts. But at one point, she said —" here McCalley interrupted himself and took out a small note pad. He leafed through a number of pages of intricate doodles before finding what he wanted. "Here it is," he said, glancing first at Markarian then at his notes, then looking up again as he spoke. He leaned back in his chair. "We were talking about hurting. She was terribly upset. I thought at first it was because she had kept everything from her husband. All Delancourt knows is that Frank died in nine-eleven."

Markarian made no comment. McCalley looked at his notes.

"I'd said, in connection with Flora: 'Do you think she hurts any less than you do?' My words made her angry for some reason. She said she didn't know how much Flora hurt but knew how much she was hurting, had been hurting."

"Well, that's natural, isn't it? As far as she knew, until just a few days ago, she thought her husband had been killed in nine eleven."

"Wait, hear me out, . . . although now that I think of it, those words seem a bit odd too. After all, she'd remarried. Frank was behind her. We have to assume she's happy in her new life, her new marriage. Under the circumstances, that phrase too seems peculiar, don't you think? — she 'had been hurting,' she said. . . . Then she went on, right after that, she went on to say — it stuck in my mind, I wrote it down word for word, after she'd left — she said, and these are her words: 'And now you come along and force me back into that whole mess because you want to find out who murdered Frank Hastings, if he was really murdered.' She wasn't mourning, Ed. She was hurting in a different way. She made it very clear. She said she was glad Frank was dead. Let's see: here it is. She said 'I'm glad he's dead. Really dead. I hope there is a hell and that he's rotting in it this very minute!'"

He watched his friend take it all in. McCalley didn't have to spell it out; he could see Markarian had understood the suggestion those words carried. They sat in silence for a few minutes. The waiter came with the check, which McCalley signed and handed back to him. Markarian shifted in his chair and turned to McCalley.

"Did she say 'Really dead'? Were those her words?"

"Yes. But what struck me at the time was the other phrase, my coming along and forcing her back — that's what hit me — *forcing her back into that whole mess.*"

"As though she'd been there, knew all about it."

"But how could she have known?" McCalley persisted. Markarian shook his head. "The 'Really dead' might tie into the other," McCalley went on, "but it didn't suggest anything to me at the time except that she had found out from Flora, and I confirmed for her later, that Frank had not died in nine-eleven but in Ottawa, over a year and a half later. . . . What about that other, phrase, though?" he insisted, eager to hear what his friend had to say. "How was I forcing her *back* into that whole mess, when she'd just learned about Frank's disappearance, his marriage to Flora, and the rest? The key word is *back*, isn't it?" When Markarian didn't reply, he added: "Am I way off on this?"

"No, I don't think so." Markarian looked at his friend with troubled eyes. "You don't suppose she had anything to do with it, if it does turn out to be murder?"

"That didn't occur to me. Not to be ruled out, I guess, but no, I'm sure she's not involved. My impression was that she's caught in something too dreadful to admit or share with anyone."

"Was she surprised at the debts Hastings had piled up?"

"If Flora Chadwick is to be relied on, Katie was shocked. Had no idea."

"And how did she react when Flora told her that Frank had been killed in Ottawa, not in nine-eleven?"

"Took it in stride, Flora said."

"Shocked at the gambling debts but took in stride the news of his death, in Ottawa. . . . Anything on Frank's connections in Canada?"

"We know he set himself up as a consultant in medical malpractice suits. Was doing pretty well, even got himself on the Board of one of the large pharmaceutical companies up there."

"Isn't that a potential conflict of interest?"

"Apparently the company didn't think so."

"Maybe they wanted an insider to advise them in legal negotiations?"

"Wouldn't they have their own lawyers for that?"

"I guess. . . ."

"Anyway, we're looking into it. Kenney is on it."

"You really think there's a mob connection?"

"It's a long shot but worth exploring."

"Would he have chanced it? After what happened in New York, the debts he'd piled up with those people?"

"Yes, I think he would have. After two years, he must have convinced himself he was safe. How would Sarace know where he was? That he was still alive? The people in New York had no reason to suspect anything. Who would even dream of looking for him, after nine-eleven? Yes, he would have chanced it. He'd covered his tracks. Besides, he was a gambler, wasn't he."

After a pause, Markarian said: "Let me do a bit of sleuthing at this end while you try finding out more about his Ottawa connections."

McCalley gave him a thoughtful look. "She was quite angry," he said, picking up the earlier thread. "Nervous, on edge all the while we talked. I thought it was because she didn't want her husband to know that Frank had deserted her. As though she was ashamed, felt guilty, the way abused wives feel responsible for their husbands' beating them. . . . Now. . . . I'm not so sure. It may be something altogether different."

The theaters had apparently let out; the dining room now had some new customers. Markarian pushed back his chair.

"I'll call you or leave a message, if I find out something during the day. Otherwise, I'll stop by around five. No dinner, though. I've got a cousin coming to visit tomorrow. Promised my wife I'd be home by six."

"Good enough," said McCalley. They strolled out into the lobby.

"You have my phone numbers, if you need me before then," said Markarian, by way of good-bye.

In his room, McCalley put in a call to Sergeant Kenney. His instructions were simple. He spoke slowly, knowing that Kenney was taking everything down.

"Take a good look at law suits Hastings handled as a claims investigator in New York; complaints, allegations of any kind that involved him in some way. I also want to know just when he began to serve on the Board of that company in Canada, who sponsored him, anything along those lines."

He paused to give Kenney time to take everything down.

"I thought you'd like to know that Flora Chadwick is back, Inspector." Kenney told him. "She wants to know where we're at."

"Tell her we're following some good leads and I'll get back to her as soon as I can. Meanwhile, we need to look through Frank's correspondence, notes, e-mail — everything you can find about what he was into."

"Will do. . . . Have you found out anything more at your end?"

"No, but Detective Markarian is following some

good leads of his own. . . . Call me as soon as you have something, Bill. I'm counting on you."

At the other end, Kenney smiled. It wasn't often McCalley gave out compliments.

It was close to midnight by the time he was ready for bed. He lay on top of the coverlet in his pajamas and reviewed the case.

Hastings's movements on September eleventh would have to be checked out. It was routine, but something new might surface. Of course, he mused once again, Flora Chadwick's story might be a false alarm. McCalley needed more pieces in place, before he came to any judgment.

He took out his pad and made a quick checklist for the next day. First, he would visit the hotel where Frank had stayed after walking away from the towers. (Flora had given him the name and some other useful details that would save him steps.) Next, he would search out the places where Hastings had purchased basic necessities (although that might prove more difficult, given the number of small shops all along Sixth and Seventh Avenues and in between, on the side streets). After that, if there was time and it proved necessary, he would visit Islip and talk to the dispatcher and others at the airport who knew Frank. He'd also try to locate the OTB where Frank placed his bets, check the airports — La Guardia, Kennedy, and Newark — to track down flights to Canada, on September 16th, when schedules were close to normal again, and, according to Flora, Frank had booked a flight to Ottawa. (Markarian might be willing to take on the last three.)

But first, they would go back into Frank's computer, more leisurely this time, for anything they might have overlooked.

He missed his Sergeant, who in his quiet way

managed to spare him a lot of leg work, as well as the more routine matters that demanded attention in any investigation. He had learned to rely on Kenney. But he couldn't really complain. Not with Markarian helping him in every way. . . .

Sleep had crept in at some point. When he woke up in the middle of the night, he was still stretched out on top of the bed, the pad in his hand, the pen on the floor. The air conditioning had chilled him.

He put the notes he had made aside, got under the covers, and turned out the light.

CHAPTER ELEVEN

The phone rang as McCalley was getting ready to set out after breakfast for the small hotel where Flora had told him Frank had stayed overnight on nine-eleven, before making it into Queens on the twelfth. Markarian, in turn, had volunteered to e-mail Frank's photo to the Marriott, near La Guardia, to see if they recognized him. It was the place Hastings had told Flora he'd stayed from the twelfth to the sixteenth, when he picked up a flight for Ottawa.

Markarian's deep voice greeted him. "Good! I was hoping to catch you."

"Don't tell me you have something already!"

"I got in early and called the Marriott. Saved us time and leg work! . . . The day clerk had just come on, the same one on duty on nine-eleven. A bit of prodding, brought up the register for the twelfth, and sure enough one of the names on it was Louis Rien. Couldn't give me a positive ID on the photo I e-mailed him, but he remembered the man who had made it out of Tower One with just his briefcase and money clip and paid cash. The name was there: Louis Rien. Pronounced "Reen," by the way."

"So Flora's story checks out."

"How's that for starters?"

"You mean, there's more?"

"I just checked flights for Ottawa on the sixteenth. That's when Hastings told Flora he'd flown out, right?"

"Yes, the sixteenth."

"Same story. They'll get back to me about an ID, when the clerk who sold him the ticket comes in, but I'm not holding my breath. He used the same name and I'm sure gave them the same pitch, because he paid cash for his ticket. Gave a phony address in Toronto."

Before hanging up, McCalley told him what he was planning for the morning and confirmed the meeting for later that afternoon.

His first stop was the midtown hotel, where Frank had stayed overnight. There he showed his badge and told the clerk he was investigating some insurance claims that had arisen, involving a certain Louis Rien — whether he had indeed been in New York on September 11th, 2001, and not in San Francisco.

The clerk had no trouble identifying Frank from the photo McCalley showed him. "Oh, yes, I remember him. Poor man! He was in the North Tower when it happened. Managed to get out just before it collapsed. I got the impression he was still in shock. Had only his briefcase and a money clip with him. Stayed the one night and paid cash. Nice young man. From Baltimore, Hope he got home all right." It didn't take long for the clerk to bring up the name: Louis Rien.

McCalley thanked him and left.

Outside, he mused on Hastings' choice of the name "Rien." He must have enjoyed calling himself "Nothing," his private little joke on the successful outcome of his escape: Frank Hastings no longer existed.

Looking for discount shops and army outlet stores where Hastings might have made his purchases that day was no doubt a fruitless search. Flora had made a list, as best she could, from what she remembered Frank had told her, but McCalley knew it would be near impossible for anyone to ID Frank Hastings two years later, or to recall what he bought.

He was pleasantly surprised, therefore, when the owner of a discount outlet store not far from the hotel frowned in concentration over Frank's photo and commented:

"Can't be sure, we're talking two years ago, but there was this one guy, came in while I was on the phone with my wife — her brother works as a handyman in Tower One, had called in sick that morning to finish putting in new kitchen cabinets for us. My wife was all excited at the close call. I was trying to calm her down, when this guy walks in, picks out a few things, including a tote, comes up to the register, takes off the price tag on the tote, stuffs the rest of the things inside it, then hands me two big bills. That's how I remember. The sale was just over a hundred, and I was thinking I might not have enough change for him. Barely made it."

McCalley showed him the list.

"Can't say for sure, but it could be that's what he bought. Yeah, there's the tote."

It wasn't a positive ID, but for McCalley it was enough. He decided there was no point pursuing this particular track any further and returned to the hotel. He made notes on the morning's interviews, had a late lunch, and called Kenney for an update. At four-thirty he went downstairs to wait for Markarian.

"I've got something interesting for you," his friend began, even before they sat down in the lounge. "I took a break late this morning and phoned Katie Hastings's office. Her secretary, Lucille Radino, answered, as I expected. Her boss had already left for a luncheon conference, so it made things easier. I asked if she could give me a few minutes of *her* lunch break to answer some questions. I'd explain when we met. We had burgers and fries at a McDonald's across from where she works.

"It was a delicate matter, I explained as we ate, and I'd appreciate her not sharing our conversation with anyone, including her boss. Then I asked her about Katie's activities in the last few months. At first, she was hesitant, but I assured her Katie was incidental to another investigation that involved someone she knew. So. Guess what?"

McCalley grinned and held out his arms, in a

gesture of helplessness. He had ordered drinks for both of them, and Markarian now paused to sip his beer.

"Ready for this?" Markarian went on, putting down his glass. "Turns out that Katie Hastings or Delancourt is related to —" McCalley let out a low whistle when he heard the name of the head of the international conglomerate that ranked almost on a par with Bill Gates' empire. Markarian went on without a pause. "That's her cousin! As you know, his business is mostly pharmaceuticals, or at least it started that way. He's into everything these days. His wife died in a car crash last January. He's moved to Paris and remarried.

"How did you hit on this?"

"On her vacation last summer, Katie went to Italy and France. At St. Tropez, she ran into the cousin. Hadn't seen him for years, she told Lucille, when the secretary asked about the trip. I also found out that from St. Tropez she went on to Paris, to spend the rest of the time, about ten days, with two college chums who work there. Oh, and at the end, she made a quick trip to Geneva.

"When I asked her if Katie had seemed troubled recently, if she'd mentioned any family difficulties, she shook her head at first, then remembered a call not too long ago that had upset her boss more than seemed warranted. Her cousin, the big shot from St. Tropez, was in New York and wanted to take Katie to lunch. Lucille said Katie was adamant at first about not wanting to see or talk to him, seemed angry in fact, then decided she might as well get it over with. He was staying at the Regis, but they had lunch at a French restaurant." He took out a slip of paper.

"I took down the name. Dropped by there, just before coming here. Talked with the doorman. He remembered her on account of the quarrel she had with the man she was with. She yelled at him all the while the doorman was flagging down a cab for her, told him she never wanted to see him again. Couldn't wait to get away. Left the poor guy standing, embarrassed, on the curb."

"When did all this happen?"

"In July. The guy was flying back to Paris the next day."

McCalley asked: "Think he told her about Frank? But how would he know?"

"You undermine my talents, that's your trouble," answered the other, relishing the moment. "I did a bit more sleuthing on the internet. Want to try guessing again?" McCalley laughed and shook his head. Markarian continued. "James Chadwick, alias Frank Hastings, was on the board of one of the companies owned by Katie's rich cousin."

"He knew him? He knew Frank was alive?"

"Not at first, maybe. But he must have discovered his true identity at some point."

"Maybe that's why Katie was angry. She may have thought her cousin had recruited Frank, had known all along that he'd deserted her and yet put him on the board of one of his companies. . . . But how would he have known Hastings?"

"He may have been at their wedding."

"There was no wedding, just a short ceremony at City Hall, according to Flora. That's what Frank told her. Katie's parents were both killed in a car accident just before she graduated from NYU. Her brother had to leave for a new job on the West coast. It was a simple affair. But Ed, even if her cousin knew Frank in some way, would Katie be so angry with him because of that?"

"Maybe not, but it's worth following up."

"What else did the secretary tell you?"

"She gave me a copy of Katie's itinerary for the two weeks abroad, the names of her two friends in Paris, where she stayed for about ten days before flying back home. And she went to Geneva overnight to buy a new watch. She was wearing it, showed it to Lucille." He handed McCalley another slip of paper. "That's the itinerary."

McCalley examined the paper Markarian had given him. "Right now, I can't see where it all fits in, but the more we know, the better."

"The magic of internet —"

"— and McDonald's!"

"That too." They both laughed. Markarian went on: "You realize, Luke, this may all be a wild goose chase. Flora may be all wrong."

McCalley sighed. "Too late for that. We can't back off now. . . . We'll have to talk with Katie again, tomorrow if possible. She's holding back, I'm sure of it. We'll have to ask her about the cousin, for starters. What happened on her trip. What her cousin may have said or done to make her so angry. Why she stayed for three days in St. Tropez, obviously had a good time, then wouldn't see him when he asked her to lunch in New York." McCalley made a note, laid the pad and pen aside and took a sip of wine.

"I guess you'll want to talk with the cousin. And the two girls she stayed with in Paris," said Markarian.

McCalley nodded and shifted in his seat. "We have to find out more about what he did up there in Canada, more about his work, if he met Katie's cousin at any time." He shook his head. "It's a hell of a case. We don't even know what we should be looking for, except that Flora is pretty sure her husband was murdered, that he'd been tracked down somehow and killed. But how would anyone have known that Frank was living in Ottawa under an assumed name?"

"The cousin, maybe? You should talk again with Flora, too."

"Not right away. I want to know more before I do

that." He took a sip of wine.

"She has a little boy, doesn't she?"

"Yes."

They were quiet for a while, each following some track of his own. The lounge was crowded now. It was close to six.

Markarian rose. "I'd better be going."

They walked together through the lobby and into the street.

"If it's all right with you, I'll call Katie in the morning and tell her to meet us here after work," said McCalley. "Five all right?"

Markarian nodded. "Are you sure you want me around? She might feel easier, talking just with you —"

"That's what I'm afraid of —"

Markarian grinned and punched McCalley's arm lightly. "So we're playing that game, are we? Which one am I supposed to be?"

"The bad cop, who else."

As it turned out, it was McCalley who hit hard.

Both men rose as Katie Delancourt strode in purposefully, put her tote on the floor beside her chair, and began talking even before she sat down. The two men had risen.

"I can only spare a few minutes, Inspector," she began, looking up at McCalley and ignoring Markarian. "We have guests for dinner." The two men resumed their seats. McCalley thought: hardly enough time to prepare a meal at this hour, but then again, maybe she had everything ready to heat and serve. . . . He watched her as she settled in her chair, pushed back her long chestnut hair, and waited for McCalley to begin.

Even with the dark shadows under her eyes and the grim set of her mouth, she could turn heads. Her slim, five-foot nine body had an air of elegant simplicity that added to the overall impression of understated, intelligent taste. She wore an ankle-length linen skirt with a brown and beige striped silk knit top; good stuff, expensive, and meant to last. She held her head high, a striking presence in spite of the tension she betrayed in the nervous movement of her hands.

"Detective Markarian is working with me and is here at my request," McCalley began, pointedly, making sure she understood Markarian's presence was official and would not be ignored. He turned briefly to acknowledge his colleague. "Two heads are better than one, especially in tracing Frank's movements in New York." Katie Delancourt made no comment. Her eyes remained fixed on the Inspector, her expression both hostile and anxious. McCalley waited out a small silence, then said, his own gaze unflinching:

"Why didn't you tell us you had a celebrity in the family?" It was clearly not the kind of opening she expected. Caught unawares, she allowed her eyes to grow wide with surprise. "Charles Benson *is* your cousin, is he not?" McCalley persisted, not taking his eyes from her.

After a few seconds, she blinked and dropped her gaze. "Our mothers were cousins," she replied. A certain wariness had set in; she was clearly uneasy.

"Tell me about him."

"I just did." Then, with a show of bravado: "Is that why you brought me here, Inspector? To talk about my rich cousin?"

"As a matter of fact, yes."

For a moment, she was at a loss for words. Then, settling back in her chair, she crossed her legs and smoothed down her skirt, averting her eyes from the Inspector's.

It was Markarian who breached the gap. "You see, Mrs. Delancourt, we have to pick up any thread at all, since we're not really sure of anything right now. It's a strange case and we'd like to get it settled as soon as possible. I'm sure you would, too."

She laughed harshly. "All this because Flora Chadwick comes to you with her wild allegations!" She addressed McCalley, still ignoring Markarian. "Don't you have better things to do with your time?" It was Markarian who answered.

"Well, given Frank's habits, his gambling and all, her allegations are not so wild. The battle against organized crime is an ongoing one for us. It never ends. Frank obviously had some connections there. We know he incurred huge debts in order to keep up the habit, the kind of loans that he couldn't possibly have gotten through ordinary channels. You really had no idea that he gambled?"

"That's what *she* told you. And you believed her."

"Oh, we checked it out. He gambled, all right. He just didn't tell you about it."

"Ah, but he told *her*!" The bitterness in her voice was all too obvious.

Markarian waved the words aside. "Does it really matter, now, what he told you or didn't tell you —"

Before she had time to answer, McCalley broke in: "When did you last see your cousin?"

She seemed to be struggling for the right answer. "Last summer. I ran into him while I was on vacation."

"I understand he had a chalet in St. Tropez. Is that where you went?"

"Did I say I went anywhere?" she challenged. Then, more cautiously, "I told you, I ran into him. He invited me to the chalet. I spent three days there.

"Have you seen him since then?"

She shook her head impatiently, trying to divert this line of questioning. "What has all this got to do with Frank's death? Are you so desperate you have to track down what I did last summer?"

"I'm trying to find out what you're keeping from us." He watched as her expression wavered, took in the full implications of his words. Her eyes moved restlessly coming to rest, finally, at a point at the far end of the room.

"I've told you everything I know."

"Not everything. You didn't tell us that you saw your cousin again, recently, here in New York. You had lunch with him."

"What if I did?"

"What did you quarrel about?" He watched her expression change, heard her deep breath for air. "We know all about it. Your secretary, Lucille, told us you didn't want to see him. You were angry, she said. And the doorman at the restaurant heard what you said to him before you drove off in a cab and left him standing there. . . . Oh, don't blame Lucille," he went on quickly. "She was just as unwilling to give us information as you are. We had to pry it from her. He came to New York to see you. What was that about?"

She reached down and took out a tissue to blow her nose. She answered, without looking at him: "It was personal."

McCalley leaned forward and crossed his hands. "When Flora came to see you, told you that Frank had escaped nine-eleven and had been living in Canada since his disappearance, she said you didn't seem surprised. Did you know that Frank was alive? How long had you known?"

She pushed back her long thick hair in an impatient gesture. Her eyes had turned bright with some emotion not altogether clear. A bitter smile played on her lips.

"Suppose I did know, what then? Run to the police? Tell them my husband had deserted me, gone to Canada, married without divorcing me, started a new career, a new family?" She looked up at the ceiling and laughed. "New everything!" When she turned back to McCalley, her eyes glittered with suppressed anger. "Should I have taken him to court?"

"Who told you?" McCalley asked quietly, in the brief pause that followed. When she didn't answer, Markarian offered:

"Was it your cousin?"

"Can you imagine how I felt?" she resumed, as though there had been no interruption. "What was I supposed to do? I felt battered. How could I share that with anyone! It was too raw, too dreadful. It was frightening too. My life was shattered. My trust destroyed. How could I face anyone?" She seemed deflated suddenly. Her body sagged where she sat, her arms hung limply over the edge of the chair, on either side. It was as though the flow of words had released the anxieties that had built up inside her, as though she was desperate to transfer the unbearable burden to the two men who were questioning her.

McCalley was stunned by the sudden change in her, the release of a deep pain fed by an even deeper anger. He himself felt frustration, uncertainty.

"Your cousin knew Frank, then?"

She shook her head. "No, he never met him."

"But he knew him?"

She waved off the words in a tired gesture. "Somehow, Frank got on one of the Boards, one of the companies my cousin owns. My cousin recognized him as the man in the photo we took, the day we were married, on the steps of City Hall."

"And he told you all about Frank when you visited him in St. Tropez?"

She nodded weakly, her hand shading her eyes. When she looked up again she said, as though she had been struggling all the while with a dilemma: "He's not really my cousin. Our mothers were cousins," she said a second time as though bent on distancing herself from Charles Benson.

McCalley nodded, aware of the fragile moment. To gain time — the breakthrough was what he had hoped for but had not really expected — he made some notes in his little book. He decided to ease up a bit.

Katie had been watching him. When he looked up, she turned away and laughed mirthlessly. "It'll check out, Inspector, rest assured. . . . You're going to Paris, I take it. . . . Watch out. He's a charmer. You might even like him." She laughed again, more weakly this time. "He's infallible! Like the Pope. Except, I don't think he has faith in anyone other than himself." There was resignation in her voice.

McCalley asked: "When had you last seen your cousin, before running into him in France?"

"Some other life ago!" she answered with bravado, throwing back her head." McCalley waited out the pause. "At my sweet-sixteen birthday party. In Larchmont. He and Aunt Millie came late. Mom scolded them."

"You don't care for him much, do you?"

"Oh, he was lots of fun when I was growing up. I think I even had a crush on him. . . . No. I don't care for him at all."

"You did enjoy your three days in St. Tropez. . . ." He waited for some kind of response. When none came, he went on. "But back in New York, you were very reluctant to see him. Why is that?"

"Do I have to have a reason?" McCalley said nothing. Katie shrugged and went on. "We don't think the same. He's all bound up in his money. Money, money, money! He thinks he can buy the devil himself if the price is right!" She looked away suddenly, as though embarrassed by her own words. McCalley felt a prickling in the back of his neck.

175

"Was that what you quarrelled about, when you had lunch with him in New York? About money?"

"I wouldn't touch his money!" She hissed the words. For a moment the tumult inside her surfaced. It swept McCalley into unexpected confusion.

"Did he offer you money for some favor?"

She flinched, as though he had struck her. McCalley wondered what raw wound he'd inadvertently touched. She had not answered his question but raised a new one instead. He waited, After a while, she let out a long sigh and went on:

"What would I want with his money, Inspector? Besides, what does it matter? That's not what you're here about, is it?"

He went on doggedly, painfully conscious of her effort to avoid answering the question. "I don't know what all this means, not yet; but, yes, it matters. Every bit of information matters. We need to know as much as possible about anyone who knew Frank Hastings, especially anyone who knew he had resettled in Ottawa."

To his surprise, she burst out laughing. It went on for several seconds, spilling from her like a flood from an open dam. He wondered if she was finally giving in to hysteria, when, out of breath, in a hoarse broken voice, she cried out:

"Resettled! That's good!" The laughter threatened to drown her words again. "Is that what you call it?"

McCalley was taken aback but gave no sign. When he spoke, his voice was authoritative but not hard. "What did your cousin ask you to do?"

She had caught the shift in his manner but knew just as clearly that he did not intend to drop the subject.

"How do you come by that, Inspector?" she tossed off, with a smirk.

"It all adds up, Katie. You wouldn't touch his money, you said. What did he offer you?"

She looked away, drumming her fingers on the arm of the chair. When she turned back, she was all seriousness again. "He wanted me to quit my job and work for him."

"Is that so terrible?"

Her eyes closed against some unpleasant vision. "No. The pressure was." She opened her eyes and stared at him.

"That bad?"

"Look, Inspector, he knows how charming, how persuasive he is. I guess you develop a flair, whatever you want to call it, especially when you have to deal with as many people as he does . . . in business . . . entertaining. . . . You learn to listen while your eyes take in everything else. You know how to be witty and how to use that as an excuse for not committing yourself. You learn how to maneuver around unpleasant suggestions, how to threaten subtly, if necessary. Always on his best behavior. Very polished. Almost bored by his ability to read another person's mind, his talent for predicting what someone is about to say. He has all the answers before you even suspect what is going on. And he likes to see people squirm. Like Shakespeare's Iago. . . ."

McCalley was getting a picture that he wasn't sure he was going to like. "What was the job?"

She arched her arm in a grand all-encompassing gesture. "Running his American public relations department. Just like that! According to him, I was crazy to refuse!"

"But you did. . . ."

"That's right. I refused," she repeated with a grimace that suggested not distaste but loathing at the very idea.

"But why the quarrel, if money was not the issue?"

"He's a cruel man. I could never work for him."

"Even though charming? Persuasive?"

She blushed, pursed her lips. For McCalley, something wasn't quite right about the picture she had drawn. It was full of emotions much too strong to be accounted for by what she had told him.

"Let me put it this way, Inspector. I don't like the man, for whatever reason. I never will." She met his gaze, unflinching. "I would never put my life into the hands of a man like that." She looked away even before she had uttered the words, as though she would have liked to take them back.

"You turned down his offer, but that doesn't explain why you were so angry when you saw him in New York."

"He kept pestering me!"

It was all very puzzling, McCalley concluded. He decided not to pursue the subject, not until he met and talked with the man himself. He moved on.

"Your secretary showed me your itinerary. You went on to Paris, when you left St. Tropez?"

"Yes."

"And flew back here from Paris about ten days later," he went on, checking his notes as he spoke. When she didn't answer, he looked up. "Or did you stop somewhere else before flying home?"

"I spent a day in Geneva."

"Did you like it?"

"It was all right. I bought myself a new watch."

McCalley put down his notebook and leaned back in his chair.

"You went to Geneva to buy a watch?"

"That's what I just said!" In spite of the harsh tone, her mouth twitched as though she was about to weep. Her body slumped in her seat. McCalley was startled by the intensity of the reaction. "Why don't you leave me alone!" she cried helplessly. Some people sitting nearby turned their way but just as quickly lost interest.

Markarian leaned toward her and said gently: "Whatever it is you've experienced is none of our business, well, it wouldn't be, ordinarily; but if Frank Hastings was murdered, we've got to get to the bottom of it, find out who did it and why. We have no choice. Obviously you're not a murderer —" McCalley wondered how far they could go with this but said nothing — "so why don't you tell us what happened before you left St. Tropez? You were pleased to remain with your cousin for three days but in New York you were very unhappy about seeing him. Why?" When Katie said nothing, Markarian turned to McCalley: "She's right, you know. It's none of our business."

"Sorry, but it *is* our business. She's holding back information, We call that obstruction of justice." He went on, turning back to Katie and counting off each phrase on his fingers, as he spoke. "One: you knew about Frank's double life before Flora came to see you a few days ago. And before I told you. Two: you decided to keep that information to yourself, even after we first spoke, knowing we were investigating allegations about his having been murdered. Three: you never mentioned your cousin in all this, what he might have told you, why you were so angry with him after you left St. Tropez —"

"Stop it!" She turned to one side, averting her face.

"You realize what it means to mislead the police deliberately in a criminal investigation?"

She turned back to him, her misery etched on every feature. "You asked me why I went to Geneva, and I told you. Is there anything else?" She glanced down at her belongings, as though getting ready to leave.

"A great deal more," said McCalley, "and the sooner you provide answers for us, the sooner you can leave."

"I told you I have guests coming."

"Well then, you'd better call and tell them you'll be late."

She rolled her eyes in mock exasperation, then looked to Markarian for help. He gave her a small smile and held out his hands in a helpless gesture. "Just tell him what he wants to know." She stared at him by way of response. Markarian leaned forward and said: "Flora told the Inspector that after Frank was killed in Ottawa, she received quite a number of calls from New York. We're looking into them, but can you help us with that? Who would Frank be in touch with, here in New York, under his assumed name? He'd been so careful to destroy all traces of his old life before settling in Ottawa —"

Katie Delancourt threw up her hands. "How should I know, for God's sake!"

McCalley's next question brought the woman's brief show of confidence to an abrupt end.

"Katie, at some point your cousin found out that Frank was not dead. He shared that information with you when you were in St. Tropez. But there something else he said to you that prompted your trip to Geneva, wasn't there? It wasn't to do a favor for a friend back home or to buy a watch. . . ."

This time she rose abruptly from her seat and leaned down to pick up her tote. McCalley rose also and laid a hand on her arm.

"Please sit down again. We haven't finished. I know you don't want me to visit you at home, but I will have to, if you don't co-operate with us now."

Her look was a mixture of anger and hopelessness as she resumed her seat, clutching her tote. McCalley too sat down again.

"So, I took an extra day to be on my own! Is that a crime?"

"You had to change your flight, no doubt pay a penalty for doing that. . . ."

"Good Lord, Inspector! Haven't you ever done something on the spur of the moment?"

McCalley decided on a new tack. "Flora told me you didn't seemed surprised when she told you that Frank had not died in nine-eleven. You seemed surprised, though, when she told you he'd been a compulsive gambler."

Katie laughed mirthlessly. "She thought she had reformed him."

"In a way, she had. He didn't resume gambling up in Ottawa. We know that."

"So, I was his nemesis, is that it?"

"You were a victim," Markarian interjected. "Just like everyone else he encountered. He used everyone to serve his purpose, whatever that happened to be at any one moment.

"Except for Flora."

"Flora was just as much a victim in the end," Markarian went on, showing genuine concern. "You'll grant that much, I think. She's left stranded, with a baby; much worse off than you. Your life has taken a new turn. You seem happy in your new marriage. You have a pleasant life now, you're confident in your job and your husband. She has none of that."

"Whatever happened, she was in on it. That's not exactly the role of an innocent observer."

Markarian turned to McCalley, trying to assess his colleague's reaction and wondering if they should continue with this line of questioning, To his dismay he saw that McCalley was drawing in his notepad — doodling, to be precise. He was about to speak, when McCalley looked up and asked Katie:

"How did you find out Frank was dead? That too you knew before Flora or I told you, isn't that so?" She lowered her head, her hands clutched in her lap. Markarian looked from one to the other but said nothing.

"It was your cousin, wasn't it? He told you."

Finally she looked up, her expression a mixture of fear and confusion. "I don't know" she said, her voice hoarse, as though she had been shouting or sobbing. "Last June I received a clipping from a Canadian paper."

"Who did you think sent it?"

She shook her head, looked away. "I don't know."

"There was no note?"

"No. Just the clipping."

"Doesn't it seem likely your cousin sent it?"

"To finish what he started?" The laugh she attempted caught in her throat. She coughed instead.

"What had he started, Katie?"

For a moment, she seemed dazed. "A figure of speech, Inspector. . . . Maybe he felt he was sending me tidings of great joy, letting me know the bastard was really dead this time!"

"When did you marry again?"

"In August. . . . But I could have married any time!" she replied angrily. "I had a perfectly legal death certificate that said Frank Hastings had died in nine-eleven. I married when I did because I was ready to do so. Frank had been out of my life for two years." There was bitterness in her voice.

"But you knew, from the time you saw your cousin in St. Tropez, that Frank had not really died in nine-eleven. And you learned, just before you married again, that he'd been killed in Ottawa. Surely that made things easier for you?"

"He was dead to me long before the clipping came, Inspector.'"

"You would have remarried, anyway?"

She stared at him defiantly. "When I was ready, yes! When I was ready, I did! Is that punishable, under the circumstances?" McCalley said nothing. "Or maybe I should have asked Flora Chadwick for a copy of her husband's death certificate?"

Her smile was more of a sneer. Watching her struggle for solid ground, Markarian felt a profound sadness. McCalley, in turn, wondered why she insisted on keeping all that had happened from her new husband, the one person who could offer her some comfort.

Katie was speaking rapidly, now, not only to escape the probing eyes of the Inspector but obviously anxious about getting home on time. She looked at her wristwatch as she spoke. Her composure was back and, with it, a certain insolence.

"No, Inspector. I didn't lie awake, wondering if I could marry again."

"Still, the fact remains you married only after you learned Frank had been killed in Ottawa."

"What are you suggesting, Inspector?"

"Just trying to fit the pieces together."

"You keep hounding me, even though you haven't a stitch of proof that Frank was murdered."

"If I had proof, I wouldn't be here. And I don't mean to hound you, but you *are* one of the key players."

"Key victim, you mean."

McCalley shrugged. "Have you heard from your cousin, recently?"

"No."

She rose again and gathered her things. The two men remained seated. As she looked about her to make sure she had everything with which she had come — her tote, a light jacket that matched the linen skirt, her pocketbook — McCalley looked up at her and said, in his calm even voice:

"I should tell you, Katie, that we have reason to believe that Frank, your ex-husband, murdered a man before he left New York." The words shot through her like a bolt of lightning. She dropped down into the chair, her belongings tumbling to the floor. Her arms gripped the wooden rests. McCalley went on, without a pause. "We believe it was as payment for his gambling debts. He owed well over seventy-five thousand dollars when he disappeared."

The two men watched as Katie Delancourt brought her hand to her mouth in an effort to stifle the sob that threatened to escape.

McCalley rose, a signal that the interview was indeed over. "Murder is never an easy thing, for those left to clean up the mess. . . . I will be seeing your cousin and your two friends in Paris, in a day or two. When I get back, Lieutenant Markarian and I will need to talk to you again. Is there anything else you want to tell me?" Katie shook her head violently, her eyes averted. "Good night, then." Markarian too stood up.

They waited as she picked up her belongings again and hurried away, her step uneven, her head lowered, Markarian said: "That was a rough one."

Watching her leave, McCalley said: "Whatever it is she's not telling us, Ed, is frightening her."

"She's frightened, all right," said Markarian. "But I don't think she's involved in any way." The two men sat down again.

"Whatever she's afraid of sharing with us will out, sooner or later," said McCalley. "I don't want her to get into trouble for withholding information." Stretching his back, he remembered, with a twinge of guilt, that since arriving in New York, he had done no exercise, as he had promised his wife he would. "It's the cousin that interests me," he went on, thoughtfully. "We're missing something, right?"

Markarian shrugged. "Yes. But what?"

McCalley frowned. "My feeling is, she'd like to tell us but can't —"

"When are you going to Paris?"

"Tomorrow, if possible."

"Is there anything in particular you want me to do, while you're gone?"

"Find out more about the people who lent Frank money."

"I'm working on it."

"Who was the man Frank killed?"

"Angel Estivo was his name. A drug dealer. We're trying to find who gave the order for the hit."

"You're sure it was Hastings who killed him?"

"At first, it was hard to get anyone to talk, but, yes, I'm sure. We finally found witnesses who identified him from photos we showed them. It was Frank, all right. He was driven to the spot and, when the job was done, got back in the car and was driven off. Couldn't get a lead on the plates or the driver, except that the driver was a big guy, maybe a boxer or a wrestler. Drove carefully. Was in no hurry, as though he knew no one would get in his way."

"Why do you suppose she hates him so much?"

"Her cousin?" McCalley nodded. "Maybe he made a play for her and she resented it."

McCalley considered the possibility, then shook his head. "No, there's deep anger there. That wouldn't explain it.... And what about Geneva? Why Geneva?"

"Why not Geneva?"

"Geneva is conferences, summits, banking."

Markarian laughed. "C'mon, Luke, They sell great watches too, in Geneva!"

McCalley smiled. "They sell great watches in Paris, as well, in New York too, for that matter," countered the other.

"I've never had a case like this!!" said Markarian after a pause. "It's like hunting shadows."

"We have to find solid points of reference,"" offered McCalley, "We seem to be floating, not knowing where the current is taking us."

"I know we've both considered this, but it *is* possible that Flora is way off —"

McCalley studied his friend's face. "Do you seriously believe that?"

"No."

"Neither do I. . . . Interpol may come into it, if we have to follow leads in Paris."

"So we carry on. . . . The good news is that as of this afternoon I'm officially free to give the case my undivided attention. Not like last time!"

"Good." McCalley had been painfully aware of the difficulties Markarian had to face during the Bantry case: what appeared at first to be a murder in Ottawa and two seemingly accidental deaths, one in Ottawa and one in New York. It had been an awkward time for both of them. McCalley's respect for the man grew as he watched Markarian take tremendous risks in order to help him solve the difficult case. Happily, in the end, the NYPD detective got the credit he deserved. This time was different, McCalley admitted. He was relieved that his friend could work with him on this case without resorting to subterfuge. Besides, Frank Hastings had left a wide trail of unanswered questions and possible criminal action in New York. NYPD had a real interest in him, alive and dead.

Markarian rose to leave. McCalley walked with him to the lobby, where they parted.

Alone, he briefly considered going to his room to make one or two calls before eating, decided against it, and headed for the dining room instead.

He ate slowly, taking in the activity around him, listening to snatches of conversation at near-by tables, sipping his wine and trying to blank out the distress he had caused Katie Delancourt. He wondered, with a pang of conscience, what she would tell her husband when she arrived home, to account for being late. He was suddenly aware of how much he wanted to spare her, how much she was hurting, how alone she was in dealing with that hurt. He had not made things any easier for her; but then again — as he kept reminding himself — he had to do what was necessary. Still, he wanted to protect her from the eventual fallout the investigation was sure to cause. Most of all, he felt a keen concern for how her new husband would respond when he learned all that had happened, when he realized that Katie had chosen not to confide in him. . . .

It was going to be hard on her, much harder than anything she'd had to take from the "bad cop"!

CHAPTER TWELVE

By the time McCalley cleared customs at Orly and found a cab to take him to his hotel, the morning was well advanced. In his room, he put away the few items he had taken for what he hoped would be a brief stay, ordered a late breakfast, and took a quick shower. Once dressed, he went to the window and opened it, in spite of the heat. The sounds of Paris filled the room; he took them in with pleasure. His last visit had been much too long ago.

After a while, he shut the window and pulled up the desk chair next to it, sat down and took the case folder from his briefcase. Waiting for breakfast, he started to scan the file; but he'd barely opened it, when room service arrived with his order of eggs and ham, coffee and toast. He'd had some difficulty getting the food, not because his French was poor (he had plenty of occasion to use it in Canada) but because it was too late for breakfast; the chef was getting things ready for lunch. Perhaps Monsieur could wait another forty-five minutes or so? He explained that he'd had only an apple and a piece of cheese since leaving New York late last night. The kitchen obliged.

The food was delicately prepared. He ate slowly, savoring every bite. When he had finished, he made his calls. Luck was with him. The great financier could see him at one-thirty. At the American Embassy, he had no trouble tracking down Katie's friend Josie. Of course, she would help in whatever way she could. Katie was a close friend, like a sister to her. Yes, she'd make sure Marge was there too when he came around that evening. There shouldn't be any problem, she assured him.

In both cases, he had explained that he was there to confirm certain information that had come to him about an ongoing investigation involving claims by Frank Hasting's relatives. There was enough truth in what he told her for him not to feel guilty about withholding more vital information. Later, he would decide how much else to add. Experience had taught him that the best way to gain entry for an interview was to minimize the situation that called for such a meeting. People did not want to get involved, especially if it was a murder investigation. He had given his name but had not identified himself as a police Inspector from Ottawa. That too would come later.

Pleased at having been able to get through easily to the people he had come to see and having succeeded in setting up appointments with them for that very day, he relaxed for a while, sipping his second cup of coffee as he stood watching the traffic and the pedestrians below. The hotel was in an attractive little square. In the distance he could see the top of the Eiffel Tower. The sounds of Paris drifted into the room, bringing back memories of an earlier visit, when he had spent a year there, taking courses at the Sorbonne. How long ago it seemed! And yet, certain faces were still as vivid in his memory as they had been when he lived with them, friends from another life, another age! He recalled the girl he was in love with, or thought he loved, at the time. He'd been ready to do almost anything to get her to marry him. When she went off with someone else, he thought he would never recover. He smiled at the memory.

Almost unwillingly, he turned from the window and settled in the large chair to review his notes.

Since Flora Chadwick had approached him in August — was it only three weeks ago? — he had grown increasingly certain that Frank Hastings, alias James Chadwick, had been murdered. The difficulty was proving it. Officially, there was no case; the inquest had returned a decision of "accidental death." The car and driver that had killed Hastings had not been found. Witnesses were hazy about what they had seen and neither car nor driver could be properly described. He had started looking into all that, before leaving for New York; his aide, Sergeant Bill Kenney had been left to continue inquiries at that end. McCalley was sure much more information would surface.

The accident had occurred near the Elgin Hotel at ten-thirty, on a busy Friday morning. Hastings had parked his car in a nearby garage and was crossing the street on his way to a meeting in the hotel. He never made it. A dark sedan, picking up speed, had plowed into him and continued on its way, as though unaware of what had happened. Efforts were made to track down the car and driver, but no one came forward with information. Those who saw it happen could furnish only sketchy details.

The accident occurred in June. Flora Chadwick had come to him in August, after the inquest and many unanswered questions. She told the Inspector everything she had learned from her husband, especially his fears during the last few weeks prior to his death. He was sure he was being followed, he told his wife, that perhaps the people to whom he owed money had tracked him down. He was worried sick, Flora had told him, anxious for her and the boy. He had even toyed with the idea of disappearing for a while, but dismissed the notion almost immediately. Leaving Flora and the child alone was out of the question.

Soon after that, McCalley had flown to New York to learn more about Hastings, especially his activities before his disappearance. Flora Chadwick had flown down around the same time, to meet with Katie.

Now, here he was in Paris, days later, searching out possible leads in a murder that was a certainty — the

Inspector had to admit — only in Flora Chadwick's mind. Did he really expect to find anything of consequence, something that proved her right? Had Frank Hastings really been murdered?

As he continued to scan his notes, McCalley realized that he had become obsessed with the case. Common sense told him that Flora Chadwick's story was probably the result of grief at her husband's untimely death. His instincts urged him in another direction. Even his better judgment, on which he had learned to rely on most occasions, did not succeed in dissuading him from following the flimsy leads Flora had provided.

It had become all too clear that Frank Hastings was a scoundrel, not to be trusted; that he was a bigamist, a heavy gambler, a murderer. Had the other solution not presented itself when it did, he would certainly have carried out his plan to crash someone else's Cessna with Kevin Masters in it, in order to stage his own death and rid himself of a wife he no longer loved and debts he could never hope to clear. He may have deserved to die; but if he was indeed murdered, it was McCalley's job to see that justice was done. It was a frustrating situation, yet compelling.

From the outset, McCalley tried to maintain his rigorous hold on reality, on the need to collect information and not indulge in speculation; but more and more he found himself wondering what secrets were weighing on Katie Delancourt. For secrets there were, his instincts told him.

A small groan escaped him. How could he have wandered into this surreal situation? How could he explain his conviction that there had indeed been a murder when there was no hard evidence to sustain that assumption? Could he ever explain it to Kenney, to all the others who had worked with him over the years, who knew him as the rigorous investigator, for whom only hard facts mattered? He could not explain it to himself, much less to others!

He was somewhat reassured remembering that it wasn't simply a matter of instincts; allegations had been made and it was up to him, and NYPD (thank God for Ed Markarian!) to follow through on them. He convinced himself that the usual procedures of gathering data and facts, building up to conclusions from incontrovertible evidence, simply would not work well in this case. Everything seemed to point to foul play, but certainty of it seemed to be beyond his reach.

There was so little to go on! The case threatened to undermine his confidence in the tried and tested methods he relied on and insisted others should follow. He was ready to accept, without a shred of evidence, Flora Chadwick's conviction, that her husband had been murdered under suspicious circumstances. For the hundredth time, he scolded himself for entertaining such a flimsy idea. Yet, here he was, in Paris, looking for leads that would prove Flora Chadwick's instincts right!

He pulled out the inquest proceedings and found the names of those who had witnessed the accident. He made a note to ask Kenney to round them up and question them again, more rigorously this time. The inquest had proved to be a mere formality, no suspicions were raised. The ruling was: accidental hit-and-run.

As though on cue, the phone rang. It was Kenney.

"Find out anything?" McCalley asked.

"For the record — I wanted to be sure so I double-checked: Hastings had not gambled at all since arriving in Ottawa."

"Ah."

"He was taking chances though —"

"How do you mean?"

"Six months ago, he started investing heavily —"

"Let me guess. Pharmaceuticals?"

"Right." He gave McCalley the names and waited a few seconds for the Inspector to take them down.

"Inside tips on new products not yet on the market?"

"Can't be sure," Kenney said carefully, "but it looks that way."

"Who was feeding him information?"

"I have no idea. But Flora thinks it might have been someone in the company he was connected with."

"Mmm. . . . How much did he invest?"

"Flora thinks as much as a hundred thousand."

"Where did he get it?"

"Boards pay hefty honorariums, plus expenses, I understand. He'd already been to several meetings."

"Mmmmmm."

"Flora said he'd saved some money in a secret account he'd closed in August 2001. He'd stopped gambling, she said, even before leaving New York. He also had some money left from a loan he'd taken out earlier. He carried the bills in a brown kraft envelope, tucked inside one of his business folders. Who would think of looking there? Simple, but ingenious, when you think about it. That's how he got the cash into Ottawa."

"So he had money to invest: eight thousand, roughly, plus another hundred thousand he'd earned, once he settled in. . . ."

". . . and close to half a million when he died. Flora said he was very excited about future prospects."

"Did she know that he might have been doing something illegal?"

"Can't be sure. It wasn't my job to tell her that, but I'm sure she knew. They shared everything, as far as I can tell. She knew all about his gambling, his loans, everything about his former life. I doubt he would start holding back anything from her at this late date."

"Had to be an insider, giving him information,

someone up high, who knows what's going on before it happens.... Find out all you can."

"I'm on it."

"What was the name of the company, the one he invested in?"

McCalley took it down, with a jolt of excitement. It was a company that was part of the conglomerate owned by Katie's cousin. Coincidence?....

"Oh, one more thing, Bill. Get to those witnesses again, lean on them. Find out everything you can about the car and driver. Show them the photos. Take down anything they can remember. Prod them. Ask lots of questions."

"Will do."

When he had replaced the receiver, he looked over the notes he had just made. For a while he sat very still, holding the paper in his hand and gazing thoughtfully at the blue sky outside the window. Finally, he placed the sheet of paper carefully at the back of the folder and resumed reading where he had left off.

The appointment with Monsieur Benson was for one-thirty. At one-twenty, McCalley announced himself to the receptionist seated inside the glass doors separating the bank of elevators from the executive suite. The woman was in her thirties, attractively dressed in a short-sleeved two-piece silk suit in a soft shade of coral. On her left was a Murano vase with fresh cut flowers. On her right were two phones.

With Benson, McCalley had decided it would be best to identify himself quickly as a police officer. The man was efficient; he'd probably had made inquiries of his own, already.... He handed the receptionist his card.

The woman picked up one of the phones and said a few words. She replaced the receiver with a smile and gestured toward a sitting area next to a floor to ceiling glass wall behind her, which looked out over the city. It was a magnificent view.

"Please. Monsieur will see you in a few minutes."

The tall, lanky young man who came forward to greet him and lead the way back to his office was a far cry from what McCalley had expected. The pictures he had glanced at did not do him justice. He knew from the information on hand that Charles Benson was indeed still a very young man and that he had managed to accumulate an incredible fortune in just a few years; but the man who now sat opposite him in the elegant, beautifully furnished room wore none of the trappings of what a colleague of McCalley's once referred to as "indecently huge success."

In his loose-fitting khaki slacks and blue and white striped shirt, unbuttoned at the neck, his blond hair an unruly mop, eyes focused, wide with undisguised curiosity, Benson looked more like a college senior than the head of an international conglomerate. His manner, easy and friendly, belied anything that resembled sophistication, although McCalley knew that the man dealt on a regular basis, not only with high-level executives but also cabinet members and heads of state.

Only a closer look — his eyes especially: a transparent blue that reminded McCalley of icy seas — forced one to reconsider the immediate first impression. Those eyes now bored into his visitor, assessing him openly, without the least effort to conceal his curiosity. His steady gaze studied McCalley's face as though deciding what role to take on, what voice to assume. He had the easy grace of someone who knows himself thoroughly, who has mastered the skills of life without the least difficulty, and who knows instinctively what will serve him best in any situation. There was nothing naïve about Monsieur Benson. He knew what he wanted and how to get it.

The general impression, McCalley had to admit, elicited genuine admiration: a man not easily ruffled by the vagaries of fate, someone who did not betray or act on his emotions and who was always in full command of things. At the same time, he recognized in all that a ruthless indifference, a latent danger.

They sat facing one another on soft Italian leather chairs, an unusual delicate shade of apricot. The color complemented the rich mahogany of the display cases, book shelves, and tables and blended softly into the oriental rug of soft pastels against a vivid cobalt blue background. The same colors were repeated in the striped pattern of the tie-back drapes at the tall windows. The effect exuded warmth, wealth, and comfort, without any hint of ostentation. The room could easily have served as a gracious living space in an expensive home, where the aim was to create and insure tasteful comfort.

In one slow movement, Monsieur crossed his long legs, steepled his hands under his chin, and gave McCalley a wide smile which lit up his face with an unexpected air of startled innocence.

"What can I do for you, Inspector? You said you were investigating something that concerns my cousin Katie — a claim of some sort?" His English was perfect, as McCalley had expected it to be. The dossier they had compiled told him that Monsieur spoke several languages fluently, in addition to French and his native tongue.

McCalley had meant to be direct and quick but on impulse decided to take a short detour.

"Yes. Some relatives have come forward with unexpected claims."

"Relatives? Besides her brother Matt, Katie has no relatives left, except for me."

"But she *was* married, has married again, in fact, as I believe you have? Wives and husbands are relatives, too, are they not?" McCalley smiled and went right on. "I didn't mean blood relatives. Claims have been put forward by people related to Frank Hastings, Katie's first husband. You know, of course, that he was killed?"

Monsieur was all attention, a small smile playing on his lips. "Inspector? Am I correct? With the Ottawa Police?" McCalley nodded. "Forgive my presumption, Inspector, but why have the Ottawa police been asked to investigate claims to Frank's estate? They are legal matters, are they not?"

McCalley recognized the skillful maneuvering which gave nothing away and evaded questions with other questions.

"Ordinarily they would be, but the circumstances of Frank Hastings' death are not altogether clear."

Monsieur leaned forward and clasped his hands between his knees. A small frown dramatized his effort at concentration. He waited for McCalley to continue.

"Did you know Frank Hastings?"

Monsieur did not answer at once. He straightened up slowly and leaned back in his chair, taking time to reply.

"I never met him. They were married just after Katie graduated from NYU. Her parents had been killed in a car crash some weeks earlier, I believe, and her brother had rushed off to a job in California. There was no one, no family there for her. Maybe that's why she sent us — my mother was still alive then— a snapshot taken outside of City Hall, right after the ceremony, just the two of them. We were her only relatives besides her brother. . . ."

McCalley noted the careful evasive wording. He shifted abruptly to other matters.

"I understand Katie ran into you while she was vacationing in France last summer. . . ."

The wide gaze did not flicker. "Quite a surprise, yes! She cancelled her three days in Nice and came to stay with us instead, before going on to Paris. We were delighted to have her."

"Did you talk about Frank any time during her visit?"

"Inevitable, wouldn't you say?"

"What did you talk about? What did she tell you about him? About his relatives? About his work?"

*His father died a while back. His mother is living in Florida. As far as other relatives, I didn't know he had any. But you say some have turned up?"

"Yes. Did Katie enjoy her stay in St. Tropez?"

"She seemed to. My wife and I — Emma, that is, my first wife, she died in a car accident, just after New Year's — gave a party for her the night before she left. Katie had a great time."

If the sharp turns in the exchange annoyed or bothered him, Monsieur gave no visible sign, but McCalley knew the man was fully aware of the fencing match they had taken on. There was no visible change in his face or manner, no hint of any worry. He seemed to enjoy the challenge: his easy smile reflected confidence; his steady gaze was alert and ready to parry any thrust.

"Your wife Emma, you said she died in a car crash?"

"Yes, and as you know, Inspector, since you mentioned it earlier, I remarried and now live in Paris."

"What did your wife think of Katie?"

"My wife was always gracious to our guests."

"Emma was alone when she crashed near Naples?"

"Yes. She was driving back from an evening with friends. It's a tricky drive, the Amalfi. Dangerous at any time, but especially when slippery and at night."

"Why didn't she wait until morning?"

"Emma was a charming woman, Inspector, but stubborn and unpredictable, totally independent. And, I am sorry to say, a rather heavy drinker. She had had quite a few that evening, before, during, and after dinner. Her friends could not convince her to wait until the next day to drive back."

He looked down at his hands and went on: "Her car swung too wide when she tried to negotiate one of those terrible curves. They've put up protectors, but cars speeding around a bend all too often ram into them and are flung below. In most places, it's a sheer drop down the cliff to the water."

McCalley was surprised at the details Monsieur offered. Then again, the newspapers, magazines, tabloids throughout Europe, South America, and the Far East, as well as the United States and Canada (Markarian had told him at one point), had carried the story for days, right through the inquest and the funeral. Emma, young and beautiful, married to one of the richest men in the world, had been big news all along. Her death was reported as a major catastrophe in the gossip sheets, a world event in leading newspapers as far removed as Japan and Australia.

There had been no investigation, McCalley recalled. None was called for. The alcohol in the young woman's system precluded anything other than a verdict of accidental death. All of this and much more was reported in the press for weeks following the tragedy.

McCalley said nothing. Monsieur looked up, with a frown. "Excuse me, Inspector, but what does my personal life have to do with your errand?"

Ignoring the condescension in the choice of words, McCalley smiled. "Nothing, it seems. But my questions may dredge up something. One never knows." A curious expression flitted across Monsieur's face, a mixture of annoyance and anticipation.

McCalley decided he'd had enough evasion. "You never met Frank Hastings, but you knew what he looked like from the wedding photo Katie sent you, is that correct?"

"Yes."

"And you had other, more recent photos of him to compare that one with, is that not so?"

Monsieur scratched the back of his hand. "Is this relevant?"

McCalley smiled. He too could be evasive. "I'm here to ask questions."

If Monsieur was disconcerted, he hid it well. His expression remained one of puzzled curiosity. "Forgive me if I sound impertinent, but your questions seem unfocused. . . ."

"It's my way," replied the other, almost carelessly, without any further explanation.

"You said you were looking into claims by relatives of Frank Hastings's who've turned up — ?"

"That's right."

"What sort of claims?"

"Allegations, really."

"Who are these people?"

"His wife, for one."

"Katie?" For a moment he seemed genuinely confused.

"No, Monsieur, not Katie. Katie had been his . . . shall we say, his widow? . . . for almost a year, when she learned he had married a second time, in Canada, soon after nine-eleven."

There was no surprise, no sign of unease, as Monsieur slowly rose from his chair, walked to a bookcase with a built-in mini-bar. He opened a bottle of Perrier and poured himself a glass, adding a piece of ice from the silver bucket that stood ready. After a sip or two, he turned to McCalley and gestured toward the array of bottles behind him. McCalley, shook his head. He watched in silence as Monsieur drank the rest of the water, refilled the glass, and returned to his seat.

"Surely you knew he had remarried, left behind a wife and remarried. You're the one who told Katie. . . . "

"So I did."

"Why?"

"She was mourning. I wanted to help."

"By telling her Frank was a bigamist?"

"It was the truth."

"And the truth would make her free, was that it?"

Monsieur laughed. "I like your style, Inspector. You have a way with words. . . . Yes, I suppose the truth made her free, but it may also have irritated her, after the initial shock wore off."

"What else did you tell her?"

"Let's see. . . ." He crossed his legs again. "I believe I told her I'd come across a picture of Frank and recognized him as the same man as the one in the wedding photo she'd sent us."

"You had a more recent photo of Frank, as well?"

"One of my CEOs invited him to serve on the Board of his company, which I happen to own. I like to find out about new people who join us from time to time. It's become routine with me. Hastings had set himself up in Ottawa as a consultant for medical insurance claims. Many of my companies produce pharmaceuticals. Frank's, or I should say James Chadwick's credentials were excellent. I thought the choice was a good one. The file included a photograph, yes."

"And so you recognized James Chadwick as Frank Hastings. . . . Which of your CEOs recommended him for the Board? I'd like names, if you would."

"Of course. Grace will get the information for you."

He went to a console and pressed a button. A smart-looking mature woman appeared at the door. He told her what he wanted.

McCalley held out a second card, on which he had written the name of his hotel and his phone and room number.

"I'll be in Paris for the next day or so, should you want to get it touch for me."

"What more can I possibly tell you, Inspector," replied the other with a little smile, as he took the proffered card, examined it, and tucked it into his shirt pocket.

Grace came back with a slip of paper. Monsieur glanced at it and gave it to McCalley. "Anything else?"

If the words were meant as a dismissal, McCalley took no notice. He shifted slightly in the comfortable chair and glanced at the paper in his hand before asking:

"Frank's being invited to join one of your Boards, wasn't that unusual?"

"How do you mean, unusual?"

"He'd been in the country only a short time, a recent arrival. Did your CEO know him well enough to recommend him for his Board?"

"Apparently Frank . . . James . . . wasted no time making contacts. A clever man. In the short time before he died, he'd accumulated half a million."

"You know about that?"

"It was in the papers."

"The Paris papers?"

"The Ottawa, papers, Inspector," replied the other, with a little smile.

"You buy the Ottawa papers?"

"No, Inspector; but my staff does. That and hundreds of other major newspapers from all over the world. They scan them daily for items of interest to our companies, or for what might interest me, particularly, and bring it to my attention. Someone in the company came upon the notice of Frank's death, recognized the man in the photograph as one of our new Board members, and sent me the clipping."

McCalley jotted something in his notepad. "Thank you." There was a brief pause while Monsieur finished the water in his glass. "When did you tell Katie that Frank had been killed?"

Monsieur seemed in no way disconcerted. "I didn't."

McCalley went on, as though he had not heard. "Did you know she was planning to remarry? Did you want to reassure her there would be no complications?"

Monsieur laughed. "Why should that concern me?"

"She *is* your cousin —"

"But not her guardian angel —"

"You didn't tell her Frank was killed in Ottawa?"

"She was furious when I gave her the first bit of news. I wasn't going to play that role again."

"She was furious when you told her Frank was alive?'"

"Wouldn't you have been? Or, more precisely, wouldn't any woman who found out her husband had cheated on her in that way? She'd been grieving all that time for a man who had not only abandoned her but had immediately remarried. A scoundrel, a gambler, and a bigamist. Poor girl! What a terrible waste, her grief!" McCalley felt a strange apprehension. Monsieur went on:

"Naturally, she felt she had been abused but, as in most cases of abuse, she felt guilty too, as though something in her had provoked Frank's rejection." McCalley made no comment. "The abused wife is apt to ask: 'What did I do to deserve this beating?' or in Katie's case: 'What did I do or not do to drive him away? How did I fail?' Her rage I'm sure was directed toward herself, at allowing herself to be duped that way. But I suppose I deserved her anger, too. After all, I was the messenger with the bad tidings."

McCalley said: "But she was still furious with you when you took her to lunch in New York, not too long ago. Why was that?"

For the first time, something flickered in the depth of those cold blue eyes, the lips closed over the smile. Monsieur looked away before answering.

"I have no idea."

"Why had you gone to New York?"

"Business, what else?" The smile and the confidence were back.

"She didn't want to meet with you —"

"Did she tell you that?"

"No."

Monsieur paused, as though waiting for an explanation, then said: "I don't know where you might have heard that, Inspector, but it's nonsense. Katie was always a bit high-strung. Sometimes my teasing was too much for her."

"What did you talk about at lunch?"

He gave it a moment or two before replying. "Nothing much. Her work. The new man in her life. . . ."

Unflappable, thought McCalley. Nothing seemed to pierce Benson's self-control. He was ready with answers that gave away nothing. And, as though adding insult to injury, he was enjoying the side-stepping, his clever maneuvering around McCalley's questions. His eyes were bright with contained excitement.

McCalley decided the time had come to show his hand, give away what he knew, in order to get a reaction.

"Didn't you offer her a job?" McCalley asked bluntly.

Monsieur knitted his brows, trying to remember, but not before McCalley caught the twitch of surprise around the mouth, the slight narrowing of the eyes. It was only a moment, then Monsieur burst out laughing. "Katie told you that?"

"You didn't offer her a job?"

"Yes, yes, I did," he went on, as though relishing a good joke. "Good Lord, it *was* funny! I offered her a huge sum of money to come work for me. She turned me down! Wouldn't budge. As though her job back there is all that exciting!"

"Yours would have been?"

"Well, certainly more interesting. One meets all kinds of people. She would have had a busy social life as well. And lots of money. Ease. Comfort. All the things she admired while she was with us in St. Tropez. All the good things most people have to fight so hard to get."

"Very generous of you."

"She's the closest blood relative I have any dealings with, Inspector. Why shouldn't I share some of my success with her? I was happy to be able to reach out that way. I thought she'd be pleased. Anyone else would have jumped at the chance!"

"But she didn't —"

"No."

"The money didn't interest her?"

"Not in the least."

On impulse, McCalley asked:

"Do you know why Katie went to Geneva before returning to the States from her vacation?"

Just a slight hesitation. "Haven't a clue."

McCalley rose abruptly. "Thank you for your time, Monsieur. I may have to call on you again. I hope you won't mind — ?"

"Not at all."

They retraced their steps to the reception area and the elevators. "Did you say you'd be in Paris for a day or two?"

"As long as it takes," was the cryptic reply.

When he reached the lobby, McCalley pulled out the map he had picked up in the hotel, on which he had circled in red the places he would like to visit, if there was time. He needed to clear his head before reviewing the meeting he'd just come from. After studying the markings he had made and working out rough estimates of distances, he decided he was in no mood for sightseeing and opted instead for a leisurely walk back to the hotel, stopping to look at the stores along the way and picking up a small gift for his wife.

Even as he gave himself to the sounds and sights around him, the French words that drifted his way as people moved past him; even as he studied the French advertisements along the way, his mind kept reverting to what he had just experienced. He stopped after a while and entered a café. As he sipped the strong hot brew, bits and pieces of the exchange with Monsieur floated back, like flotsam on a calm sea.

Katie had learned from her cousin about Frank's new life in Canada and had more or less admitted that he had sent the clipping about Frank's death in Ottawa. Benson had skilfully evaded answering the question McCalley had posed. He had admitted seeing Katie in New York. but what had they really talked about? At some point, he had offered her a job, which Katie had refused.

He seemed to know a great deal about her, about Frank as well.

Something jogged the Inspector's memory. What was it the man had said? The apprehension he had felt at the time engulfed him again. He searched for the words. *She'd been grieving all that time for a man who had not only abandoned her but had immediately remarried. A scoundrel, a gambler, and a bigamist. Poor girl! What a terrible waste, her grief!*

Gambler! That was it! How did Monsieur know Frank Hastings gambled? And, more to the point, knowing that, why would he accept him as a Board member? His success was built on judging quickly and accurately the people he dealt with. Would Benson, a shrewd businessman, take on a gambler on one of his Boards? Frank had quit the habit, even before he arrived in Ottawa, Flora had told McCalley; but did Monsieur know that? And even if he knew, could he trust Frank not to fall back into it?

More to the point: he had never met the man; he owed him nothing. He hadn't seen Katie herself in years, before she turned up in St. Tropez. Why the sudden interest?

He had allowed Hastings (Chadwick) to serve on the Board of one of his Paris-based companies. He had offered his cousin Katie a fantastic job. . . .

Why had Katie turned down that offer without a moment's hesitation . . . and with so much rancour, such anger?

He quickly paid his bill and resumed his walk toward the hotel. This time his pace was brisk. He wanted to jot down, while everything was still fresh in his memory, a detailed summary of his meeting with Charles Benson, and, as quickly as possible, before it began to fade, his impression of the man.

The phone was ringing when he unlocked the door to his room. It was the front desk with an urgent message.

Monsieur hadn't stopped downstairs, but the clerk, *pardon*, had seen him entering the elevator —

It was from Katie's friend, Josie. She and Marge apologized for not thinking of it earlier, but was he free for dinner? If he came by around seven, they could chat over a glass of wine and then enjoy a leisurely evening at a cozy little restaurant,. walking distance from their place.

McCalley smiled remembering "urgent" messages

from his own daughter, when she was away at college and, later, when she moved to California to work as a junior clerk for a large law firm. It had been her first time away from home, completely on her own —

The number he dialed turned out to be the American Embassy. Josie was at a meeting. McCalley left a message accepting their invitation.

It was five thirty when he replaced the receiver. He took a quick shower, put on a pair of black jeans and a fresh undershirt, then settled in the big chair by the window and opened the thick file he took from his briefcase.

CHAPTER THIRTEEN

He read over his summary of the interview with Benson, adding to it here and there. He missed Bill Kenney at times like these. Bill took careful notes in shorthand and had them ready for him in record time. With Kenney along, the Inspector was always free to carry on an interview without having to write things down. He refused to use tape recordings; didn't trust them. At headquarters, it had become a standard joke; but McCalley was adamant about it. Kenney had heard the stories, as a rookie in the department, and accepted the fact without indulging in the banter and friendly criticism. When McCalley had advertised for an assistant, Kenney had applied — but not before taking a crash course in shorthand. He was one of over a dozen who tried for the job, most with better credentials than his. That the young man had displayed foresight and keen judgment in preparing himself that way had not been lost on McCalley. He chose Kenney over the others....

When he'd read over his six-page summary, he dated it and placed it at the back of the folder. He then started to review the rest of the notes and reports, starting with the most recent.

An hour later, he closed the folder and put it aside. A theory was forming in his mind, but he realized that it might well be clouding his judgment. Wasn't he the one who always scolded Bill Kenney and others — even Markarian, all through the Bantry case! — for indulging in theories, letting their imagination suggest far-fetched notions and interfere with the methodical, important gathering of facts?

Still, something about Katie's cousin rankled him. The man was an enigma. McCalley was certain he knew much more than he was telling. He remembered how skillfully he'd worked his way around questions and how deftly he'd avoided answering them. His unbreachable self-confidence, his self-command as he took in what McCalley told him and gave back the obvious — these were all qualities the Inspector might have admired in the highly competitive corporate world Benson was part of, where such qualities undoubtedly gave him an advantage; to McCalley, following a potential murder trail, they were suspect.

He wondered too what Benson really felt about Katie. She was the only relative he had acknowledged, but just how important was she to him? If he felt so strongly about her, why had he waited so long to reach out to her? Or, better yet, why had he reached out at all, and with information that had caused her so much pain?

His performance had been brilliant. Except, of course, for the one little slip, which — the Inspector had to admit — might not be relevant at all. How had Benson known about Frank's gambling? Katie, on the other hand, had seemed surprised when Flora told her. What did it mean? Did Benson also know about Frank's huge debts? About the people Hastings dealt with, the mobsters who lent him the money he needed to gamble?

By now, McCalley was convinced that Benson knew much more and was hiding a great deal. Why would he want to follow Frank's movements? Or Katie's? For what purpose? And how did Katie come into this whole mess? It was as though the man had woven a subtle but intricate web to draw both husband and wife to him, manipulating them for some reason McCalley could not begin to fathom.

He rested his head against the back of the chair and closed his eyes.

He had known Frank was alive and living in Ottawa. He had told Katie, when she was in St. Tropez. Why hadn't he told her earlier? Why wait almost a year?

Why tell her at all?

McCalley wondered too about the encounter in St. Tropez. Just how casual was that meeting? A man who could get whatever information he wanted could have known she would be there and may have contrived that "casual" meeting. But why?

He would definitely have to talk with Katie again. He was certain she too knew much more than she had told him. What had happened between her and the cousin to make her furious? Pressure to take on the job Benson had offered seemed a lame excuse for the kind of rage she had displayed on leaving the restaurant, after their lunch in New York. The doorman had described in detail what had happened, as she waited for a cab.

Something jogged his memory. He picked up the folder and found the notes he had added to the file.

Benson had laughed when McCalley asked about the job offer to Katie, as though it were a good joke. He'd admitted he'd offered her a great deal of money. Why had she really turned him down? It was somewhat strange, in a way. She was an ambitious girl. With her skills and personality, she would have been catapulted into success, would have had the security, recognition, and power she was hoping to achieve. She would be on top of the heap. Even if she wasn't really interested in the money, it was a job much more interesting and challenging than her present one, or any future one she might be offered where she currently worked. Why not consider it at least?

The curious thing was that such an incredible offer should have evoked the kind of response he and Markarian had witnessed. Katie's rage and anger had seemed unwarranted.

The thought of money reminded McCalley of the slight, almost imperceptible hesitation on Benson's part, when the Inspector had mentioned Geneva. McCalley's guess was that Benson had something to do with that trip. Or was it something else? Katie's story about wanting to buy a watch simply didn't sound right, although she *had* in fact bought one.

It probably wasn't at all important, but it *was* puzzling. She could have gotten a good Swiss watch anywhere in the world, certainly in Paris or New York.

Geneva was the place for conferences, summit meetings, banking.

Something else to ask Katie about again. He jotted down a reminder. Would a practical, efficient person like Katie have changed her flight schedule at the last minute simply to buy a watch in Geneva? McCalley didn't think so.

And how had James Chadwick, alias Frank Hastings, come to be recruited for the Board of one of Benson's companies? He hoped Kenney would come up with something. Was there a connection between his joining that Board and the investments that, according to Flora, had proved so lucrative?

Mulling over these questions, the doubts and uncertainties that plagued him, he realized how much he missed Ed Markarian at that moment. He wondered once again at the coincidence that had brought them together at an arms convention some years earlier, where they had sat over a beer and talked all night.

Markarian had been invaluable to him in solving the Bantry case. The murder of the taxidermist at the Canadian Museum of Natural History in Ottawa had led McCalley to New York, to look into the death of Ellis Bantry, an importer-exporter, "accidentally" killed in cross-fire on a Soho street. Without Markarian's help, the case — a triple murder, as it turned out — might not have been solved at all. They had worked well together and had become good friends.

He wondered what Markarian would say to all

this, what "hunches" he might put forward.

In the Bantry case, those "hunches" had served them well, even though McCalley remained firm in his conviction that the most important thing in a criminal investigation was to collect quickly and carefully as much information as possible, every scrap and detail, when it was still fresh, no matter how insignificant it might seem. He insisted on efficient procedures, no matter how tiresome and time consuming, and lost no occasion to impress upon Bill Kenney and others working for him how much could be lost if they ignored immediate facts in order to test a theory prematurely. He had trained his assistant well, and Bill Kenney had proved an apt pupil; yet, even Bill at times indulged in what McCalley considered to be irresponsible speculation. Still. it *had* proved useful, more than once, he conceded with a smile.

If prodded for their opinions, what would they have to say in this case?

Listening to Benson, his own gut reaction had stifled his better judgment. Even now, much as he tried, he could not shake off the feeling that the man had gotten the better of him, that he had enjoyed the parrying, setting up foils to distract his opponent. The interview had been a kind of fencing match, a test, a game of sorts.

It also occurred to him, most unreasonably, in a flash that lit up his doubts and sharpened the dark mood they had produced, that Benson was a master at deception and would stop at nothing, not even murder.

He shook his head, trying to rid himself of such unfounded conjectures but succeeded only in part. His instincts told him with frightening certainty that Monsieur Benson could prove a formidable threat.

Was he a threat to Katie? Why was she so upset with him, so frightened by McCalley's questions?

With a start, he realized it was close to seven. He

changed quickly into the one suit he had brought with him and had worn earlier — a light-weight gray-striped wool— put on a fresh shirt and tie, and before leaving decided to make a quick call to Kenney.

His sergeant didn't have much to report. "I'm still looking into Frank Hastings's contacts here in Canada, Sir. Nothing definite, but there's one chap who got to know him fairly well, a sort of sponsor, you might say, an older man. About your age, Sir" — McCalley winced. "He might be the one who recruited him for the Board. I don't have all the information yet, but he could also be the chap who gave Hastings insider information."

McCalley gave him the names Benson had produced for him. One of them was the contact Kenney had referred to. "Don't try to talk to him, Bill," McCalley warned. "Not yet. Not until we know more. Meanwhile, check those other names."

"How much should I tell Mrs. Chadwick? She calls every day."

"Tell her we're doing our best. I'll see her when I get back." He went on to describe briefly his meeting with Benson.

"You think he knows more than he's telling?"

"I can't trust my instincts, Bill, but yes, I feel he's holding back."

"He seems to have known a lot about Hastings."

"Yes, but why? What interest could he possibly have had in Frank Hastings? We need to know lots more, Bill," he cautioned. "Keep digging,"

What he had not told Kenney was that the interview had miscarried but at the same time had provoked responses that presaged — he was absolutely sure of it! — startling new revelations. It was simply a matter of time. Patience and hard work would win out, he was certain. What he couldn't be sure of was where to start looking.

Quickly, he tucked his notepad inside a pocket and set out for his appointment with Josie and Marge. Outside, he was lucky. A cab was letting out a couple in front of the hotel. He grabbed it.

The two young women were waiting for him with a chilled bottle of White Zinfandel, which they quickly poured, as McCalley settled in a third chair they had brought out to the terrace. The evening promised to be more comfortable than the hot day; a small breeze came up, as they sat sipping their wine. The scattered sounds from the square below and the streets nearby provided a pleasant background.

McCalley found himself relaxing as he listened to the two girls describe their life in Paris — meetings, diplomatic parties at the Embassy, the Ambassador's wife always a bit late for everything, preparations under way for the visit of the Deputy Undersecretary of Foreign Affairs of Italy, a certain Jean who taught where Marge also taught and who seemed to be courting her. Marge actually blushed as Josie teased her about her would-be suitor. McCalley listened earnestly to Josie's account of her early mistakes both in protocol and in translating official documents, to Marge's stories about the children she taught, the trouble she had finding English texts for them to read. They reminded him so much of his daughter! The same energetic commitment, the same willingness to face new challenges. It made McCalley feel even older than his fifty-two years. Still, it was like a reminder of home. He liked that.

It wasn't until they were getting ready to leave for dinner, at eight-thirty, that the subject of Katie came up. He had hoped it would come up naturally, and it did. It was Josie who asked:

"Is Katie in some kind of trouble?"

"No, no. We're checking on something concerning

Frank. I'll explain later. . . ."

Over excellent mussels in a wine sauce, fresh asparagus *au gratin*, a peach soufflé, and a first-rate white wine from Algiers, recommended by the owner, Mr. Talman, the girls reminisced about their college years with Katie.

As they finished their meal, McCalley asked: "I take it, Katie told you about visiting her cousin? How she ran into him in St. Tropez?"

It was Marge who answered. "Oh, yes! Funny thing, Inspector. She called us the very first night she spent at the chalet, all excited. We were too! We had no idea her cousin was the world-famous American billionaire who has been living in France several years now! Only thirty and almost as rich as Bill Gates. He and his wife Emma, his first wife — she was killed in an auto accident on the Amalfi Drive last January — they were in the press every week, just like movie stars. We saved some back issues for Katie. But, when she got here, three days later, she didn't have much to say about her visit. In fact, she seemed not to want to talk about it at all." She turned to Josie. "Am I right, Josie? Didn't she seem a little down when she got here? Not her bubbly self, I remember thinking."

"She looked very tired," replied Josie.

Marge turned back to the Inspector. "Then later, at dinner, . . . well, we *were* celebrating —"

"What she means is, we all got drunk!" explained Josie, with a grin.

"— at dinner she said something that struck me as odd."

"How, odd?"

"Josie?" asked Marge, turning to her friend. "You remember what happened better than I do —"

"I'm surprised you remember at all. You were pretty far gone by then!"

"So, tell us. What did I say? What did Katie say?"

Josie furrowed her brow in concentration. "You had just told Mr. Talman—" she leaned toward McCalley to explain "— he owns the restaurant —" then went on, "you'd just told him about Katie having spent three days in St. Tropez with her cousin, the great American tycoon. Mr. Talman was properly impressed and treated us to espresso and cognac. We were all pretty high, Inspector," Josie said, almost apologetically. "Then, out of the blue, Katie began talking about money. 'Money, money, money. Wives and money,' she said. I don't know what she meant."

"Did you ask her?"

"She was past listening at that point. She went on rambling, all the way home — about the Midas touch, about how everything he touched turned to hard currency. That's it! Hard currency! 'Except for Emma.' I remember that especially because I laughed, it was so funny. 'Except Emma,' she said. 'Emma turns to fat'." She laughed again, remembering.

Marge seemed to be trying to recall the incident, without too much success. She smiled weakly, in response. Josie went right on.

"I remember laughing so hard I was crying. Katie too. We were hysterical, I think. But it *was* funny. 'Except Emma. Emma turns to fat.' Don't you think that's funny, Inspector?"

McCalley smiled. "Was Emma fat?"

"Oh, no. The pictures of her are gorgeous. But, rumor was, she liked to drink. I suppose Katie noticed something, maybe it was beginning to show. We never did find out what she meant. But in matter of fact, whatever she was like before, whatever anyone said to the contrary, Emma was still a knockout. Better-looking than Princess Di, than any of the Hollywood crowd. She was from Sweden. Smart cookie, too."

"That's right," Marge acknowledged.

Josie resumed: "The rest was even stranger. She was choking with laughter and talking at the same time, trying to catch her breath between one word and the next. If I hadn't been walking next to her, propping her up, I would have missed it. She said: 'He thinks he can buy me. You know? He's crazy! Off his rocker. I should know, right?' The next morning at breakfast I asked her what she meant about money and wives. She didn't remember. Said it couldn't have been important. She laughed when I told her she'd sounded a bit jealous."

They were silent for a while. McCalley sipped the last of his wine, sat back, and asked casually. "Do you know why Katie decided to go to Geneva at the last minute?"

"Something about having to run an errand," offered Marge.

"What was the errand, did she tell you?"

"A colleague had asked her to check something about his account in one of the banks," Josie explained. When she realized the Inspector was waiting for more, she added, somewhat apologetically: "That's it, Inspector. That's all she told us. We were disappointed she had to cut short her stay, even if it was only a day and night. Anyway, there was no use pressing her; she was set on doing what she had promised."

Monsieur Talman had sent coffee and Amaretto, compliments of the house. McCalley leaned back and savored the strong brew. "Nothing else?" he pressed.

"That was it," Josie said, spreading her hands wide. "We didn't ask questions. A promise is a promise. We would have done the same."

Recalling his own promise to explain his visit to them, he now told them about the investigation he was helping with, claims that had surfaced after nine-eleven. He was careful not to say anything about Frank's double life and his death in Ottawa. There was time enough to fill in those blanks, later, when the dust settled. Instead, he asked:

"How well did you know Frank?"

Marge answered first. "We met him a few times during our last year in college. He was already working."

"They were a steady item during that last year," Josie picked up. "We used to joke about it, right Marge? We'd tease her that they were like an old married couple!" Marge smiled. Josie laughed, and went on: "The idea of an older man appealed to her —"

"Frank was five years older than Katie," Marge filled in.

"— especially after losing her parents in a car crash just a few weeks before graduation, and her brother having to leave New York for a job in California. Couldn't stay to see her married. It made Katie feel very insecure, very lonely. Of course, she had known Frank for almost a year, but at that point in time he must have seemed even more attractive, someone she could rely on to support her. He was good that way."

"Even we couldn't stay for the ceremony," said Marge. "We had jobs waiting for us here. . . . But until Frank was killed, we kept up with e-mails several times a week. After that. . . well, you can imagine! Just think! Losing a husband after just a year! At that age!"

"We were ready to fly back for a few days," said Josie, shaking her head, "but she wouldn't hear of it. Promised to spend part of her vacation time with us in the Summer,"

"And so she did," commented the Inspector. Then, looking from one to the other: "Did you like him?"

The question took the girls by surprise. There was a slight hesitation. Josie replied first.

"Frank was . . . affable enough, I guess. Not my type, though."

He turned to Marge. "He didn't appeal to you, either?"

"To be honest, Inspector, I often wondered what they had in common. Katie was gung-ho about her job, always looking for new ways to make things more interesting, more efficient."

"She was ambitious and Frank was not?"

The young woman appeared embarrassed. "I didn't mean to suggest that, Inspector. But Katie had already earned a couple of raises and was up for a big promotion — actually got it, last November. By comparison, Frank seemed restless, bored even, at his job. But I could be wrong —"

McCalley looked at Josie, who nodded in agreement with Marge and explained: "Marge is right. By comparison, Frank seemed listless."

"Did Katie talk about it?"

"Not really. But once she'd let something slip, remember?" — turning to Marge, then back to McCalley. "It was the Spring before he died, she e-mailed us about Frank looking for a more challenging job."

"Oh, right!" Marge chimed in. "Said he'd gone to Canada — it was April, I think — for some convention and came back all excited about the possibility of transferring up there. She thought it would give him the kind of motivation he needed. But, she was worried, too, because it would mean leaving New York and her own job, and she wasn't ready to do that."

"Did he get any offers?"

"Apparently not," said Josie.

McCalley leaned back and smiled. "So, Frank didn't appeal to either of you?"

The two girls laughed. "It wasn't *us* he was courting, Inspector!" said Josie.

"The important thing," said Marge "was that Katie thought he was right for her. When Frank died, we thought she'd never get over it."

Josie hesitated, then volunteered: "I guess, back then, we thought she could have done better. Katie is such an unusual person, full of energy and ideas. Frank was, . . . well, he just didn't have that same drive."

"What about Delancourt? Do you approve of him?"

"We never met him, Inspector," said Marge, "but I must say Katie is a different person since Francis came into her life."

"How is that?"

"Frank gave her stability, reassurance, the things she needed at the time. Francis swept her off her feet. I think she really loves him. When she talks about him, it's a totally different thing."

"You don't think she really loved Frank?"

Marge shrugged. "I guess she did, or thought she did . . . but it wasn't the same."

"You think she might have outgrown him, eventually?"

"I can't say," said Marge, suddenly looking troubled. "I don't want to give a wrong impression, Inspector. Anything can happen in a marriage. All I know is that for the year they were married, Katie was very content."

McCalley realized he had been right in pegging Marge as the romantic and Josie as the reasonable, efficient one. Each looked the part: Marge was extremely pretty, with her long blonde hair framing small features and hazel eyes. Her skin was flawless. All in all, a very attractive young woman. Except for a touch of lipstick, she wore no make-up. Didn't need any. . . . Josie produced a different effect: her wide mouth and dark eyes reflected a quick wit, an ease with words, a knowledge of the world that was much deeper, more mature than what her years suggested.

They lingered over a second coffee. The girls wanted to know what the people in Canada thought about the war in Iraq. They discussed Mel Gibson and Jennifer Lopez, "Wheel of Fortune" and Pat Sajak.

"Sometimes we get the Italian version. It's not the same," said Josie. "Pat Sajak, especially. I love his ad-libbing and his timing!"

McCalley sat back and relaxed. The two young women reminded him of his own daughter; their chatter made him feel very much at home. Besides, he had always been a good listener.

It had been a most enjoyable evening. . . .

When he got back to the hotel, it was after eleven. The first thing he did was to make careful notes of his meeting with Katie's two friends. He tried to record as closely as possible what they had told him about Katie's remarks at dinner, her first night in Paris. Her words had raised new and puzzling questions in the Inspector's mind.

Much as he tried. McCalley could not dismiss his suspicion that Katie and her cousin were holding back what had transpired between them during Katie's brief visit at the chalet.

He remembered how frightened she had been when he brought up her cousin's visit to New York. Had money changed hands? Had Benson asked Katie to do him a favor? Was he the one who asked her to check a bank account in Geneva?

No, no, of course not, he chided himself. Why would a man with his connections and clout ask someone like Katie to do that for him? He didn't need an intermediary, he didn't have to ask for favors. In minutes, a man with his connections could remove any obstacle, get whatever information he wanted, do things most people would find it impossible to attain. The favor

— if it had been that — may indeed have been, as the girls said, for a colleague in New York; but somehow McCalley could not bring himself to accept that explanation.

He had come to question everything in this unusual case — not just the manner of Frank Hastings;'s death; also the bizarre events surrounding it. And because of Flora Chadwick's unshakable conviction that her husband had been murdered, the case had become, for McCalley, a personal challenge. He sensed, also, a certain urgency.

His mind still churning, he prepared for bed.

One good thing, he told himself, with a sense of accomplishment: he had managed to see the people he had wanted to interview, all in the one day. Tomorrow, he could fly to Geneva early in the morning and return to New York on schedule the next day.

The first thing he and Markarian must do when he got back was talk with Katie again — this time, push hard for answers.

He wondered what his colleague had found out about the loans and the man who had provided them. As though at a signal, the phone rang.

It was Markarian. "When are you due back, Luke?"

"Tomorrow night or the next day. I've finished here and fly to Geneva in the morning." He went on to tell him about his meeting with Benson.

"Cunning fellow," he said, by way of conclusion. "Didn't get much out of him, except, he let slip he knew Frank was gambling. We'll have to look into that. It's far-fetched, but there may be a connection with the fellow who was lending Frank money. . . . The girls shared some interesting gossip — "

"Anything relevant?"

"I'll hold off on that until I see you. We've got to pry a lot more out of Katie."

"That may be hard to do for a while," was the reply. "We're not sure what happened, but she was found in a coma in the elevator of her apartment building yesterday afternoon. We think she was coming home from work and someone followed her. The doorman was taking a leak, didn't see anything. Looks like a mugging. Her bag was missing, and her wristwatch and rings."

McCalley felt his heart racing. "A mugging?"

"That's what it looks like."

"Does it look like that to you, Ed?"

"Don't go paranoid on me, Luke."

"We're looking at a lot of accidents, Ed."

"Until, or unless we know more, that's what they are, Luke. Accidents. Let's go easy on this."

"What do you really think?"

"Hey! I'm trying to do what you keep telling me I should do: not jump to conclusions."

"Well, I confess even I can't help wondering...."

"Don't. There's nothing else to go on. For the moment, it's a mugging. I've got someone looking for the rings and the watch. We're bound to find them sooner or later. Or a credit card purchase."

"How serious is it?"

"As far as we know, a bad concussion, a huge bump on her head, and a dislocated shoulder. They're running more tests. The doctors aren't saying much. All they offered is what we already know: if she comes out of it tomorrow or the next day, the chances of recovery are pretty good."

"Is she in danger?"

Markarian heard his friend let out a long sigh. He understood the concern. "I honestly don't know, Luke. Nobody knows."

"Where was the husband?"

"The poor guy found her. He'd gone out for a few minutes to get a salad dressing — he had come home early and thought he'd surprise her by starting dinner—came back into the building, pressed the button, and there she was, sprawled on the floor of the elevator, unconscious. He probably just missed whoever did it. The elevator hadn't moved. No one had called it. Whoever did it must have come up behind her, hit her, and fled."

"Took quite a risk."

"It worked."

"It could easily have backfired."

"Well, it didn't." There was a brief silence. "When does your plane get into Kennedy?" McCalley gave him the information but tried to dissuade him from picking him up. "Hey, it saves us both time. You can fill me in on the way into Manhattan."

In bed, McCalley kept thinking of Katie being attacked in the elevator. Muggings usually took place in the street. If the mugger was quick, and as a rule they were, he could be out of sight in a matter of seconds. But in an elevator? In that kind of building? The doorman could easily have come back in time to see the mugger before he got away. The whole incident was too *clean*, too efficient. Was there a car waiting outside for the mugger? If so, McCalley thought grimly, the event had been carefully programmed and carried out. Katie could have been followed for days, hit at just the right moment. . . .

He forced himself to remember Markarian's warning, smiling at the friendly jab that they had exchanged roles. Ed was right. He mustn't push it. They had to find the mugger, trace the stolen items. Only then would they be able to make a sound judgment about what happened, whether or not it was indeed just another mugging, . . . or something else.

He refused to follow that thought any further and forced himself into a fitful sleep.

In Geneva, the snapshot the girls had given him,

taken in a disco when Katie was in Paris, served his purpose. In the second bank McCalley visited, the manager recognized her at once.

"You understand, Inspector, we cannot give out information about our clients or their accounts." They both knew McCalley could pull rank and eventually get information, if he wanted to, but for the moment he decided to go easy. The manager too understood the protocol. He decided to give way a little.

"Can you tell me why she came to you?"

"She wanted to close her account and send the entire sum to someone else."

"When was that?" McCalley asked, taking down the information as he spoke.

The man opened a folder he had taken out of a filing cabinet. "Last year, in August."

"Was it a large sum?"

"Depends on what you mean by 'large,' Inspector. In any case, as you know, I'm not at liberty to give that information —" McCalley dismissed the question with a casual wave. The man *was* trying to cooperate. "What I *can* tell you, Inspector, is that the same amount was deposited again, in a new account, in the same name, opened soon after that."

McCalley looked up from his notes. "When did that happen?"

"Let me see. . . . " He leafed through some papers in the folder. "Ah, yes. That was in January of this year."

"Is the account still in place?"

"Oh, no. It was closed for good in —" He glanced down at the sheet in his hand. "— Here it is. In July." He looked up, pleased with himself. "There has been no new activity since then."

McCalley thanked the man and left, feeling confused and depressed. Until that moment, he had truly believed Katie to be innocent of any complicity in whatever it was that was going on. But money had passed hands. Was it a legitimate payment for something that had nothing to do with the case? Possible, thought McCalley, but highly improbable. More likely, Benson *had* offered Katie a job and opened an account for her with an advance, a sign of his trust in her or, more likely, a lure to have her accept his offer. She had been emphatic about having turned him down. Could that explain the return of the money?

Maybe! Maybe! Maybe!

Too many unknowns!

One thing was clear: a large sum of money had been deposited in Katie's name. That had to be explained. And why would she return it twice? Or, more to the point: why had it been deposited twice? Was that the pressure Katie had talked about? What had made her so angry?

It was not at all what he had expected to find. It hurt him to think Katie might be involved in some shady deal — why else wouldn't she talk about it?

Never had McCalley had a case like this one. It was like floating on air, nothing to fix on . . . except for disturbing suggestions having to do with money, loans, bank accounts in Geneva, lucrative job offers —

Money and wives. . . .

Money could buy the devil himself. . . .

Ah, but not Katie. Isn't that what she'd said? Money couldn't buy *her*.

But someone had tried! Tried and failed.

Was it blackmail? The thought gave McCalley pause. . . .

Facts! Facts! he reminded himself!

Someone had attacked Katie, but not killed her. Was it meant as a warning? Punishment for having told McCalley about her cousin knowing Frank had escaped nine-eleven? A reminder not to talk about what she knew, what she was keeping back? Had she become a threat to someone out there?

And just what did all this have to do with Frank Hastings?

CHAPTER FOURTEEN

The plane was on time and Markarian right by the gate when McCalley emerged. He insisted on carrying the Inspector's single bag to the car, which was conveniently parked close by, an official NYPD sticker clearly displayed on the windshield. Getting out of the airport was frustratingly slow, but traffic picked up once they hit Grand Central Parkway.

McCalley had started in, even before they reached the car, with a more detailed account of his meeting with Benson. He went on to describe his dinner with Katie's two friends.

They were nearing Manhattan when he finished and asked:

"What are your thoughts about Benson?"

"From what you've just told me, a real piece of work." Then smiling and glancing surreptitiously at his companion: "Only an opinion, you understand, based on hearsay." McCalley laughed. He was used to his colleague's friendly jabs by now. Markarian joined in, then added: "That bad, huh?"

"Frustrating beyond words."

"Think he's up to something?"

McCalley shook his head, but not in denial. Markarian gave him a quick glance, turned back to the road. "I'd say you had better luck with the girls."

"It could mean nothing. We went through two carafes of wine."

"You mean *they* did. I've never seen you drink more than one glass at any time. Anyway, *In vino*, etcetera. What was the phrase again, about money? 'Money and wives'?"

"Yes, but don't ask me to explain it."

"I wouldn't dare." They both laughed again.

"Money was mentioned more than once, as I told you. What I'd really like to know is what happened between the time Katie arrived at St. Tropez and the time she left for Paris. Hardly speculation to figure out her cousin must have said or done something to rattle her. It may well have been about money, since she kept harping on it, according to Josie. Even with us, you remember. That business of a job doesn't quite fit, somehow. A girl like Katie knows how to say 'No,' if she wants to." He shook his head. "Whatever happened was something beyond her control, something that made her angry because she couldn't get out of it. Almost as though she'd been abused. A lot of resentment had built up. The mere mention of him made her go through the roof. You saw it. You heard her."

"I would say, afraid more than angry, although that too."

"Tell me about Joe Sarace, the friendly loan shark. Was Flora's information of any help?"

"Oh, yeah. We finally tracked him down. Couldn't deny doing business with Frank. A real smart-ass. He and that big guy who hangs around. He's had trouble with the law often enough, our man, but has never been charged with anything."

"But he admitted knowing Frank."

"How could he deny it? His secretary and others remembered Frank's being there more than once. A lot of people saw him, knew he was a steady client."

"Except Katie," mused McCalley.

"Except Katie," repeated Markarian, glancing over at his friend. "What I can't understand," he went on, "is why they didn't break his knee caps or an arm or a leg. He was way behind in his payments. Instead, they give him fifteen grand!"

"They wanted him for special assignments," replied the other, with more than a touch of irony.

230

Markarian sneered. "I like that. Murder as a 'special assignment!'"

"It's not exactly your routine job."

"It's not exactly a job you give an outsider. Why pay him like a hit-man? He owed them in a big way. He was supposed to be clearing debts. Why give him all that cash when he was supposed to be paying *them*?"

McCalley shrugged. "Beats me. In any case, according to Flora, he spent most of it within days. . . . What, exactly, is on your mind, Ed?"

Markarian shook his head. "I keep wondering why they left him hanging in there. . . . How much did Flora tell you he owed when he disappeared on nine-eleven?"

"About seventy-five thousand. Spent most of it on the horses. Some went for a pink sapphire pendant, an anniversary present for Katie, in August. A few thousand went into his OTB reserves, his secret bank account, but he didn't spend it, Flora said."

"Cagy bastard!"

"You have to admire his reasoning, if not his motives. He told Flora the pendant was to give Katie a sense of security — all is well, that sort of thing. A practical fellow! He continued to take out loans, Flora said, so Sarace wouldn't suspect anything. As far as Sarace knew, Frank was still hooked, but Flora told me he'd already begun to taper off on his gambling. He felt he had to continue betting on the horses or Sarace would get suspicious. He was careful to do nothing out of the ordinary. I suppose in his shoes, I might have done the same thing."

"Oh, yeah?" For a moment Markarian took his eyes off the road and turned to him. He sounded angry. "You would have killed a man too, I suppose? Or lured that young guy, what's his name again?"

"Kevin. Kevin Masters."

"You would have lured Kevin Masters into

thinking you were his friend, just so he could take your place in the Cessna, be found burned to a crisp in a deserted field, still strapped in the pilot's seat?"

Still talking, Markarian made a hard turn into the FDR Drive. It threw McCalley against the side door.

"Wait until we get there before tossing me out!" the Inspector cried out, with a small laugh.

"Sorry."

McCalley put a restraining hand on Markarian arm. "I'm just as angry as you are, Ed. But we've got so little to go on, just provocative bits and pieces floating in a vacuum. Much as I dislike admitting it, I have an unpleasant feeling that there is much more to this. Flora played a large part in Frank's wanting to clear the decks, so did Sarace. That much we know and can grasp. Why else would he go through that awful charade of playing dead? If all he wanted was Flora, a divorce would have done it, eventually. Katie would have come around, once she realized she couldn't hold on to him. It was Sarace he had to escape from, and it had to look good. That much we can be sure of. . . ."

Markarian shot him a curious look. "But, who killed him, and why? Is that it?" When McCalley said nothing, he went on: "My bet is Sarace. Frank owed him big." McCalley still had no reply, and Markarian went on: "We agreed from the beginning that Sarace would be after him like a light, if he found him. Okay, maybe he didn't do it himself? Maybe he had someone else do it."

"Or someone else gave the order."

"Who do you have in mind?"

McCalley may have heard, but he was following a track of his own. "What's nagging at me, for starters: how could anyone have found out that Frank was living in Ottawa under an assumed name? He'd burned his bridges pretty well, wouldn't you say?" Markarian leaned slightly toward McCalley, as though not to miss what he was saying. He answered promptly.

"Katie's cousin knew. He may have known other things too about Frank. But that's another story."

"Maybe not. Maybe that's part of the same story, you see." Markarian was about to answer that he didn't see at all, but McCalley went on:

"Think about it, Ed. If in some way Sarace or whoever he takes orders from found where Frank was living and had him killed, it should have been the usual execution-style murder, not a hit-and-run." He paused, as though to let his words sink in. His attention now riveted, Markarian said, somewhat sharply:

"Where are you going with this?"

"I think he was set up." Markarian's deep frown did not faze him. "There's more to this than just owing money."

"More than just owing money?! We're talking $75,000!" countered the other, shifting his body as far as he could to face McCalley.

Markarian could not hide his surprise. The fact that McCalley had been brooding about such a farfetched notion bothered him. It was no longer a matter for friendly teasing. The idea was so wild, so improbable, that he wondered briefly if McCalley hadn't perhaps reached that ultimate point of frustration that affected one's judgment. Out loud, he said:

"Katie's cousin knew a lot about Frank, but his interest in that whole sad story seemed to be to steer Katie into a new life. We may not like him, but I don't see any other motive in what he did. What would he want with someone like Frank?" McCalley shrugged. "What do you hope to find there? Or, better yet, how do you propose to go about it?"

"I've got Kenney looking into the investments Frank made during these last few months."

"What's the connection? What he did may have

been illegal but not life-threatening."

McCalley ignored the irony. "Unless, they thought he might talk."

"About what? What could he tell them, except that a friend gave him a tip? You're way off, Luke! You're reaching in the dark."

"We don't have all the points of reference yet."

"What are you talking about? I've never heard you go on like this! It worries me." Even as he spoke, the doodles in McCalley's notebook flashed before him. He was about to joke about that and "points of reference," but something in McCalley's stolid look held him from voicing the easy dismissal that had formed on his lips. Whatever McCalley was thinking had taken firm root in the Inspector's mind; he'd obviously been struggling with it for some time. It wouldn't be easy to turn him away from what was nagging him. At the same time, Markarian realized how hard it must be for his colleague to admit such an absurd idea, let alone find fuel for it.

For it *was* absurd, Markarian insisted to the skeptic in him; it was totally off base! There was nothing to give that notion even a hint of credibility. What irked him beyond reason was having to admit that McCalley — the last person he would have expected to entertain such a wild idea — was the very one holding fast to it!

Backtracking, the detective allowed himself to examine what McCalley had put forward. Was there something they had missed or someone who might have ordered the scattered events they had uncovered into a sinister plot?

He remained silent for a while, trying to grasp the full implications of McCalley's startling proposition of what amounted to a conspiracy. McCalley was right about Sarace, Markarian conceded. If the mobster had located Frank Hastings in Ottawa, he certainly would have had him killed — but would he have gone out of his way to make it look like a hit-and-run? If Frank's death had not been an accident, and Flora was certain that it was not, then someone wanted it to look that way, not look like an execution-style murder. Even if Sarace or someone connected with him had been following orders, the motive might have been altogether different from what they had assumed all along: Frank's outstanding debts may have been only a part of the reason for his death; maybe it didn't figure in it at all. Other things may well have been at stake, other people involved, other motives at work. Brooding out loud, he heard himself say:

"Frank told Flora he thought he was being followed. We should go back to that. Find out more."

They had reached the hotel, the same one where McCalley had stayed before flying to Paris. There had been no difficulty reserving a room again for the next few days.

Neither man moved. When the doorman started toward them, Markarian waved him off and pulled up as far as he could, to allow other cars to discharge or take on passengers.

"Here's how I see it," McCalley began, watching the doorman's retreat. "From the beginning, nothing but accidents and coincidences. No clear pattern. No obvious connections. Except that there was a kind of consistency in the inconsistencies."

Markarian was tempted to interrupt but decided not to. McCalley turned to him and went on:

"Frank's death may be altogether unrelated to Sarace or gambling debts. But Sarace has got to be mixed up in all this, not necessarily the way we first thought, but definitely in it. The money bothers me, too, Katie's account in Geneva. There was bitterness there, lots of emotions let loose, for reasons we still can't figure out." He paused, as though reviewing it all in his own mind. "We agreed, Katie knows a lot more than she told us.

We'll simply have to force it out of her. And I'm afraid she'll have to tell her husband about it, soon. He's bound to get wind of something and then it will be too late."

Markarian finally interrupted: "Too late for what?"

"Too late for her to make amends. He might not like the idea that she didn't trust him enough to confide in him...."

"Well, for whatever reason, she's making it very hard for both of them. She could use some support."

McCalley moved his head from side to side, his lips a tight line of disapproval. "How long can she keep it up? She will have to testify, sooner or later, may be asked for depositions; she'll have to talk to us again, maybe more than once. Lawyers and the District Attorney's office will want to talk to her. Her husband is bound to find out. How do you suppose he'll react, when he learns about all this? Or when *we* have to tell him? We've got to bring her to see it our way, Ed, the minute she regains consciousness. Or, better yet, do her a favor and talk to her husband ourselves. It might be easier, all around."

Markarian scratched his head. "She'll be furious."

"I know. But things are closing in on her. We went along for a while. But soon, it won't be her call any more. What time should we try the hospital in the morning?"

"Is ten all right?"

"Fine with me. Will her husband be there?"

"He's been there since it happened. Sleeps on a cot in her room."

McCalley got out and shut the car door. Markarian opened the trunk for McCalley's bag. They lingered a few more moments outside the entrance.

"Well then, he'll understand what we have to tell him, don't you think?" McCalley persisted, searching the other's face for the answer he needed.

"I suppose so," Markarian replied, hesitantly.

"You mean, Katie may be right? He may walk away? If he's that thin-skinned, she may be better off without him!" replied the other, with some feeling.

"Let's go easy with this, Luke. She's had a hard time." He walked around to the driver's side and got into the car. "Pick you up at ten!"

In his room, McCalley unpacked again, washed his face, and changed into his slacks and sweater. It was long past the normal dinner hour, even the after-theater crowd had thinned out, but the chef assured him that a grilled veal chop and a large salad were still possible.

Sitting back to enjoy his brief respite, he took a first sip of the Merlot he had ordered with his dinner.

McCalley hated hospitals, for both personal and professional reasons. He had seen much suffering and death in almost thirty years in Homicide; but his most haunting memories were the long hours spent visiting his mother, day after day, week after week, as she lay dying of cancer. Even now, the odor of disinfectants made him recoil; the white smocks and striped uniforms of attendants and nurses, their brisk efficiency, served as a grim reminder of how helpless they all were, in the end, in the presence of death.

Markarian led the way to Katie's room. They found her still unconscious, very pale, hooked up to tubes and machines, her upper left arm in a cast. A tall man in his late twenties or early thirties sat beside her, slowly stroking her other arm. He looked up, as the two men entered the room. His eyes were sunken, with deep shadows under them. His face was almost as pale as his wife's. He must have shaved that morning: there was a fresh nick where he had cut himself.

Delancourt recognized and greeted the detective warmly, thanking him for stopping in to see Katie. Markarian leaned down and spoke softly to him. The young man nodded and followed the two men outside, into the hall.

"Is there some place we could sit down for a few minutes?" asked Markarian, keeping his voice low. Delancourt led them to the end of the corridor, where a black vinyl bench stood in front of the only window in the entire area. Markarian introduced McCalley, who explained that he was working with the Detective on a case that involved Katie's former husband, Frank Hastings. They sat down on the bench.

Seeing him up close, McCalley realized what a strain the young man was under. Thin blue veins stood out underneath his eyes, his pallor had a yellowish cast. Surprise and confusion now brought a flush to the haggard face.

"Inspector, the man's been dead for almost two years! Frank Hastings died in nine-eleven."

"That's what everyone thought."

"What are you saying?"

"He died," Markarian picked up quickly, "but not then. He was killed recently in Ottawa."

"Ottawa! Did Katie know this?"

"Not until a few weeks ago."

"Why didn't she tell me?!" His voice had risen.

It was McCalley who answered. "It's a strange case," he ventured. "We don't have much information yet."

"Was he suffering amnesia? Is that why he didn't go home that day?"

"No, Mr. Delancourt. He didn't suffer any amnesia. He simply disappeared."

Delancourt looked from one man to the other. "Was Katie still legally his wife when I married her?"

"No. He died in June."

"My God! In Ottawa, you said. He died in Ottawa? What was he doing in Ottawa?"

McCalley leaned back and looked across Delancourt's back to Markarian, who sat at the other end of the bench. The brief glance the other cast his way told him he too was finding the exchange difficult. Perhaps they had made a mistake after all! He had truly believed that Katie's insistence on keeping from Delancourt the sordid facts about Frank's life and death had been an exaggerated reaction — perfectly understandable, but overemotional and irrational. He wondered now if it had been a good idea, after all, to break it to him this way. Sadly, he acknowledged the possibility that Katie had feared all along: that her husband might not be prepared to accept any of it.

It was Markarian who took on the hard task of telling Delancourt the details of what had happened.

"He didn't go home that day because he had planned all along to disappear. Another more elaborate plan was in place, but nine-eleven gave him an easier way out. He managed to walk away from Tower One, and in a matter of days flew out of New York to Ottawa, where he married a woman he had met earlier in the year. Within a month, he'd set himself up as an independent consultant for medical insurance claims. At the time he was killed, he was doing pretty well."

Delancourt stared at him, his mouth a grim hard line. "Katie knew all this?"

"She came to know it slowly."

"Before we were married—?"

"Not all of it." A long silence fell like a pall. Delancourt rose and walked a few steps away from the window, then back, where the two men remained seated, watching him. "Why didn't she tell me?"

"She wanted to spare you."

Mixed emotions transformed the young man's face into an impenetrable mask. His eyes were hard points of incomprehension as they searched Markarian's for answers that were not there.

"She thought she was doing the right thing," McCalley added lamely.

"Not to tell me? That was *right?*"

"She was terribly upset."

"No! *I'm* the one who's upset! I've been in agony over what happened, not knowing if she'll ever come out of the coma!"

"Katie did nothing wrong," ventured Markarian.

"You think so?" His voice had a sharp edge to it now, his eyes mere slits, his mouth a tight unforgiving line. His fists were clenched tightly at his sides.

Markarian stood up. "Yes, I do," he replied with some sharpness, closing the short distance between them. His voice was almost threatening. "You should be by her side, ready to comfort her when she wakes up, not standing here nursing your pride!"

Delancourt had taken a step back. He glared at both of them before striding off, past Katie's room, to the far end of the empty corridor, where he disappeared into an elevator.

"So." McCalley stood up. "Katie was right, after all." Markarian gave him a sharp look.

"About wanting to protect him? Keep him in the dark? She couldn't have much longer. You said so yourself. Just being here, our presence alone would have had to be explained, our wanting to question her. What, in fact, just happened—"

A nurse came toward them. "I thought I saw Mr. Delancourt with you. . . ."

"He just left, but I'm sure he'll be back shortly."

"His wife is asking for him."

The two men walked briskly toward Katie's room. "Just a few minutes," the nurse called after them.

Katie Delancourt was propped against pillows, her eyes closed. She opened them and stared, as the two men approached the bed.

"Where's my husband?" Her eyes flew to the doorway behind them.

"He's been here, with you, since you were brought in. He needed a break."

"Where has he gone?" She tried to prop herself up in the bed.

"He'll be back."

"You can't stay."

"We have to, Katie. And you've got to help us."

"I've told you everything I know." Talking had tired her. She closed her eyes again. "I don't want my husband to find you here."

"He won't, not if you help us. We'll be gone in no time." When she didn't answer, Markarian said:

"This is very important, Katie. A lot has happened and we need your cooperation. What did your cousin say or do to make you so angry when you left St. Tropez. . . and later, when he came to New York?"

"I don't remember. It wasn't important."

"Are you sure? . . . . It wasn't about a job, was it?"

She shook her head. "I don't remember. Please, leave me alone."

"We'll have to come back until you tell us what you know."

"I don't know anything!"

The nurse came in with two doctors. "So! You're back with us, I see," said the older man, smiling cheerfully as he took Katie's pulse. He took down the reading and proceeded to shine a light into her eyes. "Good, very good. How do you feel?"

"Tired. Where's my husband?"

The doctors looked at the nurse. The nurse looked at McCalley.

The Inspector said: "He went for a walk." He hoped he was right, that Francis Delancourt had not

241

gone home to pack.

The doctor gave instructions. He patted Katie's hand. "I'll look in again, later. Meanwhile, I want you to rest."

Outside, there was a brief whispered conversation. The doctors left. The nurse came back into the room.

"You have to leave now."

"How long do you expect to keep her here?"

"Not too long, once she regains her strength. Have they found who did it?"

"We're working on it," said Markarian.

Waiting for the elevator, the men conferred.

"Can you get one of your people here? asked McCalley.

"I'll try my best."

They both knew there wasn't a solid enough reason to post a police officer outside Katie's room. Who ever heard of a mugger tracking the prey he had injured and robbed to the hospital bed where she had ended up because of his attack?

Neither man voiced what was in his mind. The elevator came and went. The two men remained standing to one side. Finally, Markarian said:

"You've got me worried, now, Luke."

"And if I'm right, Katie isn't the only one who needs protection."

McCalley said nothing. This time, when the elevator came, they entered. As they crossed the lobby, Markarian asked:

"Where will you be this afternoon?"

"I'll stay put, wait for your call. I'd like to visit Katie again, later on."

"Think we'll have better luck?"

"Not unless we push harder."

"Think Delancourt will be back?"

"He was awfully put out."

"Wouldn't you be?"

"And leave my wife unconscious, just like that? I can't see myself doing such a thing."

"It came as a shock. You saw with your own eyes. He just needs to sort things out."

"I hope you're right!"

Outside, the sun was brilliant against a cloudless sky. McCalley turned down the offer of a lift and decided to walk back to his hotel. It was a long walk, but it would serve as a good excuse for the daily exercise he had been neglecting. The long trek was made easier by the promise he'd made himself, to have lunch at the McDonald's two blocks down from his hotel.

Later, he took a short nap. The phone woke him. It was just after two. He recognized Kenney's voice. "What's up, Bill?"

"Something interesting about that company of Frank's, the one he was on the Board of." McCalley swung his legs around to the side of the bed. "The fellow who recommended him for the Board and who fed him information, one of the names Benson gave you? turns out to be from New York. Joined the company less than two years ago."

"Had he met Frank in New York?"

"I don't think so. I asked Flora how well they knew him. She'd seen him only once, when he stopped by to pick up Frank for some meeting. But Frank talked about him all the time, Flora said."

"Did he know about Frank's gambling?"

"She was certain he didn't, at least Frank never mentioned anything. He was the only really close friend Frank had up there, Flora told me."

Flora had told them a lot, mused McCalley grimly. Most of their information had come from her, that single source, the bereaved and embittered widow. Once again, the Inspector wondered how much trust they should place in that information. It had proved useful so far—well, nothing had been actually *proved*, but indications were strong that a pattern was emerging and that Flora's information had given them the direction they needed.

McCalley had made some notes while Kenney relayed this information, but as far as he could tell, the news didn't add much to the intricate puzzle Frank Hastings had left them. It confirmed the presence of a man who, for whatever reason, had favored Frank Hastings or, rather, James Chadwick, and taken him into his confidence. Where all that would lead, McCalley could not tell. They were pursuing it, of course; but, at the moment, other matters pressed. He told Kenney what had happened and what he and Markarian hoped to do in the next several hours, then asked:

"Were you able to get into Frank's computer again?"

"Nothing there, Sir. I've gone through most of his papers, too, but if there was anything compromising, he must have gotten rid of it. Not many letters. Memos for the most part, reminders, notes, that sort of thing."

"What about e-mail?"

"I've pulled out everything, I can send it to you if you like, but there's nothing relevant, as far as I can make out.

He had scarcely put the phone back in its cradle, when it rang again. Markarian seemed out of breath.

"You want to be here, Luke. Grab a cab and come right away." McCalley took down the address and left as quickly as he could.

Traffic was building up, although it was only two-thirty. The cab driver, a surly Mexican, kept muttering under his breath. He had not wanted to take a fare out to Queens, but McCalley had shown his badge and won out.

It was a world far removed from that part of Manhattan in which his hotel was located. Here there were cemeteries, warehouses, an area which looked like a miniature Hong Kong, with lots of oriental specialty shops, restaurants, discount novelty stores, and colorful banners everywhere advertising the different products or services. He learned, later, it was called Flushing, the old center of the county. As they drove deeper into Queens — the driver trying to beat every traffic light in his hurry to drop his fare and get back into Manhattan — they passed *bodegas*, car dealerships, Korean churches, karate schools, and pizza parlors. The buildings were all low, most of them old, the effect somewhat depressing.

They pulled up next to a fire hydrant in a side street off the main thoroughfare. The cabbie muttered something under his breath and crossed himself when he saw the police cars and ambulance that had effectively closed off the street. His eagerness to get away was palpable.

Several police officers were holding back a small crowd gathered in front of what looked like an empty store. The yellow strips had been set up.

McCalley spotted Markarian and started to move toward him. Markarian saw him and came forward.

"Wait till you see what we've got," he whispered, as they elbowed their way inside. Two officers in uniform stood by the entrance. They nodded to Markarian, who had apparently already checked in with them. A few wooden tables and chairs were pushed against the walls, where a number of men were seated; others stood, whispering to one another. They turned curious eyes on the two new arrivals, as they moved through the front room, into the back.

A short corridor opened at the far end into a more spacious area. Facing the door was a desk with an elaborate computer station resting on it and next to it were two phones. About a dozen chairs were lined up against two of the dull ochre-colored walls. A large print of an Italian landscape did nothing to liven up one of the walls. In a plastic box frame on the opposite side of the room hung a large photograph of a smiling Monsignor in his formal robes, his arm around another man in shirtsleeves. Around that, in smaller similar frames arranged in a poor attempt at symmetry were several other photographs of what appeared to be local dignitaries accepting or giving out awards.

Here too the chairs were occupied. The men who sat on them wore jeans, T-shirts, or work outfits. Two, dressed in blue overalls, had their names and the garage where they worked embroidered just under the collar. Behind the desk a young woman was sobbing, her mascara running down her cheeks. She kept dabbing her eyes with a stained wad of tissue.

Markarian went up to her. "Gina, this is Inspector McCalley. He's here from Canada. He's working with me and the Lieutenant on this." The woman nodded. "Can I get you some fresh coffee?"

"No, I can't swallow anything."

Markarian gave her a pat on the shoulder then led the way past her, into the back room, Joe Sarace's office. This one was almost elegant by contrast with the rest of what McCalley had seen. The walls were wood-paneled. On three of them, tastefully framed and placed in sequence were hunting prints. A large signed photograph of Marilyn Monroe claimed the far wall, opposite the parquet table that served as a desk. In a corner was a medium-sized refrigerator, its door the same wood as the walls. It was flanked by two filing cabinets, these too in the same walnut as the paneling. A cheap orange plastic chair across from the desk spoiled the overall effect. The room, like all the others they'd come through, had no windows.

A trace of stale cigarette smoke lingered, in spite of the cool air coming up from the baseboard vents.

The body lay a few feet from the edge of the desk.

The medical examiner had arrived and followed them into the room.

"You're here already. Good," he was saying over his shoulder to the burly Lieutenant behind him. Markarian introduced Dr. Mackey, then greeted the other man and introduced him to McCalley as the officer in charge, Lieutenant Sean Gallagher. The two men shook hands.

A CSI unit with boxes, cameras, and other equipment followed them in, carefully avoiding the area around the body, and placed themselves to one side, to make room for Dr. Markey. The ambulance attendants remained outside the door.

"Left word to let you through, if you got here first," Gallagher told Markarian.

"I appreciate it, Sean."

The Lieutenant turned to McCalley. "Ed tells me you're looking into Sarace's operation."

McCalley chose his words carefully. "Not exactly. We're looking for information about loans Sarace made to someone whose death we're investigating."

"All the way from Canada, huh?" Markarian obviously had filled him in.

"The person we're interested in, Frank Hastings, lived in New York before relocating in Canada."

The Lieutenant nodded, his eyes fixed on Dr. Markey, who had put on plastic gloves and waited patiently for the photographer to finish taking pictures of the body. As though biding time, Markey asked no one in particular:

"The body hasn't been touched, I hope!"

They all knew what the answer would be, but it was the Lieutenant who answered:

"After CSI, Miami, and all those other shows on TV? C'mon, Doc, by this time, even kids know better!"

There were titters all around. The Medical Examiner smiled.

The photographer moved away, and suddenly Dr. Mackey was all action. He squatted down beside the body.

They all watched in silence as he conducted his examination. It didn't take long. When he stood up and took off his gloves, Gallagher nodded to someone across the room, and the team began their work of dusting for fingerprints and looking for evidence.

"So, what have we got, Doc?"

"Offhand, I'd say cardiac arrest."

"Cardiac arrest?" Gallagher made a dramatic show of opening his mouth in disbelief, as he turned this way and that, registering his reaction.

"Mobsters sometimes do die from natural causes," was Mackey's dry reply. "In any case, we won't know for certain until after the autopsy. How old was he?"

Gallagher looked around for an answer. He was ready to ask Gina when he spotted a big man in the doorway. "Ah, there's Bonz! He can tell us. Bonz found the body when he came in at twelve-thirty."

Markarian raised his eyebrows and glanced at Gallagher. The call to 911 had come in at two. He could see the time gap had not escaped the Lieutenant. What had Bonz been doing for an hour and a half in this room, with his boss dead on the floor?

The man addressed did not move where he stood, his arms folded over his thick chest. He was dressed in brown slacks, a brown patterned jacket that stretched tight over his shoulders and chest, and a brown shirt with a colorful patterned tie, mostly coral, yellows, and greens.

Everyone knew he was Sarace's bodyguard and trusted aide. They also knew they should steer clear of him, if possible.

"How old was he, Bonz?" Gallagher asked again.

"Forty-three," replied the big man, his lips barely moving.

"Young for a heart attack," said Dr. Mackey, "but it does happen...."

Gallagher asked: "When can you get back to me with the official results, Doc?"

"Sometime tomorrow, if nothing else preempts."

"Can you tell me roughly the time of death?"

"Unofficially? Sometime last night, probably between nine and midnight," said Mackey, as he made for the door. Gallagher frowned as he watched him leave. The ambulance attendants came in. Bonz unexpectedly moved forward and stood beside them as they zipped up the body bag.

"I'm going with them," he told Gallagher, in his low, thick voice.

Gallagher moved quickly to stand in front of him. "You can't, Bonz. We have to talk to you." For a moment, no one was sure if the big man was about to knock him down or move aside. After a brief stand-off, Gallagher turned away and they all watched as Bonz shuffled back to let the ambulance attendants through.

Markarian approached Gallagher. "Mind if we sit in on the questioning?" It was a formality; the ground had been cleared earlier. Still, protocol was important.

"No problem," said the other. leading the way into the reception room, where Gina still sat, glassy-eyed, stooped low where she sat.

Gallagher gestured for some chairs to be pulled in close to the desk. "I want everyone to wait outside in the front room, until they're called. Don't go anywhere, or you're in trouble," he added. The men sitting along the wall filed out. Only Gina was left.

Gallagher pulled up a chair close to the desk.

249

Markarian and McCalley sat to one side, behind him. Two officers stood by the closed door.

"I'm going to ask you some questions, Gina. Answer them as best you can. All right?"

All heads turned as Bonz came out of the room they had just left and walked slowly up to Gallagher. The Lieutenant seemed to have forgotten all about him.

"You wan' I should wait?"

"Yeah. We'll take you next, right after Gina." The man's face registered nothing. He turned, without answering, and shuffled out of the room. One of the officers shut the door behind him.

Gallagher turned back to Gina with a small smile. "You'll be out of here in no time," he said, as he took a small recording machine from his pocket and pressed the "On" button. "Just tell me exactly what happened, everything you did from the moment you came in."

CHAPTER FIFTEEN

Gina had arrived at the usual time, around nine-thirty. She had put on the large electric coffee urn, always the first thing she did, when she came in. It held forty cups which lasted through the morning. In the afternoon she made a second urn. There was coffee all day for anyone who wanted it. "Joe was good that way. Had a heart of gold."

After that, she laid out all the necessaries — stirrers, real and fake sugars, milk and the assorted doughnuts she picked up at Sergio's down the street, every morning, on her way in. Joe had asked her, when she first started working for him, if she would mind doing that. The money came from petty cash.

Gallagher waited while Gina dabbed her eyes with a fresh wad of tissue and blew her nose.

Oh, yes. Quite a few people were already waiting outside when she got there. Others continued to come in throughout the morning. By noon, both rooms were full. When Joe still hadn't arrived, some of the petitioners left. No, there was nothing unusual about that. People came in and waited their turn. That was the way it was done. If they had another appointment, they left and came back later, or returned on another day.

No, she hadn't gone into Joe's office, never did, she said, in answer to Gallagher's next question. Joe was very firm about that. He got her on the intercom, when he needed her; more often, he would come out to her desk with papers to type, or instructions. If he had ordered food, he would take the delivery from Gina, right there, in the doorway. No one went into the office, except Bonz — and, of course, whoever had come to see him. It was the first rule. The office was off limits.

"When did you learn something had happened?"

Gina dabbed her eyes again. "After Bonz got here."

"Tell me exactly what happened."

"Bonz came in about twelve-thirty. I remember thinking that Joe might be ordering lunch soon."

"You're sure about the time?"

"Yes, because I'd glanced at my watch. I hadn't realized how fast the morning had gone."

"People had been waiting all that while?"

"Some had left, like I told you."

"Do you know these people?"

She pulled out a large pad. "Sure, you get to know a lot of them." She held out a large yellow pad. The date was written at the top and underneath it were names and addresses. "They have to sign in. If they've gotten in to see Joe, I put a red check next to the name. If they haven't seen Joe, I check them out in pencil. The next morning, I type up the list and leave it for Joe."

Gallagher glanced through the three sheets of legal pad paper. "Quite a few left before noon —" He handed back the pad. "I'll need a copy. In fact, get me the lists for this whole week."

"I don't know about the rest of the week. Joe keeps them locked in his files. I can't get into those."

"Maybe Bonz can get them for us." He jotted down a reminder.

"What happened after Bonz came in?"

"He used the remote and went into Joe's office. I thought everything was all right, because he never came out until close to two. He said Joe was sick and to call an ambulance. That's when I put in the call to 911. They came pretty fast, but I was surprised to see all those police cars pull up in front at the same time!"

Gallagher asked a few more questions, then sent Gina home. He called in his aide, a Sergeant Finney, who had been told to take statements from people in the area — shopkeepers, "regulars," for starters, anyone who was around the previous night — and ask what, if anything, they had seen or heard. He rifled through the papers Finney handed him.

Nothing extraordinary so far, Gallagher told his colleagues, handing the sheets back to his aide. Most of the shops along the street had closed long before eight. During the day, everyone had been busy. Of course, there had been plenty of traffic in and out of Joe's place, but that was routine. Everybody was used it to it by now, although there were often complaints, still, about the line spilling outside, obstructing sidewalks and blocking doorways nearby. Bad for business.

By nine, the night before — Finney had learned — the place was dark, no one was around, . . . except, of course, Joe was still around, alone or with someone. . . . Or had he left and returned later, without being seen?

Gallagher excused himself and went out with Finney to make sure the area had been cordoned off properly. On his way back in, he beckoned to Bonz, waiting in the next room. The big man followed him into the reception room. This time Gallagher led the way into the inner office and seated himself behind Joe's desk. He motioned Bonz to the plastic chair opposite. Markarian and McCalley followed inside and stood to one side, near the door.

"You know the procedure Bonz," said Gallagher. "We have to tape the interview, so that we don't miss anything." He pressed the "On" button. "Tell me what happened, from the time you got in. Had you talked to Joe since yesterday? Did he ask you to come in at twelve-thirty today?"

Bonz stared at him. "No."

"Was that your usual time?"

"Sor' of. If Joe wan' me before, I come before."

"So you came in around twelve-thirty. Did Joe

usually arrive at that time?"

"No."

"But people were already waiting."

"Thass how it goes. They wanna see Joe, they gotta wait."

"Is that the normal routine?"

"Yeah."

"And twelve-thirty is usually when you get in?"

"Like I said, depends."

"What happened when you got in at twelve-thirty?"

"I wen' inside."

"Was the door locked?" The man nodded by way of response. "You'll have to speak up, Bonz," said Gallagher, pointing to the tape recorder.

"Yeah."

"You have a key?"

"Remote." He took it out of his pocket. Gallagher picked it up, examined it, and placed it on desk.

"Who else has one, knows the code?"

"Just me and Joe."

"So you punched the code and went in."

"Yeah."

"Then what?"

"I found Joe lying there, like you saw."

"Did you touch him or anything near him, anything on the desk?"

"I'm not stupid."

"What did you do then?"

There was a pause. Bonz uncrossed his arms and carefully examined his nails, then rubbed them against his jacket. "Nothin.' I was upset."

"I can understand that. You and Joe have been together for a long time, since your mother died, Gina told me."

"Yeah."

"What did you do then?"

"Tol' Gina to call 911."

Gallagher leaned forward casually, as though checking the tape recorder. Bonz watched through eyes that were sunk deep, hardly visible in his mottled face.

"What time was that, Bonz?"

The man shrugged and grimaced, as though trying to remember. "Can't remember the exact time."

"The call was taken at one fifty-seven, ninety minutes after you found Joe lying there. Why didn't you call 911 right away? You might have saved his life. What did you do in that room for an hour and a half?"

"Nothin'."

"Did you sit at the desk? Check his calendar? Call someone? His family, maybe?"

"He got no family."

"We'll be checking the phone calls, Bonz."

"Made no calls."

"So, what *did* you do?"

"Nothin'. Sat here until I felt better."

"Behind the desk?"

"I nevva once sat in Joe's chair," he said, as though he'd been insulted. "I sat right here, where I'm sittin' now."

"All that time you just sat there?"

"Yeah."

"You're sure you didn't touch him?"

The man shook his head; then, remembering the tape recorder, he leaned into the desk and spoke into it spacing his words with exaggerated care: "Like I said, I touch nothin'." His half-closed, heavy-lidded sunken eyes remained fixed on Gallagher's face.

"How did you know he was dead?"

"No pulse."

Gallagher was certain that the man was keeping back a great deal. He decided to try a new approach.

"Was Joe expecting a visitor last night?"
"Know nothin' 'bout that."
"When did you leave?"
"Round seven."
"Joe was still here?"
"Yeah."
"Don't you drive him home?"
"Said dinn' need me."
"Did he say someone else would be driving him home?"
"No. I figure he'd call the car service."
"Does he do that often?"
"Sometimes."
"Were you surprised?"
"'Bout what?"
"That he didn't go right home last night."
"Nah."
"So, you didn't drive him home. Did he eat out?"
"How should I know!"
"Bonz," said Gallagher, pushing a pad toward him. "What I need from you is names, people who did business with Joe, friends, enemies, as many as you can give me. I know; I can get some from Gina, but not all."

The big man shifted in his seat. "Doc said it was a heart attack."
"We won't be sure until the autopsy."
"Sumbody killed him?"
"I never said that. But Joe was an important man. We need to know if someone maybe quarreled with him, threatened him. We need to cover all the bases."

Bonz seemed to be ponder Gallagher's words. A troubled look transformed his face into that of a wizened old man's.
"If sumbody did him in —"
"I never said that," Gallagher repeated, sharply this time. Bonz clenched and unclenched his enormous

hands. It was the first time McCalley had noticed how large they were. "Don't read more into what I say —"

"You said —"

"I know what I said. . . . Answer me this: was there anything that happened recently, that bothered Joe? Anything he said to you about trouble brewing?"

"No. Nothin' like that."

"Did anyone ever barge in on him and threaten him?"

The man across from him thrust his head forward and stretched his lips into what was meant to be a threatening smile, as he twirled his thumbs. "No one's tried it. Not wi' me around!"

"Anyone quarrel with him recently?"

"No way."

Gallagher stood up. "We'll need to get into the safe and those files," he said pointing.

"Can't do."

"You don't have the combination?"

"There's nothin' in there for you."

"I'll be the judge."

"Joe le' nobody in there."

"It's routine," said Gallagher, hoping that would suffice.

"Don't belon' to you."

"We have to investigate."

"Why? Joe hadda heart attack."

"It could have been induced."

Bonz considered the words for a moment, then asked: "What's that mean?"

"It means, the attack could have been brought on. Maybe someone didn't want to play by his rules."

"Brought on, how?"

"There are lots of ways."

"Nobody was with'im!"

"That's what you said, that nobody was here with

257

Joe, when you left last night. Or maybe Joe left and came back later with someone? *You* didn't come back, right?" Gallagher watched the other's expression as he spoke.

Bonz shook his head. When he grasped the full import of what Gallagher had said, he got up and leaned into the desk, his face an ugly mask. "Nowway you gonna pin it on me. Joe was like a brother. 'Sides, I got an alibi." Gallagher held back a sigh. "I was atta cock fight, then had a date. Didn' get home until after two."

Gallagher was sure it would check out. "Let's take a look inside the safe, Bonz," he went on easily. Bonz quickly came around to stand in front of him, effectively blocking access.

"You got no bizness in there."

"So, we wait around two or three hours for a search warrant?"

Bonz appeared to be weighing the alternatives, but Gallagher knew it was all show. They were both stalling. The safe, and no doubt the files too, had probably been cleared of anything that might arouse suspicion. Besides, Bonz knew perfectly well that Gallagher wouldn't wait around for search warrants so late in the day. He's be ready with them in the morning.

A cunning smile broke through the scarred flesh. It lasted only seconds. Gallagher moved away with a gesture of dismissal. He wondered briefly where Bonz had stowed away what he must have taken out in the hour and a half before he called 911. To all appearances, and Gina vouched for it, he hadn't left Joe's office, once he was inside. Gallagher was certain he had spent the time hiding what might turn out to be incriminating documents. But how? Well, he'd tear up the whole floor, if he had to. . . .

Gesturing to one of the officers standing in the doorway, the Lieutenant said: "Ted, I want nothing touched in here. No one goes in or out until we've had a chance to look through everything. Then, if we have to, we'll rip up the floor."

"You won' find nothin'," said Bonz, smugly.

"Somewhere else, maybe?" He waved him off, impatiently. "You can go for now. But I want you back here at nine tomorrow."

They watched him saunter off, his thick legs far apart, his arms loose at his sides.

In the reception room, Gallagher reminded the officer on duty: "No one in or out, Ted."

The three men walked back up the corridor, through the front room, out into the street.

"You guys think there's more to it?" Gallagher asked, as they stood by the curb.

"I know it sounds crazy, Sean," said Markarian, "but so far we've had nothing but coincidences and accidents in this case, nothing blatanly suspicious. . . . This one seems to be a heart attack — and it may be just that. But the Inspector can tell you, Sarace is definitely connected with the hit-and-run victim in Ottawa. There are other ties that suggest there's more than meets the eye. But no evidence. Zilch!"

"Well, if you think it will help any, come back tomorrow, when we go into the files."

"What time?"

"Nine."

McCalley nodded. Markarian said: "We'll be here."

It was close to six, when the two men started back toward Manhattan. They decided it was not too late to stop by the hospital.

They found Katie alone, propped up against the headboard, her eyes closed. Her hair had been washed and her color was much better than it had been earlier in the day. She had put on some lipstick.

"You look much better!" said Markarian, as they

walked in. Katie glared at him.

"What did you say to my husband?" Her voice was still weak. McCalley realized with a pang that she had probably thought of nothing else, since she regained consciousness.

"Why?"

"He's disappeared!"

"He needed a break. Slept right here, beside you, all the time you were unconscious." He motioned to the cot, nearby."

"The nurse said he was here, talked with both of you, then took off!"

Markarian held his hands wide. "We don't know where he went, Katie."

"You're responsible," she said, with undisguised hostility. "You told him everything, didn't you?"

It was McCalley who answered. "We told him what he should have known long ago, Katie. You can't keep it from him any longer. We have to question you again, because we know you haven't told us the truth. And it's our job to find out everything you know. Especially now."

They watched her crumble where she lay, her face contorted by grief. "I haven't lied," she whispered.

"But, you haven't told us everything," McCalley replied sharply, "and it's time you did." She was crying softly now, the tears streaming down her face. Markarian had remained standing by the door. He glanced up and down the corridor, as though expecting a contingent of orderlies to drag them away. McCalley pulled up a chair close to the bed.

"We're facing a very serious situation, Katie, and to be honest with you, I don't know where it's leading. You're part of it, though. We want to protect you but can't do that without knowing more."

She had turned away when he started to speak.

McCalley waited for her to turn back again. After a while, she did, her eyes pleading.

"You keep saying I know more than I told you. I don't!"

"You may not realize it, but you do. And, you may be in danger."

The startled look she gave him told McCalley he was definitely on the right track. "What are you holding back?" Her silence prompted him. He went on: "Something happened in St. Tropez. What was it? What did your cousin tell you that suddenly made you so unhappy?"

Her words were barely audible. "I can't tell you."

"We'll protect you, whatever it is, Katie. But you've got to tell us. The man who'd been lending Frank money was found dead today."

Katie's eyes registered confusion, fear. McCalley took her hand in his. "Katie, whatever it is, you must tell us. We'll get to the person behind all this." She had closed her eyes again but did not take her hand away. "We had to tell Francis what we knew, Katie. I hoped I wouldn't have to. I knew how you felt about telling him."

The mention of her husband brought on a troubled look again. "He's not home. They've been calling him all day. He's not at work either."

"I think he needs time to take it all in. But he really loves you Katie. He'll be back, you'll see." He wished he could be sure of what he said.

The nurse came into the room. She seemed almost relieved to see them, this time. She smiled when she saw McCalley holding Katie's hand. "Ah, you're back. It's rather late, you know," she added, but made no effort to send them away.

"It's been a busy day," said McCalley. "Could we have a few more minutes? It's important."

Nurse fluffed the pillows and took Katie's pulse.

"Just five minutes."

As she moved past him, the woman beckoned to Markarian, who joined her in the corridor. "She's been asking for her husband all day, Detective," she said in a whisper. We've been calling the apartment, his place of work, all the numbers Katie gave us. He's nowhere to be found!"

"Keep trying, Nurse. I think he needed some time to himself, that's all." She nodded as though she understood, but left frowning.

"Why were you so angry with your cousin?" McCalley was asking. "What did he do or say to you in St. Tropez, Katie, just before you left?"

She pulled her hand from his and turned away. The quick movement made her wince in pain. McCalley remembered the dislocated shoulder.

"We need to know, Katie. You and Francis may be in danger."

She turned back slowly, but her face was suddenly animated.

"Francis doesn't know what I know!!" The words gushed out. McCalley gave no sign of what she had indirectly admitted. He pressed on:

"Others may think he does, may think that you told him what you know."

"But who would want to hurt me? I've said nothing!"

"Good. But now you have to tell *us* what you know. We can't protect you until you do."

She tried to sit up in bed, but the strain was too much. "I can't," she repeated miserably.

"I think you're protecting the wrong man, Katie. Think of Francis. The two of you. Doesn't he mean more to you than your cousin?"

Anger and despair contorted her pretty face. She began to cry, dry sobs that shook her body without a sound. McCalley waited.

"It's awful," she said at last.

"And you've been very brave, living with it, trying to spare Francis."

"If anything happens to Francis because of me —"

"Nothing will, Katie. I give you my word."

Again, he hoped he could live up to his promise.

Katie's face registered uncertainty, pain, grief, a mixture of emotions that made McCalley realize how difficult it had been for her. The secret she nurtured had taken a heavy toll.

After a while, she grew calm again. She brought her head to rest against the pillows behind her, closed her eyes, and told him everything.

The next two hours were spent on the phone with Interpol and the Italian police. It was past midnight when Markarian drew up to McCalley's hotel to discharge his passenger.

"We'll need to work on Bonz in the morning," said McCalley as he stepped out of the car. He shut the door and leaned into the open window. "Get whatever he stashed away."

"You think he hid files somewhere?"

"He had plenty of time. What else could he have been doing?"

"But he never left the room. Do you think Gina was lying?"

"No, but there has to be an answer, Ed."

The next day would prove him right.

When Markarian arrived with the Inspector the next morning, Gina had not come in yet. The two uniformed officers on duty in the reception room opened the door to Joe's office and let them in. Gallagher was at the files, looking through a folder, as the door closed softly behind them.

Bonz was already there, a massive column resting against the wall, arms crossed across his thick chest. His gaze was fixed on Gallagher's back.

"Nothing but old stuff," said Gallagher, without looking up. Four, five, six, seven years back." He closed the third drawer and bent down to open the last one. "Same thing." He shut the drawer with a bang.

"Mind if we take a look?" asked McCalley.

Gallagher seemed only too happy to step aside. "Be my guest. . . .Our friend here thinks he can get away with hiding evidence."

"Joe hadda heart attack," was the answer.

Gallagher turned back to McCalley, who had already opened the first drawer and was going through folders, pulling out a sheet of paper here and there, then sliding it back in place. The other two men watched in silence for a while.

"What do you think you'll find?"

"Nothing probably."

"I've got men looking through Joe's apartment. His too," he said gesturing toward Bonz, who had not moved all the while. "Thinks he can play games with us, don't you Bonz. . . . Got it all worked out, right? Ambrosini's lawyers will get you off? Well, let me tell you something, wise guy," the Lieutenant went on, moving slowly toward him and coming to a stop inches from the big man. "We'll get you on obstruction of justice, for starters, and then you'll really know what it's all about!" He lowered his voice and narrowed his eyes. "When you have to fight off your big roommates every day for the duration. Because, . . .are you listening? I'm going to put you away for a long time, buddy boy!" McCalley could hear the frustration in his voice. Bonz kept his eyes fixed in front of him.

The tension that had built up was relieved as

McCalley began taking out folders from one of the two filing cabinets. After a little while, there was small pile on the desk.

"Let's start with these," he said, sitting in Joe's chair. He took the top folder and opened it in front of him.

"What are we looking for?" asked Markarian, lowering himself into the chair opposite.

"I wish I knew," replied the other, handing him the next folder on the pile. "Anything that rings a bell."

Gallagher started for the door. "Take your time. Have Finney page me, if you need me. I'll be back later."

The Lieutenant had been right, McCalley decided after he'd gone trough several folders. Nothing here but old receipts for routine services, bills, memos, the kind of records you would find in an ordinary business operation. He glanced up at where Bonz stood, watching him.

"Why did Joe clutter the files with all this old stuff?"

"IRS," was the laconic reply.

Markarian looked up with raised eyebrows. "That far back?" Bonz shrugged. McCalley picked up the next folder. He stifled a groan. More of the same....

For the next hour, the two men worked silently. They had replaced the folders from the first cabinet and had started on the second, when McCalley picked up a sheet of paper and sat back in his chair to examine it carefully.

Markarian look up. "Find something?"

McCalley leaned across the desk to hand him the paper.

It was dated six years back. Joe had entered simply: "MA called about B. Said to go ahead."

"Could be Mario Ambrosini," Markarian noted, without looking up. "Or Michale Angrisani, his top

265

consigliere." Ambrosini was the head of one of the leading "families" in organized crime. Their influence extended far beyond New York, into Canada, Europe and South America. McCalley was familiar with the name and had hazarded the same guess. But what did it have to do with Frank Hastings? What had triggered his reaction?

Markarian was thinking the same thing. Out loud, he asked: "What do you make of it?"

McCalley didn't answer. Instead, he held up his hand and went back to the pile already discarded. He pulled out an earlier file, found what he was looking for, as though something had registered the first time and was now embedded in his memory.

This too was a short memo. Scrawled on the half sheet was: "MA, 5 PM." Underneath the first line, he read: "Call B at home (ST) at two PM," and in parentheses "(eight PM his time?) for a conference call in the usual place." There was an asterisk next to the hours noted, and they were circled in red. This memo carried no date, but the year on the folder tab was the same year as the other.

McCalley took out his pad and made some notes before putting the two memos to one side and continuing his search.

Gina had come in. One of the officers opened the door to ask if they wanted her to order lunch.

"Not right now," said Markarian, waving him off.

After a while, McCalley held out a third sheet. "Take a look at this."

Markarian read it and placed it with the other two. "Who's this 'B'?"

"I'm not sure, but the difference in time suggests someone in France or maybe Holland."

"Sounds like an important meeting . . ."

"Yes."

From the last folder McMcCalley extracted a fourth sheet and handed it to Markarian.

It was written in the same scrawl as the others. This one said: "MA called to say merger with D looks like a good bet. Call B that we're interested." This too had no date, but the tab indicated the contents of the folder went back six years, like the others.

"Looks like a business deal," said Markarian, studying the memos. "Ambrosini putting up money for a merger, a loan to this "B," whoever he is."

Instead of answering, McCalley looked at his watch. It was near one o'clock. He pulled out his cell phone and punched in a long series of numbers.

Markarian saw his face light up when someone answered at the other end. "That you, Josie? It's Luke McCalley. . . . No, I'm not in Paris, I'm calling from New York. Wasn't sure I'd get you. . . . Well, I'm glad I caught you before you went out. . . ." He laughed heartily at something Josie said. "Listen, you may be able to help me. . . .Thanks, I appreciate it. . . . You remember the magazines you saved for Katie? About her cousin and his wife Emma?" He nodded as Josie said something. . . ." He nodded again, then asked: "Do you still have them?. . . . Good! What I need is information that's probably in one of those stories, very likely the one about Emma's death. Do you still have that?. . . ." He nodded, smiling, as he listened. Turning to Markarian, he whispered: "I think we're in luck."

He turned back to the phone. "Yes, I'm right here. . . . Find it? Here's what I need to know."

Bonz had moved slightly away from the wall, still locked in his familiar pose. McCalley was talking into the phone again.

"What does it say about Emma? Her background, that sort of thing." He listened in silence, growing more animated as he made notes on his pad. "Read that part again, would you?. . . Was that her maiden name, Danziger?" Markarian watched as McCalley wrote it out in capital letters, while Josie kept talking. "A and E Danziger? Is that what it says? 'Family-owned drug company'? . . . . No wait, let's stay with this for a moment. What else does it say about the company?" He listened, taking notes all the while. "When did that happen?" He nodded as though by way of confirmation. "Was she the one who signed the papers?. . . .So that's how they met. . . . Does it say that?" He laughed, enjoying the joke, whatever it was. "*Now* go back. Tell me what it says about his father's business. . . . " He had started to write again, but something Josie said drew him up in his chair.

"Spell that will you?" He read out the letters as he printed them on his pad. "B I S O N N O. . . . His father was Italian?. . . . When was the name changed?. . . ."

The room was very quiet. McCalley was too engrossed in what Josie was telling him to notice how Bonz had moved away from the wall and had come forward, to stand by Markarian's chair. Markarian, trying to follow the phone conversation, was not aware of it, either.

McCalley was saying: "Do me a big favor, Josie. Put those magazines in a safe place for me. . . . I may come over to pick them up myself!. . . . Oh, you can bet on it, if I come. . . . . She's well, Josie. I'll tell her I talked with you. You've been a big help."

McCalley put away his phone and went to stand near the big man. "It's all coming together, Bonz. We may have found what we need to get to the bottom of this case. . . . Joe is dead, Bonz. There's nothing you can do for him now. But we still need evidence and you can help us get it. If someone was with Joe and hurt him last night, brought on the attack in some way, we want to punish him as much as you do."

The sunken eyes told him nothing. McCalley went to sit behind the desk again. From there, he went on:

"What the autopsy says is not really important any more. It will probably say it was a heart attack. And we may never prove it wasn't. But you can help us find the truth, Bonz. Find out what really happened to Joe."

"What's in those folders?" the big man asked, by way of reply.

"Enough to make a connection with someone who has caused a lot of trouble. Joe worked for the Ambrosini, but Mr. Ambrosini might take orders from somebody else, at least some of the time. Maybe it was that other person who wanted Joe dead."

There was no reaction. McCalley went on. "Maybe Joe knew too much. Maybe someone at the top couldn't risk the possibility of Joe talking."

Trying to take in what he had just heard, Markarian wondered how much of it was true. Did McCalley really think Katie's cousin was behind Joe's death and Frank's? Maybe his wife's death, as well? His attention was pulled back as McCalley went on:

"We need to see the more recent files, Bonz, but I'm pretty sure I'm right. If we're on track, we've got to find more evidence, Bonz. Those files you hid — you did hide them, didn't you? — they can tell us a lot. Where are they, Bonz? The folders you took away?"

For what seemed an eternity, the two men stared at one another. Neither one moved. Markarian was about to speak when Bonz turned away abruptly and walked toward the wall across from the door. For a moment, Markarian thought he was going to smash through it. He watched as Bonz took out a remote and punched in some numbers. A panel opened silently to reveal a short dark corridor, at the end of which was a sunlit yard, enclosed within a high cement wall. The two men followed Bonz into the yard, where a Camry and an Explorer were parked.

They watched as he fumbled inside the van and took out the back seats. Folders were stacked in a shallow space that had been carved out of the chassis from behind the front seats to the far back. McCalley wondered how often incriminating material had been hidden there, before the arrival of the police.

Without a word, Bonz took out several folders at a time and placed them into the outstretched arms of each of the two men, who took the load inside and came back for more. They made three trips in all. Bonz took the last batch in himself, then went back to replace the seats in the van. In the room again, he was about to close the panel in the wall, when McCalley stopped him.

"Leave it open. The Lieutenant will have to take a look out there."

"What about the safe?" asked Markarian.

"It can wait. We've got enough to keep us busy for a while," answered the other. Then, turning to Bonz: "Ask Finney to page the Lieutenant. Tell him to come here as soon as possible."

Bonz nodded and went out. He had joined their ranks, eager to help find whoever was responsible for the death of his only real friend. For although Gallagher had warned caution, Bonz was now certain, as he knew the Inspector and Markarian were but couldn't prove, that Joe had not suffered a natural heart attack, late at night, alone in his office. The attack had been — he struggled for the word they had used: — "indoosed"? yes, that was it! — had been indoosed by whoever had come to see Joe that night.

Someone out there wanted Joe dead.

CHAPTER SIXTEEN

The Italian police had nothing to add to what was already on record about Emma Danziger Benson's death. It had been ruled an accident; and without any hard evidence to the contrary, then or now, that ruling had to stand. The car had been turned in for scrap soon after the inquest. Emma's body too was not available: she had been cremated. Interpol was ready to cooperate, but nothing suspicious had turned up.

McCalley was not surprised. If someone had indeed had a hand in getting rid of Emma, that someone knew how to cover his tracks. The big question in the Inspector's mind was: how did Katie fit into the picture? Why had Charles Benson asked that incredible "favor" of her? It didn't make sense — unless her cousin had some other reason for wanting to make her his accomplice. If so, he may have been following her activities for some time. In the hospital, Katie had told the Inspector that her cousin knew she was in St. Tropez. Their meeting had not been accidental. He had sought her out.

To ask her to kill his wife? Hardly!

McCalley was certain there had to be another answer. He knew how to be patient, but how long would he have to wait before the pieces of this strange puzzle came together?

Emma Benson was dead. Frank Hastings and Joe Sarace had already been targeted and eliminated. Katie was still at risk. She could easily be attacked again (for reasons not altogether clear yet). Benson would have to be told that McCalley now knew everything that had transpired between him and Katie . . . and much else. Katie and others had signed depositions and were ready to testify at whatever trial resulted from this investigation.

If anything ever did come to trial! What they had found in the files gave the police a good excuse to pull in Benson's New York buddies for questioning, but that, as everyone knew, was hardly a threat. Rounding up the usual suspects meant nothing to a "family" like the Ambrosini, who employed a team of crackerjack lawyers, always on call. They would reduce to shreds the cryptic notes McCalley had found. No one seriously expected indictments to result from the police questioning.

Of course, they had Bonz. He had cooperated and would continue to do so. That meant that he too was now a target. And Francis Delancourt — if he ever turned up! — might also have to be protected if someone out there thought Katie had confided in him. McCalley shook his head in silent disapproval, thinking back to Delancourt's angry departure from the hospital, when he and Markarian told him the facts and tried to explain Katie's reluctance to involve him. That was two days ago. Katie was home, now, with a day nurse to help her get around. McCalley had suggested she remain in the hospital for a few more days, but she was adamant in her refusal. She had to be home for Francis, she explained, with an unshakeable determination that McCalley admired in principle and rejected in view of the risk involved. She had to be there for him when he came back, she had insisted. He could not change her mind and dreaded having to remind her of the danger she was courting, even with a nurse in the apartment, even with an officer patrolling the corridor.

With an effort, he had held back what he was about to say. In spite of her show of strength, Katie had been crippled emotionally by the hard realities she'd been forced to accept in the last several weeks. McCalley did not want to add to her fears. He wondered again if she would be able to cope if her husband did not come back but served her with divorce papers instead. The doctors said she was recovering nicely from her "mugging," but there were other, deeper wounds that would not heal for a long time, if ever. She needed her husband by her side to help her through this ordeal. . . .

McCalley sighed. He hoped, for Katie's sake, that Delancourt would come back, and soon.

He picked up the notes he had been reading and had laid aside. Surely, he'd missed something that would unlock at least the puzzle of Frank Hastings's death. Was it really murder, as Flora Chadwick kept insisting?

He read again the pertinent documents, the depositions of hotel and airline clerks; what Kenney had found, Flora's statements. Nothing jogged his attention into a new direction.

Once more he put aside the papers he had been examining, his thoughts again gravitating to Katie. The story of a job had been false; Katie had made it up on the spur of the moment, to give McCalley an answer he could accept. Monsieur had laughed when the Inspector had asked him about it. Amusing indeed to have a ten million pay-off referred to as a "job offer!"

At least they knew now why Katie had decided to go to Geneva, before returning to the States from her vacation in Europe. She was determined to fend off her cousin's largesse. She wanted no part of the one hundred thousand "no-strings-attached" gift he had placed in an account he'd opened in her name as a good will gesture. It was puzzling, all this attention, all this loving concern for a second cousin Benson had not seen since he'd dropped in at her sweet-sixteen birthday party.

He picked up the folder again and searched for the notes and copies of memos and letters he had made the day before, the originals now under lock and key in Lieutenant Gallagher's evidence room. McCalley was not sanguine about finding anything more in them. They contained nothing relating to Frank's new identity. And yet Benson had known all about Frank, McCalley was certain, even before he recognized his new Board member as Katie's husband. Had he traced back his movements, as McCalley had done? Did he know about the aborted flight plan? He knew about Frank's gambling debts — he'd let that slip in the interview with McCalley — and had actually paid them off, as McCalley had discovered (or concluded) from going through Joe's files.

The search of the folders Bonz had retrieved for them indicated that Benson (or the "B" referred to, he forced himself to concede) had been in touch with the Ambrosinis for years, long before Frank or Katie came into the picture. It also told them that Frank's contact in Ottawa had been sent from New York by the "family" at Benson's request, to keep an eye on Frank and to provide him with inside information about a merger that netted him half a million dollars, for starters. Was this meant to feed his gambling instinct in a new way? Why would Benson want to do that? Acting on insider information, as Frank had done, was potentially lucrative but risky. Frank knew he was doing something illegal. Was Benson triggering Frank's old addiction, forcing him to gamble in this new way, to run new risks, to place himself outside the law? For what reason? It seemed increasingly plausible that it was Benson who ordered Frank killed, but why?

Good God! He was doing precisely what he kept warning others *not* to do: speculating, theorizing, letting his imagination distract him from the facts.

McCalley closed his eyes and rested his head against the back of the chair, the folder open in his lap. Why would Benson want to compromise Frank? And, later, Katie? Stay with the facts, he reminded himself.

Fact: Frank had fallen into the trap — or whatever one preferred to call it — Katie had not.

Why had Benson taken all that trouble? Control?

Possibly; but not as an end in itself. Control for a reason. What reason? He put the question aside.

Fact: Benson was intimately involved with the most notorious and most influential of the current crime syndicates. Six years ago, the Ambrosini family had provided him with his first loan, a huge amount which enabled Benson to buy out A & E Danziger, a small family-owned pharmaceutical firm, located in Sweden.

Fact: The company he bought had been founded by Albert Danziger, whose daughter Emma eventually joined him in running it. She proved to be quite a good administrator. When her father decided, because of failing health, to retire, Emma talked him into selling instead. Danziger had agreed and turned everything over to her. It was Emma who negotiated and closed the deal that made A & E Danziger part of Benson's company.

In one clever blow, with money borrowed from Ambrosini, Benson had pumped new life into his father's failing business, which he had inherited. (*Fact:* the older man had changed his name to "Benson" when he set up his company, but Ambrosini must have known it had originally been "Bisonno.")

An unexpected bonus to the merger was Emma Danziger. Benson courted and married her in a matter of months. This merger cost him almost as much as the other — the price of a four carat diamond. (What went wrong there, McCalley refused to consider.)

Fact: Joe Sarace, the "family"'s "banker," had served as contact between Benson and Ambrosini. He had proved efficient in that role — the cryptic notes confirmed it — but perhaps for that very reason had to be terminated. For McCalley was certain that Sarace's death had come about because of information Joe had about Frank's death and much else. The question was: whose idea was it, Ambrosini's or Benson's? And which one had given the order?

Sarace had been in tight spots before but had always proved loyal. Like the other members of the "family," he had never been charged with anything, although the police had taken him in for questioning often enough. Ambrosini had nothing to complain about. Sarace had always come through for him. He had discharged his duties effectively and followed orders.

It *had* to be Benson's idea, getting rid of Sarace, McCalley reasoned. And much as he disliked entertaining assumptions, he couldn't help thinking that Joe's heart attack may well have been induced, just as Emma's death, like Frank's, may not have been an accident.

Back to facts!

Fact: They had found receipts, after the first initial loan, for several more large amounts from Benson to Ambrosini over the last five years. McCalley decided not to linger over the possibilities that came to mind, not right then. What mattered, what was significant, was that the relationship was an ongoing one.

The big question was: what kind of relationship had it become in recent years? And, more important, who had the last word? Was Benson paying Ambrosini on a continuing basis as a gesture of good will, for having helped him over the years, as a kind of continuing retainer perhaps? *Money could buy the devil himself.* The phrase inserted itself into his thoughts. Or, was money still changing hands for services rendered more recently?

Money was the key. It all hinged on money. *The Midas touch.* . . .

McCalley forced himself back to the facts.

Sarace's memos showed that Benson had paid all of Frank's outstanding debts — no doubt giving orders, at the same time, not to let the man off the hook. Sarace had managed that nicely, forcing Frank to kill a man to pay for debts he no longer owed. No doubt the hit would have taken place in any case, but it anchored Frank firmly in Ambrosini waters and in Benson's control.

It had to be Benson who gave Ambrosini orders to monitor Frank's activities, who paid handsomely to have Sarace watch him and keep him coming. Surely they knew about the Saturday outings with Masters, the rental unit where extra fuel, parachutes and other items had been stashed away. And if they knew that, it was easy enough, with their resources, to pick up the trail and track him down in Ottawa, where Benson had him recruited for one of his Boards.

McCalley couldn't stop himself from wondering how Benson — the superman, the control expert, the man with the Midas touch — had reacted to the discovery that Frank had managed an incredible feat, disappearing without a trace. Surely, he must have admired Frank's ingenuity, at least! Or did he resent the man's nerve, his Olympian disregard for others, the quick intelligence, the *sang froid* Frank displayed in doing what he did, on the spur of the moment, on nine-eleven? Did he see in Frank a competitor? Did he find it exciting to keep a man like Frank in sight, if for no other reason than to manipulate him, to program him for his perverse satisfaction?

Facts! Facts! he reminded himself.

Fact: Benson had told Katie about Frank — according to Katie, in order to free her from unnecessary and prolonged grieving.

Fact (?): Katie had confirmed his suspicion that it was her cousin who had sent her the clipping about Frank's death in Ottawa, the victim of a hit-and-run. Was it to free her from worry, so she could marry again without legal complications? Or was it a bribe?

Katie firmly believed her cousin responsible for Emma's death and, later, Frank's. As she had told McCalley, she felt her cousin had compromised her, trapped her by telling her about Frank's death. If it turned out to be murder, as Flora insisted, Katie could be accused of withholding information or charged as an accessory after the fact, especially in the light of the large sums her cousin had deposited in her name in Geneva.

Benson had thus effectively silenced Katie by the outrageous favor he'd asked in St. Tropez and, later, by sending her the clipping about Frank's death. When Emma, then Frank, were in fact killed, Katie was petrified. Even if she got up the nerve to go to the police with what she knew, what did it amount to? She had no proof. And how would she explain the money in Geneva? The account had been closed, but if her complaint proved correct, if there had been foul play and her suspicions surfaced, she could be putting herself in jeopardy as a suspect, a conspirator. At the very least, she could be charged for withholding evidence. Had Benson placed her in that terrible dilemma deliberately?

McCalley shook his head, rose, and went to the window. In spite of the heat, he raised it all the way for a few moments, looking down at the street below, at people hurrying home to dinner with family. He thought of his own wife and how much he missed her.

He closed the window, sat down again in the big chair and picked up the folder again. The case had turned into a labyrinth in which he had lost his way many times already. Again, he was drawn to Katie and the strategy Benson had used to bring her into his camp.

Katie's silence proved Benson had made his point. He had terrified Katie by what he had said and done. Ironically, she was safe so long as Emma's death remained an accident, so long as Frank's death was not conceived as murder. The dilemma must have worn down any resolve she may have had to offer what she knew to the police.

Nothing in Joe's files had produced a clue as to Benson's intentions. Unless Kenney came up with a name, a solid lead, Frank's death, like Emma's, would go down as an accident. And who could prove that Katie's "mugging" was anything more than just that?

He checked the time. A little after one; the morning had gone fast. He had promised to look in on Katie around two. Lunch would have to wait; he'd grab something before joining Markarian and Gallagher at the precinct, to talk with Bonz again. The big man was being held in protective custody as a potential material witness.

Bonz himself was not at all worried that the Ambrosinis might be after him. He had lost the only man who had ever befriended and protected him. What mattered now was avenging Joe. It was the only reason that had brought him around to cooperating with the police. When he learned that Joe's death may not have been a simple heart attack, he took it as fact and had given them everything they wanted, so they could nab who was responsible. As far as he was concerned, he owed nothing to the Ambrosini family. Joe worked for them, but Bonz worked for Joe.

Now that Joe was gone; Bonz refused to recognize the old chain of command. It meant nothing to him.

McCalley threw the folder on the table beside him, utterly frustrated by his inability to find anything significant that would move the case forward. He started to dress. As he was buttoning his shirt, the phone rang. It was Markarian.

Could McCalley come down to the precinct now, instead of later in the afternoon? McCalley agreed; he would reverse his plans and visit Katie later.

At the precinct, he was escorted to Markarian's cubicle and was told the Detective would be there in a few minutes. McCalley sat down to wait in one of the two worn wooden chairs across from the littered desk. Outside, he could hear the high-pitched voice of someone up front, complaining as he was being booked. A loud speaker full of static was paging someone called Garner.

Under the open window there was a burst of laughter that almost drowned Markarian's greeting as he entered the room and came around to his desk. Standing there, he pointed toward the doorway, with a dramatic flourish.

"Look who's back!"

McCalley rose and turned. A disheveled, unshaven young man, with deep circles under his eyes took a tentative step forward. McCalley scarcely recognized him.

"I wanted to apologize for my behavior the other day," said Francis Delancourt. "I think I was in shock."

McCalley's relief must have registered. Delancourt gave him a small tired smile. "I can't forgive myself for leaving Katie like that, Inspector. It was a terrible thing to do. I told Detective Markarian, and it's true, I spent the rest of that day walking around in a daze. I couldn't come to grips with what had happened. I thought . . ." he cleared his throat and went on, "I thought I could handle just about anything. But this, . . . this was . . . to think of Katie, my poor Katie, having to carry that enormous burden all alone!" His voice cracked and he turned away.

Markarian sat down and addressed McCalley. "I told him, it was perfectly natural to feel as he did. We knew he'd come around, eventually, right?"

"Of course," said McCalley.

Delancourt turned back to them. His eyes were clouded, but he had regained a measure of composure. Markarian gestured him to the empty chair across from his desk. McCalley resumed his seat next to it.

"My God, Inspector!" the young man exploded. "To drag Katie into such a mess! What kind of a man is that cousin of hers? Did he really have Frank killed a second time?"

McCalley couldn't resist a smile. "No one dies twice. And we don't know that he had Frank killed. We do know that Frank staged an elaborate scam and got away with it and that he was the victim of a hit-and-run car accident in Ottawa. Right now, we can't be sure of anything else. I take it, Detective Markarian explained it all?" When Delancourt nodded, McCaley went on to ask:

"Have you seen your wife yet, Mr. Delancourt?"

"No. I came here first. I wanted to talk with you, apologize for going off the deep end like that. I can't believe I —" His voice broke. He turned away for a moment, then continued: "I called the hospital. They told me Katie had been discharged."

McCalley nodded. "She's home, waiting for you."

He knew why the poor man was stalling. It was going to be hard having to face his wife and explain why he had gone off as he had, leaving her unconscious, alone, in the hospital. He had come to terms with himself, but could he be sure of Katie's welcome?

Watching the young man struggle with a host of emotions, McCalley hoped Katie would understand.

"I know I did a terrible thing, Inspector. I told Detective Markarian, too. I only wish I could go back and replay that whole scene. I wasn't thinking straight."

"Never mind all that. Katie is waiting for you at home. Isn't that what you want?"

"She has every reason to be mad."

"Not for long, you'll see."

"What will I say to her?"

"That you're sorry. I'm sure that will be enough."

"What if she throws me out?"

"I don't think it will come to that."

"How can you be sure?"

McCalley rose. "Why don't we find out? I was about to look in on her" — he glanced at his watch as he spoke. "Why don't you come along?"

Relief brought color into the young man's face, the hope that somehow McCalley would work a miracle for him.

Ah, the faith of the young!

McCalley glanced at his colleague, who gave him a surreptitious nod.

"Sorry I can't join you," said Markarian waving them off. "I've got a stack of paperwork to catch up on." Then as McCalley turned to leave: "I'll reschedule our appointment with Gallagher for around three thirty."

In his relief at seeing Delancourt back, McCalley had all but forgotten the meeting. He gave Markarian an appreciative nod.

It was three fifteen, when he returned. Markarian was still at his desk, sorting papers.

"You're early."

McCalley sat down with a small groan. "An hour was more than enough!" He went on to describe the homecoming, the recriminations, the tears, the grief, the relief, the loving embraces. . . . Markarian leaned back and crossed his hands behind his head.

"How does it feel to be a marriage counselor?"

"I'm drained." He shook his head. "I feel sorry for them, Ed. For Katie, especially. She's been through a lot. Much more than we ever had to cope with at their age!"

"Speak for yourself," said Markarian, shifting forward in his chair and crossing his hands on the desk. "I went around mooning for Sylvia Kabrinsky for two months. Never had the courage to ask her out. I was dead to the world. My mother thought I was sick. I guess I was." They both laughed.

"They're going to have a tough time," McCalley said. "She won't ever forgive herself for not trusting him to share her burden. And he will never forget that she kept things from him."

"They're in love. It will pass." McCalley threw him a skeptical look.

They walked the short distance to Gallagher's office. It was no bigger than Markarian's and just as cluttered. The Lieutenant was waiting for them. He had ordered coffee and doughnuts. McCalley made no effort to restrain himself. He'd had no time for lunch.

They pooled information. McCalley told them about the fruitless reexamination by the Italian police of the circumstances surrounding Emma Benson's death. No way — short of a confession — could they ever prove it was murder. Frank's death too would remain an "accident" unless more evidence turned up. Kenney was checking again Frank's colleagues and acquaintances in Ottawa, especially the man who had sponsored him for the Board. There was a slim chance something more might turn up there, but it was a long shot. They shouldn't hold their breath.

Gallagher told them the lawyers had come to whisk away the Ambrosinis — father and two sons — who had been brought in for questioning. A frustrating hour had produced nothing, and they were let go.

"The way I see it," was the Lieutenant's cheerless conclusion, "to prove that Frank's death or Sarace's was anything but what it appears to be is like defying gravity."

Markarian smiled at the analogy. He was about to comment, but thought better of it. Instead, he launched into his own dismal report. A second search of the files produced nothing more that could be of immediate interest to them.

"The only good news is that Delancourt is back home with Katie."

It was late afternoon when the meeting broke up. They had agreed that McCalley should fly to Paris that night or the next day, to confront Benson. This time he would be told what they had learned, what Katie had relayed to them, what Bonz had told them. McCalley would inform him that it was just a matter of time before they had solid facts on which they could build a case against him, that material witnesses were under police protection and that he would himself be under surveillance at all times.

"Of course, his friends must have gotten to him by now, must have brought him up to date . . ." was Markarian's dry comment.

"Still, he's arrogant enough to get over-confident, maybe let something slip," countered McCalley, with more conviction than he felt.

Gallagher rose and started for the door. "You guys are really convinced we've got three related murders and one attempted murder?"

"It does sound a bit crazy," Markarian conceded, "but Luke thinks so, and he's not given to speculation. Anyone who knows him will tell you what a stickler he is for facts and hard evidence!"

"It's a weird case, all right!" was the Lieutenant's reply, as he led the way to where Bonz was being held.

"It's more than speculation, Ed," McCalley picked up, wanting to set the record straight. "Flora Chadwick came to us with serious allegations which, given the unusual circumstances surrounding her husband's relocation to Ottawa, we felt had to be investigated."

"The way I see it," Gallagher said, "coming to it fresh, and not being as close as you guys have been to this whole business — and maybe that gives me a clearer view of things, so forgive me for being blunt, let me be the devil's advocate for a moment — as I see it, and I hate to say it, but you may never have a case. Whoever is responsible for Emma Benson's death has done a pretty good job of burying any and all suspicion. You may be convinced there was foul play, but, let's face it, you've got nothing solid except your gut feelings. As for Hastings — "

"Don't forget what Frank told Flora," McCalley interjected, anxious to justify the investigation he had taken on. "The reason she came to us, . . . especially about his being followed."

Gallagher shook his head but did not go on.

Markarian had to admit that what Gallagher had said was true enough but not what the Inspector wanted to hear. Still, out of deference to McCalley's professional integrity, and also because he had come to share the Inspector's view of the bizarre events that had brought them together again, he reminded Gallagher that what Katie had told them about her cousin, what Flora Chadwick had told them about her husband, the cryptic notes they had found in Joe Sarace's files, Benson's connection with organized crime and the money that had changed hands over the years, all those things taken together revealed a pattern . . . .

"I grant you, it's all very suggestive," Gallagher conceded, "but nothing conclusive. Not nearly enough to bring charges that will stick."

They had reached the detention cells. The only other person in the long corridor was a young officer, assigned to stand guard outside. When he saw Gallagher approach, the rookie unlocked the gate for them.

Bonz was lying on the cot, his legs apart, his hands locked behind his head. As the three men entered, he turned his head slowly toward them, swung his feet to the floor in a surprisingly swift motion for one his size, and remained sitting on the side of the bed.

"Am I gonna get out?" It was more a threat than a question.

"In a while. We have to ask some more questions."

"I tol' you what I know."

"We want you to think about the day Joe died, Think hard this time, Bonz."

"Whaffor? Like I said before, I din' hear nothin'."

"Just think hard and answer our questions. Think back, Bonz. Did Joe get any unusual calls that day? Or the day before? Or any time recently? Take your time."

The big man looked at the ceiling, shook his head.

"What sort of calls *did* he get?"

"The usual."

"What's the 'usual'?"

"People who wan' favors."

"Loans?"

"Whatever."

"Settle arguments?"

"Yeah."

"What about teaching somebody a lesson?"

"Whaddya mean?"

"Break a couple of knee caps, maybe?"

The big man looked down at his hands and cracked his knuckles. "Don' know nothin' 'bout that."

"You never hit a man?"

The mottled face grinned at them. "You puttin' me on?"

"Just answer the question."

"Hey, I gotta protect myself. And Joe. You come in here an' talk nasty, sure, I throw you out. That a crime?"

"No, it's not a crime. So, did anyone threaten Joe recently? Did you have to throw anybody out?"

"Nah."

"Okay. Let's go back to the calls. The day before Joe died. Think back. Who called him that day? Try to remember."

"Hey, Joe got dozens of calls before lunch, dozens after lunch. He was always on the phone. You expect me to 'member who called him? It was bizness!"

"I'm not saying you heard the conversations. I'm not saying they were all important. But someone out there maybe called Joe that day and set up an appointment for later on."

"So? It was bizness. People wanting things."

"But this call would have been different. Maybe Joe answered it in a special way. Was surprised, maybe?

We think somebody got to Joe, called him maybe earlier that day or maybe the day before, to make sure he'd be in his office that night, to meet with whoever it was."

"You mean the guy who killed him!" came the rejoinder, through stiff lips.

"That's what it looks like."

Bonz said nothing, but his face grew dark, suffused with contained rage. He rose from the cot, walked slowly to the door of the cell and back, to stand under the small high window that framed a tiny square of blue sky. He was still wearing the brown shirt, the patterned jacket, the colorful tie. Gallagher couldn't help thinking of what might have happened to anyone who had ever ventured to cross him or insulted or threatened Joe. Out loud he said, somewhat impatiently:

"Sit down and listen to me!" He waited for Bonz to do so then closed the distance between them, pad and pen in hand. The other two men leaned against the bars of the cell. They knew the protocol. Gallagher was first at bat. They wouldn't ask anything until he was through.

"So. What I want you to do is focus on the calls that came in. Take your time."

Bonz was making the effort. His puckered his face in a show of concentration and studied the patch of blue beyond the window. His mouth was a grim line. His jaw was thrust forward, as though challenging an invisible opponent. Gallagher remembered reading somewhere that he'd been a wrestler then a bouncer.

"Nothin' that day," he said to the ceiling.

After a pause, Gallagher prodded: "Go on. . . ."

"The day before. In the morning."

"Who was it?"

"Jimmy, Mr. Ambrosini's accountant."

"What was special about the call?"

Bonz shrugged. "Jimmy comes to check the books every three weeks. He'd done that a few days before."

"So, what did he want?"

"Said he had to double-check the books. Joe got mad and hung up."

Markarian was jotting it all down.

"That it?"

"That's it."

"So? Did he come around that day?"

The big man shook his head. "Not the next day, either."

"Maybe he came around that night? Maybe he was the person Joe was waiting for?"

Bonz was following some track of his own. "He never done that before. Came 'round every third Friday."

"Why wasn't his name in Joe's appointment book, if he was coming around?"

"Don' ask me!"

Gallagher turned to the other two men. "Anything you guys want to ask?"

McCalley came away from the door. "Bonz, did Mr. Ambrosini ever call the office?"

"Sometimes. Joe would ask how he was, how the family was. Always showed respect."

"Did Mr. Ambrosini call Joe that day or the day before?"

"No."

"Did you recognize any of the calls that came in those two days? Did Joe mention anybody?"

"They're in the book, why you askin' me?"

Gallagher brought the appointment book to Bonz and held it open for him: "Look here, Jimmy's call isn't listed. Why do you suppose?"

"How should I know?"

"Were there any other calls besides these?" He handed Bonz the book, so he could read the entries.

Bonz handed it back with a shrug.

McCalley made an impatient gesture. Markarian

chimed in: "What exactly did you hear him say when he took Jimmy's call?"

"He said 'Hello.' Then he gets real mad and yells 'Whaffor? You were here jus' the other day!'"

"And?"

"That's it. He hung up."

McCalley tried again. "Why would he do that?"

"Ask Jimmy."

"Mmm . . . . A lot of people called Joe and Mr. Ambrosini from all over, from places like Germany, Italy, France, Japan, Norway, Australia. Did someone call Benson ever call Joe from France?" Bonz shook his head. "Does the name ring a bell?" Bonz thought about it, then shook his head again. "You heard about Frank Hastings, how he was killed in Ottawa."

"He was runnover."

Markarian had taken out his notebook again. He said, without looking up: "Maybe. Or maybe it wasn't an accident. Did Joe ever talk about it?"

"The man was a loser, Joe had given up on him."

"Did Mr. Ambrosini give orders to have him killed? He owed him a lot of money."

"He was runnover."

"Maybe he was killed because he didn't pay up."

"Dunno about that."

It occurred to McCalley that he knew a great deal about it. The answers came too quickly, too easily. "Did Joe ever mention Benson, or talk with him on the phone?" he asked.

"Nope!"

"Did you know he was related to Frank Hastings? Actually, to Frank's wife, his first wife, Katie. They're second cousins."

To McCalley, watching intently, Bonz showed no surprise as he shook his head again. The Inspector wondered how much the man actually knew about

Charles Benson and his first wife, Emma, about Frank and Katie, about the intricate web that had forced all of them all under the glare of a harsh spotlight.

As they turned to leave and the rookie was opening the cell door for them, Bonz suddenly blocked the passage in one swift unexpected movement, forcing Gallagher to a stop. "What about Joe? You gonna tell me who killed him?"

"We're not sure, Bonz. And that's the gospel truth. But we think somebody killed him so he wouldn't talk."

"'Bout what?"

"If you can't tell us, how do you expect us to know?" Markarian suggested.

"Look, I tol' you everythin'. Are you gonna get me outta here? I gotta pack up Joe's things, clean up the mess you guys left behind. Pack up my own things. Close up the place."

"Not so fast! You get out when we tell you. When we have a safe place for you to stay. Forget about packing Joe's things. Or yours. You're a target now. You do what we tell you or I'll put you in the regular ward, where all the scum live."

"I gotta pack my own things."

"We'll pack for you, when the time comes. Where can we find Jimmy without too much trouble?"

He gave them the address of one of the "clubs."

"Where does he live?"

He told them.

They moved out into the corridor and the guard locked the gate behind them. Bonz stood close to the bars watching them move away.

Outside, they went separate ways. McCalley had calls to make and had to get ready for his trip to Paris. Markarian was going with Gallagher to question Jimmy.

"Talk to Bonz again. Try to get more out of him," McCalley said to them, as they parted.

Gallagher nodded. "We know where to find him."

They could not have imagined, at that moment, how wrong they were.

CHAPTER SEVENTEEN

They found Jimmy playing pool in a storefront club room near Mott Street. Gallagher took him outside, waved him into the back of the car, and got in beside him. Markarian sat up front, diagonally across from Jimmy.

Gallagher got right to the point. "What was the call you made to Joe, the day before he died?"

"What call?"

"We know you called him. What was it about?"

"Oh, yeah. There was something in the books I had to ask about."

"Why didn't Joe put it down in his log?"

"Hey, it wasn't the Queen of England calling."

"He logged all his calls."

"I guess it wasn't important enough."

"Maybe not, but he was sure mad about whatever you said to him."

"He liked to sound off."

"What was wrong with the books?"

"Nothing. Just routine."

"He seemed to think it wasn't just routine."

"He tell you that?" The man was cocky, overconfident.

"So what was it?"

"I don't remember."

"But you remember talking to him about it, right? When did you see him?"

"I didn't."

"You're lying."

"Hey, why should I lie?"

Markarian chimed in. "You went to see him the next night, didn't you?" Bingo! He thought. The man's face had taken on a wary look, his eyes shifted from one to the other.

"Who told you that?"

"Never mind who told us," said Gallagher, picking up the thread. "What time were you there?"

"I wasn't there! I told you."

"Let's see. You do all the books for the after-hours fun and games Mr. Ambrosini provides in his so-called community clubs, like this one, right?" He waved toward the place they'd just come out of. "I could get a search warrant here in half an hour. Then you'd go down for obstructing justice besides half a dozen other assorted charges. And don't count on Mr. Ambrosini or his hot shot lawyers. They're all trying to save their own skins."

Jimmy looked uncertain. The others saw the doubt in his eyes, the dawning realization that he might well be left out in the cold. They pressed on:

"What time were you there?" Markarian asked.

"I told you, I didn't see him the night he died. I told him I'd be around, that's all."

"Why did you call, then?"

"I told you. I needed to check out his books."

"You'd been there," said Gallagher, "just a few days before."

Jimmy was suddenly quiet. "Well?" Markarian persisted.

"Well what? I told him I'd be around to check the books again. That's it!"

"That's not it! Not by a longshot." Gallagher leaned toward him, forcing Jimmy into the corner. "You went to see him that night, the night he died. What time was it?"

"If you know I saw him, you know what time it was, right?" He snorted, trying to look amused.

"Try again, hotshot. What time were you there? Or do you want me to drag you in on suspicion of murder?"

Jimmy suddenly sat up straight where he sat. He

made no effort to hide his apprehension at Gallagher's suggestion. "It was a heart attack!"

"You were there? You saw him collapse?"

"You guys are crazy!"

"Well, did you? Were you there?"

"Everybody knows, it was in the papers. He died of a heart attack!"

"You believe everything you read in the papers?"

"I know what I know."

"And what's that?"

When Jimmy didn't answer, Markarian turned further in his seat, so that they was almost face to face. He was about to speak, but Gallagher beat him to it.

"The Ambrosinis are in hot water, Jimmy. It's only a matter of time. And it won't be the usual rounding up of third-raters, like you and Bonz. We're building a case that will tear this whole operation apart. We have enough right now to put the Ambrosinis away for a long long time." Markarian wondered how far the Lieutenant would go with this.

"So, go ahead and do it," answered the other. Some of the cockiness had returned.

"You think I'm bluffing?"

"Hey, you do what you gotta do," was the brazen reply. A smile played around his lips.

Markarian turned back so that he faced the windshield again.

"How about my taking you in right now and spreading the word that you spilled your guts out?" Gallagher went on.

There was a moment's hesitation, then: "Mr. Ambrosini trusts me. He knows I wouldn't do that!"

"So. Let's try it." Gallagher took out his cuffs and started to get out but, even before his feet hit the ground, Jimmy stopped him.

"So what if I was there?"

Gallagher eased back into his seat and closed the door. "Go on."

"I went around about seven-thirty, after I was through here."

"Who picked the time?"

"Like I said, I had to finish work here first."

"Why couldn't it wait until morning?"

"I gotta put in a full day."

"How long were you there?"

"Not long. I was atta there by eight. Joe had the books out for me. Didn't take long."

"What were you checking?"

"Some money that was overdue."

"Doesn't sound like something urgent, not in your line of work. What was the rush?"

"No rush."

"How come you hadn't noticed anything wrong when you checked the books earlier?"

"I guess I missed it."

"Who caught it?"

"The boys. They like to look things over."

"Don't they trust you?"

"Sure they trust me. They just like to keep on top of things. Glance over the entries. Ask some questions."

"So they asked questions when you checked out the books last time, a few days ago?"

"That's right."

"And they found discrepancies?"

"Don't know what you mean, 'discrepancies.' They were curious about loans that were still out there."

"What do they usually do when that happens?" Jimmy shrugged. "Break knee caps? Fingers, what?"

"I don't know anything about that."

"So you checked the books again. What did you tell the boys?

"Not to worry. Everything was okay."

"That's the message you brought back?"
"Yeah."
"You left around eight, you said."
"That's right."
"And Joe stayed behind?"
"Yeah."
"Was he annoyed at your coming?"
"I guess."
"What did he say?"
"I can't remember! Something about 'making so much fuss'."
"Is that when the other guy came in?"
"What other guy?"

Markarian said, without turning around: "You don't want to be the last one to see Joe alive, Jimmy." For a few seconds no one spoke. The words echoed, like distant thunder closing in.

"It was a heart attack...."

Markarian half-turned in his seat and said: "You don't want to take a rap like this one, Jimmy.... Who came in just before you left?"

"I didn't do anything!" was the reply, frustration breaking through.

"Then tell us who did."

After a few seconds, Jimmy said: "Joe wasn't feeling too good."

"Did he say that?"
"I could tell."
"So you left anyway."
"How did I know he was going to drop dead!"
"I don't think so, Jimmy. We don't think he dropped dead," said Gallagher.
"He had a heart attack. Everybody knows."

Gallagher threw down his notepad on the seat and crossed his arms. He addressed Markarian, sitting in front of him. "How about that? They're all experts, suddenly, trying to convince us Joe died of a heart attack." He turned back to the other man. "Suppose I tell you that it was induced?"

"What do you mean?"

"Maybe somebody wanted it to look that way?"

"You're crazy! Nobody can do that!"

"You'd be surprised." He waited. Jimmy stared out the side window, keeping his face averted. The two officers watched him, said nothing. Finally, Gallagher broke the silence.

"Tell you what, Jimmy. You give us what we need and we'll rough you up a bit and send you back to Mr. Ambrosini a hero."

"Come off it. He'll know I talked once you start nosing around."

"Believe me, he won't." Markarian tried to hide the excitement that was building up inside him.

"So who came in after you?" Gallagher repeated.

"They'll kill me."

"We won't. So tell us."

"It was the boys, right?"

Jimmy seemed to sag where he sat. He nodded.

"They were the ones who told you to set up the appointment, right?" asked Markarian. Again a nod. "You were the excuse. You were supposed to keep him there until the boys arrived." A third nod. "Then what?"

"I left. But they just talked to him, that's all."

"How would you know, if you left, if you didn't see anything?"

"That's what they said. They only talked to him."

"You really believe that?"

When Jimmy didn't answer, Gallagher put away his notepad and said in a brisk tone: "Here's how it's going to play. Lieutenant Markarian is going to write up a statement for you to sign, right here and now. We'll call you in tomorrow for more questioning and have a formal statement typed up, ready for you to sign. We'll release you without a word about any statement. In a few more days, we'll have enough to be able to round up the Ambrosinis. Your statement won't be needed until we go to trial. You'll be safe."

"I'll never be safe. They've got people everywhere. I'll never be safe!"

Markarian reached over and patted the man's knee. "Let the Lieutenant and me worry about that."

Gallagher started to move out again. Markarian stopped him. "One more thing," he said, turning back to where Jimmy crouched in the back. "You can help us in a big way here Jimmy. Did all this happen because of the books or was it something else?"

"I don't know! That's what I was told."

"Did you really think that was the reason?"

"I don't know what to think. The books seemed all right to me. The boys were worried, that's all."

"About unpaid loans? But that's the business you're in. Nothing surprising about that, is there?"

"I guess not."

"So, what was it that really triggered Joe's death?"

"God help me, I don't know!" said the other, with some feeling. "Joe was okay. Never trimmed, never cheated. I don't know why he had to die."

Markarian decided to give it one last try. "What about calls. Outside calls to Mr. Ambrosini, to the boys?"

"They get calls all the time. From all over."

"We know that. Were there any special calls you happened to witness? Foreign calls maybe?"

"Ambrosini is all over the place. He gets calls from all over the world."

"And you're there sometimes when those calls come in. . . ."

"Sometimes."

"Did any calls like that come in at any time in the

last week or so, when you happened to be with Mr. Ambrosini or one of the boys?"

Jimmy thought about it for about thirty seconds. "There was one call. . . ."

"Go on."

"Don't know who it was. Mr. Ambrosini just listened, then hung up.

"What do you mean, he 'just listened'?"

"He said 'Hello?' Listened and hung up."

"Just like that?"

"Just like that. He hung up and walked out—"

"What did you think?"

"— walked out with just Tommy."

"His bodyguard?"

"He's got three. Doesn't go anywhere without them. But he told Lou and Mike to stay put. When I ran into Tommy in the kitchen, just before lunch, I asked him about it. He said Mr. Ambrosini didn't need all three of them, they'd just driven to the public phone down the block. The guards outside were right behind them, he said, watching the street. They were gone only a few minutes."

"He made a call from a public phone?"

"That's what Tommy told me."

"When did this happen?"

"A few days before Joe died."

Markarian marveled again at what could be dredged up by a routine question.

As they drove back to the precinct, to pick up his car, Markarian asked:

"You thinking what I'm thinking?"

"Let's not get our hopes up," the Lieutenant answered, dampening somewhat Markarian's optimism.

"But it fits, right? A call from higher up to get rid of Joe because he knew too much and we were sniffing around. Joe was handling Frank. He knew Frank's debts had been paid off but he'd been told to keep the screws on him, forced him to kill a man as payment for what he owed . . . or thought he owed. Then suddenly, Joe himself becomes a threat. My bet is, Benson targeted him."

"You're guessing — "

Markarian shrugged. "We know Ambrosini drove a block down the street to return a long-distance call from a public phone."

"Doesn't prove he was calling Benson."

"Right. But think about it for a minute—"

"— Hard to believe that Ambrosini is taking orders from Benson."

"Not if he's getting big money for it, for doing him . . . favors, shall we say?" He glanced over at the Lieutenant. "It would explain the receipts. . . ."

The files they'd retrieved from the van had a number of cryptic notes that recorded periodic money transactions that suggested business between the mobster and Benson. They should ask Jimmy about it when they questioned him again, Markarian reminded himself; but he was sure he'd hit it right. If so, Benson was still paying money to the Ambrosini family, for some reason.

"What favors could Benson possibly need?" asked Gallagher. "He's rich enough he can get anything he wants without help from anybody!" He waved the argument aside. "We'll never be able to prove any of it."

Markarian decided to drop the subject. They drove the rest of the way in silence.

By the following morning, they had confirmation that a call had been made to a public phone in Paris from a phone booth a block down the road from the Ambrosini residence. The call was made around the time Tommy had driven his boss the short distance to that location.

Markarian was pleased. But Gallagher was right: they could never prove Ambrosini made the call or that

Benson was waiting for it at the other end.

The Inspector was settling into his hotel, when Markarian reached him in Paris to tell him about their meeting with Jimmy.

"It's circumstantial, and tenuous at that," was the Inspector's response. "We're still circling around, we haven't hit the target yet." When Markarian told him that Jimmy had signed a preliminary statement, that he was coming in to sign a formal deposition, McCalley sounded more positive, though still circumspect. "Cover him. We don't want still another accident."

"I doubt they'll try anything at this point."

"Don't underestimate them. They're pretty clever. They've managed to keep us at bay all this time."

"Not for much longer."

"I hope you're right."

Markarian sighed as he replaced the receiver. Why was McCalley always so hesitant about accepting the bright side? But even as he entertained that thought, he chastised himself. The Inspector was utterly professional in his rigorous search for hard facts and evidence. He had handled the Bantry case superbly, just as he was handling this one. No one could ever fault him for having mistaken wishful thinking for hard reality. He made no concessions to what might be obvious to some but unfounded in his eyes.

Markarian had to admit that once again he was brought to task; McCalley's common sense dissuaded indulging in euphoric visions of indictments and charges that would never stick in a court of law. Although everything now pointed to the Ambrosinis and Benson himself as fellow-conspirators in the death of Joe Sarace — and possibly in the two other deaths — there simply wasn't enough proof for an indictment. The Prosecutor would never take on the case with what they had to offer.

He was waiting in his cubbyhole for Jimmy to

arrive. The deposition had been prepared and was ready to be signed.

The phone rang. It was Gallagher calling from his own office down the hall. "That SONOFABITCH!?"

"What's up?"

"He got away!"

"Jimmy's gone?"

"Not Jimmy! Bonz! Got the guard to open up. Told him he was having chest pains. Starts making like he's dying. The poor kid goes in there, to see how bad it was, and when he gets close the guy grabs him, knocks him out and walks out of there. We made it easy, putting him in that deserted wing, right near the entrance. No one was around."

"Probably went home to clean up the place, like he said."

"Oh, he was there all right. But not to clean up the place. My men did only a brief search. There was no mess. Wasn't as though it was a crime scene. . . . He got right past Gebstadt, the fellow on duty. The man had been sitting for hours, took a short walk to stretch his legs. Just down the block and back. No more than five minutes. When he got the call that Bonz had bolted, he checked the area. Never expected to find the back door wide open! We left the guy was behind bars, damn it!"

"Sure it was Bonz?"

"Who else?"

"He can't go far, Sean. You'll get him." Markarian tried to sound reassuring.

"Just when I thought we were wrapping things up!

But, by the end of the day, they still had not located Bonz. The man seemed to have been swallowed up. No sign of him anywhere.

Why he had gone to the house he shared with Joe was not altogether clear. Gebstadt said everything seemed untouched. There was no indication that someone had been there. . . .

When Markarian reached McCalley a second time, the Inspector was getting ready to join Josie and Marge for dinner.

Markarian held back as the Inspector filled him in with the latest news. "I talked with Kenney, just after you called," McCalley began. "I'd asked him to find out more about A & E Danziger and to search out the other companies Benson bought up in the last few years. We found some interesting data that seems to fit in with what we discovered in Joe's files about those hefty sums paid out to Ambrosini from a source in France, by the mysterious "B". . . ."

Markarian let him finish. The new information was intriguing. If only they could find some way to prove it was more than a theory!

"Wonder how Benson will react when you tell him what you've found!" he ventured, when McCalley had finished.

"Oh, he's full of surprises. But he won't cave in. He knows we don't have proof."

Markarian, in turn, told him about Bonz escaping from the detention cell shortly after they'd talked with him. The Inspector agreed that his bolting confirmed their suspicions that the man was holding back information. He had some special knowledge that he kept to himself and perhaps meant to use. He knew Ambrosini would be looking for him now that he had gotten away and was no longer under police protection. Markarian expressed his concern.

"He's not safe, out there by himself. Where could he have gone? And what do you suppose he took away from the house? It had to be something important to risk going there — "

McCalley agreed. "We'll find him, Ed. In the meantime, he knows how to take care of himself." He promised to call as soon as he got back from the meeting with Benson, the next afternoon.

Before leaving, he checked his appearance in the small mirror behind the bathroom door. After showering, he had put back on what he had been wearing. The one change of underwear and socks was for the next day. That should keep him until he got back to New York. . . .

Josie and Marge greeted him like a long lost friend. McCalley had to admit he liked the attention.

Even before they sat down on the small terrace for their pre-dinner glass of wine, Josie had retrieved a large manila envelope and handed it to McCalley.

"Don't want to forget the magazines I saved for you."

He thanked her and went on to tell them about Katie being mugged, quickly reassuring them that she was fine now, mending nicely. He evaded questions about the claims he was supposedly investigating by telling them he'd come to Paris on other business. They in turn were only too happy to tell him about their work, their escapades, their friends.

Dinner was in the same restaurant where they had taken him on his earlier visit. This time they ordered veal with tiny carrots and asparagus.

"This could easily turn into a habit," McCalley told them over coffee.

"Good!" said Marge clapping her hands.

"Any time!" said Josie. "And plan to stay with us, when you come again. We've got a spare room and bath. Katie stayed for over a week."

"My wife might not understand!" he said.

"Bring her along!" said Marge, with an expansive wave.

"There'll be even more room in a little while," Josie expanded. "Marge just got engaged. She's going to be married in a few months," said Josie. Details followed, while Marge shook her head, still blushing.

The Inspector was surprised at his own reaction to the news. It was as though he'd known the two girls for years, old friends, neighbors' daughters whom he had watched growing up. He was genuinely pleased for Marge. He congratulated her and impulsively leaned over and kissed her cheek.

She held his hand, tears brimming in her eyes.

"A romantic through and through," said Josie, leaning close to rub her friend's back. She knows just what to do, thought McCalley. Not that Marge wasn't capable of fending for herself. But she must appreciate the fact that Josie was there for her, any time.

"Nothing wrong with being a romantic," he commented with a smile.

On it went until a second cup of coffee and a small glass of Curvoisier, compliments of the house.

He told the cab to wait for him as he escorted the girls to the door of their building.

"Too bad you have to leave so soon," said Marge.

"Promise you'll come again?" said Josie, giving him a hug."

He watched until they were safely inside before giving the cab the name of his hotel.

It was after eleven when he picked up his case folder. Lying on the bed in his pajamas, he leafed through it, his mind elsewhere.

His thoughts kept going back to Bonz. The man knew it was dangerous to be out there alone, so why did he leave protective custody? McCalley remembered his questions, his loyalty to Joe, his suspicions, his genuine surprise when they'd suggested that heart failure could have been induced. He also recalled that he had never for a moment shown any fear. If he was planning something, they wouldn't be able to stop him. For McCalley was convinced that Bonz had an agenda of his own and was ready to see it through.

Had they done the wrong thing, telling Bonz that Joe's death might have been induced?

When he woke up some hours later, the folder was still open on his lap. He put it on the table beside the bed and settled down to sleep.

CHAPTER EIGHTEEN

His appointment with Benson was for one-thirty. There was plenty of time, after a quick breakfast, to review the file again.

He pulled out his notes about Katie's visit to her cousin. Because of Benson's incredible offer, Katie's suspicions about Emma's death were unshakable. The anxieties and fears that grew out of the conversation in St. Tropez continued to torture her, long after she had returned to the States. Katie was convinced she had been compromised, that if Emma's death were ever questioned and the bank account her cousin had opened for her in Geneva ever came to light, she could easily be charged as an accessory after the fact, a blackmailer, even.

Not for the first time, McCalley wondered why a powerful man like Benson, who could buy the devil himself, would tease (for lack of a better word!) his cousin with the kind of impossible request he had made. Surely he didn't expect her to do the deed! And surely not by shooting! If Emma had been deliberately killed, it was done in a much more subtle way. If it was murder, it had been carried out with great care. In McCalley's mind, shooting had never been an option for Benson. Shooting Emma would have meant a police investigation, all sorts of inconveniences — things no one would want to bring on if they could be avoided, least of all a man like Benson. Would such a man place himself in a situation where the police would be given an opportunity to root around in his personal life, not to mention his business activities? Would he deliberately invite such scrutiny — not to mention having to answer questions about his deteriorating relationship with Emma? McCalley did not think so. And yet he had asked Katie for a favor that was both unrealistic and gross. It didn't add up unless — as

Katie insisted — he had meant to compromise her.

The argument was far-fetched, but it made sense if Benson really wanted to make sure she would never repeat what had transpired between them, should an occasion arise where his actions might be questioned, his motives scrutinized. The only problem with that was: nothing had compelled Benson to tell Katie about Frank or to ask her to shoot Emma. Katie would have remained blissfully ignorant of what her husband had done. As for Emma: McCalley was convinced, after hearing the whole story, that if Benson was responsible for Emma's death the plan, with any number of variations, had probably been worked out long before Katie even arrived in St. Tropez. Although Interpol had agreed there was nothing solid to go on, they were still pursuing leads. A new one was being tracked down, a garage mechanic who had serviced Emma's car just hours before she met her death on the Amalfi drive.

It sounded promising, but the Inspector wasn't banking on it. His interest was focused on Benson's motive for approaching Katie with his incredible request. What reason might he have for implicating his cousin? Why had he placed such a terrible burden of fear and guilt on her?

He remembered Katie telling him that her mother always thought her cousin Millie was "strange." At the time, McCalley had interpreted it to mean "esoteric," "outgoing," something like that. But what if there was more to it? What if a strain of insanity had crept in, somewhere along the line? something that might explain her cousin's bizarre request, his strange behavior, that grotesque favor he had asked? Was Benson a psychopath?

McCalley shook his head in frustration and shifted his attention to the memos about Benson's first merger. The purchase had been made with money borrowed from the Ambrosinis. He had bought a small

Swedish company owned by the Danzigers, father and daughter Emma, the woman Benson married soon after. He scanned again the copies of what he had found in the files Bonz had retrieved for them, memos, in the years that followed, of direct or indirect payments to the Ambrosinis, from Benson or people connected with him, right up to the present.

He placed the folder to one side and closed his eyes, acknowledging the familiar sensation that he had missed something. After a while, he sat up and started to doodle in his notebook. It was a habit he had acquired early in his career. At first, it worked merely to relax him; it still did. But he soon realized that it served another purpose as well; it helped him transfer his problems into a maze of intricate lines that eventually suggested a pattern, a design. He couldn't explain it; his colleagues, he knew, joked about it behind his back.

He turned to a clean page and began drawing a new design of lines and curves, while he ordered his scattered thoughts.

Benson was a shrewd and cunning man, rational, practical. Although he insisted on utter control and knew how to wield power, neither served him as psychological compensations. He was also, McCalley had decided, completely amoral. What might appear ruthless to others, Benson undoubtedly saw as perfectly natural within the world he had created for himself. In his eyes, nothing he did could be wrong, if he, Benson, did it. He felt himself to be exempt from existing rules and regulations, not answerable to them; he was ready to take chances, test his skills against the strictures others had to live by. He was his own law.

While thus brooding, he had managed to fill the entire page with fresh doodles. He turned to a clean sheet and wrote in large letters at the top:

FACTS:

August, 2000. K marries FH.

September 11, 2001. FH is presumed to have been killed in the twin towers collapse. Later declared dead.

August, 2002. B asks his cousin, vacationing in France, to shoot his wife. (A strange and unrealistic request!)

January, 2003. EB skids off the Amalfi drive while returning to Naples alone, late at night, after visiting friends (and, as the autopsy showed, having had too much to drink).

June. FH a hit-and-run fatality in Ottawa, where he'd settled after nine-eleven, married a second time (Flora Mosely) under the name James Chadwick, without benefit of divorce. They have a child.

Mid-June. K gets a clipping about FH death.

Early July. B in NY; has lunch with K.

Early August. K marries Francis Delancourt.

Mid-August. Flora tells Ottawa police her husband James Chadwick (Frank Hastings) was murdered.

Late August. Flora comes to NY to talk with K about FH/JC's death, etc. Mc arrives in NY, questions K. Mc flies to Paris to talk with B and with K's two friends (M and J).

End of August. Katie is mugged.

Early September. Joe Sarace, a mobster with the Ambrosini crime family, is found dead in his office, apparently from cardiac arrest. The police talk Joe's trusted aide, Bonz, into handing over JS's files to them. Files strongly suggest a long-standing connection between the Ambrosinis and B. Mc returns to Paris to talk with Josie, Marge, and Benson again. . . .

He stared at what he had written. After a while, he added, in bold big letters:

MERGERS, BENSON, COINCIDENCES, MONEY —

Money had changed hands several times since Benson had orchestrated his first merger, with the help of a huge loan from Ambrosini. The folders Bonz had handed over to Gallagher suggested a number of similar payments or gifts — nothing clear and direct (he reminded himself), just memos and notes, initials rather than names, dates scattered here and there.

Enough to suggest a pattern?

Ambrosini had started Benson on his road to success. Were those later sums connected in some way with later mergers and takeovers?

He reminded himself that Benson did not need that kind of money after the first major success. That loan had been paid back within a year. So, why was he still paying huge amounts to Ambrosini?

That first merger enabled him to pump new life into the business he had inherited from his father. The stories in the magazines Josie had saved for him recapped the entire history of the Benson empire. On the occasion of Emma's death, they described the "romantic" merger that brought Emma into Benson's life and started him on his climb to wealth and power. His own keen sense of timing, his management skills and his reckless daring did the rest.

Reckless daring. . . .

Money can buy the devil himself. . . .

Had the later mergers all been as easy as the first one? He picked up the manila envelope Josie had given him the night before. Quickly he found what he was looking for: a two-page feature that reviewed in some detail the history of Emma's life and that of the empire she helped to launch.

It was there! The rise to international fame . . . and conveniently boxed, as an interesting "filler," the names of the six corporations Benson had taken over, after the first merger!

Quickly, he returned to his folder and pulled out copies of the memos he'd retrieved from Joe Sarace's files. On his accompanying notes, he now added the dates of the takeovers listed in the story spread out before him, the names of the companies. There had been six after A & E Danziger. He made a note to ask Kenney to search them out.

He scanned again what he had written and glanced back at the newspaper story. He now read it through, carefully. When he was finished, he added under the summary he had made:

Payments.

A surge of excitement forced him out of his chair. He paced the length of the room, opened the window briefly and took a few deep breaths. Only when he sat down again did he acknowledge the wild possibility that had struck him.

He looked over what he had written.

How often and in what different ways had the Ambrosinis helped him along the way? The question stopped him. He shuffled his papers again, pausing here and there to reread his notes and other documents.

Yes. All told, plenty of payments to the Ambrosini family, right up to now, right up to . . . . If he was reading the notations correctly, if they meant what he thought they meant . . . those payments went right up to — right up to . . .September!

He underlined *payments* and put three asterisks next to the word.

For a long time, he stared again at what he had written.

How many times had he gone over these same facts! It was all there, right in front of his eyes. It had been there all along, but he'd missed it!

Was it really the key to the puzzle? Or was he simply doing what he told others not to do: indulging his imagination?

For there was nothing he could prove, even if he was dead center right! Short of a confession, no one could be charged with anything. At the very least, the money could have been gifts. The lawyers would know how to get out of it. There was no case, nothing on which this sudden insight could be anchored. . . .

After a while, he picked up his phone and called Bill Kenney in Ottawa. The conversation lasted eleven minutes. He read off the list of companies taken over by Benson and ended with instructions.

"Bill. I want to know as much as possible about those takeovers, about the principals involved, whatever you can find. . . . And talk to Flora again. Walk her through the last two or three days before Frank was killed. Were there calls from his contact? Was he to meet him at the Elgin? And, Bill, get back to me before one o'clock, at the latest, with whatever you dig up, whatever you have to that point. And stay with it."

The second call was to Markarian in New York. The desk officer told him the Detective was out, wouldn't be back until after lunch. McCalley insisted that he be paged, said it was urgent and left his name and phone number. "Tell him to drop everything and get back to me." It was eleven o'clock.

At eleven-ten, Markarian called back. He listened without interrupting as McCalley explained what he thought he'd found.

"And I've got Bill looking into Frank's death again, but I know I'm right about this, Ed. I'm even willing to bet on it."

"Never dreamed I'd ever hear you say that!"

"It's not just idle speculation." At the other end, Markarian laughed. "Hear me out," the Inspector went on. "I've looked through all the papers, I've got them here, everything we've put together so far. Ed, it all fits!" He quickly summarized what he'd found and what it pointed to. There was a pause. "Look, I know what you're thinking —" but Markarian interrupted him, before McCalley could go on:

"Then, you must know that I'm impressed."
"It's not just a theory, Ed."
"You don't hear me objecting, do you?"
They talked some more, then McCalley asked:
"Has Bonz turned up?"
"Nothing. No word. No sign."
"We've got to find him. He must know about this. Joe handled the money! And Jimmy kept the books. How could they not know!"
"I'll get to Jimmy again. When do you meet with Benson?"
"In two hours. Kenney should be getting back to me soon. I'll tell him to call you as well, and give you what he's found. Get to Gallagher with it. He's been very cooperative. We don't want to leave him out of this."

He showered and dressed, donning the fresh shirt and tie for the occasion. At twelve thirty he ordered a sandwich and coffee, which he ate in front of the TV, where a French newscaster reported the most recent suicide bombing in Iraq.

At ten minutes to one, the phone rang a second time. Kenney had found the information he wanted.

"Right on target, Sir! How did you come on to it?"
"Not now, Bill. Getting ready for my meeting with Benson." He made quick notes and hung up, annoyed with himself.

Why not admit that the possibility had come to him in a flash, that it was an inspired guess? Because — he argued, trying to convince himself it wasn't really a wild guess — he simply had missed the pattern, until he went back to the documents, memos, interviews, receipts. . . . The conclusion was right there, had been waiting, as though a curtain had been drawn back and you suddenly saw clearly what was behind it. You couldn't miss it once certain facts were reordered. Then, everything they had known before as scattered pieces of information became important, revealing — no, not evidence, exactly, he couldn't prove any of it, but it made sense. It redirected them and suggested what had been lacking all along: a strong motive for getting rid of anyone who knew too much, anyone who might talk to save his or her skin!

Nothing solid, he reminded himself, nothing that could stand in a court of law; but what Kenney had told him on the phone definitely strengthened his suspicions.

Emma may have known. Frank Hastings might have found out, somehow (a long shot, McCalley had to admit). Sarace certainly would have known (but did he pose a threat? how?).

He drank the last of his coffee and set out for his meeting with Benson.

Monsieur was still in conference but would be out shortly. Would the Inspector like some coffee, tea, a glass of wine?

McCalley shook his head and strolled to the tall windows, from where he could see the Eiffel tower not too far off. It was a wonderful view. His wife Susan had spent a year studying art history at the Sorbonne; she almost didn't return to Canada because of a young painter she met during her stay in Paris. But she did return, and she'd married McCalley. . . . On the way to the airport, she had made him promise that if he got to Paris he'd visit Versailles, even if it meant taking an extra day. "You're always scurrying from here to there," she had admonished; "this time, give yourself an extra day at least, to relax."

How he wished he could do that! Instead, he would be flying back to New York, as soon as possible, maybe as early as the next day.

The receptionist had come to where he stood.

"Monsieur is back," she said, leading the way to Benson's suite.

They moved down the same bright corridor he remembered from the last visit, past the same vivid paintings, to the same elegant room where he had first talked with Monsieur.

Benson had been at his desk, but now came forward to greet his guest. They sat as they had before, facing one another in the same exquisite chairs.

"I doubt I can help you any further, Inspector," he said pleasantly, crossing his legs and letting his arms rest along the sides of the chair.

"Perhaps you can, Monsieur Benson. Perhaps you could tell me about your connection with the Ambrosini family?"

Monsieur pondered the question, twisting his face in concentration. At last, he smiled. "Ah, yes. Ambrosini. We've done some business together."

"Could you explain?"

A little frown materialized between Monsieur's hard blue eyes, even as he continued to smile. "Business dealings are hard to explain, Inspector."

"They lent you money, when you first took over your father's company, is that correct?"

"Why yes, they did. And I paid it all back, once things started rolling. I'm forever grateful. They helped me at a time when I needed money for a merger. I bought out a small company to boost my own. It was in fact Emma's, my late wife's, company. Her father had founded it, and Emma had run it with him. When he retired, he handed it over to her. But Emma decided the best thing for her was to sell it. We were married soon after the merger, as you probably know."

McCalley had read about that romantic meeting (and the glamorous wedding that soon followed) in the newspaper and magazines stories Katie's friends had given him. "So you not only ate your cake and had it," he found himself saying, "Emma was the frosting on the cake — "

"You're mixing your metaphors, Inspector. Your clichés, to be precise — "

A fleeting memory took the Inspector back to the Bantry case and Jill Masterson, — the young NYU English Professor, who took him to task for his addiction to such phrases. . . . Jill's teasing had quickly put him at his ease; but Monsieur's remark had just the opposite effect. Still, he managed a smile and went on.

"An added bonus, then?" Monsieur said nothing. McCalley consulted his notes. "You paid back that initial loan to the Ambrosinis —"

"You've done your homework, I see," the other cut in. "Yes, as I just told you, I paid it back soon after," he added, with a hint of impatience.

"There were a number of rather large payments after that, when you no longer needed to borrow money from anyone. Can you explain them, Monsieur?"

"Of course, but I don't intend to. To be candid, Inspector, it's none of your business." He rose to get himself a glass of bottled water. "Besides, you wouldn't understand," he said, as he returned to his seat.

McCalley sat back to observe him. "Try me."

Irritation momentarily crossed those otherwise placid features and just as quickly disappeared.

"Say what you've come to say. Inspector," was the reply.

"Why did you burden you cousin Katie with that business about Frank? What purpose did it serve?"

"On to that again, are we? Has Katie been complaining?"

"My question first. . . ."

"I was trying to help her. Frank was dead a whole year, and she was still grieving for him! It was obscene! I felt I had to tell her so she could get on with her life."

"And what was the one hundred thousand for, to

start her on that new life?"

    Monsieur regarded him serenely. Not a muscle twitched. "You might say that. It was a gift. A very small one. I was hoping we've grow close again. Aside from her brother Matt, whom I scarcely know, she's my only blood relative left. I wanted to help."

    "And the rest of it?"

    "What do you mean?"

    "The ten million?"

    "Oh dear! The poor girl is really up tight! I told you about the job I offered her. She would have earned ten million in just the first year."

    McCalley had to admire the skilled parrying. Out loud, he said: "The story about a job offer was Katie's. She made it up when I questioned her. You picked up on it very cleverly." He leaned forward in his seat. "The truth of the matter is, you offered her ten million dollars to kill your wife, Emma."

    The silence was brief. Monsieur drank from his glass and put it down on the table in front of him. He crossed his hands on his knee and said, with a touch of severity: "That is by far the most absurd thing I've ever heard! Did she really say that?"

    "Indeed, she did."

    Monsieur spread his hands in a wide gesture of disbelief. "Why would she concoct such a story?"

    "Why, indeed?"

    "All I can think of is, she was terribly upset about Frank."

    "That was later. After you made the offer."

    Monsieur gave him a quizzical look.

    "If you say so. I'm surprised at your taking all that seriously, Inspector. Katie was in a bad way, when she visited us in St. Tropez. I tried to cheer her up."

    "By telling her that her husband was a bigamist?"

    "She was bound to find out sooner or later."

"Not necessarily. He had changed his name, he had a new life. Of course, you knew all about it, helped make it possible, didn't you? Paid all his gambling debts through Joe Sarace, made sure you kept him in your sights, to serve whatever purpose you might dream up. Why did you want him under your wing, Monsieur? Of what use was Frank Hastings to you?"

Monsieur gave an indulgent laugh. "I can always use an intelligent man, Inspector. I had him recruited for the Board of Directors of one of my companies. I thought he might bring fresh ideas to the operation. I also wanted to know what he was doing, for Katie's sake, to protect her, if necessary."

"But you told her, instead, that Frank had deserted her, had settled in Ottawa under a new name and, to top it all, had remarried."

"As I said earlier, I thought it best that she know."

"Were you protecting her, also, when you had Frank killed? Or was it so she could remarry without the complications of an earlier husband, still alive? Was that, too, meant as a gift?"

Monsieur opened his eyes wide with staged surprise. "My dear Inspector! You astound me with your imaginative forays into the unknown! I thought your job was to find evidence!"

McCalley shifted uncomfortably in his seat. The remark came too close to home. But he had thought hard about the approach he would have to take, had worked it out before venturing on this track. McCalley could only hope that his accusations would throw Benson off balance, that he would give himself away at some point, in some way.

No luck, so far.

"Rest assured," McCalley went on evenly, "we've found a great deal of evidence in Joe Sarace's files about money changing hands, phone calls between you and Mr.

Ambrosini, all kinds of documents that I'm sure the authorities here will be very pleased to share. Bonz — you know Bonz, Joe's bodyguard? — well, of course you do. Bonz was most accomodating, when he heard what we had to say about Sarace's death. So was Jimmy, Mr. Ambrosini's accountant." With Jimmy, he was pushing. Watching Monsieur's eyes narrow ever so little, he regretted having mentioned the names. Was Bonz in even greater danger now, if found? Having said that much, there was no point keeping back the rest. "We know that Ambrosini got a call from Paris shortly before Joe Sarace died, that he went outside to return that call, and that it was received at the other end, here in Paris, at a public phone. We have that number too."

"I'm sure he gets lots of calls from all over the world, Inspector," was the unruffled reply.

"But not many are continued from a public phone. . . ."

"You're very good at mysteries," said Monsieur, glancing at his watch. "I leave that kind of entertainment for reading at night."

"We're pretty sure you had Frank Hastings killed. Was it because he knew about your mergers, your so-called business deals, your insider trading, was that it? Had he become greedy, hard to control? Or was it something else? Joe certainly must have known about them. Had he become a risk, too?"

"I see no point in continuing this conversation," Monsieur Benson interrupted, as he rose to his full impressive height. "I suggest you call my lawyer. My secretary will give you the name."

McCalley showed no sign of leaving. "The call to Ambrosini was about Joe, wasn't it? This too must have given you tremendous satisfaction. Making murder look like a natural death; just as Frank's was made to look like an accident. Perhaps Emma's, as well? Were you afraid Joe would talk? Did he feel we were getting too close?"

Monsieur started for the door. "I really must leave you, Inspector. I'm already late for an appointment."

"And all the payments to Ambrosini over the years? How many times did you have to get rid of your competition?"

McCalley had followed him to the door. Benson stopped on the threshold, turned to him, and said rather smugly:

"I'm really quite good at what I do. Fortune, I must admit, also had a hand in it. But I was there for it, always at the right time. I knew when to strike." He seemed to enjoy the clever ambiguities he was spouting. "Few men could have done what I did."

"I'm sure you're right," said McCalley. "Few men would have taken the measures you took to clear the field for yourself."

Monsieur led the way down the corridor to the receptionist's desk. No one was there. A sign informed those who might somehow have found their way past all the security stops along the way that reception would reopen in an hour and please wait or come back later.

Monsieur leaned against the desk, his arms folded across his chest. "It's been exhilarating talking to you, Inspector. I find the intricacies of your mind stimulating, to say the least."

"You will find the intricacies of the law less rewarding, I can assure you. I don't mind telling you that the Paris police and Interpol have had you under surveillance for the last week."

He laughed, a merry sound. "Do they hope to trap me into something indiscreet?"

"You've trapped yourself already, in any number of ways," McCalley bluffed. "But *indiscreet* is hardly the word; *criminal* is more like it."

"You amaze me, Inspector! I took you for a sensible man. This banter is not only out of character for you, it's downright boring."

McCalley smiled. "I never imagined I could amaze and bore at the same time. . . . Rest assured, the investigation has been going on for some time. We already have dozens of depositions and have most of Joe's records in our possession. Jimmy's books have been subpoenaed as well. Regardless of the great friendship between you and the Ambrosinis, I suspect they will have no qualms about sacrificing you should they be trapped in the nefarious web they've spun for themselves."

"Well, then, we shall just have to wait and see," replied the other, as he turned and retraced his steps leisurely down the hall. McCalley watched him disappear into his office, before moving toward the elevators.

The interview had bothered him more than he cared to admit. His exterior calm was the result of self-imposed discipline; inside he felt as though he'd been put through a physical ordeal. Impatient to be outside, away from those elegant but oppressive surroundings, he pushed the "down" button repeatedly, as though doing so would speed things up. His unruffled exterior belied the angry churning inside him at Benson's cool manner, as though Monsieur had expected all that was said and had been ready for him. McCalley could swear that the man had actually enjoyed the encounter.

A loud commotion made McCalley turn back and retrace his steps through the glass doors. The sounds were coming from Benson's suite. They grew louder as the Inspector ran down the length of the corridor. The receptionist, who had just returned from lunch, was right behind him. Others were coming out of nearby offices.

McCalley leaned against the doorjamb to catch his breath. Inside, Benson's secretary was slowly backing out of his office, the blood drained from her face, her eyes bulging, her hand covering her mouth. McCalley took her by the arm and drew her outside into the corridor. With another swift movement, he blocked the receptionist, who was about to move past him, into the room, to see what was happening.

"Stay right here," he told the two women. "Don't let anyone inside."

The fracas was coming from the innermost room, Benson's private office — sounds of exertion, heavy grunting, small muffled cries and, as a background to these, a steady thumping. At first, all McCalley saw was the overturned desk, the chairs thrown into a corner, papers strewn over the floor.

A terrible premonition overwhelmed him as he moved closer. The thumping continued, a deadly sound McCalley would never forget. He approached cautiously and looked behind the overturned desk.

Two men were on the floor. One, lying face up, was thrashing wildly, trying to free himself from the other, who straddled him, and had him firmly pinned down. McCalley would not have recognized Benson as the man being attacked, except for his clothes, now spattered with blood. With one enormous hand against Benson's throat, the huge hulk on top of him held his victim's head in position while, with the other hand, he kept hitting the almost unrecognizable face of his victim. His blows were methodical, deliberate, carefully spaced, powerful, each one shattering and splintering more bone and tissue. Blood continued to spurt out. It had already covered most of the elegant Chinese rug under the desk and covered, also, the jacket, trousers and hands of the assailant.

McCalley backed away slowly and retraced his steps. A small crowd filled the entrance to the suite. He pushed them back into the corridor, ahead of him, then turned to Benson's secretary and said:

"Get Security up here. Stay at your desk and wait for them. Don't let anyone else in. Can you do that?" The woman nodded, still very pale. When she was back at her desk, talking into the phone, McCalley moved into the hall and closed the door behind him.

"I am Inspector Luke McCalley, with the Ottawa Police," he said in French, loud enough for everyone to hear. "This is a crime scene. No one is to go inside." To the receptionist he said, "I want you to stay at your desk. No one is to go beyond this point. The police will be here soon and they will take over. Then, standing by the glass wall overlooking the spectacular view he had enjoyed earlier, he placed his own calls to the police and Interpol.

In a matter of minutes, the place was swarming with security guards from the building and the French police. People from Interpol arrived soon after. As the officers moved down the hall toward Benson's suite, they could hear the scuffling, the pounding noise from within. They moved in quickly, but the thumping and groaning didn't stop right away. It had taken, McCalley saw — when he hurried back into Benson's suite, after the sounds had finally ceased — five of the strongest police officers to pull the attacker away.

In the eerie silence that had settled inside the room, McCalley watched as Bonz got up from the floor, offering no further resistance, and allowed himself to be led around the desk to the very chair McCalley had occupied a short time earlier. He sat quietly, as the police tied his hands and feet (cuffs were too small for his large wrists and thick ankles). He was unexpectedly calm, as though he had done his job and could now relax; but he was not answering any questions, even when McCalley tried to help by translating them into the easiest possible English. Bonz's clothes were splattered with blood, as were his face and hands, one of which — McCalley now noticed — had been turned into an even more lethal weapon by brass knuckles.

At last, the big man acknowledged McCalley's presence. "If he'd been smarter," he said, turning to the Inspector with something like a smirk: "he woudda had me rubbed out with Joe." They were the only words he would utter for the rest of that that day.

CHAPTER NINETEEN

McCalley remained in Paris for over a week, but still found no time for Versailles or even the Eiffel Tower. His only indulgence — if it could be called that — was walking to the nearest men's apparel story to buy himself two shirts, two pairs of socks and some underwear to see him through the extra days needed to wind things up.

The French police had proved most cooperative, especially since McCalley had offered to share his case materials with them. It made things easier on both sides: with the Inspector's help, the French authorities were able to establish motive easily enough, and in return they allowed McCalley free access to Bonz, who, at one point declared he would speak to no one except Inspector McCalley.

Bonz, to McCalley's great relief, turned all their scattered data into hard evidence, filling in the blanks not only for Interpol and the French police, but also for the police in the United States and Canada. The Ambrosinis — father, sons, Jimmy, and a number of other members of that crime family — could now be indicted on a number of charges, including Frank Hasting's murder. By telling what he knew about Joe's relationship with the Ambrosinis and with Charles Benson, who apparently had used the "family" for a number of "hits" for which he had paid handsomely, Bonz had provided McCalley with the connecting lines between the Inspector's "points of reference." He had also told them where to look for written evidence and had deciphered some of the cryptic notes Markarian had searched out in Sarace's files and sent the Inspector, at his request.

As McCalley later explained, it was Bonz who confirmed that Joe had gone to Ottawa on special orders "from the top" to kill Frank Hastings and make it look like an accident. Kenney's inquiries provided essential details. The meeting at the Elgin, the morning Frank was killed, had been called by Frank's contact, who worked for Benson and had been sent to Ottawa to watch him.

Joe too had been set up on Benson's orders.

Benson, obviously, had made it a habit to kill — or, more precisely, to give orders to have killed — anyone who was a real or potential threat.

Bonz also went into detail about Benson's special "deals," what Joe had told him about those, and especially the interest Benson had taken in Frank Hastings from the very beginning. He told them that Benson had had Frank in his sights long before he disappeared on nine-eleven. For reasons not altogether clear, he had paid all Frank's gambling debts and had maneuvered him into position in Ottawa, once Frank got there, luring him with big money and illegal investments.

"Leddem know what that bastard did"— was Bonz's summing up.

August Bonzeski, the son of Polish immigrants, had an air of confidence about him now, a new alertness, as though he had accomplished a heroic deed. He seemed not at all concerned about the obvious fate that awaited him; if anything, he was enjoying the limelight. He had performed what he felt was a duty, like a soldier who seeks out and kills the enemy.

When asked, he said he'd struck down the police guard, went home to pick up his passport and some cash he had hidden under the floorboards (entering through the back, when the officer on duty up front took a short walk to stretch his legs), grabbed a cab to Kennedy and boarded the first available flight to Paris. Once there, he gave the cabbie the address he had copied from Joe's little black book (still safe where he'd put it, under the floorboards, after Joe's death). He entered the building when the security guard was turned away and made his way quickly to the fire exit. The reception area was still empty when he looked out — it was still early — after climbing the thirty floors to Benson's offices. He scurried down the corridor to Benson's suite. No one was in yet. After checking out various doors, he found a cleaning closet and hid inside. It was a long wait.

Benson's secretary was the first one in, around noon. Benson himself arrived soon after. His secretary trailed him into the office to tell him that an Inspector McCalley was waiting to see him. Bonz was surprised, but it made no difference. He itched to get his hands on the "bastardsonnovabitch," but he wanted plenty of time with his victim. He could wait a while longer, until McCalley left. When Benson was back at his desk, Bonz came out of hiding and did "wha' I hadda do."

McCalley himself felt vindicated. What might have seemed to others merely unfounded suspicions had been turned into hard evidence. It wasn't mere idle speculation, he rationalized to himself and later insisted, somewhat indignantly, when Markarian ribbed him about how the answer had come to him in a flash. "I kept going back to the materials we'd accumulated, re-read our reports and memos over and over again, all the data we had found, and suddenly it was all there, right in front of my eyes. All I did was connect the dots. Everything was clear as day. It isn't proof of anything," he'd admitted, "but we'll get that eventually."

The payments to the Ambrosinis had triggered it. They were spaced out and did not suggest gifts, as he and Markarian had believed at first. Nor were they payments for loans: Benson had not needed large sums of money for a long time now. So, what was the money for? It was then that he remembered certain particulars in the background stories Josie had saved for him. More research had confirmed his suspicions: the companies Benson had bought out over the years had not all been failing; several had been doing quite well. As McCalley reviewed the accounts of purchases and takeovers, other details suddenly loomed large. What flashed a signal, what made him sit up in his chair as he went over those accounts was the fact that the heads of a number of the corporations mentioned had retired or died during negotiations. A pattern began to emerge.

Most of Benson's payments to the Ambrosinis were made soon after takeovers had been successfully negotiated. These sums could not, however, be construed (McCalley was quick to concede) as evidence of criminal activity, although the legendary entrepreneur, in his opinion, was certainly capable of using and might indeed have used illegal and criminal means to get what he wanted. That he was capable of murder, Bonz had confirmed. To McCalley, the notations they had found about money passing from "B" to the Ambrosinis, were significant. He saw them as important points of reference; Bonz had in part confirmed his suspicions.

Throughout, he had moved cautiously; but in the end he was pleased to find that his conclusions were consistent with what he'd observed about Benson.

Further review of the accounts they'd subpoenaed revealed large sums to the Ambrosinis around the time of Emma's accident and Frank's hit-and-run. On the books, those deaths had been entered (according to McCalley's reading of dates and sums) as "services rendered."

And of course, there were more recent payments, which McCalley had guessed (a decidedly "informed guess," as he described it later to Markarian) were connected with Katie's mugging and Joe Sarace's death. Bonz had been able to fill in those blanks easily enough. He was there when Joe called in Georgie and gave him instructions about the mugging. Katie was not to be seriously hurt; the attack was meant as a warning, a reminder to keep her mouth shut. Katie's watch, rings, all the stuff taken from her, Bonz had explained, were safe. Georgie had been told not to touch anything until Joe got back to him. He had also told them where they would find the loot: under the floorboards in Joe's living room.

In Frank's case: Joe had alerted Bonz about a job he'd been assigned by Mario Ambrosini himself, the head of the family. He left Bonz in charge of the office, with careful instructions, while he went to Canada for a few days. Joe had told Bonz about the conversation he'd had with Mr. Ambrosini, as the two men (with Ambrosini's bodyguards in front and back) walked the short distance, from where Tommy had parked the car on Mulberry Street, to Luigi's, a cramped little eatery that served only three dishes: fried *calamari* with regular, medium, or spicy sauce and stale rolls on the side, dunked in whatever sauce was ordered. Ambrosini loved the dish, especially the spicy sauce. He went there often, although his doctor had told him to avoid that kind of food. By the time they reached Luigi's, Ambrosini had explained that James Chadwick, alias Frank Hastings, had become a threat and that his sponsor was pulling out. He, Ambrosini, was sending Joe, his best man, to take care of it. Their friend Benson in Paris had been clear about that: Ambrosini was to send his very best man, the one he trusted most.

Of course, in court — as everyone knew — what Bonz told them would be dismissed as "hearsay." It could hardly matter, though, since the Ambrosinis (McCalley had learned) were being advised by their lawyers to make a deal — in which case, they were likely to admit to that and much else.

Also with Bonz's help, McCalley eventually was able to piece together a picture of Benson as the top man, the one who gave the orders. Benson had chosen Frank early on and had encouraged his gambling from behind the scenes, ostensibly to trap him into doing favors in return for large loans he couldn't pay back (or so Bonz had concluded). Later, it was illegal trading and the big money which resulted that kept Frank in place.

It rankled McCalley that he still couldn't figure out to his satisfaction the reason for Benson's interest in Frank Hastings. Why he had Frank in his sights long before nine-eleven. What threat Frank posed.

Or why he had asked Katie to kill Emma.

Benson had chosen a gambler for one of his Boards, monitoring his movements through the man he had sent to Ottawa for that purpose. The contact, under relentless questioning, finally admitted that he'd been sent by Benson to befriend Frank and report back on a regular basis. Through him, Frank had been given insider tips and had invested heavily.

What they could piece together about Frank himself (and McCalley gave Kenney major credit for this) was that, thinking he was safe in Ottawa and in his new identity, he had grown careless in his greed for easy money. His gambling instincts had taken a new direction; he started investing recklessly on the basis of insider information, following his own time-table, making his own decisions, his own shady deals. Given his gambling history, he was clearly becoming a risk to himself and to others. Was that why Benson decided he had to be exterminated?

Ambrosini, Bonz had told McCalley, had shared some of the details with Joe as a sign of his trust in him, and to explain why he was sending him personally, his top man, to kill Frank. The client had insisted that the job be done by the very best; no near-miss would be tolerated.

Following McCalley's instructions, Kenney had checked motels in the area and came upon a Joe Stacey, answering Sarace's description. The clerk had positively identified him, from photos he'd been shown, as the man who had checked into the motel two days prior to Frank's death and left on the same day Frank was killed. The car, damaged in the accident, was eventually found. It had been stolen. It also had been cleaned a number of times since Joe had rented it, but the police were still able to find traces of forensic evidence that tied Joe to the car.

In spite of lingering doubts and a few loose ends, McCalley allowed himself to bask, briefly, in well-deserved satisfaction. The information they had gathered assured a number of indictments. Several trials were shaping up as a result.

Bonz, of course, was arraigned in Paris, but a trial was unlikely. Nor was it likely that he would be arraigned or tried in New York on the lesser charges (withholding evidence, conspiracy to murder, accessory to murder, and so on) — although he would probably be brought to New York (and possibly taken to Ottawa), to testify. The Queens prosecutor, for one, felt there was no point pressing the other charges as a back-up, when the French police had found him actually committing the murder, with witnesses on the scene. Not only had Bonz been caught pummeling Benson to death; he was proud of what he had done.

In any case, it spared the French authorities the expense of a trial. Sentencing was all that remained.

The coroner's report noted that Benson was dead long before his assailant was pulled away from him. The victim's skull had been crushed by having been repeatedly banged on the hard oak floor, the face was smashed to a pulp, no longer recognizable. The throat too had been injured: it had deep indentations, as though an attempt had been made, toward the end, to strangle or — more precisely — asphyxiate the victim.

A lawyer had been assigned to Bonz, but it was a mere formality. Bonz refused to accept him. He wasn't interested in any kind of legal representation.

Witnessing Benson's brutal murder had been a traumatic experience, even for a hardened homicide chief. That Bonz had managed to flee from protective custody, board a flight to Paris, and murder Benson was a twist no one could possibly have foreseen. Nor could anyone have imagined Bonz turning against the Ambrosinis and providing McCalley and the other officers with so much solid proof of Benson's guilt. The irony of owing so much to the man who murdered Benson did not escape the Inspector. He would much have preferred taking Benson in alive, but he had to admit that without Bonz, they would still be floundering in a fishing expedition.

On the plus side, Benson's death had put an end to a frustrating investigation. Of course, the Inspector was quick to remind himself, a great deal of hard work had brought things to that point, which in turn had led to such an unexpected closure. They could all now breathe a sigh of relief.

Only one thing continued to bother him, even though, except for the paper work, the investigation was over. Why had Benson kept such a close watch on Katie and Frank Hastings? An easy answer was a psychological one: an obsession, perhaps, a fixation to re-establish contact with the only family member he recognized and liked — Frank coming into the picture only because he was Katie's husband. Briefly, McCalley had entertained the notion that Benson was a psychopath, but in the course of events he had dismissed that idea. The man did not fit the profile, not in any clinical sense. Although he seemed to suffer no sense of guilt and was prepared to kill without a second thought, he was not moved to do so compulsively or indiscriminately.

Benson had motives and targets that were part of a practical master plan with practical goals. His talents were all directed toward those goals. He was lucid, knew what he wanted, and was ruthless in getting it. No need for constant reassurances as to his own worth, no reason to compensate for a lack in himself. He had plenty of common sense and cunning — a shrewd operator. Dreams of power were not necessary to soothe his ego; he *had* power, plenty of it, as well as a huge fortune that could buy anything and anyone — even the devil himself!

Yet he had kept a close watch on Katie and her husband, probably from the time they were married, or soon after that. Whatever the reason, McCalley had decided, it had to be a practical one, part of the overall picture that had slowly emerged. Benson may well have wanted to protect Katie, share the harvest of his success with her in some way; but why did he nurture the same kind of interest in Frank? Why had he set the man up, lured him into illegal trading, and then have him killed?

McCalley would be the first to admit that Frank Hastings was a selfish, greedy, amoral human being. In New York, he'd paid off a large loan by killing a stranger. In Ottawa, he'd acted on insider information fed to him by one of Benson's men and in less than two years had raked in half a million. He was unscrupulous, self-serving, a compulsive gambler, and much else; and, yes, he may have deserved to die, but not on Benson's orders.

Benson knew a great deal about Frank and had used it to his advantage for several years. What made him suddenly want the man dead? To McCalley it still didn't make sense. Brooding on this, the Inspector felt a profound inadequacy that quickly gave way to an overwhelming frustration.

Still, he was grateful. Bonz's lengthy and detailed deposition would give a number of people good cause for concern. The Ambrosini family's shrewd lawyers would have a hard time getting their notorious clients off the hook this time; there were too many direct charges —

conspiracy, attempted murder, conspiracy to murder, racketeering, extortion, and much else — in addition to the memos, notes, and other documents found in the files that corroborated Bonz's information. Under oath, Bonz had given them all all that they needed. He had also turned over documents to support his testimony. For the first time in a long time, the Ambrosinis were on the defensive. Their lawyers might succeed in defusing some of the charges, but not all of them. Even if a deal was made, there would be jail time for several members of the "family" and their minions.

By the end of that long and trying day that he would never forget — when Bonz had abruptly and unexpectedly turned up and killed Benson — McCalley was exhausted. It was after nine, when he arrived back at his hotel. A dinner of prawns in a mild curry sauce, tiny peas, and roasted potatoes, together with a glass of wine (a white Bordeaus, this time) helped restore his depleted energy and brought some emotional relief.

Back in his room, he sat at the desk and made detailed notes of that eventful day. His eyes were closing by the time he had finished.

Ten hours of uninterrupted sleep worked their spell. McCalley woke the next morning refreshed both physically and psychologically. Before showering, he ordered a late breakfast. In the dining room, they were serving lunch — it was well after twelve — but the kitchen staff had come to terms with his erratic schedule and made no fuss. When the order arrived, McCalley paused in his ruminations to enjoy the delicate crepes and the strong coffee he had come to like so much. When he was finished, he opened the window and looked down on the little square below. The weather was holding; it was still warm enough for short sleeves.

He watched as pedestrians walked by in the street

below purposefully, as cars circled around the small fountain in the middle of the square, they too with a goal and a purpose. He watched a line of little schoolgirls in uniform, escorted by two nuns dressed in the traditional long black robes, white band under a short black veil — they too with a destination, a goal in view.

What was Benson's goal, his reason for keeping Frank Hastings on a long leash? He'd gone to some trouble to get him on one of his Boards, then lured him on with the promise of quick money.

Then had him killed. . . .

Restless, he considered a leisurely walk to the center, or visiting some of the old haunts of his student days, but quickly dismissed the idea: he was too distracted to enjoy such an excursion. Instead, he took one last breath of the mild, warm air and moved back into the room, leaving the window open.

He sat on the bed and thought of Benson playing God with other people's lives.

After a while, he picked up his cell phone and called Bill Kenney.

His sergeant was effusive in his congratulations. Benson's dramatic murder was already being reported as a "developing story" on all the major TV channels.

"It was team work, Bill. You and Markarian had a big part in all this."

"Ready for a welcoming reception?"

"What? No way! Listen, Bill, . . . tell them I'm exhausted, I suffered bodily injury. Anything. Tell them I need to rest for at least a year. In seclusion, got that? I can't see anybody for at least a year — !"

"The Chief himself is supervising it. The minute the news came in, he started to plan it," Kenney went on. McCalley heard a gurgle at the other end. "We've all been given tasks. I have to make sure you're there for it."

"Bloody Hell!" was the reaction.

Kenney ignored it. "When exactly will you be coming back, Sir?"

"Probably, never." McCalley held back more expletives by vigorously scratching his head. When he spoke again, his tone was properly official.

"Look, Bill, I really don't know when I'm coming back. There's a good deal still to do here, before I fly to New York. And a lot waiting for me there. It'll be a while before I can get back to Ottawa."

"Well, let me know when you're coming —"

"— It'll be some time —"

"— so I can pick you up at the airport and —"

"— We'll see. . . ."

"Is there anything you want me to do, in the meantime?"

He had almost forgotten the reason for his call. "Yes, Bill, there is. You remember my asking you some time back to check on Hasting's history on the job? Did you come up with anything?"

"Not really, Sir. I didn't get back to you on that because it was a dead-end and now, of course, the case is closed."

"What did you find?" McCalley persisted.

"If you want details, I'll have to fetch my notes."

"Just run it by me quickly, for now."

"He specialized in medical malpractice suits, as you know. During his five years on the job, he handled four cases. Three went to trial. Two of them ended up in settlements of a quarter of a million for one, four million for the other. The third went against the plaintiff. One case was withdrawn just before going to trial."

"Did the third plaintiff file an appeal?"

"Yes. It was denied." When McCalley did not respond, Kenney added: "Sorry, Sir. I didn't think we had to follow it any further —"

McCalley quickly retreated. "We've certainly had

plenty else to keep us busy," he admitted, "but there are a couple of loose ends I'd like to clear up, Bill. . . You said one case had been withdrawn?"

"That happened when the man charged, a Doctor Harold Crane, died suddenly, a short time before the trial was scheduled to open. He had a heart attack right there in the hospital. He'd just finished making his morning rounds."

"The claim was withdrawn because the doctor died? It doesn't make sense."

"Especially since the plaintiff was sure to win. Everyone agreed that the man had died because of the new drug Dr. Crane had prescribed. Crane admitted prescribing the drug. He also admitted that it had had lethal effects."

"And the drug company was never charged?"

"Apparently not."

McCalley took in this information with a slight stirring that made him rise sharply from where he had been sitting on the bed. He paced the small room, the phone close to his ear.

"Are you still there, Sir?"

"Yes, yes, I'm here. . . . Pull out your notes, Bill — I'll wait — and when we're finished, fax me everything you have on this. I'll be here for a while." He read off the hotel's fax number. "Be sure to put my name and room number on every sheet . . . and, Bill, mark everything 'Urgent' and for personal delivery, so it won't get pushed into a mail box. . . . Right now, what I need to know is —"

"Hold on, Sir. Let me get my notes." McCalley could hear the rustle of papers. "What am I looking for?"

"What exactly was the Doctor charged with?"

"Let's see. . . . Ah, here it is. That the drug was put on the market prematurely and was unsafe —"

"— But that would suggest the manufacturer was at fault, not Dr. Crane. How could he have known — "

"— and that Dr. Crane acted precipitously in prescribing it.... I don't know, Sir."

"How did the Doctor respond to the charges?"

McCalley could hear Kenney leafing through papers at the other end. "Ah, here it is.... He'd prescribed the drug in good faith.... Nothing happened until two years into the treatment, when his patients began to die. He then stopped prescribing the drug, although it wasn't taken off the market until later, after Dr. Crane died."

"What kind of medication was it?"

"An anti-inflammatory. At first, the patients seemed to find relief but eventually the tissues and bones were compromised, . . . it says here, 'compromised beyond possibility of repair'."

"You mean the bones and tissues wore away?"

"So it seems. It affected major organs too. After a while the body just closed down."

"That's pretty decisive, wouldn't you say? So, why was the suit withdrawn?"

Kenney seemed flustered. "I'm sorry, Sir. I just didn't have time to — "

"What I find strange," McCalley interrupted, "is that the company wasn't sued for negligence... Did you say the FDA had approved the drug?"

"Yes."

"That's even more strange. Was the FDA asked to investigate? When did Dr. Crane die?"

"Excuse me, Sir. I'm checking my notes...."

McCalley took a deep breath and held back the other questions that were crowding his brain. "Dr. Crane died in February of 1999, two weeks before the trial was supposed to begin. I don't see anything here about the FDA being approached."

"Then what happened."

"Some kind of settlement was arrived at. No

details available, but the charges were dropped right after Dr. Crane died. There was no trial and the whole thing was forgotten."

"How many deaths were attributed to the drug?" McCalley could hear Kenney shuffling papers.

"I only have Dr. Crane's figures here. He started treating thirty patients with the drug, early in ninety-seven. Nineteen were dead by the end of ninety-eight, two years later. Some who were started on the drug late in ninety-seven, survived, since Dr. Crane discontinued the drug soon after. . . . Here it is: stopped prescribing it in April of ninety-eight."

"When was the suit filed?"

"September ninety-eight."

"And Hastings was on the case?"

"Hold on. Yes, as assistant to a John Chisholm."

"Is Chisholm still around?"

"No, Sir. He was transferred to another location right after the suit was filed. No one replaced him."

"You mean, Hastings was on his own?"

"There were plenty of lawyers for the legal work, but after Chisholm left, Hastings seems to have taken on Crane as his client, that's right."

McCalley said nothing. Kenney waited it out.

"We may have to go back into this, Bill."

Once again, Kenney apologized: "Sorry, Sir. I didn't have time for a more thorough search—"

"I realize that," McCalley agreed for the second time. "What about Flora? Did Frank talk to her about any of this?"

"Didn't ask, Sir. It didn't seem—"

"— Listen, Bill. Ask Flora to search Frank's things again. No, better yet, go in and search with her. I have a feeling. . . . He may have left notes, a file —"

"What are we looking for?"

"Anything that throws light on Hastings' role in

all this. Why the drug company wasn't sued. Where the FDA comes into it. Why the case was dropped. . . . Did Dr. Crane have a family?"

"Wife and three children. The oldest is thirteen."

McCalley asked for the address. It was somewhere in Riverdale, in the Bronx. Markarian would know how to get there. They would visit her as soon as he got back to New York.

Finally, he asked: "What's the name of the drug and who makes it?"

When he had taken down the information, he sat staring at what he had written. Kenney was asking, "Sir, are you still there, Sir?"

"Yes, I'm here, Bill. . . . Look, I need some more dates." As he jotted them down, he resolutely closed his mind to the questions and doubts crowding in on him.

Before hanging up, he gave Kenney detailed instructions. Kenney took them down, then commented, somewhat hesitantly:

"But, Sir, the case is closed. . . ."

"Not quite, Bill." He left it at that. How could he explain that what he was about to look into might well be another murder instigated by a man who could not be brought to justice because he was already dead!

If he was right, the plaintiffs, the victim's family, had been paid well for dropping the charges. He was guessing, damn it, but what other explanation could there be?

McCalley could not ignore the exciting tug of certainty prodding him on. He had no evidence to support any of his wild conclusions but rushed on nonetheless, in spite of his better judgment, justifying his probing as perfectly natural under the circumstances.

His instincts told him, even with the little he had just learned and again, without a scrap of evidence, that Dr. Crane had not acted precipitously, that he was innocent of any wrongdoing. So the big question was: why hadn't the plaintiffs raised charges of negligence against the company or the FDA, instead of targeting Dr. Crane? The facts seemed to call for such action. And why were the charges dropped, after his death, the trial abandoned?

Why did the doctor have to be silenced?

For the Inspector was ready to swear on a stack of Bibles, even without having the full story, that Dr. Crane had indeed been silenced — but not with money.

The guilty party surely was to be sought elsewhere, or, more precisely (he would bet on it!) would turn out to be Charles Benson, who, as Kenney had informed him, owned the pharmaceutical company that had produced the drug that had killed Dr. Crane's patients.

And what if (a big "if"!) . . . what if Frank Hastings, who had become Dr. Crane's insurance representative, had stumbled on incriminating evidence that would place certain people in jeopardy?

What if he'd threatened Benson with what he had uncovered?

McCalley was sure he'd hit the right buttons.

CHAPTER TWENTY

After a great deal of paper work, McCalley finally was able to leave Paris for New York. His overnight trip had stretched to ten days. No doubt, he would have to return again, later; but first, there was unfinished business to take care of in New York and Ottawa.

On the plane, he read all the fresh stories that had come out since Benson's murder. Josie and Marge had collected them for him in a large envelope, which Josie handed him, when they picked him up to drive him to the airport.

Not surprising, the magazines specializing in the grotesque, celebrity quarrels, divorces, love affairs, assorted tragedies and escapades, reported Benson's criminal activities with something like gusto. The newspapers were less brazen, but there too the facts were laid out with a certain dramatic flair. After all, how often did a case like this come their way?

On the whole, the stories were accurate enough. For McCalley, they were painful history.

Once again, Markarian had insisted on meeting him at Kennedy. To the Inspector's embarrassment, his friend came forward holding high before him, like a trophy, a red carnation, which he pinned on McCalley's lapel before hugging him.

"You're an international hero!" was his greeting. He put his arm around McCalley's shoulder, as they walked toward the exit. "I can't believe you were there, saw it all."

"Not a pleasant sight!" was the reply. "The man was like a robot. It took five policemen to pull him off!"

As they drove into Manhattan, Markarian briefed him about the Ambrosinis.

"At least four people will be charged. Maybe

more. We've got Jimmy ready to talk, but the Ambrosinis are waiting for their lawyers to strike a deal." He turned to McCalley with a grin. "Even so, we'll get them on at least three or four counts. They're definitely looking at jail time."

Katie was doing well. Francis had insisted on a brief vacation and had taken her to Quebec for a week. Her colleagues at work had been solicitous; her boss, cooperative. She was recovering in every way.

Flora Chadwick had called. Markarian told her that she'd been right in suspecting Frank had been murdered. "That's all I said. I thought you should be the one to explain everything."

McCalley nodded. "An unpleasant task, having to tell her what a scoundrel her husband was."

"I suspect she knew all along," Markarian said, quietly. *Does love really conquer all?* McCalley wondered, knowing his friend was thinking the same thing.

They agreed to meet at the precinct the next afternoon, to compare notes for their reports.

The Inspector was early, but Markarian was ready for him. The usual clutter had been cleared from the desk, but there were still stacks of folders and scattered papers on the floor and on the windowsill. A small table had been drawn up alongside the desk to provide additional work surface.

They sorted out their papers and for the next two hours checked one another's notes, made corrections, transposed items, cross-referenced material, made a rough working index of documents and depositions to help them find information easily and quickly. At five they took a short break. Markarian went down the hall to check his mail and stretch his legs. McCalley stayed in the office, watching the traffic in the street below. In ten minutes they were ready for more.

It was six-thirty when McCalley sat back, yawned, and pulled out a folder from his briefcase.

"Thought you might like to have copies I made for you — transcripts of interviews, summaries of meetings with witnesses, depositions — " He handed the folder to Markarian. "Feel free to use them. Some of it is good reading, if nothing else."

Markarian laughed, took the folder. "Maybe you're in the wrong profession!"

"Actually, Kenney put together most of it. I added some of my own notes."

"And I've got something for *you*," Markarian said, picking up several sheets of paper clipped together, from a pile on the floor. He held them out to McCalley. "A rough summary of highlights. I'd like you to read it, . . . if you have time, that is." When McCalley nodded and reached for it, Markarian pulled it back. "Not here though. Take it with you. Call me tomorrow. I have much more to add, including some of what you just gave me. I've never had to cover three, possibly four related murders at once, not to mention any number of assorted felonies. Anyway, I'd like your reaction so far." He held out the sheets and watched as McCalley placed them inside his briefcase.

"Are you free tomorrow afternoon?"

Markarian made a face. "Good Lord, do you expect it will take all afternoon to make it right?"

McCalley laughed and shook his head. "That's something else." He glanced at his watch. A quarter to six. "It's been a long day, but if you can spare a few more minutes, there's something I want to pass by you—"

Markarian waved him on. "I have time."

McCalley went on to summarize what Kenney had told him on the phone. When he'd finished, Markarian asked:

"Why didn't the family sue Crane's estate? In fact,

why didn't they sue the company instead of Crane?"

"It puzzled me, too. I have Kenney looking into it again."

"How is it relevant to our case?"

"The drug was made by one of the companies owned by Benson. Somewhere in Virginia."

Markarian gave a low whistle. "You think . . . ?"

"I don't want to think too long about this, Ed, not until I have more to go on. But it *is* strange. . . . The trial was supposed to start early in March of 1999. Crane died about two weeks earlier." When Markarian said nothing, McCalley went on: "So, will we have time to drive up to Riverdale tomorrow afternoon, talk to Crane's widow? Is it a long drive? Where is it, exactly?"

"Riverdale? It's the posh section of the Bronx, facing the Hudson, just north of the George Washington Bridge. The Bronx is where the Yankees still play ball in an old stadium, where there are whole blocks of burned out abandoned ghettos, where mostly Black and Puerto Ricans live. Coming out of the Bronx into Riverdale is like landing in Heaven. It's really the beginning of Westchester County, where the money lives." He glanced at the address McCalley had passed on to him. "From your hotel, it shouldn't take more than forty, fifty minutes." He looked up. "What time?"

"I called Mrs. Crane before coming here. She said after lunch would be fine."

They decided to start out at one.

In the morning, McCalley called his wife and chatted with her for several minutes, then touched base with Kenney, who had nothing new to report yet, then jotted reminders to himself about things he wanted to ask Julia Crane.

When they arrived at the simple colonial house and rang the bell, just before two, there was no answer. They rang again, a long burst this time. The muffled sound of footsteps reached them.

The woman who opened the door and stood on the threshold staring at them, looked confused. McCalley introduced himself and Markarian and, pulling out his badge, reminded her of the appointment they had made. With her free hand, Mrs. Crane brushed back some stray hairs as she opened the door wide to let them in.

"Sorry. Lost track of the time. After four years, I've finally gotten around to sorting out Harold's clothes. I'm getting rid of everything, with the excuse of the annual church drive." She led them into a dark living room. "Let me get some light in here," she said, as she moved to open the blinds, adding as she did so: "We don't get many visitors."

She was a small woman in her late thirties. What should have been a pretty face was drawn and lined, almost to the point of being haggard. Fatigue and lack of sleep over a long period of time had taken their toll. From some photos on the mantelpiece, taken in happier days, McCalley guessed that before her husband died Julia Crane had been lively, her deep blue eyes bright, her expression warm and outgoing. The contrast was startling. It was as though a light had gone out inside her.

The two men remained standing as she walked away from the windows. Warm afternoon sunlight flooded the room and brought it to life, as she moved toward a grouping of two facing sofas and armchairs at right angle to them. A large, low, square table was in the center, within easy reach of all who sat around it. Like the rest of the furniture in the room, these were simple pieces, made for use, but not inexpensive. It was a room, thought McCalley, the family must have enjoyed, before tragedy struck.

Mrs. Crane sat down at the far end of one of the sofas and gestured for the men to sit opposite her. There was a careless indifference in her movements, in her way of looking at the world, even in the way she dressed. Her white cotton shirt was wrinkled, her hair was pulled back in a ponytail and held in place with a rubberband. She wore loafers and no make-up.

"What do you want to know about my husband?" she began without preamble.

"Anything you can tell us about the suit that was brought against him and then dropped," said McCalley.

The woman's face took on a hard, stubborn look. "Are you here to stir things up again?"

The Inspector was taken aback, momentarily. "We're homicide detectives, Mrs. Crane," he hurried to reassure her, "My colleague and I have nothing to do with insurance claims or legal matters, as I said on the phone." He went on to explain that they were trying to tie up some loose ends in connection with the death of the man who was representing her husband's insurance company at the time the suit was filed.

"Frank? Frank Hastings? He's dead?"

"I'm afraid so. Did you know he had moved to Canada? He died in Ottawa. Did you know him well?"

"I'm sorry to hear that. . . . Yes, we got to know Frank fairly well. At first, he was assigned to work with John Chisholm, then John got the transfer he'd asked for, to California, where his son lives. Frank was left to carry on. Well, the lawyers were always there, of course, but Harold wouldn't listen to them after a while."

"But he got along with Frank?"

"Oh, yes. Frank was solicitous, always helpful. For a while, Harold would talk to no one else. Later, he distanced himself from just about everybody, including Frank — but, why are you asking me about Frank Hastings? I don't understand what the suit brought against my husband has to do with Frank's death. We're talking about charges filed back in the Fall of ninety-eight. That's a long time ago!"

"We think there's a connection between Frank Hastings' death last June and what happened back then. You see, the pharmaceutical company that produced the drug that went on the market in ninety-seven and that your husband began to prescribe to his patients around that same time is owned by a man who is related to Hastings by marriage."

"Benson? Charles Benson? Frank was related to Benson? Wouldn't it have meant a conflict of interest for him to have worked on the case?"

McCalley decided to ignore that can of worms. "I don't think Frank knew about the connection. Benson was his wife's cousin, and she hadn't seen or talked to him in years. They were never close."

The woman was obviously trying to sort out what she'd just heard. "But, Inspector, if Frank didn't know his wife was related to Benson, how is it relevant?"

"We're not sure, not yet. But other information that has come to us makes these questions necessary. . . . You must have read or heard about Benson's death recently?" McCalley wondered how much she knew of the gruesome details of Benson's murder. Her expression told him she knew quite a bit, but her words veered elsewhere.

"Oh, I read about it all right!" she said sharply, shifting restlessly where she sat, struggling with some inner turbulence. "There's the one who should have been sued, not Harold! Putting out drugs that weren't properly tested, new medicines that had been pushed through with bribes, paying off that poor man's family, so they would drop the charges and everything could be hushed up nicely —"

"How do you know that?" Markarian interjected, even as McCalley cut in sharply:

"Could you tell us about that? You said earlier that your husband distanced himself from everyone at a certain point. Was that because he suspected something was wrong?"

"He didn't *suspect*, Inspector. He *knew*. I heard him say he had all the proof necessary to have Benson indicted. Unfortunately, he died before he could make public what he'd discovered." She pulled out a handkerchief and wiped her eyes and nose. The two men glanced at one another.

McCalley said: "That's exactly what we need to know, Mrs. Crane. What your husband found out about Benson's company, about the drug. And if he told Frank Hastings about it."

The woman was trying to read their faces as she put her handkerchief back in her shirt pocket. Markarian filled the awkward pause.

"Mrs. Crane, these last two weeks we've learned a great deal about Charles Benson and Frank Hastings. Our investigation suggests a connection between them and the suit filed against your husband. We need to know what happened before your husband died — if he ever talked with Frank about his . . . suspicions, . . . what he had uncovered. Because, as the Inspector just said, we think something happened at that time that may shed light on Frank Hastings' death and, by the way, also clear your husband of any wrongdoing."

She gave a small bitter laugh. "Too bad you weren't around when we could have used you!" Her voice turned hard as she leaned forward and went on. "You bet something happened! Harold was the best doctor in the world. I can show you the awards he won year after year. Twelve in sixteen years of practice! But all the drive went out of him on account of what he had to endure during those last two years, when he lost patients, then discovered it was the drug that was doing the damage, and to top it all, that *he* was being sued, not the company!" She looked away for a moment then resumed with fierce determination.

"Can you imagine what it did to him? He wanted to prove that he'd done nothing wrong and, yes, he was afraid too, after a while, my poor darling! The pressure was too much, It killed him at thirty-nine, still a young man!" Her mouth quivered as she spoke, but she held back the tears.

"We are truly sorry," said McCalley. Watching the woman trying not to give way to her emotions and sensing her discomfort and embarrassment, he decided to shift to an earlier question for which they still had no answer.

"What we would like to know is why the suit was withdrawn, the charges dropped after your husband died. It's unusual. Can you help us with that?"

"We heard rumors that the family who'd filed the suit had been approached with assurances that they would get their money, the full amount, if they dropped all charges."

"You mean, the insurance company was ready to pay out several million without a fight?" Markarian asked incredulously.

She shook her head, somewhat impatiently. "No, of course not."

"Who, then?"

"Benson, who else?" The two men glanced at one another. Mrs. Crane interpreted the look as one of skepticism and went on quickly, as though to convince them:

"I may look dull, but I'm not stupid. Harold learned things during those last few months that made him retreat into himself. No, I can't tell you what they were because he never told me. Protecting me, he said. Me and the children. I didn't understand it, but I went along. I could see how troubled he was. He began to avoid the company representatives. Didn't trust them any more. He felt they were stalling. They were supposed to be helping him; they'd promised to withdraw the drug, but after a whole year, patients were still dying, and all they gave him was a song and dance about having to work out details before going public, try to avoid a class-action suit. They said it could cost them billions of dollars."

She dismissed it all with a little wave, before going on: "A lot of hogwash. All the while, they were taking care of their business, quietly, behind the scenes. One day, they told Harold the charges were going to be dropped. They were vague about settlements, but they told Harold the drug would be taken off the market right after the suit was withdrawn and everything else would be taken care of then. To make a long story short, Benson made sure there would be no trial. That's when my husband went berserk."

"What?" Markarian broke in. "They took him off the hook. Isn't that what he wanted?"

"Earlier perhaps. But by then he *wanted* the trial. He felt he needed the public forum to make his case."

"What case?" asked McCalley, at the same that that Markarian threw out:

"Because of a deal? Was a deal made behind his back?"

There was an eloquent pause, as the woman considered her replies. When she spoke, her voice was softer, but her expression betrayed the kind of frustration she must have experienced watching her husband struggle silently, unable to trust anyone, trying to shield his family.

She answered Markarian first. "Harold went crazy when he heard that the company was prepared to pay the victim's family the full amount they were suing for. It was a rumor, mind you. We never knew for a fact. But they must have paid, because the suit was dropped. But that was after Harold died."

"Didn't he want the victim's family to get compensation?" Markarian asked.

"Oh, it wasn't that. Something else was eating him up. He became secretive, kept to himself. Wouldn't see or talk to Frank even. I think he suspected Frank had had a hand in the deal that was rumored, but I told him, even if he had helped negotiate a deal, that's what insurance companies do — although it soon became clear that the insurer had nothing to do with it."

McCalley watched Markarian jotting something down, then turned back to ask: "You said your husband wanted the trial, a public forum, to make his case. What exactly did you mean?"

"He felt the deal was a deal, it wouldn't clear *him*. Besides, the other thing was nagging him by then. He swore the company had falsified records to get the drug on the market. Talked about bribes. Don't ask me for details, I don't have any. He never told me more; as I explained earlier, he didn't want to put me at risk. That's the whole story: he wanted a trial to clear his name and to put the blame where it belonged, on the manufacturer for doctoring reports to get a defective drug out and reap huge profits. Getting the truth out there was the only thing that kept him going."

"Those are serious allegations," said McCalley. "Did he have any proof?"

"He said he had. But no one ever saw it."

"Is the victim's family still in New York?" asked McCalley.

"No. They moved to Austria soon after the charges were dropped."

"Austria!" McCalley echoed, genuinely surprised. Markarian, who had been taking notes all along, looked up sharply.

"That's what the lawyer told me, the lawyer Harold hired. He found out they had relatives in Austria and had decided to resettle there. The grandparents had come from Austria in the thirties."

"Who was the lawyer your husband hired?" asked Markarian.

"Sam, Sam Kramer. He was competent enough. Of course, the company had dozens of good lawyers to represent their interests in court or to negotiate a settlement; but by then Harold wanted no part of that. He had plans of his own. Kramer was supposed to fight all the efforts on the part of the insurer and the drug company to avoid a trial, or to negotiate, for whatever reasons. It turned out to be an impossible, expensive task." She took a long breath, more of a restrained sob, before going on.

"I overheard him tell Sam once that in court he would blow the case wide open and nail the true criminals: Benson and his cronies. But every time Sam asked for evidence, he'd refuse. The papers were stashed away safely, he told him. He'd pull out everything at the right moment."

"And you have no idea where they might be, those papers?"

"None. I told you, Harold wanted to keep me in the dark, by way of protecting me. He was paranoid about it. He'd become obsessed."

"Might he have told Frank about the evidence"

"I'm sure he did. But he wouldn't have shown him anything. Nothing came of it, in the end. Harold died in February. Benson must have made the deal right after that, because the suit was dropped just before the case was due in court, in March."

Again, she tried to gauge the reaction to her words and addressed what she interpreted as skepticism in their faces. "It was all hush-hush, but it had to be Benson, who else could it have been?"

But the reaction she had witnessed had been

triggered by very different emotions. McCalley worked his way back to something she had said earlier.

"How can you be so sure your husband had actual proof of the drug company's complicity?"

"I know my husband. He would never have said the things he said, without having proof. If he was so willing, no, so *anxious* to have his say in court, he *must* have had proof!"

"But he never produced it...."

"No."

"And none has been found...."

"That doesn't mean it didn't exist, doesn't still exist —"

"Have you looked for it?"

She nodded. "Believe me, I would have found it, had it been here, in the house."

"What about Kramer?"

"I told you: he was just as frustrated as the rest of us." Her eyes darted from one man to the other, as though sensing a certain distance in them, reading in their expressions a difficulty in accepting what she had just told them. She picked up, almost recklessly:

"Well, how would *you* feel, Inspector, if all your achievements of more than a decade threatened to be destroyed because of other people's mistakes?" When McCalley looked away and said nothing, she plunged ahead.

"We had to take on a second mortgage, a large one, to pay for Sam's retainer and up-front fee. I was worried but didn't complain. Harold was worried enough for both of us. I didn't want to add to his burden. Besides, I trusted him. So I gave him lots of space, supported him by not asking questions, letting him carry on as he thought best. I felt, once everything was over, we could resume our normal lives."

She paused, letting her doubts surface again, then

continued. "If he hadn't been so stubborn, he might still be alive. Clearing his name and putting the blame where it belonged was all that mattered. It bothered him more than anything else that the company was getting away with murder. Those were his words. 'It was murder,' he told Kramer. He meant it literally. He wasn't buying 'negligence'; he was saying the company had deliberately killed hundreds of people by selling that drug. . . . In the end the pressure was just too much — " Her voice broke, and she turned away, then blurted out, "It was so unfair!"

The men said nothing, waiting for her to recover and continue. Instead, she rose abruptly, her emotions still struggling inside her.

"You wanted to see his study?"

"If it's not too much trouble —"

They followed her down the hall to what had been — still was — the doctor's special room. It was lined with shelves of medical books and journals; the desk had papers and letters spread out over it, as though their owner was expected back any minute.

Julia Crane said, with a catch in her voice: "I've never cleared it out. Still can't bring myself to do it. I haven't let anyone else in here, until today. Not even Frank, who soon after Harold died asked for whatever notes he'd left behind. I told him I'd call him if I found anything."

Markarian started looking through the desk drawers, while Julia Crane stood watching. She seemed to grow more frail before the Inspector's eyes. A surge of pity swept over him. He wished he was somewhere else, not doing what he was doing.

Afraid of betraying his emotions, McCalley turned to watch Markarian before speaking again. "We would appreciate Sam Kramer's address and phone number," he said. Mrs. Crane pointed to a black telephone book lying on the desk. "It's in there."

McCalley picked up the book and held it open as Markarian copied the information.

McCalley thought of something else. "Did your husband have a close friend or colleague, someone he might have confided in at the hospital?"

"Jerry Adler, Cardiology," was the quick reply. "He and Harold played golf on weekends; sometimes, in the summer, they would take the boys fishing — John, my eldest, and Jerry's two sons."

Markarian had finished with the desk and started leafing through books on the shelves. The others watched him silently for a while, then Mrs. Crane asked:

"What exactly are you hoping to find?"

It was McCalley who answered. "Notes, letters, memos— anything that might throw light on the evidence your husband talked about, or names of people he met, talked to. . . . Earlier you said something about inadequate testing, bribes, the drug company pushing its product before it was properly assessed. The FDA itself may have been involved in some sort of conspiracy to get the drug on the market prematurely. . . ."

"You don't expect to find anything like that tucked inside those books, do you?" was the quick retort. "My husband was a careful man; in this instance, over cautious to the point of paranoia. He would hardly leave such notes or memos lying around, Inspector!"

"We need to exclude the possibility." It was clear to Markarian, however, that McCalley was in agreement. He had lost interest in Dr. Crane's papers and moved slowly out of the room into the dim hall. The others followed.

In the corridor, Mrs. Crane said: "I don't think he hid any papers in the house, Inspector — I've gone over every inch of it — or in our safe deposit box, if that's what you're thinking. I held, still hold the keys. Harold never went near the bank. He left all that business to me. . . . I can tell you exactly what's in there. Our wills— just mine, now— our marriage certificate, passports, the children's records, a few pieces of jewelry my mother left and which I haven't worn in years. The last time I went to the box was to take out Harold's will and put in his death certificate."

McCalley said, spacing his words deliberately, in a studied cadence: "Those documents, the proof we keep talking about, will exonerate your husband, Mrs. Crane. It will bring justice to bear, put the blame where it belongs. That's what you want, isn't it? Serious charges may result. That's what *we* want."

Some memory stirred in her. "Serious money. . . ." The words came forth slowly, dredged from some deep well in her consciousness.

"And serious accusations, if we find what we're looking for," added Markarian.

"'Serious money' — " she repeated in a monotone, as they moved back toward the entry hall.

A commotion and laughter outside drew their attention. Suddenly the door flew open and two little girls came running in. Seeing strangers in the hall, they came to an abrupt halt a few feet inside the threshold, the momentum throwing the smaller child against her sister's back. Mrs. Crane reached out to keep them both from falling.

They were old enough not to ask the questions their undisguised curiosity had provoked. Instead, they stared, wide-eyed, at the two men.

Mrs. Crane introduced them, then hurried them down the hall with a small push.

"There's milk and a chocolate cake in the kitchen. You can watch TV for half an hour. Then, homework."

They moved away reluctantly. As they continued down the hall, their heads bent, almost touching, they whispered to one another. At the end of the hall, they turned for one last look.

At the sight of her daughters, Mrs. Crane's face had lit up. A smile still hovered around her lips.

"You have a son, also?"

"John, yes. He's thirteen. It's been especially hard on him. Too bad you won't meet him; he's staying overnight with a school friend."

The men followed her back into the living room, where they sat down again. Mrs. Crane continued, without a break:

"I try not to come down too hard on them," she explained. "They're still very confused about their father's death. John sees himself as the protector of the family, a heavy burden for a child. He was only nine when Harold died. I try to distract him as much as possible, encourage him to go out with his friends . . . and all the while, the poor boy is trying to distract *me*! At times, he positively *hovers*. . . ."

"You must be very proud of him. . . ."

"Funny thing, Inspector; John was still a boy when Harold died. Then, suddenly, one day, he was the man of the house. Stranger still, I've learned to rely on him. . . ."

Markarian was searching through his notes; McCalley, his hands clasped between his knees, watched him for a while, then asked:

"You said something about 'serious money' — "

Mrs. Crane went on apologetically: "I'm sorry. I got distracted. Yes. I heard Harold say once that 'serious money' had passed hands. He meant bribes, Inspector. Bribes to people high up, to fix it so the drug would be approved."

"Part of the proof your husband claimed to have?"

"That's right."

"How did he come by that information, have you any idea?"

She took time to answer, as though she had not really thought about it before. "It never occurred to me until just now, and maybe it means nothing, but it was around the time that Freddie Ingersoll came up from Washington. Twice, in a short period of time. They weren't social visits."

"Who is this person?"

"An old college chum of Harold's. They kept in touch and would meet for lunch or dinner when business brought Freddie to New York. He's with the FDA."

McCalley turned to Markarian, who already was jotting down the name. "Do you have an address for him?" Markarian asked, without looking up.

"It's in the book. Let me get it for you."

The men stood up as she came back with the telephone log in her hands. Once again McCalley found the name and held the book open while Markarian copied the information. The others watched him in silence.

McCalley returned the book to her. "By the way, did anyone from the drug company ever try to contact you at any time, come around asking questions?"

"Funny you should ask. I'd forgotten about the lawyer — at least that's how he introduced himself, although I had my doubts. Came to the house about two years ago; asked for Harold's notes, same as Frank had, same as you're asking now. It was just after nine-eleven. He said they were trying to recover lab records my husband had borrowed from them for the trial, even notes Frank may have left behind. It struck me as peculiar, that second request. I remember thinking: any notes Frank may have taken belong to the insurance company, not to the drug company."

"He mentioned Hastings?"

"Yes."

McCalley turned away from those searching eyes before speaking. "What did you tell him?"

"Nothing. I had nothing and nothing to tell. But even if I did, I would never have given any of Harold's papers to anyone, least of all that fellow. After what Harold went through, I wasn't ready to trust anyone, especially somebody connected with the drug company. I told him to try the hospital, that Harold had kept all his records in his office. Apparently he'd been there and found nothing. I wondered that he'd really expected to find anything: the office had been cleared and reassigned right after Harold died, his case load redistributed, old records stored away. . . .

"He tried to butter me up, and I went along. Said he'd talked with Harold twice at the hospital. Said my husband was a brave man. Very cooperative, he said. Wanted to help. Would have been pleased to learn that the company had withdrawn the drug from circulation. . . . I wanted to yell out: Why are you telling me this; why are you here, after he's been dead for almost three years! Instead, I nodded appreciatively, all the while seething inside! I felt like shouting the truth at him. Somehow I managed to keep my cool, as Sarah would say." Again, a small smile lit up her face when she referred to her daughter, but it was gone in seconds.

She crossed her arms as though to warm herself and went on. Her voice was brittle.

"He was lying, of course, thinking he could talk me into letting him snoop around. I told him how sorry I was, that everything had been cleared out, that whatever records there were had been returned to the hospital. I enjoyed watching him squirm with disappointment. . . ." Her tone shifted again.

"Inspector, my husband had learned things he wouldn't share with his closest friends, not even with me.

Never, in a million years, would he have given that kind of information to a stranger, especially someone he didn't trust. . . . and certainly not to anyone from Benson's company! I let the fellow think I wanted to help; I even apologized for not being able to give him what he was looking for. I promised to call him if I found anything."

She laughed, a mirthless sound.

"You said the man visited your husband twice at the hospital?"

"The second time, the very morning he died. Betty, Betty Storper, was at the nurses' station, directly across from Harold's office. She had been filing. When she turned around, she saw the man leaving Harold's office. He was probably the last person to see my husband alive!"

"Would you recognize him, if we showed you some photographs?" Markarian asked.

"Yes, definitely. He had bushy eyebrows and spoke, . . . well, as though he was reciting lines he'd rehearsed. Didn't sound natural to me, more like he was playing a role. He was fluent enough, but didn't strike me as a lawyer, . . . too . . . well, let's just say he was a little rough around the edges. At least that was my impression." She looked from one to the other, as though expecting some comment, then asked:

"Why do you suppose the company waited all that time to send someone for my husband's notes? The whole business was a dead issue by then. Why would the company send a lawyer to retrieve old records of no use to anyone any more, even if I did have them, even if I knew where to find them?"

McCalley thought he had the answer to that, as he suspected Markarian had; he also knew he could not share it with her.

"You're sure he didn't keep anything like that,

maybe forgot that he had them?"

"Of course, I'm sure. Most of the records had been given over to the lawyers. For the trial. We all knew what they contained. I still don't know what else Frank or the company expected to find. And no, Inspector, Harold never forgot anything, especially something important. I wish I could help, but I can't. Just before he died, Harold cleaned out the filing cabinet in his study. I assumed he took most of the folders to the hospital. What was left, when I went through the few remaining papers, after he died, had nothing to do with his practice. There were old receipts of work done on the house years ago, personal letters, some photographs. I put everything in a carton and took it down into the basement. It's still there." She frowned, remembering, then went on: "Funny thing. . . . When Ingersoll called to express his condolences, he asked the same question. . . ." She searched McCalley's face, as though some explanation could be found in it.

"Ah! Tell us about Ingersoll."

CHAPTER TWENTY-ONE

On the drive back, McCalley marveled once again at how vital data surfaced from casual questions, and when least expected. He knew they had just stumbled on information crucial to their case. From what Julia Crane had told them, it was obvious that Hastings, as Dr. Crane's insurance representative, knew about Benson as far back as 1998, when legal proceedings first started. It was also pretty clear that he never knew anything about Benson's relationship to Katie, whom he married in 2000. Benson, on the other hand, shrewder by far and with much greater means at his disposal, surely knew about Frank's marriage to his cousin — and much else.

McCalley was pretty sure that what had triggered Benson's interest in Hastings had to do with the legal action that had targeted Harold Crane. What Julia Crane told them suggested that her husband had discovered incriminating evidence that could destroy Benson, whose company, in 1998, was just beginning to prosper. Julia Crane was sure that her husband had told Frank Hastings about his suspicions. It was hardly far-fetched on the basis of those compelling assumptions, McCalley reasoned, to deduce that Frank, always in need of cash, might well have confronted Benson or one of his top people, with what he'd learned and asked for money in return for his silence. Benson must have soon realized that Hastings held no proof; but both parties knew that proof did exist and could turn up, once the authorities were alerted. Not wanting to take that risk, Benson no doubt went along and paid Hastings from time to time, while keeping him in his sights.

Everything pointed to it.

As the insurer's representative, Hastings must have had close dealings with the company that put out the drug Dr. Crane had been administering to patients since 1997, Benson's pharmaceutical company. He must have known that in 1998 Benson had just effected his first merger. Reserves had been depleted by the purchase of A & E Danziger, owned by Emma Danziger, the woman Benson married. A setback, just then, would have been disastrous. The suit in New York, and all the others that would mushroom up as a result, had to be nipped in the bud or the company would go bankrupt.

As McCalley saw it: Hastings was playing a dangerous game by threatening Benson at such a time, but somehow he'd pulled it off. Benson must have thought it expedient to go along, if for no other reason than buying time to see what Hastings or Dr. Crane came up with, if anything.

Then, in just a few years, B & D Ltd. had become Benson International and money was no longer a problem. By 1999 Dr. Crane was dead and Hastings had disappeared in nine-eleven. They no longer posed a threat. Or so it seemed — until new circumstances brought matters to a head.

What those circumstances were McCalley did not know until late that very morning, when Kenney called to report what he had found.

A careful search and hours of scanning Hastings's computer, papers, files, CD movies, tapes of ball games, the baby's birth and christening, as well as audio tapes, uncovered some cryptic notes Hastings had recorded — Flora recognized her husband's voice — about doctored lab reports submitted to FDA by "B & D Co. supervisors, and paid for by CB." At the very beginning of the recording Hastings had noted the date: January 2003. The message was in the middle of an audio tape of Beethoven's Fifth Symphony. Kenney had found it tucked away with dozens of other audio tapes in an open carton in full view on a closet shelf.

For McCalley it was enough to bolster his initial guess that as early as 1998 or 1999 Hastings was aware of Benson's efforts to push his new drug through, in spite of its deadly side-effects; but he could not produce anything to support his accusations. All he had to go on was what Harold Crane had confided in him, when Frank still enjoyed the doctor's trust. Still, that information had paid off . . . but, for how long?

In the light of the new evidence Kenney had found, McCalley now saw, as Hastings's most compelling reason for leaving New York, not his gambling debts, or Flora Mosely, but his mounting fear of retaliation for having blackmailed Benson. The small company whose drug had caused such concern and suffering several years ago was now an international conglomerate, that early episode in its history all but forgotten. Surely Hastings could be ignored by this time. Had the payments stopped? and, if so, was Hastings in danger?

McCalley saw Hastings' disappearance as a crucial decision in these terms. He had decided to distance himself from Benson. He'd been given a new chance for a new life. Or so he'd led himself to believe.

In Canada he took advantage of all the new opportunities that came his way. But there were new temptations as well, especially insider investment tips. What Hastings didn't know was that Benson was behind his new prosperity and still had people watching him. He grew confident, reckless, no doubt justifying his actions as clever maneuvering.

Then, in January 2003, he stumbled on some crucial data about the drug Benson had put on the market in 1997. Whether he had actually seen old company reports to the FDA or had learned about their contents indirectly — perhaps in conversation with his new Canadian buddy, the man who had "recommended" him for the Board of Benson's Canadian company — was anybody's guess. Whatever the circumstances by which he came to get new data about the lethal drug Benson had put on the market years earlier, the information was damning.

What he did with it, was not hard for McCalley to figure out. Hastings, after all, was a gambler at heart. He had already proved that by his illegal, insider trading.

McCalley's rendering was this: Hastings now had dramatic evidence against Benson that could, if made public, cause tremendous damage to the company. Confident that Benson would prefer to strike a deal with him, instead, Hastings probably approached Benson again, with his new information, hoping to net big money.

It was all conjecture, McCalley reminded himself with a twinge of conscience, but more than plausible,

Weeks before he was killed, Hastings had told Flora he thought he was being followed. To McCalley, it was reasonable to assume that Benson was closing in, that Hastings, in spite of the damning information he had stumbled upon, had not been able to deliver any hard evidence. This time, Benson saw him as a loose cannon and decided to get rid of him—

McCalley decided to try his idea on Markarian.

"It still doesn't explain Katie," was the reaction. "Where does she come into it?"

"I think Benson was probing, when he made that bizarre request," McCalley answered easily. "After all, she was married to a compulsive gambler, a blackmailer. How much of that had rubbed off on her? Maybe she was an accomplice. How far would she go to get what *she* wanted? What was her price? The way I see it, Benson wanted to find out how important money was to Katie, if it was as important to her as it was to Frank. For all he knew, his cousin and Frank could have been partners in crime. When he saw the self-righteous indignation his request produced and when Katie returned his 'gift,' he knew she was ignorant of her husband's secret life and was exactly what she appeared to be: an unsuspecting wife. If and when the need should arise, a threat would be enough to keep her from repeating the conversation they'd had in St. Tropez. Or so he thought. . . . It's a plausible scenario. Admit it."

He waited for confirmation. Markarian gave a small nod. "It's possible . . . but not probable. If I didn't know you better — "

McCalley interrupted, with a touch of asperity and an impatient wave. "Consider this: Why did Benson pay off Hastings's debts, at the same time encourage his gambling, so that at one point Frank had to murder a drug dealer to make up for what he thought he still owed Sarace? Why did Benson see to it that in Canada Frank would be on one of his Boards, when he knew Frank was ready to cheat anybody if he knew he could get away with it? And when he did cheat and made a bundle on insider trading, why didn't Benson do something then? Sure, Frank was killed, but after more than a year in Canada. What was Benson waiting for?"

Markarian seemed intent on the road in front of him. He swerved around a slow car and honked his horn. McCalley wondered if his colleague had heard anything of what he'd said.

"Well?" he asked, trying to hide his impatience.

"Well what? You tell *me*!" was the curt reply. "I can't believe what I'm hearing! You of all people! I never thought I'd hear you indulge in such wild theories! Where are the facts, Luke? Facts!"

McCalley turned away to gaze out the window. "Hastings had backed off after settling in Ottawa," he continued calmly. "We've tracked down checks and cash that came in during that last year. Nothing that can't be accounted for."

"You're telling me he repented?"

"Don't be daft. We know he was making big money illegally — "

"So, tell me: what was Benson waiting for?"

"I think Benson was beginning to relax, thinking he had Hastings under control, which he did in a way. Then, out of the blue, the man pops up again, claiming to have even more damning information about the drug and what happened back in 1998 and 1999 — "

"C'mon, Luke, you don't know that!"

"— but again, couldn't deliver the goods."

"All right, I'll play along. So it was hearsay again. He had no hard evidence that would work in court. Just like the first time. . . . ."

"Oh, there's plenty on that tape, but it's Frank telling us about it, that's right."

"So, how does this success story end?"

McCalley ignored the sarcasm and went on: "Benson finally decided to kill Frank, we know that."

"Why didn't he wait, like last time, to see if Frank had access to incriminating documents?"

"He probably did wait, but decided that whatever Hastings had wouldn't hold up in court. Same as before."

"No, not the same. Well yes, the same, only this time he was killed." McCalley frowned. Markarian drove home his point. "This time, following your train of thought, which is really confusing me I'll have you know, this time Benson had him killed. You just said so. Even though Frank couldn't produce anything. He had information, but no proof. Same story. So why kill him?"

"Probably was fed up by then. We know he had enough on Frank to put him away for a long time, but that wasn't a feasible solution. I don't think Benson wanted an open confrontation. He was using Frank'a transgressions for control purposes. There was Katie, too.

The fall-out from an open confrontation would hurt her. She was his cousin, after all. I think he just got fed up with Frank. . . ."

"This is crazy!" Markarian blurted out, turning his eyes from the road to fix them on McCalley. "Are you listening? We're weaving fantasies here. . . ." McCalley studied the road ahead and stroked his chin. "What's come over you?" When there was no answer, he went on: "Anyway, it's all irrelevant. The case is closed."

McCalley seemed unfazed. "No quite. We haven't finished yet." He glanced at the clock on the dashboard. "Four-twenty. Still early. Shall we try Dr. Adler?"

Markarian let out a sigh. "Why not?"

At the hospital, Markarian parked at a hydrant and placed a police card on the windshield.

Dr. Adler was still on afternoon rounds, they were told by the floor nurse, after they had shown their badges. She pointed to the lounge at the end of the hall. "When he stops by the desk, I'll tell him you're here."

Fighting the familiar queasiness he always felt in such places, McCalley strolled to the window and gazed at the narrow street below. The sight of scattered garbage and debris was even more depressing. He walked back to sit next to Markarian, who said:

"Tomorrow, we can split up, if you like, save time. I can see Kramer while you fly down to Washington to see Ingersoll. I can meet you around four, at the hotel."

McCalley nodded approval. "I'll take the first shuttle down. Shouldn't take long."

They stood, as a tall, lanky man in his early forties entered the lounge.

"I'm Dr. Adler. Nurse said you wanted to see me?"

They introduced themselves. Markarian asked: "Is there somewhere more private, where we can talk?"

"My office is down the hall."

They followed him to a room no larger than a closet. The usual diplomas were displayed on walls badly in need of paint. Family pictures rested on a small table that served as desk. It was pushed as close as possible against the one window. This gave out on the brick wall. On either side of the desk, right up to the window, were two tall, narrow bookshelves with the usual medical books. There was just enough space for the doctor to squeeze around to his desk. Before doing so, he opened a broom closet and took out two metal folding chairs.

"Temporary quarters while renovations go on," he said, as he opened the chairs for them, "although I've grown to like it. Keeps most people from relaxing. . . ."

McCalley wondered how anybody could relax in a hospital. Out loud he explained their visit: "We've just been to see Mrs. Crane. She told us you were a good friend of her husband's. . . ."

"I was lucky to have him as a colleague, as well — but, Inspector, Harold's been dead for almost five years."

McCalley gave him a quick edited version of the connection between Frank Hastings and Charles Benson and their interest in the suit which was withdrawn shortly after Dr. Crane's untimely death. He said nothing about the possibility that Harold Crane might have been murdered. "Just some loose ends that need to be tied up," he ended briskly.

"I don't see how I can help, but sure, ask me whatever you like."

"What did Dr. Crane tell you about the suit? I understand at one point, he was fighting to have a trial, when the plaintiffs were ready to withdraw. . . ."

"That's right. Rumor was that they were bought off."

"Tell us about that."

"It wasn't the insurer, that much I know — although they were ready to negotiate."

"Who settled the claim, then?"

"Harold was sure it was Benson, personally, who paid them several million to drop the charges. After that, word spread that there was nothing to connect the drug directly to the fatalities. Most of the patients were elderly and suffered other ills. Anyway, the whole thing died down. The Press lost interest. The plaintiffs, the family of the victim, could not be found for comment, they literally disappeared. Went to live in Europe."

"Didn't it seem strange, that Benson would pay out that amount when the company wasn't even being sued?"

"Obviously, they didn't want the publicity a trial would bring. Even though they weren't being sued, the manufacturer would be targeted at some point. They wanted to defuse the situation, control it, make everyone forget that charges had ever been filed. They told Harold they planned to put everything right, once the case was dismissed. Harold trusted them at first, went along. Personally, I found the whole thing bizarre, still do."

"Serious money," Markarian threw out, glancing at McCalley, who acknowledged the comment with a slight nod and asked Dr. Adler:

"Why wasn't a class-action suit filed? I understand there were other fatalities, here and in other parts of the country, as well?"

"That's right, but there was no proof that the drug was directly responsible. That and the fact that the initial case was dropped made everybody wary. As I said, most of those who took the drug were elderly and had other ills. Culpability could not be clearly determined. Besides, the FDA had approved it."

Markarian chimed in: "So, why should Benson have worried, then? If the FDA had approved it —"

Adler interrupted with a frown: "— You know, I've often wondered about that. . . . But I guess there's more to the process than meets the eye. I don't know much about it or the paperwork involved."

McCalley felt they had brushed against something significant. He would have to ask Ingersoll about it. Adler went on:

"Harold was sure that Benson paid the victim's family several million, ostensibly to avoid a class-action suit that would have ruined him. A national report that came out later showed that the deaths from the drug were several hundred at least. Which means, big money."

McCalley stored that piece of information and pressed on an earlier point: "I understand that Dr. Crane began to suspect the company of fraud. . . ."

"That's right. He was convinced that bribes had been paid to get the drug approved, that it wasn't ready to be put on the market, that the company knew all this and went ahead anyway."

"But could produce no proof. . . ."

"He said he had all the proof he needed," replied the other, confirming what Mrs. Crane had told them earlier.

"But he didn't act on it. Why?"

"He said he wanted to make his case in court. Clear his name publicly."

"He was going to sue the company?"

Adler nodded. "Unfortunately, he never got the chance."

"Well, it's the proof, that evidence Dr. Crane insisted he had, that we're interested in, Doctor," the Inspector continued. "the documents that would not only clear his name but would lay responsibility squarely where it belongs: on the company that withheld vital information or doctored official reports, causing any number of deaths as a result. Can you tell us more about that, and where those papers might be found?"

Dr. Adler shook his head sadly. "That was the

worst time! When Harold started to talk about evidence."

"He didn't share it with you? You didn't see any of it?"

"No. . . . Oh, he talked about it all the time, but I never saw anything. Later, I began to wonder if there really had been anything."

"Do you still doubt it?"

"I'm not sure. At first, Harold convinced me that something fishy was going on."

"What exactly did he tell you?"

"That lots of money, 'serious money,' as you put it" — this to Markarian — "changed hands to get the drug approved."

"Did he think the FDA people were involved?"

"I really can't answer that; but I assumed Harold meant people in the drug company, people in charge of the testing, the labs at that end."

"Where did Dr. Crane get his information?"

"The only thing he said about that was that he had a friend at FDA, an old school chum whom he trusted. The fellow apparently came to New York a couple of times to see Harold. . . . . Fred . . . something. Can't remember his last name."

"Freddie Ingersoll?"

"Yes, that's the one!"

"Did Dr. Crane tell you what they talked about?"

"No. By then he had become secretive, suspicious of everybody, almost paranoid I would say. He did boast that his friend had information that would clear him —"

"What was Freddie's job at FDA, did he say?"

"He was — still is, I assume — one of the people who sort out applications submitted to the Agency, scanning them before sending them for final testing and final review at the top. If more information is needed or something is missing in the company's report he's the one who gets in touch with the manufacturer and asks them to provide what's missing or to answer questions about the application."

When Markarian looked up from his notes, McCalley asked:

"What else can you tell us?"

"Harold felt he had been humiliated, Inspector, compromised by the charges, and that the company was stalling, looking after its own interests, didn't give a hoot what happened to him. He was right about that!"

"How do you mean?"

"You see, the company had assured him that the charges against him would be dropped, he would never come to trial. They said, if he helped in this, the company would donate handsomely to the hospital's new wing. But first, they had to work out what was best for everyone involved. Naturally, Harold went along. The way he explained it was: the charges against him were meant to be a holding action, while the company lawyers got their act together. They couldn't risk a trial and potential class-action suits. Harold would be cleared of all suspicion of malpractice, of course, once they made a public statement and withdrew the drug. . . ."

McCalley was making every effort to follow this incredible story. Markarian frowned as he listened. Dr. Adler went on:

"But things dragged out. His contact at the company suddenly wasn't answering his calls, the drug was still on the market, although Harold had stopped prescribing it on his own. Then rumors started that the trial would not take place and that an offer had been made to the relatives of the victim, the plaintiffs that were suing Harold."

"How did he take that?" McCalley asked.

"He was angry. He grew openly hostile toward the company. Started talking about a conspiracy. About information he had that the company knew even before the drug went on the market that it wasn't ready for distribution. That they had compromised him into prescribing a drug that proved lethal. He accused the company of keeping the drug on the market in order to reap huge profits, at the expense of innocent victims."

Adler paused at some painful memory before going on. "By then the company was avoiding him. They did drop all charges, but after the plaintiffs had left the country. And after Harold had died."

"He convinced you he had real evidence to prove his allegations?"

"Yes, he did. As I recall, it was late in 1998 that he told me he'd come by hard evidence. He said, if they didn't go through with the trial, he would sue them himself."

"And what did you think when the case was dropped, just after Dr. Crane's death?"

"That Harold was right. Once that happened, the company was off the hook. No one was willing to resume the legal battle."

"He didn't believe having the charges dropped was to his advantage? That he'd be off the hook as well?" McCalley pressed.

"As I said, Inspector, Harold wanted to bring down the company, put the blame where it belonged; make sure the families involved were compensated. He felt the company had reneged on all their promises. It was up to him to put things right. He wanted his day in court, where he would present his evidence and bring about Benson's ruin." He let out a heavy breath. "When rumors began, about charges being dropped, about a deal being made, Harold decided to go it alone. I tried to talk him out of it, but it was no good."

"How did you feel about that?" asked Markarian.

"I commiserated with him, but at that point I was skeptical, too. On the realistic side, he was knocking his head against a stone wall. But he never gave up. I remember his telling me one day — it was the only time he referred to it in specific terms — he said, 'Jerry, wait till you hear what those scoundrels did! They paid bribes, big bribes, to alter data and lab results, to push the drug through'."

"But he never showed you any of the documents that would prove it."

"No. At that point I'd given up. I wasn't doubting him, I was worried about him. He'd become obsessed."

"Did he ever talk about Frank Hastings, the insurance agent who represented him?"

"Oh, sure. Frank tried to be helpful; they got along. But when Harold thought the insurer was ready to settle out of court too, Hastings became *persona non grata*."

"Do you know if Harold ever told Hastings what he told you? About the bribes?"

"I'm sure he did, because Hastings kept coming around, pumping both of us for details. He'd promised Harold he'd do everything he could to get the message out there but that he needed proof. Harold wasn't giving anything away, to him or anyone else. Not until he was good and ready." After a pause, he went on. "He wanted his own trial. A public forum. . . . He'd already hired a lawyer . . . but he died before he could do anything."

McCalley stood up. Markarian put his notepad away. "Thank you for your time. You've been very helpful." As they walked toward the elevators, Adler said:

"Harold was very confused, at the end. And angry. The morning he collapsed — he died in his office, you know — I was on the floor. I was going to stop in and ask him to meet me in the cafeteria for lunch, at noon, but someone paged me and I had to rush off. I keep thinking, I might have saved him. . . ."

McCalley patted his arm. "Don't," he said kindly.

"I doubt anyone could have saved him," he added, as he stepped into the elevator.

The first shuttle out of New York, the next morning, brought him into Washington without any delays. He reached the Pavilion (also referred to as "the old Post Office building") in plenty of time for his eight-thirty appointment.

He now stood at the bottom of the grand staircase, in the Food Court. It was like being at the bottom of a huge well; the interior of the historic landmark building reminded McCalley of an old version of the modern Hyatts, with their high open floor-to-ceiling lobbies and rooms arranged in tiers surrounding the open central area to the very top. The rooms, in this case, were — for the most part — federal offices.

In a brochure he picked up as he walked in, McCalley read with interest the history of the massive structure and its equally massive bell tower. The building was old but well-kept. Built at the turn of the century, it was Washington's first skyscraper — all of twelve stories high! Its steel and granite frame housed both the US and DC Post Offices. At the time of its completion, it ranked as Washington's largest and tallest government building, boasting its own electric power plant, with engines that activated close to 4,000 lights. Fifteen years after its completion, the building was marked for demolition to make way for a more modern structure. Delays and preservation movements saved it from destruction.

His curiosity fueled, McCalley walked around, examining the unusual interior. On the entrance level, one floor above the Food Court, he had noticed stalls (still covered at that hour) and stores (not yet open to the public) that sold inexpensive jewelry, knick-knacks, the usual tourist fare. On the lower level too, there were retail stores along the walls, carrying the same kind of inexpensive goods. At the front of this area was a large stage, where at lunch time (McCalley read) the public could enjoy performances by school bands, cabaret singers, local guitarists, Caribbean and American steel drum artists — all sorts of talent. At the rear entrance to the building were more food concessions along three walls, many already serving a variety of exotic and ethnic breakfast foods, in addition to the usual fare. Near this area and in front of the large stage were dozens of tables and chairs, where customers could take their food or just rest for a while.

McCalley was not surprised to read that the elegant Romanesque atrium, with its grand staircase, had served in the past, and still served, as a perfect venue for receptions, balls, and special events. It could take up to 1,900 standing guests and accommodate up to 500 at a sit-down dinner. Several presidential inaugural balls had been held there, as well as New Year's Eve galas and important charity events.

McCalley bought coffee and a pastry and found a table that gave him a clear view of the stairs and anyone who came down into the lower level. He rose when a tall, lanky man in his early forties approached, his hand outstretched, and introduced himself. On one of the empty chairs, he put down a plastic bag and the raincoat he carried over his arm.

"Mind if I get some coffee first?" McCalley waved him on. Back at the table, Ingersoll plunged right in.

"Harold was an old friend from high school and college. We grew up together. Saw a lot of each other all through high school and Columbia: I was Law, he was Medical School. He stayed in New York, I ended up with FDA in Washington." He took a long pull from the plastic cup. "Once in a while, when I came to New York on business, we'd have lunch or dinner. That petered out after a while. When he called me about that malpractice suit that was filed against him, I was stunned. I could tell he was worried, but I didn't realize how serious it was until I came up to see him."

"When was that?"

"Late in 1998, the first time. Then a few weeks later. He asked me if I knew anybody at the labs where the drug was made. He was sure something was wrong and the application pushed through prematurely. All this behind the closed doors of his study, after a nice dinner. I could see he was really troubled."

Ingersoll stopped long enough to sip some coffee.

"I knew what he was going to ask, and at first I was annoyed. But he was so upset, I went along. It happened, I had a good friend working at Benson and Danziger — it's Benson International now — so I called her, when I got back from seeing Harold that first time. What she had to tell me, when I met her after work one day, got me thinking."

"What did she tell you?"

"Randy, my friend Randy Stowe — she's on the team that did the testing on that drug — she told me that in the summer of ninety-six, the supervisor closed down the B and D project and assigned the team to something else. They were worried because they'd discovered serious and irreversible side-effects in the animals they'd tested, but the supervisor assured them they'd come back to the project in a few months."

He finished his coffee and went on.

"Then, one day, out of the blue, she finds out that the drug had been approved. When Randy and the others asked about it, the supervisor told them the FDA was satisfied with the report submitted."

"Who had sent in the report?"

"That's just it. The team usually prepares a first draft, with all the test charts, for the supervisor to check out. The supervisor returns it for corrections and a final draft. That never happened. Randy thinks the supervisor put it together from the working notes he had collected from each of them, including hers. Used what he wanted; left out the rest. She was sure he'd acted on orders from the top. Probably got a bonus for his trouble."

No doubt about it, thought McCalley.

"That set *me* thinking again. I dug up the report the FDA had received from the company and read it, made a couple of copies after hours and took them home. Everything was on the up and up. Nothing in it about potential hazards or serious side effects. I had Randy read it one evening, when she visited me, and she was stunned. She told me the results described there were the very opposite of what the team had found. She had brought her notes — she'd made copies for her personal files — and sure enough, it was a totally different story."

"And you brought copies to Dr. Crane?"

"Yes. I flew to New York on a Saturday, to show him what I'd found. He read everything through twice, slowly, but refused to keep any of it. He told me it was too dangerous for him to have those documents in his possession and asked me to hold on to them until the time was right. I could see he was excited. I left, wondering what the hell I'd gotten myself into." Ingersoll paused, frowning, then went on.

"That second visit made me nervous. But the matter did warrant some kind of review. I told him I couldn't get involved without revealing my source — and I certainly didn't want to get my friend into trouble — so we decided he would ask his lawyer, when the time was right, to subpoena the FDA report, together with all the notes on the lab experiments, as well as the company's report. So I took everything back with me. I put it all under a storage bin in the basement."

"What exactly did you make of your friend's information?"

381

"The testing showed something definitely wrong. The animals were dying. But in the report, the way the drug was described, you'd think it was the miracle cure of the twenty-first century."

"You believe the notes were doctored somehow?"

"Had to be. . . . Oh, I almost forgot. Something else Randy told me. The Vice President visited the lab with the supervisor a couple of times, asked questions."

"Was that unusual?"

"Well, yes, according to Randy. Vice-Presidents don't come strolling in to look over the shoulders of the lab technicians." He looked at his watch. "Have to run, I'm afraid." He pulled the plastic bag from under his coat and pushed it toward McCalley. "It's all in there. Copies, of course. Randy and I thought we'd better hold on to our originals."

McCalley nodded agreement. "I appreciate your telling me what you know." When he started to look inside, Ingersoll stopped him.

"Not here, Inspector," he said, while his eyes swept casually over the area. When his gaze came to rest again on the Inspector, he said: "Remember, you found that envelope when you went through the few remaining files Mrs. Crane had put in storage, after her husband's death. The documents were tucked away inside personal letters and household documents."

McCalley nodded again. Ingersoll went on:

"There's notes in there he took, when I visited him. Randy's name comes up; and mine, obviously. If this is going anywhere, we'll be called on to testify . . . but, until then. . . ."

"I'll be discreet."

McCalley knew he couldn't lie about the source of his information if questioned under oath — as he was bound to be, once the legal machinery was set into motion. . . .He'd worry about that later.

Ingersoll picked up his raincoat.

"By the way," McCalley asked, as he too rose, "did anyone else ever approach Randy or others on the team?"

"As a matter of fact, one of theirs lawyers stopped in once, Randy told me. He asked about the testing they were doing. She answered some of his questions, but when he asked for printouts, told him they couldn't give anything out until all the tests were completed."

"Would she be able to identify the individual, if we showed her some photographs?"

"I'm sure. She remembers faces, sketches in her spare time. Said he reminded her of someone in *The Godfather*."

He held out his hand. "I told them at work I was waiting for the plumber to fix a leak in the bathroom."

"Was I able to fix it?"

They both laughed. "In record time!"

When Markarian arrived at the hotel, just after four, McCalley had started to read for a third time the contents of the envelope Ingersoll had left with him. He listened as Markarian summed up his visit with Sam Kramer. Dr. Crane's lawyer had little to contribute.

"He confirmed what we know, that's about it," said Markarian.

McCalley handed him the folder.

"It's all there, Ed. The supervisor knew something fishy was going on. He probably was paid handsomely to do what he did." For a while, he watched silently as Markarian read through the sheets he'd handed him then, closing his eyes, seemed to doze off.

Markarian put down the sheaf of papers. "This explains a lot —" he wondered if McCalley had fallen asleep. "I don't know how far you want to carry this, Luke," he began again, more loudly, "but the fellow who was with Dr. Crane the morning he suffered his fatal heart attack was our old friend Sarace. The nurse at the hospital — Betty, was it? — identified him. So did Mrs. Crane." McCalley's eyes flew open. (So he hadn't been napping.) "There's irony for you!" Markarian went on, in his normal tone. "That the man who killed Dr. Crane was murdered the same way!"

For McCalley, his friend's words recalled images etched in his memory: Julia Crane's lined face, her wrinkled cotton blouse, her hair held back with a rubberband, the small smile that lit up her face at the sight of her two little girls, the doctor's study, with unopened mail from four years ago still on his desk; the lives of that bereaved family stretching out before them, full of sad memories. . . .

When he finally spoke, he had closed his eyes again, his head was resting on the back of the chair.

"You know Ed, I'm for going along with the coroner's report on this one. The Ambrosini brothers will have to answer for Joe's murder, Bonz and Jimmy gave us what we needed for that one; but to suggest that Dr. Crane was murdered — "

"You don't think Sarace did it?"

The eyes flew open. "Oh, I'm sure he did. But what good will it do to bring it up now, at this late date? We can't prove it, can we." It was a statement, not a question. "Why put Julia Crane and her children through another ordeal? They deserve some peace, after so many years of frustration and pain. We can clear Crane's name; let's give the family that!. . . . If Sarace killed Crane, and I'm sure he did, he's already been punished. Justice has been done. And with Benson dead, what purpose will it serve to accuse him of ordering yet another 'hit'?" Markarian was studying the ceiling. "It was just a loose end, . . . to satisfy my curiosity."

Markarian turned to study the impassive face. McCalley went on:

"We'll subpoena the FDA report and get whatever else we need. When the dust clears, Dr. Crane's integrity will have been restored and those guilty of deliberately selling a drug that caused hundreds of deaths, will be brought to justice."

With a small nod, Markarian replaced the papers inside the manila envelope and handed it back to McCalley.

"It's your call," he said.

McCalley visibly relaxed in his seat. "I think poor Emma must have found out about her husband's shady deals early on, . . . overheard or came across something. Benson didn't kill her because she drank and had become an embarrassment to him; he had her killed for the same reason he had Frank Hastings, Joe Sarace and Dr. Crane killed. She had become a threat. . . . What do you think?"

"I think *you're* the one who's become a threat!" was his friend's retort, as he raised him arm with a dramatic flourish and waved several sheets of paper in the air. "I have incriminating evidence here that proves you're too smart for your own good. Would you mind explaining how I'm supposed to use these notes you gave me for my report?"

He held out a bunch of doodles and waved them in front of McCalley's face.

"Well?"

ALSO BY ANNE PAOLUCCI

FICTION

- *IN WOLF'S CLOTHING (A MYSTERY NOVEL)*. Griffon House Publications, P.O. Box 98, Smyrna DE, 19977, 2004.
- *DO ME A FAVOR (AND OTHER STORIES)*. GHP, 2003.
- *TERMINAL DEGREES*. (A novella). Potpourri Publications Co., KS, 1997.
- *SEPIA TONES*. (Short Stories) 1st Ed. Outrigger Publishers, New Zealand 1985; 2nd Ed. GHP, 1986.
- *EIGHT SHORT STORIES*. (Introduction by Harry T. Moore.) H. Prim Co., NJ, 1977.

POETRY

- *(TRANS.) SELECTED POEMS OF GIACOMO LEOPARDI*. GHP, 2004. Winner, 2005 Award of the Italian Ministry of Foreign Affairs.
- *QUEENSBORO BRIDGE (AND OTHER POEMS)*. (Introduction by Nishan Parlakian.) Potpourri Publications Co., KS, 1995.
- *GORBACHEV IN CONCERT (AND OTHER POEMS)*. (Preface by Diana Der-Hovanessian.) GHP, 1991.
- *RIDING THE MAST WHERE IT SWINGS*. GHP, 1980.
- *POEMS WRITTEN FOR SBEK'S MUMMIES, MARIE MENKEN, AND OTHER IMPORTANT PERSONS, PLACES & THINGS* (Introduction by Glauco Cambon.) H. Prim Co., NJ, 1977.

PLAYS

- *THE SHORT SEASON*. Produced, USIA/NATO, Naples Italy, 1967. New York Premiere, Cubiculo Theater, 1970. Selected scenes, Ch. 31, NY, 1970.
- *THE APOCALYPSE ACCORDING TO J. J. (ROUSSEAU)* by Mario Apollonio. Original translation from the Italian by AP, 1969. Showcase production, The Classic Theater, NY 1975. Selected scenes, Columbia University, NY 1975.
- *IN THE GREEN ROOM*. (A play with music.) GHP, 2000.
- *CIPANGO!* (A short play in several sequences). Available on video and diskette. Distributed by Educational Video, 1991-1993l currently available through GHP.
- *THREE SHORT PLAYS*. (Introduction by Mario Fratti.) GHP, 1994.
  MINIONS OF THE RACE (award-winning short play). Available on video and diskette.
  INCIDENT AT THE GREAT WALL.
  THE ACTOR IN SEARCH OF HIS MASK.

FOR INFORMATION ABOUT BOOKS, ARTICLES, TRANSLATIONS, MONOGRAPHS, ETC. ON DANTE, SHAKESPEARE, LUIGI PIRANDELLO, EDWARD ALBEE, HEGELIAN DRAMATIC THEORY, THEATER OF THE ABSURD, ETC., VISIT:
www:annehenrypaolucci.com and *griffonhse@AOL.com*

The New York Times
Book Review
February 16, 1986

FICTION

SEPIA TONES: Seven Short Stories. By Anne Attura Paolucci. (Rimu Publishing/Griffon House, Box 81, Whitestone, N.Y. 11357. Paper, $10.) If more Italian-American writers do not speak up soon, much of their experience in the 20th century will go unrecorded. Anne Attura Paolucci's slim volume helps dispel the silence. The scenes alternate between the farmland north of Naples and the outer boroughs of New York. Cast in an implicitly documentary mode (owing, partly, to the photographs that herald each story), the tales have the sentimental "sepia tone" the title suggests, with several of the same characters figuring throughout. The author, who teaches English at St. John's University, is often in danger of turning characterization into tribute; one feels the taboo against exposing, and thereby dishonoring, the family and community. The exceptions are two New York stories. In "Rarà," a priest in Little Italy helps a 9-year-old girl drag her sick, drunken father to bed, then learns he is terminally ill when he visits his old friend, an atheistic doctor. He then goes on to help a young woman with college applications. The "and then" quality creates a sense of the daily jumble of events. "The Oracle Is Dumb or Cheat" begins and ends with the neighborhood women. The rambling narrative is written as if learned secondhand, the narrator's voice yet another gossip. In this way we hear of Louise Quattrocchi and Frank Guardino, two young lovers torn between their new American freedom to choose as individuals and their old imperatives to live as the family and community dictate. By the end of the book, the author has invoked the world of an ingrown community where family pride cautions, "Keep your eyes shut and say nothing. . . . Dust always settles."

—*Nancy Forbes*

Outrigger Publishers

RIMU PRESS, P. O. Box 13049, Hamilton, New Zealand

[USA Distributor: Griffon House Publications.

After immigration

by Rita Signorelli-Pappas

The Voices We Carry: Recent Italian/American Women's Fiction, edited by Mary Jo Bona. Montreal and New York: Guernica Editions, 1994, 376 pp., $18.00 hardcover.

The final section is a tribute to the pioneering first generation of Italian immigrant grandparents. Although it too is somewhat misleadingly titled, it contains some of the best writing in the book. The jewel in this section—indeed the masterpiece of the entire anthology—is Anne Paolucci's "Buried Treasure," a brilliant, haunting memoir of an unforgettable Italian American man narrated by his daughter-in-law. The admiring portrait of an impassioned painter who lacked formal training but possessed the sensibility and discipline of a real artist has clear, eloquent power:

> Perhaps it was simply his lack of training; but I like to think it was his vision, quirky and poetic, strangely haunting in its stiff configurations, its lines never quite straight, never quite even, that had such an ambiguous effect on me. I saw the effects all too clearly, always; but at the same time I saw his soul trying to tell me something, everything. (p.344)

THE CRITICS

"These seven short stories, beautifully written and utterly absorbing, are the work of a genuinely literary artist. The author's insight into her various Italian characters is of such clairvoyance as to make them universal. Anne Paolucci combines qualities seldom found in the same writer: a sure sense of narrative, a marked talent for writing effective dialogue, and a distinctive style that constantly engages the reader with its warmth. SEPIA TONES should bring its author the recognition she merits as an important American writer. I cannot imagine any discriminating reader experiencing the pleasure of reading these stories without wanting to read more of the author's writings."
JERRE MANGIONE, *Award-winning novelist*

". . . versatile . . . sensitive . . . they portray accurately; they interpret life among Italian Americans [with] the mind-probing of Pirandello, here and there Verga, and maybe O'Henry in "Rarà." But no, it's straight Anne Paolucci."
PETER SAMMARTINO, *Educator*

"Una lezione eroica di vita, e anche un'occasione per sentire tutta l'aderenza ad una doppia cultura, la coscienza chiara di appartenere contemporaneamente a due mondi che, all'apparenza cosi lontani, finiscono invece con il ritrovarsi vicini e quasi coincidere."
FRANCO BORRELLI, *"Due Mondi," Il Progresso, Jan. 5, 1986.*

". . . un elegante volume di novelle . . . . Sonoteneri ritratti di paesani, vicini, parenti, amici in un ambiente umano e familiare. Stile impeccabile. Centoventisette pagine di alto valore letterario. [Da ricordare che . . . A. Paolucci ha scritti nella bella antologia 'Dream Book'–cinquantasei scrittrici a cura di Helen Barolini.]"
MARIO FRATTI (*Playwright*), *La Follia, March/April 1986*

ALSO BY ANNE PAOLUCCI

iN WOLF'S CLOThiNG

A MYSTERY NOVEL

ANNE PAOLUCCI

GRIFFON HOUSE PUBLICATIONS / BAGEHOT COUNCIL)
griffonhse@AOL.com

ALSO BY ANNE PAOLUCCI

🏛 THE SONS OF ITALY BOOK CLUB

CIPANGO! (THE STORY)
By Anne Paolucci

Marco Polo's description of *Cipango*, (Renaissance Italian for "Japan"), inspired Columbus to cross an ocean to find it, as we learn in this short but powerful biography of the greatest navigator of the Renaissance by noted Columbus scholar Anne Paolucci. She starts with Columbus' early life in Genoa where he began sailing at age 15 and ends with his tragic fourth and last voyage when a storm sank almost his entire fleet of 32 ships. The facts are enhanced by excerpts from Paolucci's award-winning play, also named *Cipango!* A "must-read" for adults and teens. *[$14.95; paperback; 144 pages; Griffon House; to order call: 302/677-0019]*

Fall 2005 Selection

GRIFFON HOUSE PUBLICATIONS / BAGEHOT COUNCIL)
griffonhse@AOL.com